HEART OF THE MATTER

QUEENS OF KINGS: BOOK 1

LAQUETTE

HEART OF THE MATTER

QUEENS OF KINGS (BOOK 1)

LAQUETTE

DEDICATION

To the late James and Doris Davidson (Granddaddy and Grandma): The giants upon whose shoulders I stand.—Isaac Newton

To my husband, Damon, my original hero, my KING!

To Laura C. from JMC, this one is for you. Sorry it took so long.

ACKNOWLEDGMENTS

To God, from whom all blessings flow. Thank you for the gift, the desire, the support, and the opportunity. To Damon, this does not happen without you. Love you forever. To Sterling and Semaj, my heartbeats, the best parts of me. To my family and friends, thank you for putting up with my craziness. To the Sarah and Hot Ink Press, thank you for the opportunity and the support. To Piper Kay, I will never be able to thank you for making me, "Push the fucking button." To Elizabeth, thank you for making my crazy sound amazing. To Lexie, thank you for supplying me with my new motto, "Hustle until you don't have to introduce yourself" (unknown). To all of my JMC and LIJ people, your love strengthens me. To Alicia & Samantha, thank you for doing what you do. To my Loungers, you guys hold me down and keep me going. Thank you so much for the loyalty and encouragement. To the readers, you will never know how much I have loved writing Heart and Kenneth for you. This has been an amazing journey.

Keep it sexy,
    LaQuette 💋

LaQuette

Savvy, Sensational,
& Sexy Romance

Keep
It Sexy!

Brooklyn
Girl Ink

www.LaQuette.com

Heart of the Matter
Queens of Kings (Book 1)

Heart "Mac" MacKenzie is a tough police lieutenant in the rough streets of Brooklyn, New York. She's a strong leader who doesn't mind getting in the trenches with the men and women she leads at the seventy-four precinct. Her house, her people, and her family—both blue and blood—are the only things that matter. She would live and die for the blue wall that shields her from a traumatic past.

When her captain assigns her a high-profile kidnapping case that she doesn't want, and insists she allows the missing girl's irritatingly sexy uncle to tag along during the investigation, her blood boils. Mac has no choice but to do what she always does when things get out of control, lay down the law—her law.

Kenneth Searlington is a rich playboy from the Upper East Side of Manhattan. With stunning looks and an unlimited source of wealth, he's used to being the center of everyone's attention, especially the women that he comes in contact with.

His life is fun and carefree until his niece, Merridith is kidnapped, and he's forced to seek out the help of his godfather an NYPD police captain, David Porter. Afraid and frustrated, Kenneth defers to his uncle's expertise and his promise that he's putting his best cop on the case, Lieutenant MacKenzie.

When Kenneth discovers "Mac" is actually a sexy as sin lady cop with a fiery temper to match, he decides mixing a little business with pleasure might be just the thing he needs to distract him from long-standing family issues that are trying to crawl their way back into the forefront of his life.

Each used to having their own way, can these two work together long enough to bring an innocent child home? Or will they settle their differences and unyielding attraction in a more carnal way and get right down to the heart of the matter?

CHAPTER 1

*H*eart pulled into the right lane on the Belt Parkway West. Her ten to six shift— which always turned in to a ten to ten, or ten to twelve shift—assured her commute from Cambria Heights, Queens was relatively quick every day. She put on the right indicator of her navy-blue sedan, and headed for 17W.

In a matter of minutes, she was on Linden Blvd headed toward that familiar right turn on Essex St. She crossed the intersection of Essex St. and Blake Ave, slowing her speed down just before she reached Sutter Ave. She took a deep breath and shook her shoulders a little. The fatigue she'd been wearing for the last six weeks began to quickly peel away as she made the left turn into her house—NYPD seventy-fourth precinct.

Relief began to slide down her worn-weary body. She'd spent the last six weeks on a joint task force of federal, state, and local law enforcement. Thanks to the huggie-feely mayor who wanted his cops to play nice with the feds and the troopers, she'd been forced to go on this kumbaya-fest and pretend to give a fuck about bonding with the assholes she'd met from the other agencies and forces.

If she had to listen to one more of her so-called colleagues verbally thump his chest with stories of his latest big bust, while trying to size up whose dick was bigger among the other Neanderthals in the room, she was going to pull her weapon and shoot someone. Namely that ball-less mayor who was chocking the shit out of the police commissioner with a tight-as-hell leash he'd snapped on when he'd taken office two-terms ago. *Thank fuck that son-of-a-bitch is leaving in a few weeks. Hopefully the incoming mayor won't be such a dickless wonder.*

Hopefully once he was gone, the top cop in New York could let his people get back to doing what they should be doing, policing, crushing a few skulls when necessary, and keeping the streets safe for the people in this city. *Gawd, so glad I'll never make captain, too much political bullshit to have to put up with. The streets, that's where I need to be.*

She headed for the familiar direction of her assigned parking spot. The thought of not having to circle around the area looking for a decent spot alone was reason enough to cherish her highly envied spot. The fact that she didn't have to contend with alternate side of the street parking rules—or even worse—parking too far away from the precinct, and leaving her car vulnerable to the mishaps that could happen to recent model, well-kept sedans parked for long hours unattended on an East New York street, was enough to sell her soul for.

It was the one luxury she happily indulged in since her latest promotion to NYPD Lieutenant a year ago. She had fought it, the promotion. Happy with her Detective firstgrade status, she was a part of the elite class of investigators that were charged with solving the city's worst crimes and putting away its worst offenders. She loved every minute of her time as a detective. She'd never wanted more than the coveted gold medallion that formed her detective's badge. She'd never wanted the headache and heartache of administration and a command detail. Yet somehow she'd found herself smack in the middle of both. She always questioned how her career had taken that fateful turn and came up with only one answer. Captain David Porter.

Almost a decade before she finished her final year in college, Captain Porter—then Sergeant Porter—had sat at a table in the middle of the quad at her school, pulling her counterparts aside, explaining the joys of being a part of the brotherhood that was the NYPD. She'd watched several students with the awestruck wonder of a kid on Christmas morning painted on their faces. *Suckers.* That was the only way she could describe them, standing there soaking up everything the uniformed man had to say.

He spared her a glance, one that beckoned her to join the rest of his followers; she shrugged her shoulders and laughed. He kept a friendly smile on his face, and when she didn't come to him, he excused himself from the students surrounding him, and walked to where she was standing.

He stuck out his hand, "Sergeant Porter," he said, as if she were supposed to be impressed with his title.

She looked at his hand hanging in mid-air and firmly ignored it, shoving her own hands in her jacket pockets.

"...and you are?" he asked with expectation.

She looked up to him, he was probably only two or three inches taller than her own

five feet nine-inch height. She was contemplating walking away, but there was something in the openness of his face that made her answer him.

"Mac," she said in a short, clipped tone.

"Mac?" he repeated in disbelief.

"Short for MacKenzie," she provided on another clipped breath.

He nodded, accepting her quick explanation. "Okay Mac," Porter began. "Have you ever—"

Heart lifted a hand and stopped his words abruptly. "No I haven't and I never will.

There's a slot waiting for me in the Marines as soon as I take my last final." She turned around to take her leave and noticed him following her.

"So, you've already enlisted then, signed on the dotted line?"

She stopped and turned sharply in one motion to get a better look at him. "No, but

I've already spoken with a recruiter and the minute I'm done with school, I'm going down to enlist. Far as I'm concerned, it's a done deal."

He nodded again, something he seemed to do every time she

answered one of his questions. "It's an admirable thing you're doing young lady, enlisting, deciding to serve this wonderful country we live in," his words escaped from a full smile as he spoke.

That was a first. Every time she mentioned her plans to enter the military, someone was always bringing up something negative to say about it. Her grandmother especially. The only person who seemed to encourage—or maybe a better word was accept—her decision was her cousin, True. According to her grandmother, Ida-Mae Amare, True's opinion couldn't be trusted because she, all three of her older siblings, and both her parents had either served, or were currently serving in varying branches of the armed forces.

According to her grandma, "All those crazy damn fools drink from the same looney juice. Ain't none of them sane in the first place, how the hell they gonna stop you from doing something crazy and stupid if they all sippin' from the same brew you swallowin'?"

Heart shook her head and focused on the sergeant before her. "Thanks, surprised you're not trying to stop me though, tell me all the ways the NYPD is better than the

Marines."

He shrugged his shoulders. "You seem like a levelheaded young person, I'm sure you've done your research, you know what the benefits are to serving as well as the consequences. I'm sure I don't have to tell you them."

She nodded her head and prepared to turn away. "You're right, you don't."

"What I will tell you is that you're gonna go too far off lands to do some really good work, help some people who really need you, and defend the rights of our very own citizens at the same time." She nodded her head agreeing with him. "The only thing the NYPD has to offer you over the military, is that you'd get to do the very same things, but do them here in the country you love, in the city you live in, protecting the people you know and love," he said with a glint of pride in his eyes.

He stopped talking and walked away, and she stood still there in the quad thinking one thing—*what the hell just happened?*

HEART OF THE MATTER

When the opportunity came for her to take the Lieutenant's test, she'd firmly decided to pass until Porter had taken her to the side once again, as he had many times over the years since their initial meeting on her college campus, and educated her without pushing her on why taking the exam was the only option for her.

She'd fought him, but once he'd explained that as a black woman in the NYPD, it was her obligation to push forward, and create opportunities for those following her, not to mention the opportunity to affect change within the department, she'd crumbled. She didn't just take the test; she slaughtered the damn thing, and was summarily offered her pick of precincts. These were positions where she would be top cop in the house, if she'd wanted. Much to Porter's frustration, she'd declined those positions, and requested to remain at the seventy-fourth becoming Porter's second-in-command.

She loved this house, and she wasn't walking away from it, or her tight team of five detectives that she had trained, cultivated, and worked with during her time here. This was her house, and the only thing she loved just as much as her house was her reserved parking spot that would be waiting for her to pull into just as soon as she made one last left inside the parking lot, behind the building structure.

She turned her car in the direction of her spot and didn't see it. *Damn*, she thought. *I must have driven past it while I was daydreaming.* She put the car in reverse and slowly backed up where she knew the spot should be, but the only thing she could see was a line of parked cars, with no gap in between them big enough for her parking spot to reside. She put her car in park, got out, and walked closer to inspect the signs on the designated spots. Porter's was to her left, filled with his 4x4 truck, and directly to its right should have been her empty parking spot. She checked the sign that read, *Reserved: Lt. MacKenzie* on it. It was there, marking what should have been her empty spot, but instead, she found a silver luxury sedan with glistening wheels, expensive rims, leather interior and wood-grain trim.

Ain't this about a bitch? Who the fuck is in my spot?

She went back to her car, moved it to the empty space marked

13

with a no-parking grid across its asphalt. She grabbed her gear from the backseat and headed inside. As she walked she became conscious of the added weight on her hip. Her holstered weapon always felt a little heavy when she had ideas on using it. It was as if the ebony piece of metal was saying to her, *you know I'm here if you need me, right?*

She burst through the doors that led to the squad room, ready to ask about the illegal occupant of her parking spot when she heard her name being called.

"Hey Mac, how's it going?"

Heart's concentration yanked away from her intended task, she turned in the direction of her partner—technically her former partner now that she was a lieutenant and he was lead detective of the team she oversaw—Bryan Smyth's voice.

"Hello Bry, did you miss me?"

Bryan's shoulders rumbled with laughter. "I don't know how I passed the days without you, baby."

"Yeah right, liar, you were probably sucking up to Porter for all of the good cases while I was gone."

He smiled, revealing the truth in her statement. "You know me so well, MacKenzie. How did you enjoy your time at touchy-feely camp?"

"I didn't, I only did it because Porter pretty much threatened my badge if I didn't go, something about it doesn't look good when a command leader doesn't follow the rules all the subordinates are forced to follow," she grumbled that last bit as she motioned for him to follow her to her office.

"Hey Bry, you know who owns that silver piece-of-shit that's parked in my spot out back?"

Bryan's eyes took on a weird look, kind of nervous, rushing quickly from side to side. "Porter might know more about that than I would."

Slightly thrown by confusion, she looked back at Bryan to ask what he meant when she heard her captain's voice crash through the open squad room.

"MacKenzie, my office now!" he bellowed.

She turned back to look at Bryan again. "How the hell does he always know the minute I step foot back into this building?"

Bryan just laughed again, "It's a gift, he prides himself on knowing all things MacKenzie at all times."

"Sounds a little stalker-ish, don't you think?"

"You said it, I didn't," he answered.

"MacKenzie!" her captain yelled again.

The good officer in her snapped to attention, and followed her commanding officer's voice directly into his office. She tapped the clear acrylic panel of the door to alert her captain that she was walking in. She found Porter seated at his desk with his head bent as he read from the scattered papers taking up residence on the old metal desk before him.

"Sit down, MacKenzie, I have a job for you," he said as he took one final glance at the papers in front of him.

"What's up, Cap?" she asked. She was eager to find out what her captain was planning for her. Since taking her command detail, the opportunities for her to actually take part in an on-going investigation were minimal. As a lieutenant, her duties had become more administrative. She still supervised her team of detectives out in the field, but she rarely took part in the footwork that usually accompanied an investigation. She couldn't even remember when she made a collar last.

"MacKenzie," he stopped to gather the strewn paperwork from his desk and neatly organized them into one pile. He shoved them in a plain manila folder, and handed the folder to her. He nodded his head, giving her permission to open it.

She opened the folder to a 5 X 7 colored headshot of a man. Caucasian, waves of shoulder-length coal-colored strands framing the hard angles of his face and the palest blue eyes she'd ever seen. The contrast between his hair and eye-color made those ghostly eyes seem to stare straight out of the picture and directly through her.

"That is Kenneth Searlington," Porter's voice said, dragging her from the pull the picture had on her.

"Who is he, and what's he done Cap?" she asked. She didn't recognize him as any of the usual suspects she normally dealt with in her professional life. He didn't look like a pusher; the clean subtle look to his style took him off her pimp/hustler radar. For damn sure she knew he wasn't a thug, not with that mean-ass blowout falling in silky strands around his shoulders. If he didn't fall into any of those categories, she had a hard time understanding why her captain would bring him to her attention.

"He hasn't done anything; it's what's being done to him. He's a real estate mogul, he and his family own most of Manhattan. He's been receiving some troublesome messages that I want you to look into."

She stared at Porter through squinted eyes. "Cap, are you really trying to saddle me with look-and-see non-sense because this big-wig pissed off the wrong debutant and she keyed his car or something? Honestly Captain Porter, I'm not really feeling something like this right now. My team is still looking for a lead in those recent night elevator murders over in Cypress, I can't spare the manpower to babysit some rich kid," she said as she closed the file in her hand and stood in front of her captain's desk.

"MacKenzie, this wasn't a request. You're taking this case."

"Captain this is bullshit and you know it. If this was Starasia from Fountain Ave, you would not be bothering me with this, but because this dude has money, we gotta jump to it. Nah, Cap, not happening. Tell him to take this ish over to one of those precincts in the city that have the manpower and the resources to coddle silly-ass rich people. Cops in BK ain't got time for this," she huffed out, placed the file on his desk.

"MacKenzie!" his tone sharp and loud. "You are taking this case!"

"Cap, after all that time you had me wasting at touchy-feely camp, I don't have time for this. I did not join the force to babysit some playboy who pissed off the wrong socialite."

Porter stood at his desk, his hands on his hips, and his voice barking his words. "Just in case you forgot, Lieutenant, I am top cop in this damn house. You and your team work the cases I either approve, or tell you to work. I don't really give a damn why you joined the force, but as long as you're on it, and as long as you're in this house, you do as I say do. Are we clear?"

She took in the picture of Captain Porter. Brown skin usually the color of fudge was tinted with a red hue from what she assumed to be his boiling blood. His chest was moving in hard, fast motions up and down, and the nostrils on his wide nose were flaring open in quick intervals. *Damn he's really serious*, she thought to herself.

Porter was usually and even-tempered boss. He encouraged his subordinates to think for themselves and feel comfortable with expressing their thoughts. He had good cops who could think for themselves, and as long as you didn't do anything stupid, and followed protocol, he usually allowed his cops to work from a long leash. This argument shouldn't have even been enough to register on his piss-Porter-off radar. Yet the way he was beasting at her, she understood something was wrong.

She slowly sat back down in her seat, and leaned forward, placing her forearms on his desk.

"What's going on, Captain?"

He took in a large, noisy breath and settled back down in his seat.

"MacKenzie, this is a serious case. It isn't just someone sending him stupid messages in the mail. This investigation is more than a look-and-see. Someone kidnapped

Kenneth's niece. He came to me and not the cops in the city because we've had dealings in the past. He wanted someone he could trust to get the job done. You, Smyth, and the rest of your team, you're the only ones I would trust with this..." He ran a silent hand down his face and allowed some of the tension in his body to fall. "...trust to get this girl home safe, trust to keep this quiet, and out of the media."

He pushed himself back in his chair and she followed suite like-wise, taking the folder with her. She opened it and began flipping through it, reading and processing the information as she spoke.

"Should we involve the Feds? This guy is a VIP, if this goes wrong we could both be up shit's creek. I don't mind taking the possible hit, but my guys," she said of her team,

"I'm not willing to put them at risk."

Porter nodded his head. "I understand where you're coming from, Mac, but I want this handled in-house first. You keep me posted every step of the way during this investigation, and if I think we've hit a wall, I'll bring this to the Feds myself. I'll also publicly take the hit if this goes to shit."

She nodded her head, and collected the file, heading toward the door. When she reached it, she stopped and turned her head toward her captain. "Cap?"

He nodded toward her, acknowledging her coming question. "When you're finished with Searlington could you send him to my office please?"

Her captain laughed. "What makes you think I have him, or know where he is?" he asked.

"Cuz the only fool who would be brave enough to park in my parking spot is someone you told it was all right. Everyone in here knows I don't listen to anyone but you."

He chuckled, but said nothing.

"And Cap?"

She watched him nod his head again.

"Tell Searlington if he doesn't move his shit out my spot in the next five, I'm having it towed to the impound and making certain they 'lose' his paperwork on the way."

~

*K*enneth entered into Captain Porter's office through the side-entrance door. He had been standing outside of it listening to the battle between Porter and his lieutenant for the last fifteen minutes or so.

"Was that the infamous Lieutenant MacKenzie?" he asked a sitting Porter.

"The one and only."

"Damn, hellfire is a moderate way of describing her. I don't know if I'm scared or attracted."

Porter laughed and waved Kenneth into the office. Kenneth sat down in front of Porter taking a moment to glance back at the door behind him.

"Is she always that…" he stopped to think of an appropriate word to describe the lieutenant. "…difficult?"

Porter laughed out loud. "That was actually mild for her, we've had some knockdown drag-out fights in here."

"You let your subordinates get away with being that rude and disrespectful to you?"

"Don't try to judge what you don't understand, Kenneth. I may outrank MacKenzie, but she does not work for me, she works with me. She keeps my precinct running like a well-oiled machine. My cops respect her, because she's the hardest working of them.

Even when she doesn't agree with my mandates, she helps me sell them to my officers and detectives. She's an amazing second-in-command, and an even better investigator. I couldn't run this place without her."

Kenneth watched the middle-aged man sitting before him. His usually gruff features seemed to brighten and soften as he spoke of the lieutenant.

"Uncle David?" Kenneth asked with a lifted brow, using the moniker he had grown up using for the man sitting before him. "Is there something going on between you and the young lieutenant? Are you and she…?" he waved a hand between them. "…sleeping together?" he finally said.

"Kenneth, not every man in a position of power looks to use his office or title as a means of getting his dick wet. That girl is young enough to be my daughter, and despite her age, I respect myself, this office, my cops, and myself too much to be chasing after her like some dirty-old man. The only thing I feel for Mac is camaraderie, and concern, the same as I do for any of my cops on the job in my house."

Kenneth raised his hands up in surrender. "All right, Uncle David, you don't have a thing for her. I get it," he said with one corner of his mouth lifting in smile.

"Kenneth, the only thing you should be focused on is getting Merri home. The only interest you should have in MacKenzie is as a resource to make that a reality. Don't get in her way, if you try to distract her, I promise, she will make you pay. Now go in her office, and talk about this case."

Kenneth watched as Porter returned his gaze to the files on his desk. He'd been dismissed, no question about it. He stood up and walked toward the front door of the office when he heard Porter's voice.

"Oh and Kenneth, unless you want your car impounded, I'd suggest you move it out of Mac's spot, quickly."

Kenneth looked at Captain Porter hoping to see levity in his face. What he found was the same serious face that had dismissed him only moments before. He snatched the door open, and quickly made his way back to the parking lot, having his baby towed was not an option.

≈

The ringing of her office phone brought her out of her trance. "Lieutenant MacKenzie, how can I help you?"

"So you are back, and you didn't bother to call and tell me?" She smiled as the familiar voice of her grandmother filled her ear. "Hello, Mama, I just got in a few minutes ago, I haven't had a chance to call anyone yet."

"When am I going to see you?"

"Mama, I would love to make plans with you, but Porter just handed me a new case that I have to start working ASAP. Once I get settled in, I promise I'll come over and you can spoil me with your awesome cooking skills." Heart smiled tentatively, hoping the feisty senior citizen on the other end of the phone would give her a break for once.

"You'd better do just that, or I'll skin you alive."

She smiled, loving the familiar sound of her grandmother's voice. "I know you will, Mama, I'll talk to you as soon as I can."

"I love you, baby, tell that Captain Porter he'd better take care of my girl, or he'll have me to deal with."

Heart chuckled. Porter was six feet tall with a solid build, and trained in firearm use and hand-to-hand combat, but she had no doubt who would come out the victor between himself and the five foot two inch elderly woman on the phone. She'd wager Porter had no doubts about his odds against her grandmother either.

Heart looked up at the tap on her office door.

"Mama, gotta go," she said quickly before hanging up the phone. She waved in her visitor and watched him as he entered the room.

Six-two, six-three. If he was an inch shorter she would turn in her badge. Muscular enough that the tight-ass muscle shirt he was wearing was actually fashionable and not just wishful thinking. Lean hips were adorned with low-hanging jeans that seemed to be grabbing at the curves of the muscles in his ass and thighs. His long dark hair was resting freely around his shoulders and those penetrating pale blue eyes were looking right through her. *Damn, the real-deal is prettier than the picture, that's for damn sure.*

She blinked her eyes to give herself a moment to clear her head, get back to the purpose of the meeting. She watched him walk to her desk, offering her his hand in greeting.

"Lt. MacKenzie, I'm Kenneth Searlington," he said with his mouth lifted in a small smile.

She looked at his face, then his hand, then back to his face.

"Please have a seat, Mr. Searlington," she said, completely ignoring the hand presented to her. She looked down at the case-file sitting before her, but she could feel those eyes on her, could almost feel them walking down her skin.

Time to focus on the case, MacKenzie.

She pulled the picture of his niece from the folder and slapped it on her desk in front of him. "So tell me about your niece."

⁓

Kenneth sat watching the woman sitting behind the desk. Why was he watching her so intently? She wasn't his type. He preferred more dainty women. From the glimpse he caught of her in Porter's office she looked to be four or five inches shorter than his own six feet three inches. She was very well built, strong, lean, defined. Her hair was pulled back in a tight ponytail, not even one strand escaping. Everything about her rigid, controlled. Not his type.

No, she wasn't his type at all, and most of all, she wasn't his family's type. He had to admit, his mother and sister were not-so-in-the-closet racists. High society dictated that they appear inclusive to every skin-tone under the sun. But Kenneth knew from years of existing with his family that anything darker than a tan, just wouldn't do. And with that rich creamed-cocoa complexion, there was no hiding that she was an African American.

"Tell me about Merri," she said, pulling him out of his own thoughts and into reality. "First I need your niece's full name."

"Merridith Searlington Grant," he answered.

"How old is she?"

"She's five."

"When was the last time she was seen, and who were the people she was seen with?"

"She was last seen with her mother two days ago while shopping."

"Can you tell me exactly where they were shopping?"

"On Fifth Avenue. Karolyn, hates going to stores to shop, she likes the stores to come to her, but Merri always liked being there with all of the other people around."

"What's your sister's full name?"

"Karolyn Margaret Searlington-Grant."

"And her father's name?"

He startled a little at her last question. "His name is William Grant."

"Why'd you look so strange when I mentioned him?"

"Nothing in particular, it's just that he hasn't been around much lately."

"Doesn't his wife have something to say about that?"

"My sister and Merri's father are no longer married, they were divorced a year ago."

"Was it an amicable divorce?"

"No, not at all, he fought it tooth and nail, but my sister got her way, and had the divorce granted regardless of his contesting it."

"Was there a custody battle?"

"No, the question of custody was never even posed. William wasn't that kind of man, he loved his little girl more than life, and he couldn't bear to tear his daughter from the mother she adored."

"Did he ever contact your sister?"

"Only to talk to Merri, but Karolyn put an end to that. She wouldn't allow him to see or talk to Merri. I don't know whom it destroyed more, Merridith, or William. Once the divorce was final and Karolyn refused to let William see Merri, the poor guy was heart-broken, he left the country."

"You seem very fond of your sister's ex-husband."

"He was an upstanding guy, my sister took him for granted, and used him; he didn't deserve anything my sister dished out to him."

As he spoke she wrote, he wondered just what it was she was jotting down on her note pad, but he couldn't make it out from the angle he was sitting at.

"What is that you're writing?"

"Nothing you need be concerned with," she said, not even lifting her eyes to look at him as she wrote.

"Dammit, MacKenzie, you'll not exclude me from this investigation, she's my niece!"

She continued writing, her eyes still focused on her notepad, seemingly unfazed by his outburst.

"A fact I am well aware of, Mr. Searlington. Here's something you need to be aware of. My team and I are working this case, we are not swayed by, nor do we answer to you or your family. Our sole focus is to work the case the best we know how, and ultimately, bring your niece home. I know this must be a tough time for you and your family, but your money and clout notwithstanding, you will not interfere in this case beyond being a resource for possible informa-tion that may lead us to your niece's whereabouts," she finished calmly.

"You expect me to sit back and just do nothing?" he asked through tight lips.

"I expect you to let me and my detectives do our job," she said. Her voice colored with annoyance.

"Lieutenant, Captain Porter may get off on your flip-mouthed answers, but I don't. I don't know who you think I am—" He didn't get the chance to finish.

She stood up, walked around her desk and then leaned her long form atop its front while standing between his spread legs.

"Mr. Searlington, I know exactly who you are, and exactly what a man like you is more than likely used to," she said in a hushed tone as she reached for the shiny metal handgun fixed to her hip by her holster. He could feel his eyes grow wide as he watched her pull the weapon from her hip, cock it, and rest it flat on the desk and place her hand next to it.

"What you don't understand is that your wants, desires, and usual modes of operation don't really matter much to me. So if you want to get into a pissing match with me about who's dick-size is bigger, whose rules will be followed, know that since I'm the one with the badge and the gun, I win on both counts. Now, do we understand each other,

Mr. Searlington?"

Kenneth felt a familiar stirring in his groin that he couldn't understand for the life of him. When had fear become one of his kinks? Because there were only three things he was certain of at this moment: 1-this woman was very much in charge, 2-he was very much afraid of her, and 3-he was very much turned on by facts 1 and 2. What the hell was he going to do now?

CHAPTER 2

*H*eart walked toward the Park Avenue apartment building. Before she could reach the door, the smiling doorman opened the door and ushered her inside.

"Morning, ma'am," he said with bright teeth twinkling.

Goodness it was too early for this; she hadn't even had her first cup of coffee yet. She'd spent more hours than she cared to count huddled with her team, laying the ground work for the start of this investigation. It was well after one in the morning when she left the station, and here she was being greeted by the happiest person in the world it seemed.

Her head couldn't take it.

"To whom should I announce you to this lovely morning?"

The tips this guy must get from this perky-all-the-time act must be fan-fucking-tastic. No self-respecting New Yorker is ever this damn happy, especially at seven in the fucking morning.

She pulled out her badge and flashed it in front of the happy doorman.

"Lieutenant MacKenzie," she nearly growled at the man. "I don't need you to announce me; I know exactly where I'm going and who I'm looking for."

She left the shocked-quiet man standing with his hand on the still-opened door. She walked onto the elevator and pressed the button marked Ph.

She stepped off of the elevator, and walked to the single door sitting in the middle of the floor. She pressed the bell, and waited for the maid—or whomever it was that was responsible for opening doors in the Searlington household—to answer.

She waited for a respectable amount of time, when she didn't hear anyone come to the door, she followed her previous ring with two rings in quick succession.

"Come the hell on already, I really don't have all day for this."

Finally she heard the telltale sounds of someone shuffling to the door. Preparing herself for the kindly old woman the Searlington's probably had answering their door, she was stunned quiet when a shirtless Kenneth answered instead.

"Lieutenant, what are you doing here this morning?" he asked with a smile.

Her brain wasn't quiet able to form an answer. It was still stuck on the site of this half-naked man standing in front of her with the thick strands of his hair plastered to his neck, shoulders, and face by whatever water he had been standing in very recently.

Stop standing here with the stuck-on-stupid look on your face. Stop gawking at him, open your damn mouth, and speak.

"Lieutenant, I'm surprised to see you here."

"Why, I am working your niece's case, and I did tell you I would contact you?" she asked quickly, finally regaining her ability to speak. "Obviously you didn't believe me, or do you usually answer the door half-naked?"

Kenneth looked down at his naked chest and then returned his cool-blue gaze to her.

"I was just getting out of the shower when I heard the bell ring; I had just enough time to grab a pair of close-by jeans before you started pressing on the bell again."

She laughed at that, she was a bit impatient at times, especially when she thought people were taking her time for granted.

"Sorry for that. May I come in, or should I conduct the interviews I have planned here in the hall?"

He nodded and stepped aside, ushering her into the apartment.

"Yes, I know, but I didn't think it would be so soon. Has there been any news on

Merri yet?"

"I'm sorry, I don't have anything yet. I came over today to speak with you and your family; I need to get a background check on everyone involved."

"Whatever for, you don't honestly believe one of Merri's own family members would kidnap her?"

"I'm sorry, but I have to, as well as looking at outside sources, I have to look inside the inner-circle as well."

"That's absurd."

"It may very well be, but I need to do everything necessary to find your niece, and I don't intend to cut any corners because I might offend one of the all mighty Searlingtons. I need to find out why your niece is missing, and I intend to find out why she's missing, regardless of who it offends." She wasn't quite sure what to make of his expression, but he didn't keep her in suspense much longer.

"I was just about to go into the kitchen to get some breakfast, we can talk in there." She followed him expecting a uniformed cook to be inside, but when she stepped on the other side of the door, there was none. She sat at the table staring unbelievingly as he pulled out a skillet, a carton of eggs, and a packet of turkey bacon.

"Would you like some, Lt. MacKenzie?"

"No thank you."

"I take it you're shocked I can actually cook."

"Yeah it does shock me you can cook, but what shocks me even more is that you do. I would have thought your family has a full house staff that cooks, cleans, and answers to your every beck and call."

"We do, but I rarely make use of them. I'm not here most of the time to use them. I don't think it's necessary to hound someone down to do something I could do without any difficulty."

"How many people live in this house with you?" She quickly

changed the subject; she didn't need any personal insights into Kenneth Searlington.

"There are only four of us here, my sister Karolyn, my mother Jacqueline, Merridith, and myself."

"What about your father?"

"My father died quite some time ago."

"Does any of the staff live here?"

"No, each of them arrives on a daily basis."

"Why didn't your sister come down to the station to make the report?"

"She was busy trying to find William, and she hasn't been quite well since Merri disappeared."

"Has she contacted Mr. Grant?"

"Yes, he's flying in from Paris, he should be arriving soon."

"Is your sister at home, I'd like to speak with her, in fact, I'd like to speak with your mother as well."

He sipped his cup of coffee, and then answered her. "The two of them are upstairs;

I'll tell them to come down. You can speak with them in the den."

"Mr. Searlington."

"My name is Kenneth, Mac."

She nodded, if her calling him by his first name made everything run easier, then so be it. "Kenneth, I would like to speak with each of them privately."

"Fine, I'll send Karolyn down first."

She waited in the den for his sister. When she entered, she was shocked at the resemblance between them. She'd remembered him saying they were twins, but she didn't think that fraternal twins could look so much alike. They looked exactly alike; they even shared the same beauty mark above the right side of their upper lip. His sister's features were just softer than his. Where his face was chiseled and hard, hers was rounded and delicate.

They shared the same long dark hair, and the same light shade of blue eyes. The only real difference between them was their sex, she was female, and a few inches shorter than he, other than that, they were almost identical.

"Mrs. Grant."

"I've reverted to my maiden name, but please, call me Karolyn."

"Karolyn, my name is Lt MacKenzie, but everyone calls me Mac."

"Mac?" she asked with a false look of surprise pasted on her face. "What an odd name for a woman."

"Your brother said the same thing when we first met."

"Yes, well you know what they say about twins."

Heart smiled briefly, hoping to make the other woman more comfortable in her presence. "Karolyn, I know this must be a difficult time for you, but I really need to ask you some questions, your answers could give us a clue to your daughter's whereabouts."

"I've never been away from my daughter this long. Mother and Kenneth are doing all they can to help me."

"Kenneth tells me your ex-husband will be arriving soon from Paris."

"Yes that's true, I can't tell you what a relief it is. I truly need him here with me."

"Forgive me for seeming intrusive, but haven't you and your ex-husband been estranged for the past year?"

She seemed uncomfortable with the question, her high-heel covered foot twitching

just the slightest bit, but answered it nonetheless. "Yes, my husband, and I have been estranged for a great amount of time, but we've always done what was best for our daughter."

"Is that so?"

She didn't seem to like Heart's tone, her eyes squinting an almost imperceptible fraction. "Yes, as a matter of fact it is."

Heart's bullshit meter started screaming at her. Something wasn't right. "I don't intend to sound negative, but how could the two of you decide what was best for your daughter, when you haven't allowed him to see her? Tell me, Karolyn, why did you keep

Merri's father from seeing her?"

The woman sat straighter now. Her cool surface disturbed briefly by the slight tick in her jaw. "I don't think that's any of your concern, Lieutenant."

"Karolyn, if you kept William from seeing his daughter, there had to be a very good reason; the police need to check that out."

"Are you insinuating William kidnapped our daughter, is he a suspect?"

Heart raised and dropped her shoulders quickly. "Karolyn, until we know anything, everyone is a suspect. I can't exclude anyone from my suspicion until your daughter is home safe."

That small almost undecipherable tick in Karolyn's jaw turned in to outright teeth grinding. Her already stiff posture turned more rigid as she leaned forward in her chair.

"I appreciate you doing your job, but if you're going to sit here accusing me and my family, instead of finding the real kidnappers, I'm going to have to ask you to step down as head of this case, I want my daughter home, and you don't seem competent enough to bring her home to me."

She watched Karolyn for a moment. Her words were definitely sharp, intending to get a rise out of Heart. Conversely, there was no heat behind the cool tone of her voice. Heart surmised this was just how rich people expressed their displeasure. She guessed real rage was too much like being common, something she doubted Karolyn Searlington would ever allow herself to be accused of.

Heart was about to respond to Karolyn when she heard a familiar voice at the door.

"I think you owe Lt. MacKenzie an apology."

"Whatever for? She's wasting time accusing my husband when she could be out looking for actual kidnappers. I'll not have her sullying William's name."

Kenneth had moved into the room and placed a calm hand on his sister's shoulder.

"I have it on good authority that Lieutenant MacKenzie is the best in the department, and if you truly want your daughter to find her way home safely, I have every confidence that it will be Mac that brings her home."

Karolyn said nothing, she simply walked out of the room as quietly as she'd come in, taking the icy chill she'd brought into the room with her.

"Please excuse my sister, Lieutenant; this is a very trying time for her right now."

Heart simply nodded her head. "An apology isn't necessary," she said softly. "I'm sure my tolerance for being interrogated might be a tad bit low if it were my own child in danger."

~

$\mathcal{H}$e could feel the tense muscles in his face relax at MacKenzie's mention of her children.

"Are you very close to them?"

"Them?" she said with raised eyebrows, as if she'd just realized what he'd said. "I don't have any children," she shook her head, eyes bright as the words tumbled quickly from her mouth. "I think it would be very hard to throw myself into my work the way I do, while being a single parent."

Single, his ears almost twitched at the sound of the word crossing her lips, she was single? Why was this disturbing him so much? Why should he care whether she was single or not?

"I take it you spend an awful amount of time working."

"Yes," she said, with a small smile climbing up her face. "Being on the job means, most times, everything else in my life is secondary to what my duties demand."

"You're dedicated to the job then?'

She nodded her head again. "I bleed blue as they say. I suppose the same goes for you when you're doing whatever it is you Searlingtons do."

"Real estate, and it's not what *we* Searlingtons do, just me. My mother and sister just sit around raking in the family business profits."

He watched the question form in her brown eyes before it crossed her lips. "Your mother doesn't have a say in your family's business?"

"No, my father left his estate solely to me, he didn't trust my mother."

"I'm sorry."

He chuckled briefly. "For what, I don't trust my mother or my sister for that matter. I love them dearly, but I would be a fool to trust them. If they could, they would usurp my authority, and take the company in a heartbeat, trusting them would be a silly mistake."

MacKenzie appeared as if she had something more to say, but her words never had the chance to slip into the air.

"Are you Detective MacKenzie?" The sharp voice caused them both to look toward the door where his mother stood angrily.

"No, I'm Lieutenant MacKenzie."

"It makes no difference."

MacKenzie shrugged her shoulders at the obvious insult. Saying simply, "Actually there is." Her light words seemed to annoy his mother more. *Point one to the Lieutenant.*

"I don't care what your rank is," his mother said through the thin line of her lips. Her shoulders set back in a stiff locked position, immovable, unshakable. "When I am finished talking to your superior about your tactics here today, you won't have a job, let alone be concerned with inconsequential things such as your rank."

"Mac, this is my mother, Jacqueline who has obviously lost her manners."

"Manners, if anyone needs to learn manners, it's this poor excuse for a police officer," his mother said, not taking her eyes off of MacKenzie as she spoke.

"Mrs. Searlington, would you like to tell me what the problem is?"

"The problem, Detective—"

"Lieutenant," MacKenzie interrupted with an easy smile on her face.

She was enjoying this, Kenneth realized. He'd seen grown men crumble in the face of his mother's glare, but MacKenzie was smiling as if she were having a conversation with an old friend. *This should be fun.*

"Whatever," Jacqueline almost spat. "My problem is that instead of trying to find my missing grandchild, you're prying into my daughter's personal life like some seedy tabloid writer. What exactly did you ask my daughter to upset her so much?"

"I asked her some very blunt questions as I intend to ask you," MacKenzie said, her lips still curved in a friendly smile.

"You won't be asking me anything, I want you out of this house and off this case now. I will be speaking to your immediate superior momentarily; I don't want you anywhere near this investigation."

Kenneth watched MacKenzie, waiting for the fire she'd shown him in her office when he'd attempted to intimidate her the way his mother was trying to do now. It hadn't worked out so well for him then, and he surmised it probably wasn't going to work out well for his mother either.

"You can refuse to answer my questions," MacKenzie said, her tone still pleasant. "However, that would only force me to arrange to have you officially interrogated down at my precinct in Brooklyn." The mention of Brooklyn made his mother fidget just a little bit. The ever-present snob in her would consider Brooklyn a far-off barren land of desolation, destruction, and primitivism, instead of just another borough that was actually only a short bridge crossing away from their expensive luxury apartment on Park Avenue.

"You could also throw me out of your house, but I'd only be back later with a warrant giving me permission to search the premises," she said as she took a confident step landing her directly in front of his mother. "The one thing you can't do is throw me off this case, you weren't the one that came down to the station to make the report, and even if you had, the only way I'd be taken off of this case would be if my superior decided to take me off. Now are you going to answer my questions here, or should I suggest you call your lawyer, and have him meet us at the Seventy-fourth precinct?"

MacKenzie's lifted brow lingered after the question, and awaited an answer from his unusually quiet mother. *Strong work Lieutenant, I've been trying to shut her up for years.*

This woman really took no shit from anyone. She hadn't been intimidated by him, his sister, his mother, or the threat of the connections and power their money afforded them. Yes this woman was the perfect person to cut through the bullshit that might prevent a lesser investigator from finding out what happened to his precious niece. This woman was what Merri needed to get home.

Kenneth stifled a small chuckle under a fake cough as he looked at his mother. Jacqueline sat quietly, eyes filled with scorn for the young lieutenant that stood before her. He turned his gaze to the lieutenant and felt that familiar quickening of attraction that had come unexpectedly in her office when she brandished her service weapon to him.

She sat in one smooth motion on the chair opposite his mother and smiled as she said, "Thank you for your cooperation Mrs. Searlington."

~

"*D*on't thank me, just get on with this."
Heart could almost feel the burning venom dripping from the elder woman's lips.

She wasn't really bothered by it. Her captain knew how she operated, knew she wasn't one to kiss ass in order to climb the ladder. She was all about the job and didn't give a good goddamn about whose feathers she ruffled in the process. He put her on the case because he knew they didn't come better than Lt. Heart MacKenzie when it came to solving complicated crimes, and she had every confidence that he wouldn't pull her off of this case simply because this entitled old woman and her privileged, bratty daughter were offended at how she spoke to them, and what she asked of them.

"When was the last time you saw your granddaughter?"

"The day she disappeared, that morning before she and Karolyn went shopping."

"Did your granddaughter seem agitated or angered in any way?"

"No, she was as happy as she always was. Merridith is like a ray of sunshine in this home, she makes everything better and brighter."

"What was your granddaughter's relationship with her father?"

"She didn't have one, he walked out on her when my daughter divorced him. A man like that doesn't deserve a wonderful daughter like Merridith."

Without letting anyone on, she calculated the discrepancies in the two stories she'd heard of the breakdown between Merridith and her father. Kenneth said his sister stopped communication between the two, but their mother said William stopped coming around on his own.

The doorbell interrupted them.

"Please excuse me."

"It's all right, Mother, I'll get the door. You sit here until Mac is finished with you." His mother didn't seem happy at all, the doorbell was her only viable escape, and her son sealed it right before her eyes.

"Don't worry, Mrs. Searlington; I won't need you here much longer. I only have one more question. Do you think William would have any interest in kidnapping your granddaughter?"

"No, he hasn't wanted anything to do with the child for over a year. Why on Earth would he take her now?"

"Thank you, Mrs. Searlington, if I have any more questions, I'll contact you." She walked out into the living room, where she found Kenneth, along with a strange man holding Karolyn. William Grant she assumed, and his timing couldn't have been more perfect.

"William, this is Lieutenant MacKenzie, she's the lead investigator on Merri's case."

William was as tall as Kenneth, a little leaner, but still a significant presence in the room. He and Kenneth looked like opposite sides of the same coin. Where Kenneth's skin was pale, almost alabaster in color, William wore a bronzed sun-kissed tone. His blond locks cut into a short tapered style that was popular among young Caucasian men, very much unlike Kenneth's long, thick strands that flowed well past his shoulders.

"MacKenzie is it? Has there been any news of my daughter?"

"No, Mr. Grant, I would like to speak with you privately about your daughter."

"Anything to help find my little girl."

"Follow me into the den."

They sat opposite each other, and for the first time she noticed large brown eyes looking at her. They seemed tired...weary even. Was it his long trip from Paris, or was it worry over his daughter that left his eyes sad, dim.

"Mr. Grant, when was the last time you saw your daughter?"

"A little under a year ago."

"What kind of relationship did the two of you share?"

"We were the best of friends, I loved her dearly. I loved spending time with her."

"It must have broken your heart when your wife refused to let you see her. Why did your wife keep you from seeing your daughter?"

She watched him carefully, hoping to find some small thing—a sign of whether he was answering truthfully or hiding something.

"To tell you the truth, I don't know. I don't even know why my wife divorced me."

Interesting. "Would you care to elaborate on that?"

"Karolyn and I spent seven happy years together, and then one day out of the blue, she slapped divorce papers on me. I fought that divorce with everything I had for two years, but in the end, Karolyn's lawyers were better than mine, and they convinced the judge there was no marriage to salvage."

She nodded as she took notes. "What were Karolyn's legal grounds for divorcing you?"

"Irreconcilable differences, differences I didn't know anything about. When I confronted Karolyn about the divorce, she simply told me she was tired of being married to me, and she wanted out."

"That's the only explanation she gave you?"

"Yeah."

"That's so strange, your ex-wife was just singing your praises when I questioned her about you. She wouldn't even tell me why she wouldn't allow you to see Merri."

She saw the muscles in his face tighten. His hands were tightly laced together. He wasn't happy at the moment.

"I don't know why she wouldn't let me see my daughter. After our

36

divorce came through, it was almost as though she became angry with me; as if it was my fault our marriage came to an end. Then she refused to let me come anywhere near Merridith. Again without any notice, or forewarning."

"Why didn't you file for custody?"

"I loved my daughter, and I wanted nothing more in life than to be with her. I didn't want to drag her through something so ugly."

"Where were you the afternoon your daughter was reported missing?"

"I was working in Paris."

"What exactly do you do in Paris?"

"I'm a designer, I have a clothing line in Paris."

She nodded, continuing to take notes. "Is there anyone that can verify your whereabouts at that time?"

"Yeah, hundreds of people in my office building, but I wasn't aware I would need an alibi when I came back to the States."

"I'm sorry, but I have to ask these questions."

"I understand, you don't have to apologize, I want you to do whatever is necessary to find my little girl."

Huge difference from your former in-laws it seems. "When did you find out about your daughter's disappearance?"

"Yesterday. Karolyn called me begging me to come to New York, when I asked why, she told me Merri had been kidnapped."

Heart stopped writing and lifted her eyes to the sad father sitting across from her. "Well, that's an over exaggeration on Karolyn's part, this hasn't yet been classified as a kidnapping yet, we can't call this a kidnapping until we get some sort of demand for ransom, or a witness that says they saw Merri being taken." He nodded his head, attempting to take in her words.

"MacKenzie, have you ever handled a case like ours, where the child of a wealthy family was taken?" he asked in a small voice that bellied the amount of hurt she saw written across his entire being.

"Yes I have."

"And when the ransom was paid, was the child returned?"

She held her gaze on the notepad in front of her. "Would you like me to tell you what you want to hear, or the truth?"

"Please, the truth."

"First off, William, we don't know that Merridith has been kidnapped. My team is scouring the streets as we speak, trying to discover any news. Maybe she's in a hospital, maybe she got lost, whatever the case, there's no evidence that this is actually a kidnapping yet."

He nodded his head, "Yeah, but what if this is the worst-case scenario. What should we expect?"

She didn't want to answer that. She had been in law enforcement for the last nine years, and she'd seen the ugly things people were capable of doing. Sometimes people committed the most heinous crimes with great motivation, sometimes with no perceivable reason at all. But looking in this man's tired eyes, she could see he wanted the truth— however painful—he needed to know the worst of what could happen.

"On most of the cases I've worked, when the kidnappers got the money, the hostage was killed." She saw the worry building in his eyes. "But don't worry, we'll find her before a cent of any ransom demand is given. I promise you that my fellow officers and I will do everything possible to bring your little girl home."

She hoped he could tell by the look in her eye she would keep her promise. She wrapped up her interview with William and headed back into the living room. She was about to leave the penthouse apartment when Kenneth stopped her.

"So did you get all your questions answered?" he asked.

"Most of them." She turned to face the door, but he stopped her once again.

"Mac, would you come into the den, I'd like to discuss your findings with you." She knew if she said no, he wouldn't give up, so she followed him into his den.

"So has questioning my family given you any insight?"

She shrugged her shoulders. "Kenneth, I really don't have anything right now, it's useless discussing this."

"I don't think so, this is my niece, and I don't care how tiny the detail, I want to know what's going on."

She respected his need to know, unlike his first time he'd demanded to know what was going on in the case; there was no trace of the then obvious arrogance that he wore so openly. Now, he was a concerned uncle asking about his beloved niece.

"Whatever I relay to you remains between you and I, no one is to know what I share with you. Not your mother, not Karolyn, and not William, absolutely no one. And if I find out that you've divulged anything, and believe me, I will find out, because people can't keep secrets, I will shut you completely out of this case."

"I understand, MacKenzie, and I thank you. Now that you have my word, tell me what's going on."

She questioned her sanity agreeing to something like this. But having to fight this constant battle with this man was going to wear her nerves thin.

"The first time you and I met, and you told me of the forced estrangement between Merri and William, my alarm immediately went off. In a lot of cases, when a child is kidnapped, the parent that lost custody takes the child. When you told me the story, I felt like the man got a raw deal, and I sort of expected him to have taken Merri."

"But something changed your mind, what?"

"When I spoke to your sister, my suspicions were heightened, but there was something signaling me that I couldn't understand. So I spoke with your mother, and she totally threw me off. Your mother told me Karolyn never stopped William from seeing Merridith, she said William just deserted her after the divorce was final."

"What? I can't believe she said that." Then he became quiet, she could almost see the wheels turning in his mind.

"I don't know how she got that idea, but that's what she told me. At any rate, it made me wonder what the real story was. You offered me one story, your mother another, and Karolyn would barely tell me anything. In fact, she refused to tell me why she refused to let William see their daughter; she wouldn't answer any of my questions about her relationship with William.

"The only thing she did say about the two of them was, she really needed him right now. She said the two of them were always there for one another in times of crisis when it concerned Merridith. Said they always made decisions together concerning the welfare of their child."

Kenneth's eyebrows drew together in to a sharp point. His hands went to his hips and he leaned his weight in to his right foot.

"I don't know why my sister lied to you, but that's exactly what she did. The only

Searlington that keeps in contact with William is me."

Heart rolled her eyes, the dynamics of this crazy family were giving her whiplash.

"I'm not certain if she was intentionally lying, it seemed almost like wishful thinking. After all of the stories I'd heard, I knew there was a strong possibility that William did take his daughter, but after I spoke to William, I doubted very seriously he kidnapped his daughter."

"You doubted seriously, that isn't a complete declaration of his innocence."

"I can't give that, everyone is a suspect until Merridith is home."

"So if everyone's a suspect, why are you telling me all of this?"

"Keep your friends close, and your suspects even closer."

CHAPTER 3

"So what do you have on this case MacKenzie?"

In three days she'd had absolutely no clues. "I'm sorry to say, but I don't have anything, Cap."

"What do you mean you have nothing?" he asked in a gruff voice.

She wasn't sure if it was a criticism or a statement of disbelief. Maybe it was a little of both. Either way, she was just as pissed that her efforts kept coming up empty.

"Captain Porter, I want this little girl home just as badly as you do, but there just isn't anything for us to go on. There's been no demand for ransom, we couldn't find one witness that saw the girl leave with anyone, or even remembers seeing the child with her mother. Cap, it's like this child just disappeared into thin air, I can't find anything."

"Bring me something on this girl; I don't like the idea of this young child out there with some maniac. Find that girl, Mac, and do it quickly, talk to the family."

"I've already spoken with the family."

"Then speak with them again!" he barked at her.

She nodded her head. "Yes, Captain, I'll speak with the family again. First I need to have a team meeting with my guys, and then I'll make my way over to the Searlingtons."

Captain Porter nodded in acknowledgement of her plan of action. He dismissed her from his office, and she went in search of her team in the squad room.

"Smyth, Jenson, Thomas, Ramirez, Santini, my office now!" she barked without even looking in their direction as she took quick, long steps inside her office.

Barret Jenson, Adam Thomas, Ada Ramirez, Sage Santini, and Bryan Smyth were the five detectives that made up the best damn investigative team in Brooklyn North. It didn't matter the sector, if the crime was big enough, they were tagged to cross jurisdiction whenever Brass wanted results—quick, effective, and most of all accurate results.

"What do we got L.T.?" Smyth said as he sat down.

"Fuck if I know, Smyth," she said through clenched teeth. "Why the hell don't you tell me why I don't have dick to give to Porter after three days of the five of you scouring the streets? Why the hell did I just spend an unpleasant visit in Porter's office having him chew my ass out over our lack of progress? Could it be that the five detectives that are supposed to be the best of the best can't seem to bring me shit that's useful in this investigation? What the fuck are the five of you doing out there?"

"Come on Mac—" Smyth attempted to speak, calling her by her familiar name.

Out of her five subordinates, Bryan Smyth was the one that knew her the best, they'd partnered for half of her career. Heart was never one to surround herself with an abundance of friends, connections didn't really come easily to her. But if she'd classify anyone as a friend, it was Bryan Smyth, the man who was now sitting trying to take the sting out her as she pressed her team.

"Smyth, Mac was the one in Porter's office trying to convince him you were doing your best. Lieutenant MacKenzie is the person that's standing in this room now. You're direct superior, and dammit, you'd better have something better to tell me today than you've done for the past three fucking days you've been on the street canvassing."

She stood in front of the white dry-erase board where five pictures were taped against it. In the center, an 8 X 10 of the missing dark-haired child that was almost the mirror image of her mother and uncle. Pictures of the three remaining members of the Searlington family as well as the little girl's father, William surrounded the smiling child's face.

"Do we know anything more about the adults in this little girl's life other than the fact that they all have more money than God?" Heart asked her team, waiting for her five detectives to gather around the rectangle table sitting on the inside of her office. Their meetings were always conducted in the privacy of her office. Their cases were always played closely to the vest, with usually their captain being the only other cop in the house that knew something about their working agenda.

Ramirez stood up and walked to the dry-erase board Heart was standing in front of. She was a Dominican Republic-born Latina who migrated to Washington Heights in her youth. She was a wonderful mixture of all of the stereotypes ever heard about Latino women—a fact she wholeheartedly embraced and celebrated. She was tiny, no bigger than five-five or five-six, she was possessive of everything from her ballpoint pen on her desk, to her husband—and she didn't share either. Her temper was legendary, and she didn't have a problem getting physical, and even though she was small, she was a formidable opponent. Not that Heart and Ramirez had ever mixed it up that way — seeming to have an unspoken respect for each other, and their respective personal limits.

She watched Ramirez point to the photograph of Kenneth Sear-lington.

"Actually L.T.," Ramirez said, her words flavored with just a hint of her native Spanish tongue. "Kenneth is the only one in the family that is actually rich. With the exception of William Grant, who owns some sort of fashion design house in France,
Kenneth is the only one that has money."

Heart looked at the photo and then returned her gaze to her detective.

"What do you mean, Ramirez? Searlington mentioned he runs the family business ever since his father died, but how does that leave him as the only one with money?"

"He doesn't just run the company, Lieutenant, he owns it. And it's not just a company, it's a real estate empire. Put it this way, if Trump owns half of Manhattan, Searlington owns the other half, along with part of Long Island, a good chunk of

Connecticut and some pretty lofty parts of the Eastern seaboard." Heart let a low whistle escape her pursed lips.

"The company is national, Ramirez?"

Ramirez shook her head. "Try global. I was able to look into his financials and past tax returns; this man has money coming in from all over the world like you wouldn't believe. Apparently his father changed his will about five years before he died. He cut the sister and the mother out of it, and left everything to Kenneth."

"Damn, after meeting Jacqueline Searlington, I can't say I blame the old man, she's not exactly the warmest person in the world. He really didn't leave her anything?"

Ramirez shook her head again. "Nope, left every red cent to the son. The old woman didn't take it lying down though. She contested the will, it took a few years for the courts to decide that she didn't have a leg to stand on, and that everything would go to Kenneth. The only thing the father demanded of Kenneth is that they always have their basic needs met: shelter, clothing, food, resources, that kind of thing. He gives them each a considerable allowance each month, but make no mistake, Kenneth is the source."

Heart walked around the rectangular table that her other detectives were sitting at. It was the way she thought, the way she processed information. She walked, and digested every detail Ramirez offered her.

"What about the girl's father, William? Where does he fit into all of this?" Heart asked, and Detective Jensen stood up and walked to the board.

"Ramirez is right, Searlington is Mr. Money Bags in this family. Don't get me wrong

Grant is no slouch when compared to a cop's salary. But when you compare what his fashion house clears to Searlington, it's like comparing the working poor to royalty.

Searlington has a long line of generational money behind him, no contest." "Is Grant hurting for cash?" she asked Jenson.

"No, his business does well and it seems to be thriving."

She continued to walk then stopped to ask, "Is there any reason to suspect the amount of money these guys have has anything to do with this child disappearing?"

Smyth jumped in. "We don't know if it actually had anything to do with her disappearance, but we have to consider it a possible factor until we know for certain that

it isn't."

"What?" Heart asked.

"Merridith Grant is the sole beneficiary of everything Kenneth Searlington owns," Smyth said.

"He left all that money to a little girl? She has more than a decade before she's even legal. How is she gonna manage all of that money?"

"She's not," Santini said. "Her father is. William Grant is named as the executor of Searlington's will and empire. If anything happens to Searlington, Grant will manage the estate until the girl is thirty and receive an annual commission for doing so."

Heart stopped walking, crossed her arms over her chest and took a deep breath. "All right folks, time to find out if somebody is trying to get an early payday."

~

Kenneth Searlington sat in the high-backed leather chair behind the custom-made desk he'd commissioned when he took control of his father's company. The chair, the desk, the office, the position, all of it had made him feel confident, accomplished, in control. To experience such power in his late twenties had been a heady experience. He'd beaten his mother and sister in the courts, and at the same time shown his naysayers at his father's company—those who had doubted he could successfully shoulder the troubles of a leader and continue to make his father's legacy thrive—that he was in fact, the man in charge. He'd shown them all, shown them all he had the stones to do whatever it took to run his father's company, and that in truth, Searlington Real estate no longer belonged to

Kalvin Searlington, it was all Kenneth's.

It was all his. Not just lock, stock, and barrel, but from everything from concept to product, it was all his. His father had created an incredible business, he had left him such an amazing foundation upon which to build. But, Kenneth, forever guided by his unfailing instinct when it came to the business of real estate, had nearly quadrupled the already monster-sized company his father had grown and left him. Kenneth had taken it from the national success that it was to the global Goliath it was today.

The ages between twenty-seven and thirty-three had passed him by without much notice. Spending most of his time in this very office, he had lost interest in pretty much anything that wasn't work-related. Everything, with the one exception being Merridith.

That little girl had always been his bright spot. She was the one thing in his life that made all of the slaving he did in his work-life—his only life really—worthwhile. He was happy to put in the hours, put in the labor, endure the unimaginable stress and fatigue that came along with the long working days that led to too many sleep-less nights. Every single moment of the last six years had been worth its weight in gold, because Merridith would be safe, she would be free of his mother and sister, and able to live whatever life she chose.

The thought of his mother and sister simply made him feel heavy. They were both like an immovable albatross around his neck. The two women who were his closest blood relatives would sooner see him succumb to destruction than any of his competitors or enemies.

The two had fought him tooth and nail in the legal system to attempt to steal his father's company from him. Their schemes and manipulations had nearly worked too, were it not for his father's fore-thought to put certain failsafe measures in place prior to his death, the duo might very well have succeeded in taking what they wanted—Kenneth destroyed, and his father's company in shambles.

Kenneth thought about his sweet Merridith again. He could hear the pounding of his increasing heartbeat in his ears. He wanted—needed Merridith home, and he wanted whomever was responsible for her disappearance to pay for daring to harm his precious niece.

Kenneth had never been a violent man, he'd never sought to solve his problems with physical violence. He'd like to think he was just above that sort of thing, that he left that sort of behavior to people of a more common station in life. He'd like to believe there were too many alternate, more effective methods at his fingertips available at his leisure, to fix whatever problem he was facing at the moment. But Kenneth knew the truth. He knew it wasn't that he couldn't use violence, be it a moral opposition to it, or a physical inability to purport it, he just chose not to.

His father, Kalvin had spent several years in the armed forces, and many years practicing one form of defensive arts or another. By the time Kenneth was five, his father had hired a personal instructor to teach him how to master the defensive arts. From that point on, Kenneth had known how to defend himself physically if necessary, but his father had always taught him it was a better man who fought his battles with his words, that violence of any kind should be a last resort, not a first option.

But sitting here now, wondering what was happening with or—God help him—to his niece was making the trained black belt in him beg for an opportunity to unleash on the monster that took his niece. The police had better come up with something soon, or he would resort to his own devices in discovering what had become of his niece.

He pulled his smartphone from his pocket and swiped his thumb across its dark, idol screen. No missed messages, no missed calls, just nothing.

"Dammit, MacKenzie, what the hell is going on, why haven't I heard anything from you yet?"

He stood quickly from his chair and leaned over his desk, bracing himself on fingertips. He took in a breath, calling the vision of David Porter's second in command to his memory. He had at least five inches in height on her, placing her somewhere around

5'9" in her bare feet. She was solidly built, not skinny and frail like most of the women that he surrounded himself with. She was cut and carved, supple brown skin over tight, taut, lean muscle. The day they'd met she'd been wearing a fitted pullover long-sleeved shirt that hugged every curve she had. It provided a perfect silhouette for the wellconditioned body that lay beneath it, especially the high, firm globes that looked as if they would fit his hands perfectly. Just thinking about the elevated, firm curve of her ass that those damn fitted cargo pants she'd been wearing did nothing to hide, had his groin tightening in a deliciously uncomfortable way.

"Damn it, Searlington, get it together," he said to no one. He turned around to face his wall-length window and cupped a determined hand on his crotch to readjust himself.

"Acting like a horny teenager is not going to get Merridith home."

He didn't quite get why his body was reacting to MacKenzie this way. She was beautiful yes, in both a traditional and exotic sense. *Exotic*, he almost laughed as the word crawled across his mind. Was that the correct term to describe her? Or was she only exotic because she was such an explosive splash of color in his ridiculously homogenous world. He was certain if he asked her, she would probably pull her weapon on him again.

"Damn," he cursed again. Just when he was beginning to get his wayward cock under control he had to go and think about those long slender fingers wrapped around the hard metal of her service weapon.

"It's just been too long since I've gotten laid, that's all." That was the only logical explanation he could think of for why he couldn't reign in his body's reactions to just the thought of this woman.

An intrusive buzzing sound brought his head around from the window and pulled his gaze to the intercom button on his office phone.

"Mr. Searlington," the cool monotone sound of his secretary's voice came through the speaker.

"Yes Abigail?"

"There is a Lieutenant MacKenzie here to see you, are you avail —"Abigail's voice stopped abruptly. The next time she spoke, her voice seemed to climb higher. "Ma'am, you can't just walk in—"

That was the last he heard of her voice before a brazen MacKenzie walked into his office with a flustered Abigail trotting quickly behind her.

"Mr. Searlington, I tried to stop—"

Kenneth raised a quieting hand. "It's okay, Abby, I was expecting to see the lieutenant today."

He saw the smirk on MacKenzie's face; obviously she found his bullshit amusing.

He motioned for MacKenzie to take the seat directly in front of his desk and sat down in the familiar comfort of his chair. Before they began, he looked up to see Abigail still standing at his door.

"Abby, please make certain Lieutenant MacKenzie and I aren't disturbed. Whatever is on my schedule move it, I don't want so much as a phone call while the lieutenant is visiting with me."

Abigail nodded her head, and quietly exited the room. Once she was gone he turned his full attention to MacKenzie sitting before him with a crossed leg resting over the opposite knee. She readjusted herself in her seat, her hand briefly touching her holstered weapon to a more comfortable position on her hip. Once she found a comfortable position, she pulled the edge of her blazer effectively concealing her weapon from his view.

"Please don't be shy now, Lieutenant," he said with a smile. "Your weapon and I have been well-acquainted during our last meeting."

Her full lips, covered with the barest of pink tints by the lip gloss she was wearing spread in a full smile.

"I'm not being shy, Mr. Searlington. If I'm not in uniform, and I'm outside of the station, then my service weapon must be concealed from plain view." Her smile still plastered across her face.

"You wear a uniform?" he asked.

"Yes, white shirt, navy blue pants. Usually only wear it for official purposes, or when there is some sort of meeting with the higher-ups. Other than that, I'm usually in plain clothes."

Kenneth swallowed hard as his unruly member chose that moment to twitch beneath his zipper. Damn, the thought of her in uniform was an image he didn't need in his head at this moment.

Head out of your crotch and in the game, Searlington, he chastised himself. He quickly readjusted his position in the chair to give himself some relief while he remained in the lieutenant's presence.

He cleared his throat, and hopefully his head of the errant thoughts it was producing of MacKenzie.

"Lieutenant MacKenzie, has there been any news on my niece?" He was pleased with the sound of his voice. He'd managed to affect his usual business voice—controlled, even register, giving nothing away.

She shook her head steadily. "No, I'm afraid there have been no new developments." Her eyes quickly crawled over his face before she spoke again.

"Actually, Kenneth, I'm more concerned about what we haven't found." He quirked a brow and nodded his head for her to continue.

"Neither myself nor my fellow officers have been able to find anything that would lead us to Merridith. We can't find any witnesses that saw her leave the house that day, no one seems to remember her being on the street with your sister. We've scoured hours of camera footage from various sources and not one frame has an image of your niece. It's like she's invisible, a ghost." She reached inside her jacket pocket and retrieved a small notepad and pen then continued. "I'm also bothered by the fact that there hasn't been any ransom calls, we don't have a clue as to where she is. Something just feels wrong about this."

He slapped his hand against the heavy desk before him. Shaking all of its contents with the blow's force. Everything jumped, with the exception of MacKenzie. She hadn't seemed fazed by his outburst at all.

"Damn, that poor little girl is somewhere frightened, and no one knows where to find her!" he yelled. "God when I get my hands on the bastard that snatched her, I swear I'll kill him with my bare hands!"

The only reaction she gave was a small glint of her eye, so small it was almost unnoticeable.

"That isn't wise to threaten death to another human being in front of a police officer. It becomes a problem should testimony ever be called upon. But for now, I'll just take it as an uncle's frustration."

At first he wasn't able to discern if she was serious or not, then he saw the slight lift

of the corner of her lips, the only inkling that she was joking.

He smiled, something he hadn't done in any of their previous meetings, and even though it'd only been a short while, they're had been many. "Thank you for your cop's attempt at humor, I can't remember the last time I smiled. It's been agony not knowing where Merri is."

"You look like hell, have you eaten yet?"

He paused for a moment to think on her question. "No, I find myself burying my head into my work to forget what's going on around me. I think the last time I ate was last night some time."

"I feel like I owe you something. I don't feel like I'm doing my job, I usually have something to go on by now. Let me take you out to dinner, we can tell each other about the misery in our days."

"Are you asking me out on a date, Mac?"

She stopped, uncrossed and then re-crossed her legs in the opposite direction before she answered him.

"Kenneth, when I tell you what I'm about to tell you, I don't want you to take offense."

"Fine, I won't, say what's on your mind."

"There are two very distinct reasons why I would never ask you on a date," she said with the barest of smiles on her face.

He leaned forward, fingers steepled together on his desk. "Please do enlighten me,

Lieutenant."

"The first is the obvious, you're involved in a case I'm working on. I will never cross that line," he nodded, waiting for her to continue. "Second, you're just not my type."

That one made something jump inside of him. What the hell was that supposed to mean? Kenneth knew he was no slouch, he had what most considered to be traditional good looks. Angular features, a well-maintained physique that was awe-inspiring when adorned with the expensive fabrics and designers that he regularly patronized. Let's face it, he was sexy as all hell and he knew it. His money just made him irresistible to both women and men alike, if they weren't trying to sex him, they were trying to be his friend, excited with the thought of what his money, position, and prestige could do for them. Not her type? He'd bet his milky white ass that he was her type, and everyone else's type to boot. That is unless…

"Are you a lesbian?" the words slipped from his lips before he could call them back in.

Both her eyebrows lifted and she smiled. "Oh, I get it, the only reason I couldn't possibly be attracted to you is the fact that I'm sexually attracted to women?" She shook her head.

"Lieutenant, please forgive me, that was out of line."

She stood and smiled. "Just be glad I'm on the job, or I would give you an answer to that question." She laughed to herself. "Trust me, you wouldn't like my answer either, but I'd give you one. So are we going to eat or are you going to sit here analyzing my personal preferences in men?"

He reached into a drawer and removed his wallet and grabbed his smartphone from the desk.

"Oh believe me, Lieutenant; I plan on finding out the answer to my question while I eat the meal you're treating me to. Let's go."

~

She took him to a barbeque house. The air was filled with the sweet and spicy scent of mesquite. She couldn't imagine him in a place like this, but he seemed to adjust quite well. She watched him as he looked around, apparently trying to get a better feel for his surroundings.

"What's the matter, never eaten barbeque before?" she asked, her voice dripping with sarcasm.

"No, I was just thinking how long it's been since I've had good barbeque. Does this place grill ribs?"

"I don't know, check the menu and see if they serve beef ribs."

"Beef ribs, I don't remember saying I wanted beef ribs. I want nice greasy, cholesterol covered, artery clogging, barbequed pork ribs."

"You eat pork? I would have thought you were a health nut."

"Don't get me wrong, I normally eat a balanced healthy diet."

"And exactly what is a healthy diet to you?"

"Not too much of anything. I try to balance everything out, it keeps me healthy."

"That's a good way to balance yourself out. I see these people starving themselves, for the sake of being healthier."

"Yeah, and I refuse to let myself become one of those people. I workout regularly, and I eat right. I'm allowed to splurge on pork ribs every now and again."

She was quiet through most of their meal, concentrating on the food before her.

"So are you going to tell me why exactly I'm not your type?"

Heart shook her head, taking a moment to wipe her mouth with her napkin before speaking. "Are we back to this again?" she asked.

"Yes. So if you aren't attracted to me, what kind of man are you attracted to?"

"Why are you so interested? You don't fit the criteria."

"I'm curious."

"You mean nosy."

"So humor me," he said with a shrugged shoulder.

"Listen, I'm sure our conversation could be better spent talking about your niece's case."

He shook his head. "You said you didn't have any new developments in her case, this conversation will help keep me distracted while you and your team come up with something," he said with a sickeningly sweet smile that drew out her own smile.

"So what is it, MacKenzie, you don't like tall, built, white, rich men with long hair?"

She rolled her eyes and chuckled softly. "I will admit, Mr. Searlington, long hair is generally a turn off for me, but you really do make it work for you. You sorta look like one of those dudes on the cover of a romance novel. All you need is the wind blowing through your tresses and you'd be a perfect model."

He waved an accusing finger between them. "You're not getting off that easily, Lieutenant. Why don't I turn your crank?"

"Turn my crank? Do real people really say things like that?" She laughed hard and loud, her stomach contracting in tight spasms. "You sound like a poorly written porno right now." She raised both hands in surrender to his questions. "If it will make you shut up and never say things like, 'turn your crank,' to me ever again, I will tell you." She watched him lean forwarded in expectation, the simple move made her stomach pinch even harder as she laughed again.

Finally getting her laughter under control she said, "The one trait that I just can't tolerate in a man, a trait that you seem to have in spades is…" he leaned even closer, as if she were about to gift him with the most sought-after secret of the universe.

"…arrogance," she said quietly. "It's a turn off for me, men who appear to believe they can have anything they want simply because they want it, most times without even working for it, or worse, without asking for permission." Her words had become soft, quiet. "Those are the men that leave me cold."

She felt a familiar chill pass through her, a frigid cloak covering her from the inside out.

She'd tried for years to leave that horrible memory in the dark recesses of her mind, but it always found some way to crawl to the surface.

The surrounding noises became distant as her mind travelled to that far off place that held all of the darkness inside of her. Her mind was just about to unlock that first disgusting memory when she felt an electric jolt pull her from her reverie. It was the unfamiliar, and usually unwelcomed feeling of skin on skin. Someone else's skin touching her skin. She snatched her hand away quickly and dropped her hand to the side where her weapon lay hidden. It was a reflex many cops had when they perceived danger, it was drilled into them to always be on their guard, and she was.

"Hey, what's wrong, where were you?" she heard him ask. She blinked the remnants of the black fog from her eyes. Trying to focus on his face and voice.

"Don't ever touch a cop without permission, and without having her full attention, it could get you killed."

She took in a breath, and motioned for the waiter to bring their check. As far as she was concerned, this dinner was over, time to get back to work.

They were driving back to his office when the blue-tooth speaker device attached to her visor began to beep. She tapped it once and said, "MacKenzie," before she heard the voice of Smyth coming through the speaker.

"Mac, we just got a call from dispatch that Karolyn Searlington received some sort
of package from the kidnappers. The team's headed over there now with CSU to check it out. Are you near?"

She took a brief glance at Kenneth and returned her focus to the road. She flipped on her flashing lights and sirens and said, "I'm not far from Searlington's office, he's in tow, be there in ten." She gave Kenneth one cursory look to make certain his seatbelt was secured across his broad chest, then she made what could only be described as a wild-ass U-turn across four lanes of traffic before laying her foot on the accelerator and heading to the Searlington family home.

When they stepped off of the elevator, her colleagues filled the corridor, and the door was open. She nodded at the officers that she passed and motioned for Kenneth to follow behind her. She found her team members placed at various stations throughout the room. Smyth and Santini were sitting on the couch with Karolyn, taking her statement it appeared.

"Smyth," she said in a clipped tone. Motioning for him to follow her on to the terrace. "What happened?"

"She found an envelope containing a cell and instructions to await a call that will provide detailed directions on how she is to pay for the return of her kid."

Heart nodded. "Did we check out the phone yet, what do we know?"

He shrugged his shoulders. "Right now, all we know is that it's a throwaway. We can't trace it. It seems to be brand-new, no calls have been made to it or from it yet.

We're hoping we can get some info on the caller at the time of the scheduled ransom call. As for right now, CSU is still working on it."

She braced her hands on her hips. "Tell the Crime Scene Unit they need to work faster on this. I need as much info as possible before this damn call comes in. How long do we have?"

"Thirty minutes."

"Get me everything you can, Smyth. She nodded her head again and turned toward the doors to re-enter the apartment. "You go back inside, keep me posted on what's going on, come get me when the call comes through. I've gotta run this by Porter, he's playing this one close, wants to know all the haps."

Smyth gave her a two-fingered salute. "So glad I didn't take the lieutenant's exam,"

he called out over his shoulder as he left her alone on the terrace.

"Funny son-of-a-bitch," she grumbled as she pulled her phone from her pocket and began to dial her captain.

"Porter," he answered in his familiar brash voice.

"It's MacKenzie, we've got contact instructions left at the Searlington residence. We expect them to call in thirty minutes."

"On my way."

"Captain, there's no reason for you to come here, my team and I are handling this."

"On my way, MacKenzie," he said, then she heard the distinctive click of the phone and the resulting tone of an ended call on her cell phone.

"Fuck, this shit is about to get really funky."

~

*S*he walked through the terrace doors, searching the buzzing room for one of her detectives.

"Santini," she called. She watched a full head of thick dark hair turn toward her.

Santini's Italian heritage gave him the same midnight hair color that Kenneth wore, but that was where the similarities in the two men ceased. Santini's perma-tan, as he called it, and his noire eyes were generations in the making. They were gifts from his Italian grandparents that traveled across an ocean or two to settle in New York at least fifty years before his own birth.

He was the same height as Heart, and he stood eye-to eye with her when he stopped in front of her.

"'S'up, MacKenzie?"

"Find whoever's leading the CSU team. Find out if they came prepared to monitor and trace a call. If they aren't tell them they'd better get someone from their team to bring whatever they need to make that happen."

He nodded and walked off in the opposite direction to execute her directive.

Her eyes scanned the room again, looking for the Searlingtons. One more pass of the room and she found them. Karolyn sitting on the couch with their mother Jacqueline, her head nestled on her mother's shoulder as her body shook with small shivers. Kenneth standing to the side of the couch, his arms crossed over his chest, his eyes fixed on his mother and sister.

Why does this feel off? She'd think about that later, right now, her time had to be spent prepping for this anticipated phone call. She walked over to where the Searlingtons were seated and squatted down in front of Karolyn and Jacqueline.

"Karolyn, we're gonna attempt to monitor this call, trace it, hopefully get some idea of where these people might be hangin' their caps. We need you to keep him talking, ask questions about what he wants you to do, make it seem like you're just trying to double check the information he, she, they are giving you. If he asks for money, doesn't matter how much or little he asks for, you're gonna tell him you can't get your hands on that kind of cash at this time of night. You're gonna tell him you have to go through the approval process at your bank to liquidate that kind of cash. Basically, you're gonna tell him whatever's necessary to keep him on that line for us to get a fix on his position."

Karolyn nodded, and then turned her head back into the waiting shoulder of their mother who sat perched perfectly on the edge of the couch staring down at Heart.

Is this bitch really mean-muggin' me while I'm trying to help find her damn grandchild?

Heart locked down every muscle in her body to keep from rolling her eyes at the statue-like woman sitting on the sofa.

Heart raised her eyes to Kenneth; she saw the small shift of his head that asked her to follow him. She stood, followed him into the silence of the kitchen and waited for the question written behind his still features.

"If they ask for a ransom, you do know that getting whatever sum they ask for is not a problem? I can have any sum of money they ask for within fifteen to twenty minutes; it can all be done wirelessly."

She motioned for him to sit at the table, watching him as he slowly unlocked his rigid body and moved to the side of the room where the table was.

"Kenneth, it's not a matter of you being able to get the money or not. The truth is, I don't want you to pay these bastards shit. I just want your sister to keep them on the phone long enough so that I can find these sons of bitches and shut their asses down."

The muscle in Kenneth's jaw twitched, his words crawled through the thin line of his pink lips.

"Your need to see justice fulfilled notwithstanding, I want my niece home. If paying these people their money will make that happen faster, I will give them whatever they ask."

"Don't you think they know that, don't you think they're banking on that?" She watched a spark fly across those crystal blue eyes of his that she had such a hard time turning away from. She closed her eyelids for a moment, needed a break from that penetrative gaze of his locking her in place.

"Kenneth, if your only plan is to give these people what they want, I promise you, you will never see her again. They will use your willingness to get her back to suck you dry of everything, and I'm not just talking about your money. They will keep taking and give nothing in return. Paying the ransom almost never gets the abducted home."

He sat quietly, fists clenched. She watched a rose tint climb from that fist beyond his sleeve-covered arm. When it reappeared again it was slowly walking up the v in his collar beyond his neck, and onto his face. His skin usually the color of smooth porcelain now colored with the slightest rose blush, she would have smiled if they were sitting here under more favorable circumstance. But now, sitting here waiting on some information about the person or persons involved with his niece's kidnapping, there was no room for smiles. The tight lines of his face and his slight blush were the only signs of anger that his cool veneer allowed.

She leaned forward, just a little, to give him reassurance. "Kenneth you seem like a man that is used to handling his own problems, and trust me, I get that. But you gotta let me and my team take the lead on this. I can't promise you this is all going to work out the way we all hope, with Merri home safe and sound. But I can tell you we're your best shot at making that happen."

She glanced at her watch and stood. They only had a few more moments before the anticipated call was to come through. She headed through the door separating the kitchen and the living room and listened for Kenneth's long strides behind her. She gave a brief glance at the Searlington women still huddled together on the couch and found them joined by a new member of the Searlington clan, William Grant.

Heart kept her stride even and walked to her waiting team members. They had already taken up the necessary posts to gather as much info during this call as possible.

That's what she loved about her team, they had been working together for so long she rarely had to voice her commands. They knew what she wanted, how she worked, and executed her desires by sheer instinct.

She checked over their surveillance plan once, then walked over to the sofa where the Searlingtons were being coached on what to do during the call by the CSU technician. When the technician was finished she nodded to Heart and moved to the side of the coffee table where a host of telephone surveillance equipment rested, waiting, at the ready. She handed Heart a set of headphones and they both sat down on nearby highbacked chairs that were placed in front of the table.

The waiting throwaway telephone began to ring, bringing a practiced silence to the buzzing in the room. Her team had done this before, the only wildcards were the Searlingtons. Barring any hysterics, she hoped to come through this call with as much useful information as she could get.

"Hello," Karolyn answered carefully.

"Hello, Ms. Searlington," a mechanical voice came through the headphones Heart was holding to the side of her head. "I'm going to talk, and you're going to shut up and listen. Are we clear, do you understand?"

Karolyn released a shaky, "Yes," as she nodded her head frantically.

"I got your kid, and you got somethin' I want too. When I get what I want, you'll get this pretty lil' kid a'yours." The distorted voice coming through the headphones laughed a little and continued. "I want 237 million dollars wired to an account. I'm gonna call you back some time tomorrow or later in the week, cuz I wouldn't want your cop buddies to find me through this call. So sit tight, get'cha paper together, and wait for my call. Oh, and tell that bitch-cop MacKenzie I said stay outta my way if you want dis kid back in one piece." Then the line clicked.

Heart looked down over to the CSU technician and watched her shake her head. The young Asian woman let out a low sigh. "Not enough time. Twenty-six seconds. I needed at least thirty to get a full lock on where he is. The only thing I can tell you is he's somewhere in a 718 area code."

Heart threw the headphones onto the coffee table. "Shit."

"What does that mean?" She heard Kenneth ask from behind the sofa.

"It means this fool could be anywhere in the Bronx, Brooklyn, Queens, or Staten

Island. He wasn't on the line long enough for us to get an accurate fix on his location."

"So what's your next move now?" He spoke again, his words deliberate.

She was forming her answer when she heard the bark of her superior at the door.

"What happens now is the Searlingtons are gonna be putting up a couple of NYPD's finest for the foreseeable future," Captain Porter said.

"Stay here?" Jacqueline questioned.

Heart nodded. "Whoever was on the other end of that voice distorter called me by my name. That either means one of two things. He either has inside knowledge about this case and how it's being worked, or he can see inside of this apartment. Either way, there's a leak somewhere. We gotta be around at all times to make sure it gets plugged.

You guys could be in danger."

CHAPTER 4

$\mathcal{K}$enneth stood at the top of the stairs and waited for the two police officers following him to finish the short climb. He turned right and walked to the end of the hall stopping in front a door.

"Detective Smyth, this is your room." Kenneth opened the door, and stepped aside so that the detective could walk in. He watched as Smyth walked in, stood in the center of the room and turned around in a full circle taking the room in.

"Damn Searlington, this is like a five-star hotel in here. It's almost too pretty to touch. You sure you want my downtown carcass in your uptown digs?"

Kenneth gave a small laugh and nodded his head. "Detective Smyth, if you getting a good night's sleep helps bring my niece home any sooner, hell, I'd give you the Master Suite. Having you two spend a few days in our empty guestrooms is a small price to pay.

I'll leave you to get settled in."

Smyth nodded and Kenneth closed the door as he walked back into the hall. He gave his subsequent guest a quick glance and continued to walk down the hall in the direction they'd originally come from. As he walked, his mind catalogued the free rooms remaining on the upper floor. There were three in total, all ready to accept guests, all equipped with the same comforts: en-suite bathroom, balcony, king-sized bed, walk-in closet, state of the art wall-mounted flat-screened television with an equally exceptional entertainment center.

He passed two of the rooms and finally stopped in front of the last one which was adjacent to his master suite. He twisted the knob and opened it, then stepped aside to let the detective walk through.

"I hope you find the room to your liking, Lieutenant MacKenzie."

He watched her place her bag on the floor, and walk through the room. She silently opened the doors to closets and the bathroom; she walked carefully onto the balcony, seeming to search for something and nothing at the same time. She walked over to the bed and knelt, pulling up the expensive curtain of the silken linens. She looked under the bed and when she seemed satisfied with her findings—whatever they were—she stood and returned to her bag, pulling a small electronic device from a hidden pocket the size of a small mp3 player.

"What are you—" he attempted to ask, but was cut short by her singular finger standing in front of her lips.

She turned the device on and re-traced all of the places she'd previously scanned the first time. When she seemed satisfied with whatever readings the device gave her she turned to him and finally spoke.

"This is a cute little gadget from our tech department. It scans for radio frequencies that are usually signatures for bugs."

He gave a quick wave of dismal with his hand. "Of one thing I can assure you, Lieutenant MacKenzie, there are no bugs here. I pay a small fortune in professional pest control services to make certain of it. You don't have to worry about that."

Her lips curved into a lopsided grin and her shoulders rippled slightly with the brief chuckle she let escape.

"I was referring to electronic monitoring paraphernalia such as listening devices and hidden cameras. But I feel so much safer knowing I don't have to contend with vermin as well, just makes my job that much easier."

He could feel the slight rose tinting that was climbing up his chest, neck, throat, and face. It was the closest thing his alabaster skin had ever managed to a blush. He dipped his head slightly, allowing his dark tresses to cover some of his embarrassment.

"Please forgive my ignorance, Lieutenant."

She smiled again. "Please forgive my not being clear. I didn't mean to imply that you had vermin," she laughed, "I'm certain your floors are clean enough to eat off of."

She was joking with him, or at least joking as much as he'd ever seen her. She still stood more than an arm's length away from him, her arms were still crossing her chest. But her face seemed a bit lighter, her usual scowl only being half present in this moment.

"I'll...I'll leave you to your unpacking, if you need anything, just let me know and

I'll see to it."

He turned around preparing to leave when he heard her voice call his name.

"Kenneth?"

He faced her again, his eyes wide in question.

"There was a locked door in the back of the walk-in closet. What is it connected to?"

"That is the door that adjoins this room to the one adjacent to it." He saw her eyebrow raise, her lips forming questions. "There's actually a door in each room that locks from the inside of each room. They face each other. Even if one door is opened, access can't be granted into the second room without its corresponding door being unlocked and opened as well."

She nodded. "Who has the keys to both doors?" "I do," his tone clipped.

"And who sleeps next door?" she asked.

"I do," his breath hitched slightly. "When I took over the master suite, I had the locks changed to both outside and inside doors and I am the only one who has possession of them. I sometimes work on proprietary projects for work in my room, I had to make certain no one could access them without my permission."

He turned to leave the room again and heard her call his name again.

"Kenneth?"

"Yes?"

"I'm going to need the keys to both the front door and the adjoining door."

"I assure, MacKenzie, I won't be entering your room without permission." She shook her head and placed her hand on her sidearm.

"It's not a matter of entering or not without permission. I am an armed NYPD officer, there are certain rules I need to adhere to because of that. When not on my person, I have to make certain my weapon is always secured properly where no one other than myself can gain access to it. I'll need those keys."

He nodded, reached into his pocket, feeling for the familiar platinum key ring and removed two keys from it. He handed her the keys and watched as she carefully pulled them from his fingers by their ends. He stared at her momentarily watching her thoughtfully place the keys on her own ring.

She lifted her head, query in her eyes as they fell upon him standing there watching her.

"Is there something else, Kenneth?"

He paused for a second, but shook his head, clearing whatever question or suggestion he thought his brain was attempting to create.

"Ahh, no, nothing else, I'll leave you to settle in. If you need anything to make your stay more comfortable, please let me or my staff know and it shall be done to your satisfaction."

She nodded, but said nothing else. Her silence was his cue to exit the room. He walked through the door and closed it with a silent click. He stepped forward, then stopped, feeling as if something was pulling him to her room. He turned and raised his hand to knock. Hand raised in midair, he was just about to bring it down against the door when he heard the defined snick of the lock tumblers falling in place. *Paranoid much, Lieutenant?* Kenneth turned around and walked down the hall to the staircase. He had work to do, and the oddness of

Lt. MacKenzie, no matter how much it piqued his curiosity, would have to wait until a later time for further inquiry.

~

*H*eart swept the room a second time after Kenneth left. She found the adjoining door inside of the closet and tested the knob again. Just as before, she didn't trust it, she couldn't risk being caught unaware in unfamiliar surroundings. She tried one of the two new keys on her ring, the first didn't fit, but the second did. She opened it, and just as Kenneth had said, she came face to face with the adjoining door from his side of the closet. She closed the door back, and secured its lock. She looked at the locked door, and still felt uneasy.

"Needs something else," the whispered words fell into the air softly, only meant for her ears to hear. She walked out of the closet, and took another look around the room. Her eyes fell on two high-backed chairs sitting in the corner carefully arranged around a small circular coffee table. She took one, carried it back inside of the closet, and pushed it firmly under the knob.

She tested the door again, and when it didn't budge she felt a small hint of relief. "It won't stop someone from getting in, but at least it will alert me if someone does try to get in."

Her chest was rising hard and fast, deep tufts of air pressing in and out of her lungs. She needed to get herself together. She wrapped her arms around her cold torso, squeezing herself into a warm hug, imagining the soft kiss her grandmother would be giving her right now if she'd witnessed Heart about to lose it. For so long those hugs were the only thing that made the darkness go away. Her grandmother's gentle hands formed the only touch that made the ache stop.

"It's been fourteen years, let it go already."

She paced back and forth, trying to break the crackle of energy buzzing inside of her. She glanced up and saw her reflection in a wall mirror. A little more relief washed over her. On the outside, she looked solid, she looked focused, she looked...normal. As long as that was what everyone else saw on the outside, she was golden. No one needed to know what was going on inside of her, no one ever had, and she wouldn't allow anyone to ever know. In fourteen years she had never let the mask slip, and she didn't plan on letting it slip now.

She glossed her hand over the tightly secured strands of her hair, lying flat against her head, pulled into a tight knot at the back of her head. There were no strands loose, there never were, she always made certain of that, nothing loose, nothing out of order, nothing out of control.

She looked at her watch. *Damn it's late.* After her captain had ordered her team to stay at the Searlington residence, she made a plan and decided she and Smyth would stay at the residence, and the other detectives would canvas the streets. It's the only thing that would have worked. Porter seemed to be on overdrive about this damn case and without him having to say it, she knew he wanted his most senior investigators closest to the family if there were some sort of danger.

That decided, the rest of her team kept watch while she and Smyth went back to their cars to get their go bags. Every cop had one; you never knew when you'd be away from home for long stints at a time. She had become so skilled at packing hers over the years, she was now able to fit a week's worth of clothing into what looked like an average sized gym bag.

Once they'd returned, she gave a few final instructions to her team and then Searlington had escorted her and Smyth to their respective rooms. It was late, and she couldn't remember the last time she'd eaten anything. She walked down the back staircase that led to the kitchen. Happy to find it empty, she decided to look inside of the fridge for something quick and painless to eat.

She stood in front of the transparent refrigerator door. "Shit, I guess rich people can't be bothered to open the door and look inside, they need to look through the door to see if they want to be bothered enough to open it in the first place." She shook her head and let a little laugh slip through her lips. She saw what looked like some deli fixings. She scanned the dark counter tops, some kind of expensive dark marble no doubt, it was pretty, but she wasn't sure how smart it was to have such pretty and delicate looking things in a kitchen. Weren't kitchens supposed to be messy, weren't you supposed to spill things in them? Guess that didn't apply to the Searlingtons.

Her perusal finally found the desired item, a bread box. She opened it and found several different types of exotic looking breads there. Hell, if she could just find something she recognized like wheat or Italian, dammit, she just wanted a fucking sandwich, not something she needed a gourmet chef to create.

She heard footsteps coming down the back staircase and waited to see Kenneth walk into the kitchen. When she saw his curtain of long, dark hair swinging around his bare shoulders, she smiled to herself. Her cop's senses hadn't waned in her time as a commander. She could still detect whom and what was around her without having to rely only on what her eyes showed her.

"Looking for something, MacKenzie?" His eyebrow cocked in question making her want to slap the smug off of his pale face.

"I would offer to make you a sandwich, Kenneth, but I can't seem to find a single slice of regular bread in this bread box of yours."

"Regular bread?"

"Yeah, you know, like white, or wheat, damn, I'd settle for rye right now I'm so hungry. All I see in here is shit that looks pretty, but doesn't look like it tastes worth a damn."

He laughed, an honest-to-goodness laugh with his shoulders shaking and his eyes squinted. His curtain of hair draped over his face and rippled as his laughter quivered through him. She'd never seen him like this. Since the moment they'd first met the two had been in a decided battle of who would control this investigation. He'd shown her anger, conceit, over-confidence, even arrogance, but never something this beautiful.

Wait, hold up, did she just call this grown-assed man beautiful? She blinked hard, trying to dislodge the thought from her head. She watched him as he composed himself, leaning against the counter to brace himself for a moment, then he walked over to the bread box and removed a golden brown loaf.

"I'm not exactly certain what kind of bread this is, but our chef,

Brady; he usually makes it for me to make sandwiches for myself. I tend to get in pretty late, and a heavy meal is the last thing on my mind when I walk through the door."

He handed her the bread and opened a cabinet door to remove a cutting board, then opened another cabinet and removed two plates and glasses. Once he'd rested them on the counter, he opened the refrigerator and pulled on a sliding drawer that held a platter with several types of sliced meats on it.

She watched the meat for a long time before she raised a finger to touch it. These weren't the cold cuts she had in her fridge, damn, these were carved. Like, real roast beef, and real ham, and real turkey breast. *Damn, these people can't even eat normal.* Her hungry stomach rolled a bit and reminded her that it needed her to stop playing games and fill the growing hole inside of it now.

She grabbed a knife and sliced the bread while Kenneth went back into the fridge for something else. It appeared to be a small transparent glass dish, covered with clear plastic wrap. It was an odd mix between a cream and a gold color.

"What's that?" she asked.

"To tell you the truth, I don't really know. It's some sort of sauce slash sandwich spread that Brady makes and it is better than any mayonnaise I've ever tried. I promise you, it will make your taste buds dance."

He must have seen her reservation; he grabbed a spoon out of the drawer, and then dipped it into the creamy concoction. He guided it toward her lips and for some strange reason she opened her mouth, and let him place the spoon inside of it. Her eyes locked on those crystal blue pools that held her captive in the center of his kitchen. It was only the burst of flavor that forced her eyes closed. The flavor was sweet, with a mix of tanginess and just a hint of spice. She heard the moan escape her lips, the sound of pleasure almost unrecognizable as her own voice.

He simply nodded his head and smiled.

"I told you it was good, Brady is ridiculously talented. I've learned over the years to just eat whatever he puts in front of me.

Half the time I don't even want to know what it is, I just eat it, and enjoy it."

She took the knife she'd been working on the bread with and began to spread the concoction on the four slices of bread lying face up.

"Beef, ham, or turkey?' he asked.

"Beef," she answered.

She watched him gather several slices of the roast beef on one of the plates, and then layered what looked like provolone cheese on top of it before sticking it in the microwave to heat. She went to protest, exactly what she wasn't sure, but before she could speak he raised a pointed finger at her.

"Wasn't I right about the sauce, trust me with this too. I'm king of needing to eat fast, but good food. This is going to floor you, Lieutenant."

She crossed her arms over her chest and lifted a skeptical brow. At the ding of the timer, he pulled the smoky mountain of melted cheese covered meat and waived the plate under her nose. The aroma wafting up was almost intoxicating. He forked equal portions of the heated beef onto the waiting slices of bread that were blanketed with pretty greens and juicy, red slices of sweet tomatoes. He finished constructing the sandwiches, and then sliced them diagonally. He turned around and opened another cabinet, and out came a huge bag of potato chips. He poured them carefully on each plate, and then returned the bag to its original hiding place. He made one last trip to the fridge, returning all of the used trays and then he pulled two bottles of water from the refrigerator placing them under his arm. He picked up the plates with their food, and walked toward the benchstyle seating at the breakfast nook.

She followed him, still a little unsure she had witnessed this whole performance and sat down across from him at the table. He motioned for her to take a bite of her sandwich, already chewing on his, and thoroughly enjoying it if the wonderful sounds coming from him were any indication. She picked up her sandwich, bit into it and paused, unable to move. When the moment had passed, she took another bite, and savored that one as well.

"Dear God, even rich people's sandwiches taste better. What the hell have I been missing all of these years?"

She didn't give Kenneth the opportunity to respond. She went right back to eating her sandwich, and he did the same with his. They sat in relative silence eating their food, the only sounds between them were the equal echoes of pleasure erupting from their chewing lips.

She took a final drink from her water bottle and found a smiling Kenneth staring at her.

"What?" Her eyes widened with the simple question.

His smile broadened showing the neatest set of white teeth she'd ever witnessed.

"All of the woman that I have had the opportunity to share meals with would never allow themselves to enjoy a meal like that. From my mother, to every skinny little waif

I've dated acts like they're allergic to food, like it's poison to them. It's refreshing to see a woman act like a human being and enjoying the food on her plate."

He continued to smile as she allowed her gaze to pass over him. Her head tilted to the side as she measured him in that moment.

"Did you just call me a fat hog, Mr. Searlington?"

A smile pulled at her lips as she watched him cough up some of the water he was drinking.

"I said no such thing, Lieutenant. All I meant was..." His words drifted off and he squinted as he watched her in earnest. She kept her face straight for as long as she could, then she began laughing and he joined in. "You shouldn't scare a man like that,

MacKenzie. I thought for sure you were going to shoot me."

They were both laughing as they each stood up from the table. She went to grab for their now empty plates, not watching as she should have been when she felt his hand on hers. It was like fire to flesh and she instinctively pulled back as her skin burned where he had touched her. The loud crash of the splintering plate snatched her from the internal freeze that had locked her muscles in place.

"MacKenzie...Mac, are you okay?"

She stepped-stumbled back placing distance between the two of them. The simple act helping her to kick-start her brain again.

"Sorry...you just...you startled me, that's all. If you can just show me where the broom is, I can clean this mess up. I'm sorry about your plate, if you want, I'll replace it for you."

She was trying like hell to sound normal, normal people wouldn't be bothered by something so simple, she needed to be normal in front of him, normal.

He stepped forward. "It's all right, I'll clean it up."

She instinctively stepped back again. He stopped, and so did she.

"I'm sorry, Kenneth. It's just been a really long day, and I get a little goofy when I'm sleep deprived. If you don't mind, I'm gonna head upstairs, check in with Smyth, and then knock out."

She turned and quickly headed back up the stairs, not looking back to see if Kenneth was following.

Damn, MacKenzie can't you be fucking normal for one moment in your life.

Apparently not.

CHAPTER 5

*S*he'd spent two days in the Searlington penthouse. She was so uneasy there. Her skin felt prickly, like something was crawling on it. She was jumpy, restless, and having a hard time focusing on anything other than what it felt like for Kenneth Searlington to touch her two nights ago in his kitchen. Like any other man's touch she was still disturbed by it. But with Kenneth there had been something added to that usual mix of anxiety and fear that notoriously exploded inside her head and body when her skin was touched. All of the other touches had felt wrong; her body had instinctively known to retreat, there was never a question of staying in place when it happened before. In that kitchen, for just a split second, she had forgotten to move, she had completely forgotten to protect herself. In that one moment, it had almost felt good to have his long fingers softly caressing the minute piece of skin on her hand where his fingers had connected with her.

And that right there was why she'd ran. That quick passing of pleasure that was almost unrecognizable to her scared her more than any of the fear and panic she usually walked around with after coming in physical contact with a man.

She'd spent the entire night after that encounter in the kitchen questioning why her usual defenses hadn't recognized Kenneth as a threat, why she hadn't reacted like she usually did, like she was supposed to. Damn this fucking case, she had to find this little girl, catch this bastard that was playing with her and get the fuck out of dodge where Kenneth Searlington was concerned. She wanted to go home to her little basement apartment in Queens and hide in the darkness until she forgot the brief indescribable mixture of fire and pleasure that started at her hand, and ran like a spark up her arm, finally exploding in her chest like a stick of dynamite. She needed to go home.

From the first thing in the morning, to the last thing at night, Kenneth was always in the house. He wanted to be a part of the investigation, she couldn't blame him, but she didn't know how much longer she could take being around Kenneth Searlington.

"Good Morning, Mac, it's about time you got your butt down here."

She smiled as she watched a yawning Bryan Smyth. They'd decided he would take the night surveillance, and she the day.

"Hey, I'm right on time, I have from twelve in the afternoon, to twelve at night, my shift doesn't begin for a couple of hours, I'm going to get me something to eat. Want a cup of coffee while I'm at it?"

"Sure, Mac, and some breakfast too, I'm starving."

"I don't think I've ever seen you when you weren't."

When she walked into the kitchen, Kenneth was at the counter drinking a cup of coffee. She had avoided as much contact with him as she possibly could, hoping to find solace in her work, but there was no such luck.

"Good morning, Mac."

"Good morning, Kenneth."

"I haven't really seen much of you in the past couple of days, except for when you're supervising down here."

"Police work keeps you busy."

He nodded at her response, and she hoped her answer would satisfy him enough that he would leave her the hell alone and drop the subject.

"Not that busy, you've been avoiding me, and I want to know why."

She rolled her eyes hard. No such fucking luck with getting rich boy to leave her the hell alone.

"Don't you ever stop it with the questions?"

"No, I don't."

"You're like a dog with a bone."

"Bow wow, baby."

She looked at him from the corner of her eye before she spoke.

"I don't know how you go from Ivy League educated, wealthy businessman speak to porn star vocabulary words in one breath."

He laughed, not looking up from his coffee cup as he spoke.

"That's the second time you've referred to my porn star quality vocabulary. Should I take that to mean you're a student of all things pornographic?"

She rolled her eyes again. Damn, why did this guy piss her off so much?

"Kenneth, you act as if we have some long drawn out connection with each other, we don't. I'm just working your niece's case, that's it. That fact doesn't give you the right to be all up in my business."

"Why are you playing the role of the bitchy cop?"

"Maybe I'm not playing a role."

"You are, when we were in that restaurant together, you almost acted human, I think beneath that badge beats a heart."

"Why are you so interested in me, don't you have anything better to do than nose around in my business?"

He answered with a smile plastered across his face. "No, as a matter of fact, I don't." She couldn't help but smile at that one.

"Now see, I knew there was something human about you. Come on, I don't want to fight you; we're on the same side. You're just different, and I've always been curious about things that are different. You have to tell me why you don't like men who are arrogant."

"Don't forget having something to do with my job."

"So if I had nothing to do with your job, you'd date me."

"No."

"Because I just happen to be—as you've surmised—arrogant?"

"Yes."

"That makes no sense."

"It doesn't have to make sense to you, it's my preference. Something that appeals, or in this case, doesn't appeal to me." She turned away from him and began pulling things from the fridge.

"Can I ask you something?"

"Not like I can stop you," she mumbled as she continued searching in the fridge for more items to cook.

He went ahead ignoring her minor rant. "Is my arrogance really the problem, or is it something else?"

That got her attention, she stopped what she was doing and turned around to face

him across the counter.

"What else could there be?"

"Maybe you've got something against rich people, or perhaps, I'm just not your cup of tea because I'm white."

She felt like he had just struck her. Flinching as his words filled the air.

"I'm not a racist if that's what you're asking me. I'm a black woman in a commanding position in an organization that has been known to have abysmal race relations with minorities and the poor. I do this job so that more people that look like me, who have been marginalized by the system, can understand that there are people in the system that represent their interests and uphold the law at the same time."

He nodded as he said, "I believe you."

"Why must this be a race issue with you?" she asked him, voice firm.

"Because I get the sense that your arrogance garbage is just that, trash. I think it's something bigger. Our racial and financial differences are the biggest things I can think of between us that might keep you from dating me. I've never believed in discriminating against anyone because of their race and I don't intend to suffer the same. Now what is it exactly you don't like about rich, white men? Have you ever dated a rich, white man?"

"No, I haven't dated any white man, be he rich, poor, or working class."

"Then how do you know you don't like us?"

"I never said I didn't."

"Not in so many words, but yeah, you kind of did."

She flung a pan a little more rigorously than she had planned and it clattered in the metal sink.

"So you lied just now when you said you believed I wasn't a racist." It was a statement, not a question. She was beginning to lose her patience with this man. She took a breath, trying to calm herself.

"I do believe you, or at least I want to believe you," he continued. "How about you prove it to me?"

She busied herself with making breakfast, still unable to ignore him.

"And just how am I supposed to do that?"

"When all of this is over, and Merridith is home safe and sound, go out with me. Let

me take you out and show you that arrogance is not always such a bad thing."

She heard the timer on the oven go off and pulled a platter of golden biscuits. She placed them on the counter to cool, and began plating the other breakfast items she'd made during their conversation.

"Kenneth, why does it matter to you so much? I'm nobody to you, after this case is over, you'll probably never see me again. Why do you care what type of man I do or don't like to date?"

He leaned over resting his elbows on the counter, locking his gaze on hers. "Because it does."

"MacKenzie, when the hell is breakfast gonna be ready?" Smyth bellowed through the swinging door that separated the kitchen from the family room. She looked down, breaking the force of his gaze, and focused on the various platters in front of her.

"I'd better get this stuff out there before Smyth eats your furniture." She picked up a couple of the platters and Kenneth mirrored her actions. They walked into the family room, arms laden with food.

~

*S*he placed the steaming platters atop the table. She stopped to fix her partner a plate. Kenneth watched the way she handed it to him; almost trying to make sure their hands didn't touch. But no matter how careful she was, Bryan's hand managed to touch hers, and just as she did with him, she pulled her hand away from Bryan as quickly as she could.

What was this thing she had with physical contact? Maybe it was just his imagination, maybe he was making too big a deal out of it. She sat down across from him, and began serving herself.

"The food's great. If Brady's not careful he's going to find himself out of a job."

"I'm glad you like it."

"So where does a full time cop learn how to cook like this?"

"I haven't always been a cop."

"What were you before you were a cop?"

"A college student."

"You joined the force straight out of college?"

"Yeah, it was going to be the Marines first, but Porter talked me into the NYPD instead."

He chewed his food, turning over her explanation as he did so.

"How long have you been on the force?" "Nearly a decade," she answered.

"That's amazing, at twenty-nine, you've been a detective, and now a lieutenant."

"How do you know I'm twenty-nine?" "Just a guess."

"I'm not twenty-nine."

"Older?"

"No, a year younger."

"You're twenty-eight, how did you manage to climb the ladder so quickly?"

She paused a moment and reached for her coffee cup. He was afraid she was going to throw up another wall in front of him, refusing to answer.

"I graduated early from college and entered the academy. As soon as I was eligible to sit for the detective's exam, I took the test, and passed it with flying colors. After that, I closed a couple of high profile cases, and received a number of commendations for my work. When I was eligible, Porter convinced me to take the lieutenant's exam. I passed really well, ranking in the top ten percent of the thousands of cops that had taken the test with me. I also earned a graduate degree in organizational management and leadership.

Then I found the creep who was stalking the mayor's daughter. With his recommendation, and all of the other stuff I just mentioned, I was fast-tracked into becoming an NYPD lieutenant."

"What made you want to become a cop?"

She looked distant for a moment; he thought she wasn't going to answer the question.

"I liked helping people, and hated to see the bad guys win, so I promised myself that as long as I could, I would help those who were victimized by the deviant and criminal."

If anyone else had said those words, Kenneth wouldn't have believed a single word of that confession. But from MacKenzie, every word tingled with truth. He could see that there was something there, something so simple that would explain why all of these qualities would seem so understandable in a young woman such as herself, but he just couldn't put his finger on it. Just couldn't figure it out, yet.

"How much time do you usually spend working?"

"I don't know, a lot. I see more of the seventy-fourth precinct than I do of my own home."

"Is there really that much police work to do?"

"My shifts are usually eight hours a day, but I put in an awful amount of overtime. In all the time I've been on the force, I've never taken a vacation, and I've only taken days off when I was sick, or had to take care of urgent business."

"But isn't it mandatory that you take a vacation?"

"Kenneth, I'm one of the best cops in the precinct, so Cap sort of overlooks things like that. I've never cracked under pressure, and my psyche report is impeccable. I have no need to take a vacation."

"So what do you do in your spare time?"

"Work if I can, if not, I'm in the gym, or working on some case during my off time."

"I thought I was a work-a-holic."

"I wouldn't think real estate keeps you up late at night."

"That's because you're probably thinking of real estate in small terms, you know, selling houses and things like that. I own the company that hires people to buy and sell houses, but mostly I deal in terms of large corporate buildings."

"And those large corporate buildings keep you up late at night?"

"Yes, I'm just as dedicated to my work, as you are to yours." She stood up from the table, taking her half empty plate with her.

"Where are you going?"

"Since my shift doesn't start for a few hours, I'm going to make a few stops."

"But what if the kidnappers call?"

"Smyth will be here, and he has my cell-phone number in case anything happens and I'm needed. Everything will be fine, don't worry."

~

Ida-Mae Amare smiled as she opened the door. "Now who is this standing on the other side of my door?"

"Mama, you darn well know who it is."

The elderly woman smiled and lifted a cautionary hand waiting for Heart to grant permission. Heart stopped for a moment. She wanted the embrace, but her nerves just couldn't let her give in. She saw disappointment clouding her grandmother's eyes and reached out to drop a quick peck on the elderly woman's cheek.

"Well, it's been such a long time since I've seen you, I almost didn't recognize you."

"Oh Mama, it hasn't been that long."

"Yes it has, my sweet Lieutenant MacKenzie."

She smiled as her grandmother used her title, knowing how much she hated calling her that. "Mama, I can't stay very long, I just dropped by to check on you."

"Why can't you stay long, I'm your family, your grandmother, and you're my grandchild, my one connection to my beautiful Diamond."

Heart thought of her late mother, named after the brightest and most treasured of gems. She'd never known her, but her grandmother kept the memory of her only daughter alive.

"Diamond, she was my precious jewel. Your grandpa named her. When she was born, we were dirt poor, and had only been married a year. Your grandfather wasn't able to give me a diamond engagement ring when he proposed, he couldn't afford it, but he promised me he would give me a diamond, and that he did. More precious than any diamond he could have ever bought me, he gave me the rarest of gems."

"You loved her so much, I don't know why you don't hate me. You really should, because of me, she's dead." Her voice was dripping with guilt and pain, self-blame coloring her eyes.

"Oh, my dear Heart, you can never blame yourself. How could I hate you, when my Diamond loved you enough to give her life for you? You were the world to her; I'd never seen my Diamond as happy as she was when she was pregnant with you. She wanted you to live more than she wanted to live herself, you were your mother's heart, don't you ever forget it."

She smiled at her grandmother, as the elderly woman renewed her confidence once again. "Thank you, Mama, I needed that." She glanced at her watch. "Mama, I gotta be going."

"Working on another big case?"

"Yeah, and if I don't get back to relieve my partner, he'll have my head."

"I love you, baby."

"I love you too, Mama."

"And you'd better stop by for dinner one of these nights, or I'm gonna have your head. And bring a male companion."

"I don't have one of those."

"Then find one, you need someone in your life."

"I have someone in my life, you."

"Baby, I'm eighty years old, I'm not gonna be around much longer, you need to start your own family, so you won't be alone."

She hung her head as she spoke to her grandmother. "You know that isn't possible." Then she disappeared into the hall, making her way back to her assignment.

~

Ohen she walked into the penthouse a sullen silence enveloped her. She looked around the room, trying to gain some insight.

"What happened?"

"Mac, the kidnapper called again."

"Did we get a trace?" Her partner shook his head.

"Damn Smyth, what happened?"

"The bastard didn't stay on the line long enough. He only stayed on for twenty-six seconds. It's as if he knows how long it takes to trace a call, like he's playing with us."

She inhaled deeply. Either this perp was the luckiest son-of-a-bitch alive, or he knew police procedure intimately.

"All right Smyth, leave me your notes, and go get some rest, I'll take over now."

"I'm sorry, Mac."

"Don't be, Smyth, it's not your fault, you did all you could. I don't fault you. Now go get some sleep."

"But Mac, I'd rather stay down here and work."

"That wasn't a request, Smyth."

He followed her orders, leaving her downstairs with the technical crew. She sat going over his notes, scrutinizing them carefully. She was so engulfed in her work; she didn't realize Kenneth was standing next to her.

"Finished making your stops?"

She stared up at him, she could feel her annoyance boiling up, getting ready to spill over. "Yes I did."

"So everything went smoothly?" he asked.

She returned her view to the papers in her hand. "Why do you give a damn?"

"Mac?"

The question in his voice brought her anger to a halt.

"Kenneth, I'm sorry. I'm angry, but not with you. I'm pissed, all right. This maniac is making my life hell. He's toying with me now; he knows I can't track him unless he stays on the line. So he hangs up just in the nick of time."

He said nothing, and that brief reprieve gave her just enough time to reign in her emotions.

"Where are Karolyn and William?"

"William is upstairs, I finally convinced him to take a nap; he hasn't slept once since he got here."

"And Karolyn?"

"I honestly don't know where she is, can't say I've seen her at all today."

That was weird. Why wasn't the child's mother home? She made a mental note to question Karolyn when she caught up with her. For now she would just concentrate on

Smyth's notes.

Kenneth eventually left when she didn't raise her head to acknowledge him. When she heard the door close behind him, she took a deep breath. "I thought he'd never leave."

She worked her shift, but there was nothing, the only calls that came through were personal calls for Karolyn and her mother. When her partner came to relieve her she was more than thankful. Every muscle in her body ached with tension.

She went into her guest bedroom, pulled a wife-beater T-shirt, sweat pants, and thick pair of socks out of the borrowed dresser along with a bath towel from the linen closet. She walked into the bathroom, and began running a bath. She needed to sit and soak; her body ached from the tension she'd held in it all day. She'd worked out earlier, but the workout had served to only make her sweaty, her anger still rooted deep within her.

Talking to Karolyn Searlington about her whereabouts had also added to her current state of pissedivity. That woman wouldn't know a straight answer if it bit her on her lilywhite ass. Realizing she wasn't going to get any clear answers from the penthouse princess, Heart decided to take matters into her own hands.

Water running, bath salts dissolving, Heart walked back into the bedroom and picked up her cell phone. She pressed the familiar speed-dial button for the contact she desired.

"Ramirez," the familiar voice with the Latin flavored tongue spoke.

"Ada, it's MacKenzie."

"S'up L.T.?" she questioned.

"I can't seem to get any straight answers out of this Searlington chick. Her kid's missing, you would think that would give her reason to keep her ass home and cooperate with the cops to get her kid home safely. Instead, she's always pulling these disappearing acts. I'm starting to think Ms. Searlington may know more about her daughter's disappearance than she's been letting on."

Ramirez let out a slow whistle. "Mac, you really think this bitch took her own kid?

What for?"

"Money would be the obvious reason, but my gut is telling me I don't have all the answers yet. I think it may be more than money. I really don't want to think this way, but the chick just keeps raising my suspicions. Everything in me wants to treat her like a suspect instead of a victim. I've been doing this too long to not listen to my instincts.

"I want you to gather as much information as you can on her. And do it quietly, I also want you to put a tail on her, and find out if she has any alternate cell phone numbers besides the one we already have on file. Run her LUDS. I want to know everything about this chick, something just isn't right."

"Will do L.T.," Ramirez answered.

"Oh and one more thing Ada, make sure to keep this quiet. I don't want anyone else knowing about this, not even Porter. You got me?"

"10-4, L.T."

Satisfied, she ended the call with Ramirez and headed back into the bathroom. The massive tub was halfway full with water and bubbles. She undressed, feeling her tense muscles ache with her movements.

She stepped inside of the warm lather. She relaxed there for a while, until the water began to turn cool. She dried herself off and slipped on her clothes. After brushing her hair, she pulled her weapon from its holster, checked to make sure the safety was on it, then placed her pillow atop it. She slid into bed, almost instantly falling asleep.

This was the first time in days she'd gotten any sleep, the firm mattress covered with its sanity sheets sent her into pleasant slumber, the likes of which Mac had almost forgotten existed.

~

*I*t had been two hours since she'd gone to bed, Kenneth wondered if he should wake her, or wait until morning to tell her what he needed to tell her. He finally decided to wake her. "She'll want to know, if I don't wake her, she'll never forgive me." He tapped on the door, but there was no answer, he called out to her, but still there was no answer.

He twisted the knob to the door, and found the door unlocked. He stepped inside, to find her lying on her side, with her hands pushed beneath her pillow. She looked so gentle; nothing like the bloodhound she was when she was working.

Her hair fell against her breast, he'd had no idea how long and beautiful it was, she'd always worn it in a ponytail, but now it was free. He wondered how it would feel to run his fingers through it, to have her firm body pressed against his own, to have her be a real person with him, instead of the tough cop she wanted him to believe she was. "Stop it, Searlington, she doesn't like your kind."

He called to her, but she still slept. He sat slowly on the bed, gazing at her. He knew he shouldn't be in her room, not in this way, but he couldn't help it. She would never allow him to see her looking so feminine under normal circumstances. He sat watching her, and she didn't stir. She slept so peacefully, something he hadn't done in ages.

Work kept him busy, but why? He knew the answer to that question. He was lonely, and the women he met didn't attract him at all. They were either too shallow, like his twin, or brainless. They all wanted him because of what he could offer them, not for the man he was.

Maybe that was why Mac spent most of her time working; maybe she was just as lonely as he was. Maybe all of the men in her life didn't appreciate her strength, or her love for her work. He thought of what it would be like for the two of them to find solace in each other, but as before he reminded himself she didn't want him.

Why was she so narrow minded about dating him? Arrogance was her excuse, but somehow, that didn't feel right to him. The only differences he kept seeing between them were race and wealth.

It would be easy to label her a racist, and walk away. But there was something pulling at him that said that wasn't true. Mac was a hard case, she was, she didn't take shit from anyone and if he were honest, that turned him on more than any of his usual kinks. But something about her being a racist didn't fit. It wasn't because she was black. Porter had disabused him of his notion many years ago that racists were all white men living in the rural South, or the Midwest.

Porter had taught him over the years that bigotry came in all shades, shapes, and colors. There was something about the way he often saw her with her staff. She was kind, and she didn't seem to give a rat's ass about what corner of the world they came from. She led and they seemed to follow without so much as a second thought. Bigotry didn't garner devotion like that, hard work and respect did.

So what was the problem then? Fuck if he knew. He couldn't even understand why she seemed to intrigue him so. *It has to be the badge and the gun; chicks with guns are hot.*

Why was he even wasting his time thinking about this? She hated the world he came from, and neither his world, nor his family, would accept her. In his world, women were supposed to be dainty, and ladylike, not strong and self-sufficient.

If there was one thing Mac wasn't, it was dainty; one could tell that by the sound of

her name. Mac, what a name for a woman, but God, he'd never been more intrigued by a name than by hers. It held mystery, told nothing of what was hidden behind her deep brown eyes. Nothing of the woman she was before she earned a badge.

He lightly touched her, expecting her to slightly stir within her sleep, but she did much more than that. When he laid his hand on her shoulder, she shot up from her sleep, with her gun in hand, cocked and pointed at him.

CHAPTER 6

"*P*ut your hands up in the air where I can see them, and move slowly off of the bed," her voice calm, her hand steady, the gun still as it pointed directly at him.

"Mac, what the hell is wrong with you? Put the gun away," he said in a rush. In his mind he was yelling at the top of his lungs, but the quiet voice that filled his ears was shaky and faint. Guess that whole being a man in the face of adversity was bullshit, because right now the only thing he was actively trying to do was not piss in his pants.

"Get off of the bed now before my finger slips on this trigger," she directed.

He did as she said, totally confused by what was going on. She turned on the light, without taking her eyes off of him, or her pointed gun.

"MacKenzie, what the hell is wrong with you? Put that gun away, please let's not do anything stupid," he said with a still shaky voice. Again, in his mind he sounded a great deal more masculine, but every time he opened his mouth he sounded like a pleading little girl.

"I think I'm the one that'll be giving the orders, and asking the questions. Now what the hell are you doing in my bedroom at two in the morning?"

"I needed to tell you something."

"Something that couldn't wait until daybreak?"

"Look, it was really important. Smyth was in the middle of things, and he couldn't leave to come get you. He tried to call your phone, but you didn't answer. I volunteered to come and retrieve you."

"It was so important you couldn't knock on the door? Instead you had to sit on the edge of my bed, and touch me?"

"I knocked on the door, MacKenzie, I even called out to you, but you didn't answer. I expected the door to be locked, but it wasn't. I only came up here to tell you the damn kidnappers called again!"

She stared at him measuring the level of truth in his statement. She retracted her gun, returning the safety to it. "Are you out of your fucking mind, Searlington? Sneaking up on an armed police officer while she's sleeping is a sure way to get yourself killed!"

"Excuse me for wanting to relay information to you. God, are you trigger-happy or something? Why in the hell do you sleep with a forty-five under your pillow?"

Her lips curved in to a genuine smile. Of all things to make her smile, it was a comment about her gun that she found humor in? *What the fuck?*

"No, I'm not trigger happy," she answered. "But there are all sorts of crazies who would love to do all sorts of twisted things to a single woman living alone. A woman has to protect herself."

"Even when there's a house full of cops under the same roof?" he asked.

"It's a habit. When I'm home, I'm there alone, and I have to take necessary precautions. I'm sorry, Kenneth, but you shouldn't have been in here without me knowing. You startled me, that's all."

"Well I'll remember to knock harder next time." He stood there watching her, her gun still in hand, no longer pointed at him, but still in her firm grip. His heart was still racing and he felt his cock twitch a familiar beat in his pants. How the hell he could be turned on right now he didn't know. What he did know was watching her standing in the middle of the semi-dark room, an A-cut T-shirt hugging the curves of her full breasts, baggy sweat pants hanging from hips that looked as if they were made for a man's hands.

He closed his eyes and took a breath, this woman had just pulled her service weapon on him, and instead of running away, everything in his body screamed for him to walk toward her and rip those damn sweats right off of her.

Reason won out, he walked slowly to the door—partly because he didn't want to startle her while she still held her gun in her hand, partly because his erection only allowed him to make careful steps for fear of injuring himself—he needed to leave her alone.

"Oh, and Kenneth."

"What?"

"This isn't a forty-five, it's a forty caliber semi-automatic."

He gave a half smile. "Oh forgive me, I'll make sure to remember that next time someone points a gun in my face." His voice filled with cynicism, he left the room, and listened as her footsteps fell quickly in step behind him.

"Mac, the bastard called again," Smyth said.

Kenneth watched as Smyth brought her up to speed, replaying the call for her, as well as giving her his handwritten notes. Kenneth watched her; she was all work, as if nothing had just happened.

He couldn't understand her, there was something going on with her, and if it was the last thing he did, he was going to find out what it was. Never before had he seen a woman behave as strangely as she did, so distant, so solitary, and so anti-social.

After making a few notes of her own, she went back upstairs to her bedroom. He heard or saw nothing more of Mac that night. He finally went to bed himself, trying to forget the episodes of the day and night.

~

*W*hen he awoke, Mac was nowhere in the penthouse, apparently she went out at first light to go jogging. Exercise, something he enjoyed regularly, but something he hadn't thought of doing since the disappearance of his niece. Instead, he went to work. Perhaps he could clear his mind there.

He was right, his work did take his mind off things, before he knew it, night had come, and it was time to go home. When he came in that night, she was sitting in his living room, sifting through stacks of paper piled on top of the table with Captain Porter sitting next to her. He said nothing, just nodded toward the captain, and he headed straight for the stairs.

After a long shower, he changed into his sweat pants a sleeveless t-shirt, the matching jacket to his sweat pants, and cross-training sneakers. As he opened the door, the telephone rang, since he was the closest household member, Mac summoned him to answer the phone. On her count, he answered the phone, and the tracking devices were set in motion.

"Hello."

"Who is this?"

"Kenneth Searlington."

"Good, the man of the house, now don't talk, just listen. Did you get my money together yet? You're going to put my 237 million into a separate account. Then you're going to bring the access codes and routing numbers to that account with you to the iceskating rink in central park, at midnight, tomorrow night."

"But this is the middle of summer."

"Yes, which means there will be no one there. Come alone, or your niece dies, and you'll be the next to take her place." The line was dead, and the scrambled voice was gone.

Kenneth stood for a moment just looking at the disconnected phone in his hand. He placed the handset down and reached inside of his jacket pocket to remove his cell phone.

"Who are you calling, Kenneth?" Mac's question stopping his finger midair, hovering over the buttons on his touchscreen.

"I'm about to call my banker and get the money together."

He looked back down to his phone only to have it snatched from his hand before he could touch the first digit.

"What the hell, MacKenzie?"

"You're not calling anyone," she said quickly.

"The hell I'm not!" He turned to her captain. "Bring your dog to heel, Uncle David."

The words fell out of his mouth before he could stop them; he cringed at the sound of them, reaching out to her in immediate apology.

"MacKenzie—"

She waved her hand in dismissal. "Really, Kenneth? You think you're the first man to think of a semi-clever way of calling me a bitch? Not the first, not the most astute, and more than likely won't be the last. You're not getting anything together. NYPD will handle this; get some dummy accounts set up."

"But the kidnapper said—" Her raised hand stopped him.

"I don't care what the kidnapper said, Kenneth. Here's the truth of the situation. If you pay this person, these people, they will more than likely kill Merridith. The goal here is to make it look like they're getting what they want while setting a trap for them at the same time. Trust me, paying them isn't going to get that little girl home safely."

Kenneth watched her for a moment, then moved his gaze to his godfather's face.

Porter simply closed his eyes and gave a single nod. That was enough for Kenneth, he took a breath and turned to MacKenzie. He swallowed his need to fix this and deferred to the lieutenant. This wasn't his show. His soul was screaming with the need to make this right for his niece. Looking between the two cops in front of him— one he'd trusted all of his life, one he was learning to trust day by day —he understood one thing, he was way out of his element.

"What do you have in mind, Lieutenant?"

"I need to locate this sick fuck. I need to know where he is. He's not staying on the lines long enough. I need you to get him angry," she said.

Kenneth lifted a skeptical brown and locked his eyes to hers.

"Are you kidding me?" he asked.

She shook her head. "No, I have a feeling this guy isn't as smart as he thinks he is, get him distracted so that he forgets just how long he's been on the phone."

"And exactly how do you expect me to do that?"

"When he calls, tell him your bank won't transfer that large of a sum without prior authorization. Tell him you can't get the bank to set up an authorization meeting earlier than nine in the morning. Just stall him until the phone surveillance people tell you they have him, once they do, I'm going to get this bastard tonight."

～

*H*er phone rang. She looked at the flashing name of the caller, then looked up to Porter and Kenneth.

"Sorry, I gotta take this." Heart left the two men standing in the living room and headed toward the den. "Hey, Ramirez. What's up?"

"L.T., I've got something for you on Karolyn Searlington."

Heart sat down at the desk and pulled out her notepad and pen from her pocket.

"What'cha got?"

"Well, looks like the princess has been sneaking in and out of the building via the service entrance in the back of the building."

"So why didn't we know that, why didn't this come up in the initial canvas of the building?"

"Because the entrance is pretty much hidden and no one uses it. Supposedly there was some sort of structural issue so it was closed off and hasn't been available for use in over a year. There are no surveillance cameras back there, no lights, nothing. It's almost impossible to navigate for anyone who isn't familiar with it."

A bucket of cold washed over Heart, the resulting chill making her hand tremble in a visible tremor.

"Please tell me this fucking woman didn't snatch her own kid, Ramirez," she asked quietly.

"Truly, Mac, I don't know. What I do know is that it's starting to look like Ms. Searlington has something to hide. She's disappearing at all hours of the day, and whenever she's leaving, there's this same dark sedan waiting for her.

"I ran the plates, it's registered to a Martha Selwyn in the Pink Houses."

Heart shook her head. "What connection could Karolyn have to a woman living in the projects in Brooklyn?"

"Well, it's not a woman that's driving the car, as far as I can tell, Ms. Selwyn has no priors, but her son, RaQuan is another matter. Photo rec from the pictures I took of the driver confirm it's RaQuan that's been driving Ms. Searlington back and forth to the projects."

Heart ran angry fingers across her scalp, needing something to ground her in this unbelievable madness she'd found herself in.

"Ramirez, I'm gonna try and get you in contact with one of the UC's from narcotics.

I'm gonna call Sergeant Benjamin, and tell him to put you in contact with someone he may have working in the drug trade in that area. I don't want you walking up into the

Pink Houses just yet. They will make you, and if the girl is being held there, they'll move her, or worse. Just continue to keep track of Karolyn until I get you the contact. Once you've got info from the inside, get back to me, and we'll come up with a plan."

"All right, L.T."

Heart closed the phone and walked back into the living room. Kenneth and Porter were sitting on the couch talking when she entered the room.

"Cap, are you gonna be around for a while?"

"What's wrong, MacKenzie?"

She shook her head. "Nothing, Benjamin just called, he left some approval forms on my desk that need to be signed off. Even though I've been living it up in the lap of luxury for the last couple of days, I still have to keep your house in order, Captain."

"Benjamin?" Kenneth asked.

"He's one of my sergeants at the precinct," she said. "He's in charge of some operations that I need to approve. Police work is continual, but paperwork is endless."

"Regretting taking that lieutenant's exam, MacKenzie?" Her captain's laughter made her smile.

"Every day of my damn life since," she answered, with the same laughter coloring her voice.

"Cap, can I speak with you in private for a moment? Just need to run a couple of house things by you."

Kenneth excused himself, leaving the two of them alone to talk.

"Hey Cap, I wanted to ask you, just what did Searlington mean when he called you

Uncle David? Are you related to the Searlingtons?"

Captain Porter shook his head, his gaze falling to the floor as he spoke. "Not in the way you're thinking. There's no blood relationship between the Searlingtons and me. Kenneth's father and I were best friends. We grew up together in Van Dyke, in Brownsville. When the twins were born, he named me their godfather. Kenneth is as close to me as any of my own children."

Damn, damn, damn. "So this is why Searlington brought this to you instead of going to his local precinct. This is why you trampled all over jurisdiction to get this case.

Captain, no disrespect, but have you lost your fucking mind?"

"MacKenzie," he said, his voice still, no anger or bite in it.

"Captain, with all of the money, manpower, and resources you're dedicating to this case, if anyone ever discovers your connection to the Searlingtons you could be looking at dismissal. There's a reason cops aren't supposed to land on cases where they are intimate with the key players."

"MacKenzie, I know. I know I should have turned this over to the local PD the minute I found out about this. When I tell you that boy is a son to me, he is. That little girl means the world to us. I couldn't trust her safety to just anyone. I knew you were the only one that could bring her home safe."

She ran a hand down her face trying to bring her focus back in when she heard her captain speaking.

"I was closer to Kalvin Searlington than any blood relative I ever had. When Kenneth and Carolyn were born, Kalvin asked me to be their godfather. From the moment the two of them could speak, I've been their Uncle David. So if the detail I have commissioned seems a bit over the top, it's because my dead brother's son is in trouble, and I'll do anything I can to try to protect him and his family."

Her blood was boiling, the secrets in this case were beginning to piss her off. But she understood about protecting family. She didn't have much by way of blood, not many that she was exceptionally close to. But she understood what it was when the person you cared for most was in trouble, and that switch that tripped in your head that made you do anything and everything to protect them. She nodded her head.

"I got it, Cap, I understand. I'll do what I can to get this girl home. I gotta get to the precinct so I can hurry up back here. I'm tired of following this asshole, I'm bring the fight to him instead."

~

*H*eart walked through the doors of her precinct and straight into the squad room. She didn't look around, she didn't stop. The officers milling around cleared a path for her as she walked.

"Benjamin," she called out over the noise in the room. Still not stopping, she headed to her office, certain that her sergeant would find his way into her office.

Before she could settle in the chair behind her desk, her office door closed and Sergeant Benjamin was standing in front of her desk.

"Lieutenant MacKenzie?"

Heart looked at the man standing in front of her. Sergeant Michael Benjamin was probably only an inch or two taller than her own five feet nine inches, but he was wide with bulky muscle and a thick neck that looked like it should belong to a linebacker instead of a decorated cop. His head was bald, and he had a thin goatee that lined his lips and chin. She wasn't quite sure what part of the world his people hailed from, he was white, yes, but he seemed to blend into the streets of the hood the way no white man she'd ever met could.

This wasn't just a job to him; he'd lived these streets at some point in his life.

"Benjamin, do you know anything about a Martha and RaQuan Selwyn that live in the Pink Houses?"

Benjamin nodded and sat down in front of Heart's desk.

"Martha is a churchgoing middle-aged lady who works as a nurse's aide in a local hospital. As far as we can see, she really is all that she appears, hardworking, law abiding."

"If that's the case, then how the hell did she end up on your radar?"

Benjamin slid down in his chair a little more, making himself more comfortable.

"Because of her son. He is a big-time hustler in those projects. He's one of the big names in narcotics around these parts. He's started several bloody wars with his competition over in the Cypress Houses and even as far down as Van Dyke too. We've tried several times to build a case against him, but he's very careful about doing the dirty work himself, and we haven't found anyone that is willing to roll on him yet. I have a man on the inside; in the last eight months he's been able to get inside of Selwyn's operation."

She nodded her head, soaking up the details Benjamin gave her.

"All right, tell your boy inside to get ready for a stop and frisk on Autumn and

Loring Aves. Let's say around 11:23 tonight. He's gonna be busted by Ramirez. She'll be the only female officer on the detail. Text me a pic of him, and I will forward it to her so she'll know him when she spots him."

He acknowledged her mandate with a nod. He poised himself to get up, but stopped just short of lifting out of the seat.

"Is there any reason in particular you need to know about Selwyn?"

"I have another case I'm working on, things are being played closely to the vest right now. RaQuan may be involved in something else besides slinging and hustling in the projects. I will tell you that things can blow up really quickly from here on out. If you've got enough to bring charges against this piece of shit, do it quickly.

Depending on how this all works out, it may all be blown to hell in the next twenty-four to forty-eight hours. I will keep you posted as necessary. Let me know the minute your boy is in-house. I gotta go."

Benjamin nodded and left her office. She pulled out her cell phone and dialed a number that was burned on her brain. Whenever she dialed, her call was always answered, or at least returned within a reasonable time. The line rang twice and the familiar voice warmed the cold ache that had been hiding somewhere inside her since the last time she heard her cousin's voice.

"Speak," said the voice, bringing a smile to Heart's face.

"True, what's happening little cousin?" She heard True snicker on the other end.

"Little? Bitch please, you're only three months older than me. What do you want?"

Heart gave out a hearty laugh, True always got straight to the point. No beating around the bush.

"I need some information."

"On what, orthopedics or rehab? Did you get hurt, Heart?"

"No, nothing like that. I don't need Dr. Amare, I need the chick that does that other thing you do."

"What do you need?" asked the cool voice on the other end.

"I have a delicate kidnapping case on my hands and I think some, if not all of the victim's family may be involved. They're definitely hiding something. My captain is really close to these people and he seems to have blinders on where they're concerned. If I run information on them, he's gonna know what I'm doing, and he may impede my investigation. I don't really give a damn who is involved, I just want to get a five-yearold girl home. I'm also concerned that there may be some kind of leak in my house, so I need to reach for outside sources."

True was quiet for a moment. Heart knew her cousin was processing the information she had revealed to True.

"Who's the target?"

"Karolyn Searlington," Heart said. Bile rising into her mouth as she said it.

"Searlington? I used to know someone by that name. Kenneth Searlington. Is he any relation?"

"As a matter of fact, yes. Twin brother. You know him, how?" It would figure, her cousin seemed to have ties to everyone, it didn't surprise Heart in the least that her cousin had some inside connection to the Searlington family.

"He went to school with my two partners, Genesis and Faith. He and Faith became really close. As I recall, they dated quite seriously for about three years. When he finished grad school and went back home, they both agreed to let the relationship drop.

As far as I know they're still really good friends, and keep in contact. I've met him once or twice, he was cool, didn't raise any flags and he treated Faith very well, so he had no issues from me. Although he seemed to care for Faith very much, I got the feeling that he was never going to be able to completely commit to Faith."

"Why?"

"He's loaded, but he never really acted like a rich jackass if you know what I mean.

He was actually kind of cool. But, I did get the sense that his family wouldn't be too happy about him doing the coffee swirl with a black chick on scholarship from East New

York, Brooklyn. As far as I know, Faith never met his family."

"I don't suppose she would have. I've met them, she wasn't missing anything. The mother's weirdly protective of the daughter, and the daughter is sneaky and secretive. I can't really get a read on her, but I think she may have something to do with the missing girl. I need info on her and I need to find out why she might have some sort of connection with a RaQuan Selwyn, resident hustler in the Pink Houses."

"That shouldn't be too hard to find out. Give me a few, I'll get back to you by tonight with that info."

Relief flooded through Heart, True was always at her back, it was one of the few assurances she had been able to depend on in her life.

She ended the call and then dialed Ramirez with the information she needed to pass on. She wrapped up a few more loose ends from her desk, and headed back to Manhattan.

This shit was about to be done if she could help it, it was time to find out what Karolyn Searlington was hiding.

Just as she was poised to leave, Heart heard the familiar chime of her office line buzzing.

"MacKenzie," she answered.

"Lieutenant, it's Madison at the front desk. I have a Mr. William Grant here, he says he needs to see you immediately."

She wiped her hand down over the length of her face. *Fuck does he want?* She rubbed her temple and took a deep breath.

"Send him in, Madison."

William Grant walked into her office bringing sunshine with him. That golden yellow thing he had going with his hair looked stark and shocking compared to the drab institution white/gray dingy walls of the precinct.

God, looking at all of these beautiful rich people is really starting to make my head hurt.

His tall lithe frame walked unobtrusively inside her office, and slowly took the seat she offered.

"How can I help you, Mr. Grant?"

She watched him, worried creases etched years onto a face that she knew was only five years older than her own.

"Lieutenant, may I ask you a question?"

She nodded. "Please call me MacKenzie, what do you want to know?"

"I wanted to talk you at the house, but I thought it would be better if we spoke within your walls," he took a brief glance around her office, "instead of theirs."

She watched him for a moment more before she silently stood up and walked to the mini-fridge hidden in the corner. She retrieved two bottles of water, pulled a chair next to

William's and sat down. She twisted the top off of the first bottle and handed it to him, then she opened her own, and took a sip.

"What's on your mind, Mr. Grant?" she asked as she leaned back and relaxed into the seat. The man next to her was wound so tightly, she was afraid he was going to snap soon, if she gave him a calm exterior, maybe it would induce his own nervous system to calm down too.

"I wanted to know if you are going to pursue justice in my daughter's case no matter who the perpetrator is revealed to be."

"You sound as if you have some idea of who this perpetrator might be," she said before calmly sipping another mouthful of water from the bottle in her hand.

"I think I might," he said slowly lifting his eyes to her. "I just need to know you're going to follow this up and not sweep it under the rug because of the power and privilege behind the person."

She considered him for another moment before she answered. She had seen very little of him during the course of this investigation, often thinking that his presence was too sparse for a concerned father. But the truth of the matter was, she had no real model for the image of a concerned father, so she'd decided to wait and watch and reserve judgment for later. Give William the opportunity to show and prove.

"I'm worried for my daughter, Lieutenant, worried for her mother too."

"How so?" she leaned forward, inviting him to finish his thoughts. She watched him fall back into the seat, his sagging shoulders making his chest sink further into a humped position.

"This is my fault," he whispered quietly.

"What exactly do you mean?"

"Karolyn and I split up because I couldn't deal with her manipulations and lies anymore. I left Karolyn because I found her in bed with someone else. When I refused to take her back, she told me she would make me pay with the thing I loved most in my life, my daughter. And she did, she made me pay, she practically stole my daughter from me, and ruined any chance I had of endearing my daughter to me at all." He looked down at his ringing hands, as if they held the secret to his musings. She said nothing while he flexed and released his linked fingers, letting him work through his process however he saw fit.

He looked up at her, appearing to be armed with whatever it was he came to say. She leaned back into the arm of her chair, inviting him to come to her. He accepted the invitation, leaning forward just a little and finally opening his mouth to speak.

"I thought she had fulfilled her plot for revenge until she discovered I'm planning to marry again. It's as if that piece of knowledge set her off again, because she called me a few weeks before Merri's disappearance and told me again that she was going to make me pay. I don't want to believe Karolyn would do something like this, but I have to know what's going on with my daughter."

She nodded her head giving herself time to organize her thoughts before she spoke. There were too many variables in this case, too many things that could cause this case to go terribly wrong, she had to be careful about what she said and to whom she said it.

"Are you accusing your ex-wife of orchestrating your daughter's disappearance?"

His gaze found hers, where it was shaky before it was strong and steady now, pinning her to her seat, unwavering in its consistency.

"Yes, Lieutenant, yes I am."

She didn't flinch with his revelation; her face and body language were a schooled image of neutrality. Giving away her true thoughts was never an option when she was working; people only ever saw what she wanted them to see, calm, cool, and concerned.

That's what most people were looking for when they were talking to you, giving them that made them feel comfortable and helped them ultimately relax enough to give you what you needed from them in terms of information.

"What makes you think Karolyn is behind your daughter's disappearance?"

"Have you ever realized that Karolyn seems to be very moody, I mean more so than your average person?"

She shrugged her shoulders. "Yeah, but I don't spend a large amount of time around exceptionally wealthy people either. I just assumed it came as par for the course when it came to the lifestyles of the filthy rich and snobbish."

"It can, but she's higher strung, higher maintenance than any other pampered princess I know, and there's a reason for that. She's constantly ingesting some form of mood altering drug or another. She's a career pill popper, and in the last few years of our marriage she graduated to illicit drugs like cocaine."

She raised an eyebrow and leaned forward a little more. "We did a thorough background check on all of you. If that were the case it would have come up. Do you mean to tell me all of the Searlingtons are covering something like this up?"

He shook his head. "No, Kenneth doesn't know."

"How could he not, he's her twin brother, wouldn't he notice above all if this was the case?"

He shook his head again. "Kenneth and Karolyn may be twins, but they are anything

but close. Kenneth is not about money, he enjoys the benefits of it, but it doesn't define who he is. Karolyn and their mother, they believe money is everything, and the fact that they can't control Kenneth's is problematic. Kenneth spent six years in California between college and grad school. His education allowed him to escape the craziness of his family. While he was over there, Karolyn was on the east coast living up the socialite lifestyle. When Karolyn and I married, Kenneth had just returned from school and we took possession of one of the Searlington luxury apartments in Riverdale. Kenneth wasn't around her to know, and I cleaned up enough after her that he never became aware."

His leg began a subtle bounce that gave away his nervousness. The rhythm becoming more steady and pronounced as he talked. He stood up and began to walk back and forth in the office, worrying the battered tile beneath his feet.

"So when you got tired of dealing you just left your daughter in the hands of a drug addict?"

Her words had the desired affect and stopped his movements. The muscles in his face pulled tighter, straining against the tight angles of his face. Her inner-cop smiled and she marked a line in the win column for herself. Enough of this bullshit with these people, time to find out what they were really doing behind closed doors in this goddamned family.

"Fuck you, Lieutenant," he growled. If she hadn't been intentionally poking the bear, she might've—but not really—been the slightest bit alarmed by the bass in his voice.

"I did not abandon my daughter. I fought as hard as I could for her, but I couldn't prove that Karolyn was a junkie, she had too much power, and too much money for me to sway the courts in my favor. If I didn't agree to her terms, I could have lost Merridith completely."

She made a mental note to recheck the details of their divorce and call in his attorney, see if there was any truth to the tale he was weaving.

"So what's changed, William? What makes you think that she could do something like this? I mean, even drug addicts can sometimes function enough to not kidnap their own children."

He shook his head, falling back into the seat he'd vacated earlier. "I don't know what it is now. It's nothing I can prove, but everything in my heart tells me she had something to do with this. I just don't trust her."

She watched him carefully, crossed her arms across her chest as a singular thought crossed her mind. *I don't trust that bitch either.*

~

Heart followed Sargent Benjamin down the dark concrete corridor until they stood in front of the iron bars that constructed the large holding cell in the bowels of her precinct. Her eyes combed through the prisoners being held looking for one man in particular. When she found him, she stood in front of the door to the cell, legs locked at shoulder width; arms crossed in her familiar, "stay the fuck back," fashion.

He was sitting on a bench that lined the back wall of the community cell. His forearms resting on his thighs, hands steepled, head hanging down. Anyone else might have thought he was sleeping, or not paying attention to his surroundings, she knew that he had everyone and everything in and around that cell tracked. Eyes still focused on him she waited until he lifted his head, her gaze drawing his from the floor to where she stood at the cell's gate. Without saying a word she gave him a half smile and then nodded her go ahead to Benjamin.

"Del Torro," Benjamin called it, silencing the buzzing noise of the prisoners' grumbling conversation.

Carlos Del Torro, right-hand man of Brooklyn Drug Lord RaQuan Selwyn lifted his dark head of ink-black loose curls and laid his jet-black gaze on Heart. His cold stare walked down and then up her frame, then turned to the sergeant at her side.

"Así que la perra que se ejecuta?" he said with a sneer painted across his full mouth.

Heart's brows lifted in amusement. Many people mistook Benjamin for Latino, he was too down for most to recognize him as a Caucasian man in this neighborhood.

"En realidad, las únicas perras en aquí es que usted y el resto de la basura que se guardó en esa lata con usted. Y aquí hay otra noticia de última hora, todos ustedes me pertences," she finished with the perfect roll to her tongue.

"¿Morena, hablas español? Yo no sabía que ellos enseñaron nigger-perras como tú a hablar una lengua tan hermosa como mi lengua nativa."

Heart laughed and pulled a wide smile against her face.

"Yo diría que lo hablo mejor que la puta que te parió," she said.

Carlos jumped up and ran against the cage that separated them. She stood firm, didn't so much as blink when his body hit the cage with all of his weight behind the hard thump that made the metal bars sing a low, dull resounding tone that traveled through the catacombs that housed the prisoner cells.

She laughed as Del Torro thrashed about, trying fruitlessly to reach her through the bars. She turned to Benjamin and nodded her permission. She turned around and began to walk back up the stairs, knowing Benjamin and the prisoner would follow. She continued to laugh as she walked up the stairs.

These were the things she loved about her job. Yeah, police work could be dangerous, but most days, most days it was just comical as all hell.

~

*K*enneth heard the rumble of footsteps coming down the stairs.

"Cap, I'm going for a run, I need to clear my head to get some stuff together for this case," she said as she walked toward the apartment door.

Kenneth glanced up from the work file he was reading in his hand. His eyes doing a double take as they fastened on the image before him. MacKenzie in a form fitting black running suit that hugged every one of her imaginable curves in just the right way that made his dick jump between his legs.

She bent from the waist to tie her sneakers and he had to bite the inside of his cheek hard to keep the slow moan that wanted to escape him from leaving his mouth. Damn, the curve of her ass was perfect and round, and high, and damn, he wanted in there in the worst way.

When was the last time he'd sexed away his frustrations? He needed to find a willing partner quickly or he was going to combust from his need to slide in between the lieutenant's lovely cheeks.

He watched as she left, and kept his eyes on the door, remembering every exposed curve. It was only the sound of his godfather's voice that pulled his mind from the living memory of that ass.

"Kenneth, close your mouth and stop drooling," Porter said.

"Uncle David, it hasn't been that long since you were in the game, that woman's body is a work of art."

"That woman's body is a lethal weapon that will drop you before you can say your own name."

Kenneth couldn't help but shiver at the thought of MacKenzie manhandling him, pressing him close, doing whatever she wanted to him.

"You are such a little perv-boy, Kenneth. You really need to keep it in your pants and focus on the case," Porter said with a lifted brow at his godson.

Kenneth smiled again, his uncle David had always laughed off his playboy ways, but for some reason he was blocking hard where his second in command was concerned.

"Are you sure you aren't getting a taste of that, Uncle David?" Porter leaned forward and swatted him against the side of his head.

"Not everyone thinks with their dick, I keep telling you that boy. Nothing has or ever will go on between my second and me. I think of MacKenzie like a daughter, not someone to toy with. Why the hell are you so taken with her, Kenneth?" Kenneth took in a deep breath and crossed his arms over his chest.

"I don't really know, Uncle David. It's probably because she won't pay me the time of day, but mostly because she's the sexiest thing on two legs that I've seen in a long time." He closed his eyes and brought up the vision of MacKenzie in that second skin running gear. *Damn.*

"Kenneth, your playboy charms notwithstanding, Mac will never fall prey to you." Porter's mood changed, a seriousness pouring over him that Kenneth had only seen a few times over his lifetime.

"It's very apparent you're attracted to MacKenzie," Porter said.

Kenneth conceded Porter's observation; there was no need to deny it. He had practically humped her body with his eyes. It didn't take a trained detective to figure out he had a thing for her. "She's a beautiful woman, any man would be a fool not to be attracted to her."

"I'd like to know what your intentions are toward her."

"Uncle David, I truly don't intend to sound disrespectful, but I don't think that's any concern of yours."

"That's where you're wrong. I keep telling you, she's like my daughter, Kenneth. I'm just as protective of her as I am you and your sister."

Kenneth's stare carefully walked over Porter's face, looking for any chink in his armor. "Are you certain the two of you aren't involved, Uncle David?"

"Last time I'm gonna say this, young man," Porter snarled through clenched teeth, squaring his shoulders and pulling himself to his full height. "I'm a married man with two grown children that are older than Mac. Mac is like a child to me. And as such, I love her like one of my own. Like any father, I'll protect mine from all I can, including you."

Kenneth folded his arms across his chest, partly to show his godfather he couldn't be intimidated, partly to hide the chill Porter's words had poured into him.

"Uncle David, I have no intention of hurting MacKenzie."

Porter shook his head; he walked over to the sofa and motioned for Kenneth to join him.

"The truth is, you'll never have the chance to hurt her directly. Mac isn't going to allow you to get close to her, but if you pursue her, you're going to do nothing but hurt her."

"How?" Kenneth asked.

"Mac isn't interested in having a man in her life."

"I've been wondering about that, why is she so put off by rich men?"

"Kenneth, it isn't just rich, men, it's men in general. Mac wants nothing to do with men. She never has, and she never will."

MacKenzie had told Kenneth as much during several conversations, he just couldn't wrap his head around the why of the matter.

"Are you trying to tell me MacKenzie is gay?"

"No, she's not a lesbian." Kenneth let out a sigh of relief.

"Kenneth, she isn't homosexual, and she isn't heterosexual."

"She's bisexual?" he asked with a bright smile climbing up his face. God, the thoughts that little possibility brought to his mind.

"No," Porter barked, snatching Kenneth out of the fantasy his mind was scripting in that very moment. "She's neither of those things, she's asexual. As far as I can tell, Mac isn't interested in sex or relationships, she's only interested in her work."

Kenneth became curious. He wondered just how much insight Porter had into Mac.

"How could you possibly know that?"

"I know that, because she told me. There are some things that came up in her psych eval when she became a cop that I became aware of. I don't know the exact details, but something happened to her that made her just shut down and focus on work."

Kenneth felt a tight squeezing in his chest, his breath hitching in his throat as his mind wove conclusions in his head.

"Are you saying she suffered some sort of abuse?"

Porter shook her head. "I don't know that for certain. The eval never could pinpoint if she was actually abused. The shrink that administered the test said that Mac passed all of the markers for mental health with flying colors, she was almost too perfect. The examiner couldn't exclude her because she'd passed the tests, but she did say she felt as if MacKenzie experienced some emotional trauma prior to joining the force. She suspected it had something to do with MacKenzie's mother dying when she was a child, but she just didn't have enough information to go on at the time."

Porter laced the fingers of his hands together and intermittently flexed and relaxed them as he spoke to Kenneth.

"MacKenzie is the best cop I have in my house, I have never regretted making her my number two. She's damn good at what she does, and I don't want to see that fucked with, because you can't accept that there's one woman on this planet that doesn't want to let you hump her. Leave her alone, Kenneth, just let her go."

Porter stood up and walked into the kitchen leaving Kenneth alone to think on his words.

"*She wants nothing to do with men. She wants to be alone.*" How could a woman so beautiful, with so much to offer want to stay alone?

∾

*W*hen Kenneth returned to the living room, Mac was scrutinizing some papers in her hand.

"Anything new on the case?"

She was slightly startled to find Kenneth hovering over her. "No, this has nothing to do with the case at all."

"Then what are these papers about?"

"They're personal."

"So you're reading personal papers on the job?"

Her annoyance was quite clear in her voice. "Don't you have something do, like buying a plot of land or something?"

"Nope, so you see, there's nothing left to do but harass you. Think of it this way, you might as well tell me what you're reading, the sooner you do, the sooner you'll get rid of me."

It was only the promise of being left alone that led her to divulge her personal documents. "My landlord is selling the house I live in. I couldn't find an apartment I liked, so I decided to buy a house. These are the mortgage papers, I've been trying to take time out to go over them, but I just haven't found the time."

"Lieutenant, if you were looking for a house, why didn't you tell me, I could show you hundreds of wonderful houses, as well as beautiful condos."

"Thank you, but no thank you, I'll find my own home, my own way, without your

help."

"Would it kill you to let me help you? I'm an expert at real estate it's my livelihood, no one can find you a better house than I can."

She stood about to walk away, but she thought better of it, and decided to answer him. "I am only here because my work causes me to be here. Once Merridith is home, I'll go my way, and you'll go yours. It could take a very long time for you to find me this perfect house or condo, I don't have that time, and I don't make it a habit of letting instrumental people on cases I've worked on know where I live."

She closed the file, ascended up the stairs, and shut the door behind her. Did he ever stop? Why wouldn't he leave her alone? Since they'd met, he'd been poking his nose into her business one way or another. God, he of all people should understand a person's need for privacy, yet every chance he got, he tried to poke and prod into her life.

Thank God for the lead they'd gotten, the sooner she found this little girl, the better.

She didn't know how much longer she could spend in the presence of Kenneth Searlington.

She paced the floor for hours, she had to find some way to work off the unusual amount of energy she had. Why was he getting to her like this? No other man had been able to make her this angry, or get any sort of emotion out of her.

His room was next to hers, and he could probably hear the constant movement. She was usually quiet this time of night, but for some reason she was unsettled. She was about to grab her badge, gun, and keys off of the night stand, hoping a walk on the streets would help calm her when the shrill sound of her phone ringing brought her to a halt.

"MacKenzie," she answered.

"L.T., we gotta move."

Mac shoved the phone between her ear and shoulder while she snapped her hip holster in place. "Report," Heart said in a clipped tone.

"We found the girl, MacKenzie," the low-speaking voice said.

A shiver ran through her. The thudding of her heartbeat felt like a hammer to her insides.

"Alive?" she questioned softly. Fear taking hold of her as the breath stopped in her throat.

"Yes," the voice said, bringing a gush of relief over her.

"Text me the details, then delete everything, including your call history."

"I know the drill, I'm on it."

Before she could fully pull the phone away from her ear, she felt the definitive vibration of her cell phone notifying her that she had an unread message. All the details of Merridith's location were before her.

"Only one thing left to do," she said while walking toward the door.

≈

*M*aybe he should go in and check on her. "No Kenneth, remember what happened the last time you went into that room? She pulled her gun on you, that's what happened."

Instead, he lay still on his bed, listening to her movements, imagining what it was she was doing. Imagining what it was that kept her up so late. Could Captain Porter's words be true? Could she really want to be left alone for all her life? It just didn't seem natural to him, to be alone by choice.

Yes, he was lonely, but it wasn't because he wanted to be that way. He was determined to find someone he could love, and trust. Maybe it wouldn't be the greatest love the world had ever known, but it would be something that was solid and real, and most of all, his. Mac had to want the same thing that was every human's dream, to find someone to share their life with.

Captain Porter had described her as an unfeeling woman, who cared about nothing but her work. He didn't believe that, he couldn't believe that, not about Mac, not about the caring cop he'd known.

Why was he so intent on believing beneath that badge beat the heart of an erotic, sensual woman? She'd shown him nothing to support his beliefs, she'd never stared at him through hooded eyes, she'd never caressed him, hell she hated the slightest physical contact between them. Mac had never so much as flirted with him, but he couldn't let himself believe that as beautiful as she was, she wanted to be alone.

God he couldn't get her out of his head. "The two of you don't belong together." No matter how much he told himself that, he still imagined being the man to break through her many barriers. "You come from different worlds, she's black, you're white," he rolled his eyes even as he said it. He knew damn well that he didn't have a problem with the warm chocolate hue of her skin. He'd spent more than three years exclusively dating Faith while they were in school in California. Hell, the two of them had indulged in forold-times'-sake sex on several occasions, whenever they met up in the world. His family's hang ups weren't his own, and race had never caused him to discount a partner. He took a breath, on that particular issue, he had to call bullshit. So he moved on to the next.

"She's a cop, and you control an entire empire built upon real estate." Again he rolled his eyes. Mac couldn't give a shit about what he did and how much money he made. She wasn't impressed by any of the things that most women found enticing about him. "There's only one thing the two of you have in common, this case. You are nothing but a case to Mac, nothing more. How many times must she tell you that before you listen?"

He stopped thinking long enough to hear the silence coming from the room next to him. She'd settled down, she was probably sleeping now, as he should have been. He couldn't sleep, not with so many thoughts of a woman he couldn't have running through his head. A woman he shouldn't have been attracted to, a woman who lay only on the other side of his wall.

He walked out onto his balcony; the sight of the city at night, with all its glittering lights had always seemed to have a calming effect on him. He'd spent many nights looking out over the city when something troubled him. He stood there quiet, taking in the skyline, when he sensed another presence.

He turned to find her standing next to him on the balcony. She was wearing a simple wife-beater t-shirt and dark denim jeans with a pair of black workman's boots. She was the typical replica of urban style. Simple, laid-back casual wear, but on her form, the items looked regal, tailor-made, only for her.

Her arms were bare, something he had never seen before in the short time they'd known each other. He couldn't help himself, he needed to feel that luscious brown skin that called to him. He stretched out his hand carefully, watching to see if she would turn away from him. When she didn't, he let his hand continue to move forward until it made contact with the top of her arm.

She was like nothing he'd ever seen; there was this preciousness about her, this air of innocence. As if she was untouched, or was that just his imagination.

After all, the woman was twenty-eight years old; she had to have had at least one lover in her lifetime. What he'd give to be able to get close enough to find that out. Yes, making love to her was something he wanted, but what he wanted even more than making love to her was to know her. To know her secrets, to know her doubts and her fears. To know her dreams, what she wished for most in life. He wanted to know Lieutenant MacKenzie, Lieutenant MacKenzie, Mac, he didn't even know her first name, yet he felt so compelled to be a part of her life.

She lifted a hand to her loose hair—something else he'd never seen on her—pushing back a loose tendril. Usually bound in a tight knot, it fell so freely down her back and shoulders, full of body and beauty. What he wouldn't give to be able to run his fingers through it.

"Good God you're beautiful," he said on whispered breath.

CHAPTER 7

For the first time, she didn't shy away from him; instead she stood proudly, facing him.

"Why are you watching me like that?"

"You mean in awe? The look that one has when he's stunned by beauty."

Her eyes fell from his, breaking the contact they were making. He lifted her face by her chin, forcing her to look into his eyes.

"Don't you know how beautiful you are, hasn't any man ever completely fallen under your spell? God knows I have. Mac, I want to know you, I want to know all about you. I want to know who the woman is behind those beautiful coffee eyes."

The feel of his hand on her face was doing strange things to her. She immediately backed away, putting some space between them.

"Don't pull away from me, Mac."

"I-I can't."

Before she could stop him, he closed the space between them and said, "Why do you do that, why do you back away from me, are you afraid of me?"

Her eyes still closed, she answered, "I'm not interested in starting a relationship with you." He moved closer tightening his hold on her bare arm. She felt so uncomfortable, but not for the reasons she should be feeling out of sorts. His touch made her fight against her instincts. She was literally fighting with herself to stand still. But she couldn't win; soon, she moved her arm so that his hand fell away from her.

"Why is it you can't stand to be touched?"

"I don't know what you're talking about."

"The hell you don't, every time I remotely touch you, you back away."

Her back was facing him now, trying to conceal all that he wanted to see. He placed his hand on her shoulder, and as always, she shrugged it off. "Why can't you stand to be touched?"

"I just don't like it when people touch me that's all."

"That's bull and you know it. When you handed Bryan his breakfast plate, his hand slightly touched yours, and just as you do every time I touch you, you pulled away from him."

"I told you, I'm not comfortable with people touching me, and I would truly appreciate it if you would stop."

"MacKenzie, why are you so distant? You know just as well as I do, there's something happening between us, it's been happening since the day we met."

"I know no such thing, all of this is in your imagination." If only her constant wishing could make that statement true.

"Don't play games with me, Mac, you'll lose."

"What do you want from me, why can't you just leave me alone? I've never asked anything of you, I've tried my best to keep this a strictly business relationship. Why can't you just understand that I don't want this?"

"Because I care, and I want to get to know you."

"No, what you want to get to know is my body."

"That too."

"I knew it, all you want from me is quick lay in bed. Admit it, the only thing that you're interested in is fucking me, and moving on."

He appeared shocked by her words. The lines of his face suddenly pulled taut, and something sharp and fierce crossed his eyes, like an errant streak of lightening. It seemed to pass directly from him, and spiraled down her insides. She attempted to step back again, her instinct to flee and protect loudly clicking in place. He pressed forward, forcing her back against the door fixture to the bedroom. She went to push off the wall, but suddenly felt the crushing weight of his body against hers followed by blistering lips that singed across the smooth flesh of her own.

The kiss was never slow; it was full on, hard from the first time skin met skin. The first touch ignited a blaze in her that seemed to start growing from somewhere deep inside of her that she didn't recognize. Her mind screamed for her to free herself from this onslaught. Her body and soul kept her planted right where she was mashed between the doorjamb and him.

Her lips seemed to have made up their own decision to respond to his ministrations. She opened her mouth, attempting to pull in much needed air for her lungs, when he saw the brief moment as an opportunity to deepen the kiss by inserting his tongue inside her mouth, and stroking her tongue with sure, certain caresses.

She felt strong fingers climb her arm and roughly plant themselves in her hair. So skilled, there was only a brief pinch of discomfort before that strong hold pulled her closer to him, heightening the sensations he was stirring inside of her. The soothing motion of his fingers in her hair was eliciting a long, soulful moan from her.

That sound must have broken the spell because when the last note of her emotional release left her his lips lifted from hers.

Disoriented by the departure of his lips, of its own volition her mouth began searching for the remembered warmth his lips invoked. He tightened his grip in her hair, and tilted her head back until her eyes met his.

"MacKenzie, I am very attracted to you," his voice a low, powerful rumble of bass. "...and yes, fucking you—as you so bluntly put it—is something I am very interested in. But if fucking you was all I wanted, I would have been bored with the back-and-forth bullshit we've been doling out since the first time we met. I don't chase women they chase me. I bed them, and move on, and forget about them. The last serious relationship I had was while I was in college and grad school, and I haven't had one since, haven't wanted one. But there is something about you, something that makes me want more, and the way you just melted in my arms tells me you want more too. I intend to give us both what we want."

He pressed a final soft kiss against her lips. She closed her eyes, and steeled herself, trying to remember why she had come into his room in the first place. Just that quickly, like frigid water sliding down over her head, the cop that was always in control clicked back into place.

"I need you and Grant downstairs now, we found Merridith."

~

*H*eart watched the white and yellow lights of the Midtown Tunnel whiz by as she let her car hug the tight curves of the left lane. It was late in the night; there was no traffic from Manhattan going into Queens at this hour. She radioed ahead before they'd left the apartment. The toll plaza had a lane open and waiting for her to sail through once she reached the other side of the tunnel.

She forced her eyes to stay focused on the road ahead of her. She'd taken these curves at higher speeds without much effort before. But now, with Kenneth sitting next to her, and the memory of how his lips felt and tasted against her so freshly imprinted on her senses, she constantly felt like stomping on the brakes. For fear of tail-spinning out of control, she placed both hands on the wheel and let her training take over. They had to make it out of this tunnel, a little girl's life depended on it.

She flew through the toll plaza and was at Exit 19 in a matter of moments heading toward the Rockaways. She lit up her lights and sirens, there were too many traffic lights up Woodhaven Boulevard that could hold her up. She cleared Woodhaven, making a quick right onto Atlantic Ave. Atlantic to Crescent, Crescent to Euclid. When she reached the intersection of Euclid and Belmont Avenues, she killed her lights and sirens, not wanting to alert any lookouts that 5-0 was on the move. She continued down Euclid to Linden, and within moments she was nearing the all too familiar housing project. She parked behind a blacked out van and pulled her cell from her back pocket.

"What do we know, Ramirez?" Heart said evenly.

"The girl is in apartment 9c. We've got snipers watching in through the windows. It's a one-bedroom apartment. Kitchen is open on both sides to the living room. Bedroom is to the right of the living room, bathroom to the left. There are two windows in the bedroom, one in the living room, and one in the kitchen. We have a closet in the living room, one in the hall adjacent to the bathroom, and one in the bedroom. One entrance in and out. No fire escape. Two staircases and elevators in the middle of the floor. Apartment is to the left when coming off of the elevators. Once we are inside and upstairs, we will kill the elevators. We will have someone waiting at the bottom of the incinerator chute just in case someone decides to get creative if there's a chase."

"Sounds like you have the layout down pat, who's inside?"

"The girl is in the bedroom with two guards. There's a third adult in the bedroom with the child, but we can't make out who or what the individual is. Selwyn is in the living room with two of his cronies, and Karolyn Searlington."

Heart swallowed hard and glanced quickly at Kenneth and Grant. Both their eyes trained on her. She pulled her eyes away and returned her focus to the black van sitting in front of them.

"Ramirez, what is Searlington doing in there?"

There was silence for a minute, just long enough to make Heart look at the phone to see if the call dropped.

"Ramirez, are you still there?"

"Yeah L.T., it's not pretty...they seem to be running a train on her."

"Come again?"

"Karolyn Searlington, Selwyn and his two guards are currently having sex with her simultaneously."

Again, another beat passed before either of them spoke.

"Ramirez, are they forcing her?" The words made her sick as she said them, the images that they created made her stomach roll.

"Honestly, Mac, I can't tell. She doesn't appear to be fighting them. None of the men seem to be holding any weapons against her, she's just sort of lying there and taking it. She could be high out of her mind right now. I can't really tell from the feed without any audio attached to it."

Heart nodded, and decided on their plan of action.

"All right, seems like now is the best time to go in, while Selwyn literally has his pants down. Everyone goes in with a partner, everyone wears protective gear. These damn projects are like a warzone and I want my people dressed for the part. Tell the tactical guys to cover all entrances and exits, no one gets in or out of the building while we are inside. I want complete shutdown until we clear this building. You got me

Ramirez?"

"Yes, copy that, Lieutenant."

"I have Searlington and Grant with me. Give me five, then I will bring them to the van. They can stay there with the surveillance team while we are inside."

Heart turned to look at Kenneth and William. She could see the worried expectancy painted across their faces.

"Karolyn is inside of the apartment where Merri is being held." She watched as something seemed to break inside of each man.

"Let me just say this, we don't yet know what her involvement in all of this is. Our main goal right now is to extract Merridith and her mother, secure the bad guys and sort this out once we get back to the precinct."

Kenneth's eyes never left hers, he seemed to be chewing on the information she had just provided them.

"Are you going to arrest my sister?"

"Kenneth, I don't know why your sister is in there. The fact that she's with her missing child, and that she hasn't been cooperative with this investigation leads me to believe that she has some sort of involvement in Merridith's abduction. But I can't arrest anyone until I find out what's going on. If she didn't do anything, then she has nothing to worry about. But if she played even the slightest role in this child being taken, then there isn't anything I won't do to bring her to justice."

She watched him nod his head up and down and saw the slight crack that was slowly spreading down the wall of his armor.

"I need for the two of you to get into the surveillance van. Stay there, until I come get you. You do not move unless myself, or one of my officers tells you to. Do you understand me, am I clear?"

She passed her eyes back and forth between the two men. They each nodded quickly as she made eye contact with them.

Satisfied that they understood, she opened the car door, and they followed in kind. She rapt a finger twice in quick succession against the back of the dark van and waited for the doors to open. Once open, her team members hoped out, and Kenneth and William climbed in. She raised a hand, and waved a single finger, giving the signal for the other strategically placed officers to prepare themselves and step onto the playing field.

Bryan handed her a bullet proof vest. She quickly secured it, then attached a thigh holster providing her with an additional semi-automatic weapon and ammo at her fingertips. She looked at Smyth, and they began the same ritual they always performed just before walking into a dangerous operation. They each checked their personal weapon, kissed it, cocked it, and let their carrying arm fall to their side. "Smyth, let's go bring a storm to that bastard's front door."

Bryan nodded. "I'll bring the thunder."

She smiled. "And I'll bring the rain."

She took her single pointed finger and aimed it at the building they were targeting. All of the police officers strategically placed throughout the complex began to spread out like a quiet swarm. Heart nodded toward Bryan, they were about to follow the rest of their brethren when she heard Kenneth speak-whisper her name.

She turned around to see wide, crystal blue eyes staring back at her filled with worry, and something else she wasn't quite able to define at that moment.

He reached out his hand and she instinctively grabbed on to it.

"Please be careful in there."

She smiled, hoping to reassure him.

"This is what I do, Kenneth. I will be fine. I will bring your family back to you." His squeezed her hand tighter.

"I wasn't just talking about them. Please, stay safe."

Her colleagues had always watched her back. Porter had always watched her back, Bryan had always made sure she was never alone when working. Other than the people at work, her grandmother, and her cousins, there had never been anyone who gave a damn about her. She assessed him just a minute longer, looking for something that would tell her he was lying, he was bullshitting. She checked his face, his body, and finally his eyes. There in those crystal depths, there was nothing but truth. He was really worried about her.

More than ever, that revelation scared her. She never cared about what happened to her in her line of work. There weren't many people who would mourn her loss. The world would move on if she drew her last breath in the line of duty, and that knowledge had never made her once fear walking into danger. In fact, it usually gave her the drive to push forward, first in line if she could help it. But somehow, knowing that this man was concerned for her—although she wasn't quite sure why yet—made her fear what she would find on the other side of those walls.

"I'll be fine, Kenneth," was all she could find to say. She took one last look at him

and turned with Bryan toward the apartment complex.

"Let's do this, Smyth."

～

*H*er team, and the weapons and tactical team had already been briefed. They each knew what their roles were going into this little apartment. The tactical team would be the muscle. They would take a battering ram to the door, and rush in and secure the place. Her team was there for extraction. They were there to get the girl, get her mother, and get the hell out of there. Preferably with everybody alive, if not, the bad guys dead, the good guys and victim alive.

She stood against the wall, her gun secured with both hands, pulled back at the ready, waiting for the moment it might be needed. She took a deep breath, and then gave a slow nod for her people to move into action. Before she could bring her head back to center position, the tactical team swung the big key back and let it come crashing down against the metal door. There was silence followed by a loud thud. The organized chaos ensued. Just as planned, her guys took down the room, unfortunately, two unaccounted for guards by the door gave Selwyn and his men just enough time to grab their weapons and hold their positions before the police could advance.

Heart moved to the front of the line, her weapon drawn, her eyes quickly scanning the scene, processing the information before her. She saw a half dressed Karolyn at the foot of Selwyn. He stood no more than five-seven, or five-eight. His ebony skin marred by the jagged ink of prison tattoos. His low-cut hair was covered by a black du-rag and in

Heart's estimation, his close-set, small, black eyes coupled with his long protruding nose made him look more like some type of rodent than a man.

Heart held her place at the front of the line and locked eyes with the ferret-man standing in front of her.

"Selwyn, I'm Lieutenant MacKenzie of the NYPD. I'm here to take Ms. Searlington and her daughter home. If you want things to transition smoothly, I would suggest you and your men put your weapons down and let us through."

RaQuan Selwyn looked down at a weeping Karolyn, sitting at his feet like a dog come to heel. He passed a rough hand through her tousled hair and smiled as she sat there almost completely unresponsive. The only thing that told Heart she was alive was the unbalanced nod she would wake herself up from when her body felt itself falling too far to one side, instinctively pulling her back to center, or as close to it as possible.

Damn, this beautiful, rich-as-hell woman is sitting here doing the damn junkie nod.

Heart could feel the disgust crawling up her skin. If her training didn't have her arms locked in position to fire her weapon at the ready, she would have dragged her nails up and down her arms to get rid of the itchy sensation this image was creating.

Heart and Selwyn locked eyes again, his thick, wide mouth curved into a sinister smile. He licked them, as if this standoff at gunpoint had become some sort of perverse sexual enticement for him.

"Damn, Ma," he said to Heart, his ridiculously large tongue lapping at the bottom of his lip as if he were some type of dog. "You 'da head bitch in charge? You got all these ma-fuckas round here sniffing behind you like '*dat*."

"All you need to know, Selwyn, is that I *am* in charge, and I'm telling you the only way for you to make it out of here alive is to put down your weapons, and let the

Searlingtons go."

He laughed at Heart. A hearty chuckle that seemed to almost bring tears to his eyes.

"Ma, 'dat right there ain't 'bout to happen," he laughed. "'Dis bitch right here is the best cocksucker I have ever had. I mean, I ain't ever had a bitch suck my dick the way this bitch does. I mean she get my shit all nice and wet, you cain't ask a brother to pass up on that shit. And the kid, well, I ain't really much for kids, but the truth is, she won't stay unless I keep the kid, so, I think I will just keep both of them."

He tightened his grip on the semi-automatic handgun currently holding it to the side, gangsta style. *When will these fucking idiots learn how to hold a fucking gun properly?* She watched him, the smile in his eye was one of sincere pleasure. This son-of-a-bitch was enjoying this. And she was beginning to suspect Karolyn wasn't necessarily here because she wanted to be. *Time to stop playing games with this asswipe.*

She was about to signal her sniper to take Selwyn out when she heard the man yell out, "A-yo Carlos, bring that little bitch out here."

Heart could hear the creek of the wooden door opening in the back of the apartment.

Some of her officers took aim, anticipating any assault that could come from that direction. What they found was the man known to Selwyn as his second in command, Carlos Del Torro, walking slowly with his gun arm aimed, extended, ready to shoot, and his other hand holding the shoulder of a very tiny little girl who had the same crystal blue eyes that her mother and uncle both possessed.

"Merri, I'm Mac, your uncle Kenneth sent me for you. Just do what I say and everything is going to be just fine. You understand?"

The little girl's eyes, way too large for that small delicate face quickly looked up to Mac and nodded in acquiescence. Mac only saw a slight moment of hesitation, but the mention of Kenneth's name seemed to quiet any doubts the little girl had stirring inside of her.

Heart looked up and met the eyes of the man that had sat in her cell a few short days ago. He was an arrogant asshole, but he definitely knew what he was doing. Selwyn was a flashy wannabe, Del Torro, if he really were in charge of this operation, he would be someone to fear.

"Si no es el pequeño perritta," he said in a warm voice that seemed to wrap around her when he spoke.

"Te lo dije la última vez que nos vimos, Del Torro, que el único perro que sabía era la puta que te parió," she responded, with no smile.

Del Torro tightened his grip on the girl's shoulder and said, "Veo que viniste a jugar duro esta noche."

Heart nodded, watching the man, and his gun carefully. "Yo lo hice. ¿Crees que puedo ganar?"

"Yo de verdad," he nodded again as he spoke, "pero creo que hay que tener cuidado de ella, algo no está bien con ella."

Heart's brows drew together in question as she asked, "¿La madre? Sí, puedo ver que ella es alta su culo."

Del Torro kept his body very still, to everyone else around them it seemed he was just having a fun time playing with the female cop, but to anyone in the room who spoke proper Spanish, they might have glimpsed that there was something else going on when he said, "No, no la madre, la abuela."

"¿Abuela?" Heart asked, her eyes scanning the tiny apartment for the missing person in question.

"A-yo, Del Torro," Selwyn interrupted. "Cut out all that—¿qué tú quieres—bullshit you over there talkin'. Stop runnin' your gipper and bring the little bitch to me."

As Merridith seemed to instinctively turn toward Selwyn, Heart stepped in front of her, acting as a barrier between the child and the hoodlum.

"Selwyn, if that child steps one foot in your direction I promise you won't make it out of here alive."

Heart heard the momentary crackle of the communication link inside of her ear canal. Technology was so wonderful, she hardly even felt the thing inside of the small crevice of her ear, so small, it could barely be detected by even her.

"Lieutenant MacKenzie, this is Sergeant Greggs of the sniper team. We are in position and we have all three gunman in our sights. I can't get a clear shot of the guy in the middle. If I hit him, the bullet could pass through him and into you. Move thirty degrees to your right and I can take him."

Heart glanced around, they were in a tight space, too many bodies, too many guns, there was no place for her to move.

"Go to work," she said with a smile on her face. Selwyn, looked at her strangely.

"But Mac," Greggs said.

"Go to work," she repeated through clenched teeth. She watched as Selwyn became edgier. He was gripping his handgun harder, and raising it higher in front of her.

"MacKen..."

"Goddammit, I said go to work!" she yelled. It was the only way she could get this kid out of here safely. If they started firing weapons in such a small space, the casualties could be immense.

"Copy that, L.T., on my one. And three..."

She signaled the room full of officers to move back and away from the windows.

This just left her and detective Arroyo in the small living room with three gunmen.

"...two..."

Before she heard the one she lunged for the floor taking the child with her, covering

her little body. She hoped to god Detective Arroyo was wearing his earpiece. The rest of the team was connected, they all could hear the same conversation she heard while communicating with the sniper team. It was why none of them had fired, why they had all moved out of firing range. They all knew what she had planned to do, but Arroyo, she wasn't sure of.

She turned her head to see Selwyn and his three men lying lifeless on the floor. She would have to clear the room to make sure they were no longer a threat. She began to uncoil herself from the child's body. She ran her hands quickly over her limbs, making certain the tiny body hadn't been injured in all of the commotion. No noticeable injuries present, she picked up her gun, checked the bodies, one by one, kicking their weapons to a safe distance. Before she could get to the last man's body, she heard a crash and a thump.

Arroyo, she thought. She scanned the room, finding him lying on the floor, blood gushing from a cut in his head leaking crimson liquid. *Oh God no.* Her eyes moved from floor to ceiling only to see another gunman, or in this case, a gunwoman, standing over her officer.

Heart drew her weapon, and stared the individual down. She'd known something was off, but she didn't think this was it. The woman waved her hand in a beckoning motion. Before Heart could speak, she saw Merridith walk over to the woman. The woman positioned the girl in front of her and placed the heavy metal of the gun barrel to the little girl's head.

"Let her go, and we can talk about you getting out of here safely," Heart said in a calm voice.

"My dear, your 'take charge' voice doesn't work on me. I've known since I first met you that you couldn't beat me, and I'm even more certain of it now. You have an obvious flaw, Lieutenant."

The woman gave a slow crooked smile at Heart, making her skin crawl. Selwyn was a delusional greedy bastard, but this crazy bitch standing with a gun to a small child's head was one thing—evil.

"Oh yeah, since you know so much about me, why don't you tell me what's my flaw." Heart took a small step closer.

"You're just too easy," the woman said. "Just like it was too easy for me to figure out that Del Torro wasn't really working for Selwyn, he was actually working under cover for you."

Heart said nothing, admitted nothing.

"You don't have to agree, I know the truth. I discreetly acquired one of Detective Arroyo's fingerprints and had a friend of mine find out who the man really was that they belonged to. Turns out, this hooligan-like thug was actually a highly decorated officer. And like you he shares the same single flaw that will always ensure that you lose against people like me, he cared. You care, Lieutenant, and that little fact is going to cost you your life at the end of this. Now, please get my son up here so that I can finish what I started. This is after all a family affair, and Kenneth is most certainly a Searlington."

Heart took a deep breath, trying to assess what actions she could take. The gun against that little girl's temple forced her hand, at the moment she had to give in, do what this woman wanted.

"This is Lieutenant MacKenzie, does anyone copy?"

Bryan Smyth answered. "Copy, Mac, this is Smyth."

"Smyth, I've got a bit of a situation here. Apparently Mrs. Jaqueline Searlington is here. She has a gun, and it's currently resting against Merri's Temple. Arroyo is injured. She made him and took him out. I'm armed, but I can't take the risk of firing right now.

She's demanding to see Kenneth, now."

"Mac, just stall for a few minutes, we'll get the sniper team in place, take her out like

Selwyn."

"That's a negative. I'm standing directly in front of the window. They won't take a shot that would hit me directly. With a through-and-through that might have hit me when they took out Selwyn, I would have been grazed or mildly injured. They won't take the shot directly through me, doesn't matter what my rank is. They won't kill one of their own just to get her."

The smile that crept on the woman's face made Heart's blood bubble to a raging boil.

"Smyth, do as Jaqueline Searlington says, bring her son up here. Get me Kenneth Searlington."

~

*E*very muscle in his body locked as he watched the scene unfold on the monitor before him. Kenneth wished the events that were passing in front of his eyes were nothing more than a poorly made cop-flick with the cheesy dialogue to boot. Unfortunately, this wasn't a TV show, and the characters involved were very real. His mother was holding a gun to his niece's head, his sister seemed damned near catatonic, sitting on the floor half-naked and cross-legged.

How had this happened? How had the people in his family completely lost sense of reality? How had his family members become involved with a known criminal? Why was his mother holding a gun on his niece? With each question his heart rate inched up just a little higher. More than anything, he wanted Merridith to be safe, away from the two women who had placed her in such terrible danger, but just as equally, he was mad as all hell, and ready the strip both his mother and his sister's skin for daring to cross this line.

This could only be about one thing and one thing only. The money. Somehow, those two conniving witches had cooked up this scheme to get their hands on his father's money, now his money. And they'd hurt his niece to get it. *Unh-unh, no way, not going to happen.* No one fucked with what was his and got away with it. If his mother wanted him, she'd have him, and he was going to end her for her troubles to boot.

His hand had just touched the handle of the back doors of the van when they opened on their own. On the other side he saw Bryan

Smyth. Usually an easygoing man with a smile on his face, now, there was no smile. His face was a canvas of hard lines cutting into the hard marks of his muscles. This was cop Bryan, this was focused Bryan, this was a warrior preparing for battle.

Bryan reached inside of the door of the van and pulled a black piece of material from a concealed compartment. Bryan shoved it into Kenneth's hand.

"Put this on."

Kenneth looked down at the tough material and realized what he was holding, a vest, a bulletproof vest. He looked up at Bryan.

"Do you think it will come to this, will I need it?"

Bryan looked away for a moment, took a breath, and then focused on Kenneth.

"I don't know the details of what's going on in there, but your mother somehow managed to take out one of my brothers. That man is skilled, so if she got him, then she intended to do so. Right now Mackenzie is the only thing standing between your niece and a loaded weapon. Your sister is there, but apparently incapacitated. I don't know what her role in all of this was, so there's no way to tell if she's there to help your mother, or if she's simply a liability to MacKenzie.

"The cards are really stacked against MacKenzie tonight. If she were any other cop I'd say there was a real possibility that everyone in that room was going to die. But it's not any other cop, it's Mac, and she's damn good at what she does. She makes shit happen, Kenneth. Shit that none of the rest of us can figure out. She earned her command, her stripes were won through hard work, sheer will, and a cunning mind. Did you know that they tried to give her the L.T. position like three years earlier because she ticked off all their special little boxes like diversity because she was young, black, and female?" Kenneth shook his head.

"She turned them down, she was ready. Hell, from day one in the academy I knew that girl was heading for a captain's chair, but she wouldn't take it simply because she felt she hadn't earned it. The only reason she took it the last time was because Porter had to practically threaten to keep her on permanent desk duty if she refused to move up in the ranks."

Kenneth laughed. He could so see his godfather throwing his weight and title around to get his way. He'd threatened Kenneth with lock up every time Kenneth came close to one of those imaginary lines his father or his godfather had drawn in the sand. When you're a smart-mouthed sixteen-year-old with a cop for a godfather, you learn quickly to keep your shit in check, or he will check it for you. It didn't surprise him one bit that Porter had shown MacKenzie the same tough love to keep her career on track.

"The point of this story is, that woman up there is the best. She will give everything to bring your niece home safely; she's the one you want in there with all of that crazy."

Kenneth nodded and glanced back into the van for a brief second. His eyes caught the broken sight of his former brother-in-law. He was so focused on the monitor, watching his child's life hang in the balance; he hadn't even realized that Kenneth was no longer next to him. William seemed to be savoring every line of that little girl's face. God he hoped that William had the chance to see his precious little girl again, that this wasn't the last memory to be impressed on his mind for the rest of his life.

He turned back to Bryan. "That little girl is something special, Bryan. We have to get her back."

Bryan rested a strong hand on Kenneth. "And so is Mac. That woman is a miracle maker. She will come through. Now you're going to go up there, and you are going to do whatever MacKenzie tells you. You got me?" Kenneth nodded.

"No Kenneth, I need you to really understand what I'm saying here. The slightest wrong move could tip this powder keg over into a direction that neither of us wants to see it go. You do exactly as she says. You don't improvise, you don't guess, you don't go off script. Whatever she says, you do. It doesn't matter how stupid it seems, no matter how counterintuitive it feels, if she tells you to do it, you do it, end of story."

Kenneth understood completely. "Whatever it takes to bring

Merridith home safely."

Bryan nodded, giving Kenneth a worried smile. "Then let's take you to see your mommy."

Bryan led Kenneth through the throngs of officers that lined the halls of the apartment complex from the entrance all the way to the apartment door. Before he walked in, Bryan withdrew his weapon from his shoulder holster and positioned himself in front of Kenneth. He yelled through the open door.

"Mac, I've got Searlington, I'm bringing him in."

"Copy that, Smyth," Kenneth heard in response. Her voice was calm, so unlike the panic he thought should be filling her. When he finally laid eyes on MacKenzie, she was standing with her weapon drawn, arms locked in place, ready to fire if she had to.

He realized now that the day they'd met, the day she'd placed her gun on her desk and threatened him without really threatening him, she'd just been toying with him. The fixed determination that painted her face hadn't been there that day. Even that crazy night where she'd pulled her weapon on him when he'd surprised her from her sleep. He realized now that there was a hint of fear there, but no intent to hurt. Now, now he saw it. That focused, all her senses assessing the scene around her, her instinct, looking for the right time to turn the tables in this situation.

"Tell your lackey to drop his weapon, MacKenzie," his mother said. Her voice pulled his eyes from MacKenzie. His stomach felt like it was rising too fast, that sick uneasy feeling you get when an elevator drops too quickly, or you take that unexpected dip on a roller-coaster. His sweet precious niece was standing there with that unsightly piece of metal pressed angrily against her head. There was confusion in her quickly moving eyes, tears falling; fear taking over, even though she couldn't possibly understand what was going on around her. He couldn't even process it. How the hell was this baby supposed to?

"Not on your life, Jacqueline. You're lucky I don't take you out right now." His mother laughed.

"You wouldn't dare take a shot with me holding Merridith. You wouldn't risk her life like that."

Heart gave a chuckle before she said, "You really believe that? Let me tell you something. If I wanted to take you out, I could do it without much effort; I'm just that skilled. The only reason I haven't, is because I don't want to traumatize your granddaughter by watching her grandmother lose her life. But if you press me, I won't hesitate to end you, old lady. Try me if you will."

Kenneth watched the muscles of her throat tighten then loosen as she swallowed.

MacKenzie had hit a nerve. His mother's focus fell on him, a chill poured down his spine. He'd always known his mother was selfish and superficial. He'd never thought she was evil though. It just goes to show you how well you really know people.

"Kenneth, this is all your fault. If you would have just given me what was rightfully mine, I would never have been forced to take such unseemly measures."

Kenneth was tempted to roll his eyes. His mother was standing there with a gun pointed at his niece's head and yet her upper class breeding led her to classify her actions as *unseemly. God her pretentiousness knows no bounds.*

"I presume you're talking about Dad's will? It's been six years since the man died, you'd think you'd be over this by now. He never wanted you to have control of his business or his money. It's obvious he knew what you were capable of."

"I stayed married to that slum-dragging father of yours for all those years. Even though he'd rebuilt his family's wealth by the time we'd met, he was determined to keep this ungodly attachment to the ghetto that his family was forced to live in when they lost everything. I mean it's one thing to donate to places like that, but to actually visit there, and keep contact with those people. He demanded that Porter and that vile woman, Pamela that he's married to be your godparents. Your christening should have been a society event; I couldn't even invite the right people to something like that with those two and their mangy brats there. I endured the embarrassment of your father's sick fascination with everything and everyone that was poor. I deserve to enjoy the rest of my life the way

I should have always been living it all along."

He watched her anger fill every crevice, line, and space of her face. This was a deepabiding grievance that his mother had been harboring long before he and Karolyn's birth more than three decades ago.

"You're going to sign that money over to me now. You're going to use that handy little smartphone you're always playing with, and you're going to transfer every cent of my money into an offshore account."

Kenneth went to take a step forward and felt the press of Bryan's hand in front of him stopping him from going any further.

"Will that bring this ridiculousness to an end? If I give you the money, will you let Merridith go? Will you disappear and never bother us again?"

"Kenneth, we do not negotiate with people like your mother," MacKenzie said. "If you give her what she wants, there's no reason for her to honor anything she's saying. She could still end up hurting the girl. Let me handle this."

"MacKenzie..." a low moaning sound interrupted Kenneth.

Before any of them could turn around to recognize what it was, Merridith screamed,

"Mommy," and broke free of her grandmother's grasp, darting for her mother on the floor behind MacKenzie.

He watched his mother raise her gun at Merridith's retreating back. His heart raced, pounding out a raging drumbeat of fear. He opened his mouth to say...something— exactly what his brain hadn't determined yet. He heard a distinctive clicking sound that pulled his attention toward MacKenzie.

"Put down the damn gun, Jacqueline, or I will drop you where you stand," he heard MacKenzie say. Her voice calm, her hands steady, her aim and gaze focused on his mother.

"Bryan, get the girl out of here now," MacKenzie commanded. Bryan swooped down, pulled Merridith away from his sister and ran out of the room with her flailing limbs tightly secured in his arms.

His mother swung her gun in the direction of Bryan and Merridith and he heard a loud explosion fill the room. He ducked, instinctively covering his head and face with his arms. When silence followed the loud clatter he slowly peeled his arms away from his face to see both his mother and MacKenzie still standing with their guns pointed at one another.

"You missed," his mother said.

"Did I?" MacKenzie followed.

His mother started blinking quickly, as if she was processing something she didn't understand. He looked, and saw a thin line of muddy red liquid crawling down her ear, onto her neck. She must have felt the wet drop traveling down her skin, because she took her fingers and touched them against the wetness. She looked at them almost unbelievingly. MacKenzie had shot her, or in the very least nicked her. From this distance he couldn't really tell how severe or superficial the wound was. But on this was certain, Mackenzie had hit her mark.

"I don't miss, Jaqueline. That was a warning shot. You put down your weapon now, or the next one goes between your eyes. That's the last warning you're going to get."

Again, MacKenzie's voice was calm, unhurried. If you couldn't see the situation unfolding, you would think she was having an everyday casual conversation with a random person. Nothing about her mirrored the intensity of the situation at hand.

"She made me do this."

It was a ragged whispered sound. Small, unassuming, but in the heavy silence of the room, it filled the air like a crashing wave. MacKenzie's gaze never left his mother, his eyes left the two armed women to find his sister sitting on the floor behind MacKenzie, looking as if she had just awoken from a deep sleep.

"Karolyn?" he managed to say. His sister almost unrecognizable to him. Her beautiful alabaster skin seemed dull, tinted with a mossy green hue. Her glorious ebony mane, usually shiny, healthy, lay matted to one side of her head. She sat crossed-legged on the floor in nothing but a bra. He felt the jagged crack stagger right down the middle of his heart. Looking at her in such a pitiful condition, he swore he could hear the moment his heart started ripping in two.

"I was clean," she said. "For over a year, I had managed to stay clean. She's kept me high since I was thirteen years old. She made me take her sleeping pills when I was a kid, then she started making me pop her oxy. By the time we were nineteen, I was hooked on heroin."

"How did I not know this Karolyn?" he questioned.

"You were away at school, it was easy to hide on the few times you made it home," Karolyn muttered.

"But why didn't you call me? I would have come for you, I would have made Dad help you."

"I didn't want you to know because I didn't want her to ruin you like she was ruining me. Dad found out, he sent me to rehab as soon as he did. But when I got out, she had a stash waiting for me, and I fell right back in."

Karolyn seemed to take in a long pained breath. She was holding her side, sitting very still, as if it were too painful to move.

"Ever since Dad died and he left everything to you, all she's talked about is getting that money back. She somehow found out that you were leaving everything to Merridith in your will, she also knew that William was named as your co-executor with your lawyer. She knew you had made it so she could never touch it, not even if she somehow gained custody of Merridith. I knew then that my daughter was in danger, and that I had to get myself together so I could protect her. I was going to take her to William, but before I could contact him, she'd taken Merri."

Karolyn stopped talking again. Taking another set of seemingly painful breaths before she continued.

"I didn't know in the beginning where she'd taken her. Then one day when I left the house, this man walked up to me and told me if I wanted to see my daughter alive, I would come with him.

"I did as he said, and he brought me here. When I walked inside, Mother was sitting on the couch stroking Merridith's hair. She said she had figured out a way to get her money back from you. She said RaQuan promised to hold Merri for safekeeping if I would provide certain services when and wherever he requested."

She closed her eyes tightly, trying to shield herself from whatever she was seeing through her mind's eye.

"I couldn't do it at first, he made me shoot up, then I didn't care. He made me do things…"

That was it, the final tear in his heart. He crawled over to his sister, pulled her into his arms, covering her with his body, protecting her from further exposure to their mother's evil.

"For the love of God will you please shut up," his mother's words dripped with disdain. "You were always such a sniveling, whiney little brat. I came up with a brilliant plan to get that money back and all you had to do was spread your legs a few times. It wasn't like you'd never done it before."

Kenneth felt his sister's body quiver in his arms. His need to protect her caused his muscles to tighten around her.

"Don't listen to her; this is not your fault. You have nothing to be ashamed of; you have nothing to fear. You protected your daughter the only way you knew how. That's all that matters Karolyn, nothing else, not one single detail of how you did it is as important as that," Kenneth said to his sister.

"God I'm so sick of the two of you," Jacqueline said. There was something dark about the sound of his mother's voice that made Kenneth turn toward her. He could see the minute lift of the weapon his mother was holding.

"Jacqueline, this is your last warning," MacKenzie said. "Put the gun down on the floor, kick it over to me, and put your hands in the air. If you don't, I am going to shoot."

Don't do this, Mother. His heart screamed, even though he couldn't bring the words to cross his lips. There was a look of misguided arrogance in his mother's eyes. If he saw it, he knew MacKenzie saw it too.

His mother made a quick snapping motion to aim at MacKenzie. By the time Jacqueline had squeezed her trigger once, MacKenzie had already fired two times. He saw MacKenzie's bullets make impact, causing his mother's body to jerk violently then fall.

MacKenzie kept her gun trained on his mother. She stepped carefully to where Jacqueline lay on the floor and kicked the discarded gun out of her reach. MacKenzie secured her own gun in her holster, and then leaned down to place two searching fingers at the base of his mother's neck.

"She's alive," she said on breath filled with relief. "This is MacKenzie, shooter is down; I need three buses quick. Shooter took two to the chest area, pulse strong, but irregular." She quickly stepped over to where Karolyn and Kenneth sat. He relaxed his arms and looked down at his sister. Her head fell back, her shoulders slack.

"Karolyn?" he called. He shook her, but she didn't respond.

MacKenzie pulled her from his arms and laid Karolyn on the floor. When Kenneth went to help he felt a wet and sticky substance on his fingers. He and MacKenzie looked down at his hand and each saw the same thing. He looked as if he was wearing a glove made completely of blood.

MacKenzie moved her hands quickly all over Karolyn's frail body looking for the source of the bleeding.

"Shit," he heard the clipped expletive pass her lips and rested his eyes on

MacKenzie's cause for alarm. There, embedded in his sister's side was a large thick piece of glass. It looked very much like the thick shards from the shattered window that were strewn haphazardly across the floor.

"My God," he said.

"I think she must have fallen over onto a piece of glass when the snipers' bullets penetrated the window," MacKenzie said. "Kenneth, I think she's punctured something, she's bleeding pretty badly."

He had watched MacKenzie's calm withstand all of the intense, crazy moments of the night. But right now, her voice was trembling, her hands shaking just as badly, and her eyes filled with fear.

"This is MacKenzie," she yelled. "Get those buses here ASAP! I have a victim down with a puncture wound that's bleeding a lot!" She looked around the bodies on the floor, found a discarded piece of clothing, and reached for it. She balled it up and pressed it to Karolyn's side. She grabbed Kenneth's hand, and used it to replace her own over the wound. She leaned down closer to Karolyn, feeling for a pulse, and listening for a breath.

He had taken several CPR classes over the years, he knew the steps of emergency resuscitation.

"She's not breathing, and I can't find a pulse, Kenneth." She quickly tilted Karolyn's head back into the sniffing position and began CPR. "Get those paramedics here now," MacKenzie said to whomever was on the other end of her earpiece. "I'm starting CPR."

Everything seemed to happen in a series of individual slides. MacKenzie was pumping on his sister's still body, and breathing into her slacked-jawed mouth. It seemed like she was pumping forever. Then there was a flash and the room seemed to be filled with all sorts of uniformed people. Cops, paramedics, the room was busy, filled with noise, and people were crowding around Detective Arroyo his mother and sister.

In a rush the injured were cleared out of the room, including the undercover officer that his mother had assaulted earlier. After having the paramedics look over him, and having the police question him, he just wanted to be free of this entire scene. He looked around and caught a quick glimpse of MacKenzie leaving the apartment.

He followed quickly behind her once the officer taking his statement allowed him to take his leave. He reached the elevator just in time to jump inside before the metal door slammed shut. When he stepped inside, MacKenzie's head snapped up and her eyes met his.

"Kenneth," it was the only thing that crossed her lips. She looked at him, then went slack against his body. When he looked down, her shirt sleeve was damp. He put her on the floor of the elevator and ran his hand up her arm. There, at the top of her shoulder was a hole and blood was seeping through it. His mind instantly clicked back to the moment MacKenzie shot his mother. His mother did discharge her weapon, he'd only assumed the shot had missed its mark because MacKenzie never wavered, she never slowed down during the entire aftermath. MacKenzie's hands were covered in blood, but he'd assumed it was Karolyn's not her own.

"Fuck, she's been shot."

The door opened. He yelled out to whoever could hear, "Help, MacKenzie's been shot!"

CHAPTER 8

*J*ustice Amare sat in the familiar lumpy couch of the hotel room. When your job caused you to travel ninety percent of the year, you had an intimate understanding of how hotel furniture was made for sight and not use.

The cell phone resting on the couch lit up demanding attention. Justice looked at the familiar name on the screen and rushed to pick it up. Answering the call without thought,

"Bryan?" rushed across suddenly dry lips.

"Jussy, is that you?" his familiar baritone filled that empty space that had been vacant for so long inside of Justice's soul.

"Jussy, I mean...Justice," he stammered. "I'm sorry, I know I don't have any right to call you that anymore."

Justice thought of that special name only Bryan had used. It brought back memories of happier times. Times that were filled with love, devotion...passion.

"Bryan," Justice said. "It hasn't been that long since you've called me that. I don't have a problem with you using it now, I never did. What's going on? You sound a bit off."

There was a brief silence before Bryan spoke again. "Jussy, I don't know how else to tell you this, so I'm just going to come out and say it. MacKenzie has been shot."

Justice sat straight up, placing both feet flat on the floor. "Is she alive?"

"Yes, a case went to shit real fast in the projects tonight. Mac took down the perp, but not before she licked one off. Caught Mac in the arm, but she's lost a lot of blood.

The bus just took her out of here now."

"Does my grandmother know yet?"

"Porter just left to tell her and bring her to the hospital." "Which hospital?" Justice asked.

"County. Are you in town, Jussy? Can you come by? I'm really worried about your cousin."

Justice could hear the worry pouring off Bryan; it was almost palpable. Justice knew Bryan wanted a shoulder at this moment. He might have called Justice because Justice was Heart's blood, but he'd also called Justice because there was no one else that could understand how much his partner meant to him other than someone who loved her equally. *Dammit to hell.*

Justice would give anything to be there for Bryan, for Heart, but work…yeah work. Work always kept Justice separated from family and friends, and usually at the worst time. Work was the reason that Bryan had left Justice a year ago, the reason Bryan had finally had enough of being in love with a ghost.

"Bryan, I'm in D.C. with my pops on business. I will call my sister. True is in

Brooklyn right now. As soon as I tell Pops what's going on, I will be on my way."

Justice heard an audible release coming through the phone. Bryan hadn't believed Justice would come. Damn that stung, but Justice had to admit, it was warranted. Past disappointments far outweighed the times Justice had managed to be there for Bryan. That was not going to happen this time, not if Justice could help it.

"Keep your cell with you, Bryan. My sister will contact you for more info. I'll send a text once I hit the road."

"Thanks, Jussy, I really…"

"Bryan, you don't have to thank me, I should be there for you and Heart, I should have always been there."

Justice ended the call and hit the speed dial button for True.

"True, get over to County Hospital now, Heart has been shot in the line of duty. Porter's on his way to pick up Big Mama, I'm gonna tell Pops what's going on, and we'll be on the first thing moving to New York."

The only thing Justice heard on the other line were two words, "Copy that," and the line clicked dead.

$\approx$

Kenneth sat in the hard plastic chair. His back ached from the hours it had been forced to endure the special kind of torture the chair was delivering. He stood and walked around the small room to give his tired muscles and ligaments a break. The nurse had come in several times to ask him if he wanted to go downstairs to the cafeteria to get something to eat, but his answer was always the same, "I'm not leaving until she wakes up."

MacKenzie had been out of surgery for nearly two hours now. She remained in the same still position she had been in when they'd wheeled her into the room, and transferred her to hospital bed she now lay in. At least she had color to her now.

He shook his head and laughed, that sounded almost comical since MacKenzie was a black woman. Standing in that elevator had been no laughing matter though. When she'd collapsed; her sweet coffee complexion had morphed into this unhealthy greyish-blue pallor that marked the slow ebbing of her life.

According to her doctor, the injury in and of itself hadn't been life-threatening— thank God his mother was a crap shot—but the fact that MacKenzie had lost so much blood between the time that she was shot, performing CPR on Karolyn, and staying to give her statement, when her adrenaline levels dropped, her body crashed.

He'd never been so grateful in all his life when the surgeon said everything was going to be fine. He expected her recovery to run smoothly. Now he sat next to the sleeping doll-like figure lying in the bed, waiting for her to open her eyes, curse him out, and show him that she was really all right.

He heard the whining creak of the door, and looked up to find an elderly woman slowly pushing through the entrance. She was slight in build with deep silver strands pulled tightly in a large bun at the nape of her neck.

He stood up, a habit his father had drilled into him anytime a woman entered the room.

"I'm Ida-Mae Amare," the mature woman said with a warm smile curling her lips.

"Now, just who the hell are you and why are you in my grand-daughter's hospital room?" He froze, a soft smile slowly inched up one side of his mouth.

"Ma'am, I'm Kenneth, I'm a..." he tried to quickly think of a word that would describe what he was to her. An acquaintance, a former suspect in a kidnapping? No, none of those seemed quite right so he went with, "...friend, I'm a friend of

MacKenzie's."

He watched her lift a single grey-haired brow and instantly he felt a familiar chill pour down his spine one vertebra at a time. It was the same look that MacKenzie had given him the day he'd entered her office using more bravado than she cared for. Kenneth had seen it a moment shy of her pulling her gun from her holster and placing it on the desk in front of him. But here before him, this little old lady stood, and somehow, without the gun—at least he hoped without the gun, the large handbag hanging at her elbow was big enough to hide a body inside of it, no telling if there was an arsenal in there or not— she seemed more deadly than her armed granddaughter did.

"Young man," she said as she placed a honeyed-brown hand aged by time on her hip.

"I don't know who the hell you think you're foolin', but it certainly ain't me. Now, I'm gonna ask you one mo' 'gen," she paused just long enough to put her remaining hand on her other hip, "who the hell are you, and why are you in my grandbaby, Heart's hospital room?"

"Big Mama, I thought I asked you to wait until I'd spoken to the doctor before you came in here messing with..."

Kenneth's eyes fastened on the door as his ears perked up at the sound of the recognizable voice.

"Kenneth?" the voice questioned.

He blinked, bringing the face in to focus, it had been nearly six years since he'd seen her last. She hadn't changed much. Her hair was still pulled back in a ponytail, her body still fit and athletic, her gaze still deadly and foreboding.

"True, what are you doing here?"

"True, you know this here fella?" MacKenzie's grandmother brought him from his not so distant past. A time when the sight of True would have instantly meant another more endearing face was close behind. He looked just behind True to see if that welcoming smile that he once knew so well would be following her, but she closed the door behind her, effectively stopping his heart's journey down memory lane.

"Yes, Big Mama. Kenneth's an old...acquaintance. He used to be really good friends with my friend, Faith."

The older woman nodded her head, and trained her gaze back on to Kenneth.

"Well why you didn't say so, young man. I like that girl, Faith. My granddaughters

tend to get into stuff they ain't got no business gettin' into. I 'clare these girls is 'gon be the death of me."

Kenneth leaned his ear in, thinking he'd missed something.

"I'm sorry, did I mishear you? Did you say, Heart?" The elderly woman nodded.

"You heard right, that's her given name. Heart Diamond MacKenzie, my only daughter's baby."

There was a slight flash of sadness in her brown eyes, greyed-blue by time. He remembered then that his uncle David had mentioned that MacKenzie's mother had died when she was a child.

"What did the doctor say about your cousin, True?"

"He said the surgery went well, and that he anticipates Heart making a speedy recovery as long as she follows orders. He will have more information for us once she wakes up and he examines her."

MacKenzie's grandmother nodded.

"Well then, I'm gonna take a seat right here next to this little girl, and wait on her to open up her eyes."

～

$\mathcal{K}$ enneth sat in the semi dark hospital room, still waiting for MacKenzie…the name had always seemed wrong to him, it never fit. Heart, it was what her grandmother had referred to her as, and it seemed more appropriate. This woman was definitely all heart.

She had so much courage, and she didn't blink at putting herself in harm's way to save others. That took heart, more heart than anyone he knew.

The soft light over her bed gave her skin a serene glow. She still slept the sleep of the battle-weary, not moving once since returning from surgery. True had finally convinced their grandmother it was pointless staying at the hospital when Heart still slept. The two women had left him alone with her in the quiet hospital room sitting in the same spot, planted next to her bed, waiting for her to open those chocolate eyes.

She looked so still and unreal lying there. His hand lifted of its own accord, needing

to touch her to make certain she was in fact real. He slowly moved his hand until it was just above her flesh. He fought with the knowledge that she didn't like to be touched. He still didn't understand why, but he knew deep down that he was so wrong for thinking of violating the barriers she had hammered in place, but he couldn't stop himself.

His hand gently rested atop her smaller hand. It was cool to his touch, unlike the fiery burn he had experienced the few times he's had the opportunity to briefly feel her skin on his own. He let his thumb draw slow circles across the back of her hand, hoping that the simple touch would warm her.

"You will never understand how grateful I am for what you did tonight," he said quietly, the rhythm of his voice matching the slow tempo of his circular touch on her hand. "My mother was going to kill us all in a dingy apartment room. I saw it...there in the distance of her eyes; she was going to kill both her children and her only grandchild.

The only thing that stopped her, the only thing that shielded us from her, was you."

He touched her again, needed the simple connection to her, needed feel her life force for a little longer. "You nearly died because you left your own injuries unattended to try to save my sister," a slow breath left him, unable to speak or even think of his sister's name at that moment. No, this moment was for no one else, no other, just her, just Heart.

He felt a soft touch against his shoulder. He didn't have to look up to know who it was.

"Kenneth, please don't, she doesn't like to be..." True's voice traveled off.

"Please, True, I know. I just need a little bit longer," he said.

"Kenneth..."

"She saved my life tonight, she saved my family tonight. I just need to make sure she's still here, that she's safe, that she makes it through this."

True moved from behind him and sat in the chair on the other side of the hospital bed.

"Is that what prompted you to tell the medical staff that you were her husband?"

Kenneth's eyes didn't moved from where his and Heart's hands were joined. He simply nodded his head in answer.

"It was the only way they would let me ride in the ambulance. She'd collapsed in my arms after the entire ordeal was over. I thought I'd lost her."

True was silent for a minute, he knew from his past dealings with her that she usually sat quietly while she observed her surroundings and the people in it. He still didn't look up from his hold on Heart, he just couldn't pull his eyes away from her right now.

"Kenneth, Porter filled me in on the details of what happened tonight. You have been through a tremendous ordeal. You should probably leave and go talk to someone about this. You shouldn't be here fixated on my cousin. It's not healthy for either of you."

"I can't walk away, True. I need to…"

"To what, Kenneth?" she asked softly. "I suppose you've spent enough time with my cousin to know that she will never let this go beyond being a case. Whatever it is you think is going on inside you, chalk it up to the intensity of the situation you've shared with her, and nothing more. Heart will never allow there to be what I suspect you think you want between the two of you. She won't let you, Kenneth."

That drew his eyes up, for the first time since she'd returned to the room, he glanced upon a face familiar from both his past, and almost reminiscent of his present. Now that he saw the two women in the same room, he could see the family likeness that passed between them. True was a shade lighter in complexion, her skin more golden-brown to Heart's sepia-colored hue. They shared the same nose, the same almond shaped eyes, the same kissable lips. Except on True, the package just looked pleasant and attractive. On Heart, those very same features called to something buried inside of him, made something swell inside of his soul that beckoned him to find and possess her.

"Why?" he asked True, not completely certain exactly what he was asking her. *Why is she like this? Why won't she let me get closer? Why is she afraid of me?*

"It's not for me to share. It's not my story to tell. If she ever wishes to disclose that to you, that's her decision to make."

"What if I refuse to give up?"

True took a deep breath. "Part of me hopes that you don't heed my warning. She's spent so many years locked inside herself that I wish someone could break through to her.

But the truth is, she'll never let you get close enough to touch her.

You'll only hurt her by trying to make her. Heart doesn't do force, she controls everything in her life, and if she hasn't calculated for you, then the simple fact is, you can't exist."

A small squeeze applied to his hand drew his attention from True and placed it on Heart. The eyes behind tightly closed lids began to move rapidly back and forth. Her lids loosened, then tightened, then loosened again, trying to pry themselves open. When she was finally able to pull them open, her lids fluttered quickly, seeming to blink away the fog that she'd been trapped behind since the surgery. Cracked lips peeled apart to reveal a rough, small sound.

"True?" the voice questioned.

"Yes, baby girl. It's me, I'm here, and you're all right." "Arm...hurts," she said barely above a whisper.

"I'm sure it does, that's what you get for allowing someone to shoot you," True said.

"Flesh wound, why's it hurt so bad? Why am I in the hospital?" Heart asked.

"The bullet entered just below the anterior shoulder and passed through the posterior. The problem is, it nicked your axillary artery on the way out. With all of the physical activity you were involved in, and with all of the adrenaline you had pumping through your system, you lost more blood than your body was willing to part with. If Kenneth hadn't been there to get you help so quickly, you might not have made it."

Heart smiled softly, her still-sleepy eyes turned to him, and widened ever so slightly.

"I can go if you want me to, Heart. I...I just wanted to make certain you were all right," he said quickly.

She looked at him with quiet contemplation, then she gave him a small smile that did strange things to his insides. Despite all that he'd been through tonight, that tiny smile made something warm and indescribable swell inside of him.

"True," she said in a quiet voice without taking her gaze away from Kenneth. "Could you leave Kenneth and me alone for a minute? I want to talk to him privately."

True said nothing, almost without perceivable sound or motion she was gone from the room, leaving the two of them to sit in the soft glow of their semi-dark surroundings.

She gave his hand, the same one that had been surrounding hers for so long now a gentle squeeze.

"Heart huh?" she chuckled slightly. "You spend a short amount of time in my grandmother's presence and instantly you're calling me Heart."

"How do you know your grandmother is the one who told me your first name?"

"Because True keeps secrets like it's her profession. Her lips are locked tighter than

Fort Knox. Porter and Smyth wouldn't dare reveal it on pain of death. That only leaves a feisty little old lady who refuses to address me by my surname. Up until this moment, I don't think I've heard anyone else call me that in years. I'm not really certain how I feel about that yet." The tired smile she wore slowly began to drop as she looked to him once again.

"Kenneth, I don't remember much after discharging my weapon. I remember everything clearly up until then. After that, I just see kind of fuzzy images. I think I remember starting CPR on your sister, but the truth, much of it seems like a dream."

He felt a small tremble pass from her hand to his. He swallowed, trying to push down the emotions that he knew these memories would bring.

"After you got the gun away from my mother..." "I shot her, is she okay?" Heart interrupted.

He nodded his answer. "The paramedics were able to stabilize her until the doctors could remove the bullets. She is at the hospital across the street. They would not allow the two of you to be brought to the same emergency room. She's recovering in their

I.C.U. under police guard."

Heart nodded, a small breath of what appeared to be relief seeping from her lips. His mother had terrorized them all, and yet Heart still seemed to find value in sparing her life.

"And Karolyn?" There was a lilt of hope in her voice as she spoke his sister's name. A name he had been trying hard not to think of in order to focus solely on Heart. The thought of that name, ripped the delicate bandage that was covering a gaping hole that he had yet begun to think about how to dress, let alone repair it. For the few hours that had passed since they entered the stark walls of this hospital he had pushed thoughts of his twin, and the connecting emotions down deep somewhere in the pit of his stomach. Everything had been focused on Heart.

His eyes began to burn with tears not yet shed. He could feel the heat of hurt climbing up his chest to his face, making his alabaster skin flushed with an almost fuchsia-pink shade.

"We discovered that my sister had been severely injured by a very thick and long shard of glass from the window. It was deeply embedded in her side, it punctured some of her internal organs including her lung and her liver."

"Karolyn?" she questioned softly as he closed his eyes to the bloody images that raced across his closed lids.

"Died at the scene, you worked so hard on her until the paramedics came. The CPR and adrenaline is what caused you to lose so much blood. Did you know that you were injured?" he asked.

"Yes. I knew it was a through and through. I could still move my arm so I didn't think there was any real damage. The important thing was to secure the scene and to try and save the injured. I'm so sorry…I failed you, Kenneth."

He pressed a button on the side rail of her bed and waited as the head of her bed lifted so that she was in a reclined sitting position. He quickly moved from his perched position in the chair at the side of her bed, to sitting next to her, facing her in the bed.

"You saved us, Heart. Merri, me, Arroyo…"

"Damn, I'd forgotten about him. Your mother injured him somehow."

"She hit him across his temple with the butt of her gun. He was unconscious for a long while, but according to Porter he will likely make a speedy recovery. They're just observing him to make sure the injury doesn't worsen."

He moved his hand up to cup her cheek and she gentled into his touch. "You did your level best to help Karolyn; you nearly sacrificed your life to help us all. I will never be able to thank you enough for that. No matter the outcome, I will always be in your debt for what you did for my family."

He bent down to place a soft kiss across her lips and she opened for him. There was something about the taste of this woman that made his senses scream with need. But she was injured, and he knew taking this any further was the wrong move at this time. Just as he was lifting his lips from the softness of her own, he heard someone clearing their throat. He turned to find his godfather standing there, watching the two of them.

Kenneth smiled at the older man, he had no shame where Heart was concerned and he intended to follow this connection with her through to its end—hopefully and in his mind more likely, beginning.

"Mac, Internal Affairs is talking with your doctor. As soon as they get the all-clear from him, they will be in to question you. It might not be a good idea for Kenneth to be here when they get here."

"Is everything all right?" Kenneth asked.

Heart nodded. "Yes, this is just standard procedure. You should go, I will be fine."

Kenneth took one long glance at her and nodded. "I'll come back later. I need to go home, check on William and my niece, and shower. Once I'm done, I will come right back."

She shook her head. "Kenneth, I'm more than likely going to be in and out of sleep because of the meds. Stay home and get some rest, you can visit another time." Kenneth shook his head and leaned a little closer to her.

"Not an option, MacKenzie." The use of her surname raised a questioning brow. He kissed her one last time and headed for the door.

~

"What the fuck was that?" Porter asked after the door closed behind Kenneth.

"Fuck-all if I know." She shook her head, still looking down at the hand Kenneth had been cradling for so long. There was a faint tingle there now, as well as on her lips. She rubbed her opposite hand over the tingling flesh savoring the unusual sensation. The feel of his skin against her seeded an excitement that was foreign to her.

Where is the fear?

Fear is what human touch usually brought, terror from a distant past her mind fought to forget. Never...*comfort?* Yes, it was comfort she felt every time Kenneth had touched her, a soothing comfort that set her usual fears aside. *What the hell is this about?*

"How do you feel about it?"

She looked at her captain, the man who had been her mentor for so long now. "I don't think I know yet. I've never been able to..."

Porter sat down in the chair that Kenneth had abandoned earlier. He leaned forward, bracing his elbows against his knees.

"MacKenzie, sometimes, out of the ugliest situations, life has a way of bringing beauty into our lives. If we only let it."

Heart nodded her head, liking the sound of Porter's philosophy, so desperately wanting to believe it, embrace it. She smiled until her cop's mind pushed forward through the fog she had been operating under since she awoke.

Jacqueline Searlington had said something that was nagging at the back of her mind. Something she knew she needed Porter to know immediately. In a click, the memory fell into place, and she fastened her eyes on Porter.

"Cap, we got a problem in the house. I need to ask you something based on some of the crazy shit Jacqueline was saying to me."

Her captain nodded waiting for her to continue.

"Jacqueline made Arroyo, she said she had someone run his prints. Cap I don't want to ask this, but I gotta. Were you giving that witch intel on our case?"

Porter leaned back, crossed his arms across his chest, and let out a small breath. "I understand why you had to ask me that. I'm connected to the family, and this case is about to get all kinds of messy. I'm not gonna be able to keep the Searlington connection quiet. I know you're just doing your job Mac. But the answer is no. I love my godchildren, loved their father more than any brother. But not even for Kalvin

Searlington would I have willingly placed one of my people in danger."

The audible gush of air that left her chest took with it the uncomfortable pressure that had been pressing against her torso like a weighted ball.

"Then we've got a serious problem, Cap. 'Cuz there are only a few agencies and personnel that have access to a cop's information, let alone his fingerprints. We have a leak in our house."

◈

A heavy weight rested on him the minute he pushed the door to his family's apartment open. Family? What family? His mother was handcuffed to an I.C.U. bed in a Brooklyn hospital. His sister was lying cold in a morgue. His niece would soon be preparing to leave with her father to a foreign country, and he would be the one thing he'd always thought being the first-born of a twosome would never make him—alone.

He didn't want to think about any of this right now, he just wanted to wash himself clean of the hell this night had heaped upon him. Heart was all that mattered now. He ran up the stairs two at a time, walking briskly to his room. If he stood still too long, all of the hurt he was attempting to keep at bay would just smother him.

As the familiar click of his bedroom door snapped into place, he peeled the bloodsoaked clothes from his skin. He dropped every piece of clothing he'd taken off directly in the garbage, he needed no reminders of this horrible day.

He opened the large glass-enclosed shower, turned the hot water on, and step inside of the multi-directional sprays. The water burned him. He looked down and watched the water at his feet bleed red as the hardened blood of both his dead sister and Heart slipped from his body being carried down the drain.

His sister, Karolyn, his twin. Gone. Over these last few years they hadn't been close.

He'd run from New York to California to remove himself from under his mother's thumb, leaving his sister alone to fight for herself. How could he have not seen it all those years? How had he not known the torture his sister was living? The torture his own mother was inflicting on her.

He felt the tears fill his eyes. He closed his lids, and they fell, mixing in with the steaming sprays of water hitting him from all sides. They were lost in the mix of individual drops that were pooling, swirling, and sinking into the drain. They were gone, just like his sister, just like his father, just like his entire family.

He gave a quick turn of his wrist and shut the water off. He wanted to sink into the water, and let it drown both his sorrows and himself. As much has he wanted to let the pain and hurt wash over him, he couldn't. He needed to see to Heart.

He stepped out of the now silent shower grabbing a towel to dry his dripping flesh. He walked naked into his adjoining bedroom heading toward the walk-in closet, shivering at the chill that met his skin. He found a black pair of boxer-briefs, black jeans, and a comfortable white t-shirt. He searched until he found his favorite red and black long-sleeved argyle sweater. He pulled it over his head and let it settle in place across his muscled chest. He moved to the opposite wall of the closet where his footwear was organized in shoebox-sized squares that housed every individual pair of shoes, sneakers, and boots that he owned. He pulled out a pair of classic low-top white basketball sneakers. He pulled his large-faced watch from the jewelry stand, and then stood in front of the mirrored wall. He found himself smiling. The only thing Heart had ever seen him in was designer tailor-made business suits. Casual Ken had never had the opportunity to make an appearance during Merri's disappearance. He wasn't quite sure how Heart was going to respond to him, but he was just too damn exhausted after the day's events to be Kenneth Searlington Billionaire at this time. He'd take whatever shit Heart was gonna give him about his urban casual chic attire. Right now, he just wanted to get back to her.

Kenneth laughed some more. He'd dare to say he'd spent enough of his childhood in Brooklyn with David Porter and his family that urban, casual wear was second nature to him. He stepped in front of the vanity mirror inside the closet, pulled a brush through his damp hair and secured the midnight strands in a low-sitting ponytail. He walked over to the wall of his closet that displayed his collection of designer fitted baseball caps. He pulled a red cap from the wall and pulled it down over his head. Now he was ready to go.

Keys and wallet in hand, he pushed them in the back pocket of his jeans with one hand and pulled the door of his bedroom open with the other. He was instantly rushed by a quick moving blur that slammed into his midsection. He looked down to find his niece Merridith with her arms securely locked around his belted waist.

"Uncle Ken, Uncle Ken," the excited voice squealed.

"Sorry Ken, I tried to keep her in her bed, but as soon as she heard you come in she was determined to see you."

Kenneth pulled the small girl up into his arms so that he could look up into her beautiful eyes, her mother's eyes, his eyes, as he'd done so many times over her young life.

"It's all right, William, my favorite munchkin doesn't need an excuse to see me, ever," he said as he brushed stray tresses from her small face. "How you doing, Merri?" The tiny girl wrapped her arms around his neck and buried her face in his shoulder.

"I want my mommy," her muffled voice almost lost in the cushion of his shoulder.

"I know, I wish she were here too, but she was just too sick." He stopped, and looked over to William. Kenneth hadn't had a chance to talk to him and ask him how much of tonight's events he had revealed to the child.

"I've talked to her, she knows," William said, reading the concern etched in

Kenneth's face.

Kenneth ran his hand down the child's back; this was just too much for the little person to have to bear. He kept running his hand up and down her back, much like he'd done when she was a newborn. Just like then she fell into his touch until her muscles slackened, her breathing became steady, her body still. She'd fallen asleep in his arms, given in to her need to finally rest.

"Poor kid, she's had a rough day," William said. He reached out, waiting for Kenneth to place his sleeping daughter in his arms.

Kenneth gave her one final squeeze followed by a gentle kiss to her temple before handing her to her father.

"Are you heading out?"

Kenneth nodded. "Going back to the hospital to check on Lieutenant MacKenzie."

"NYPD going to let you? She's a cop who was shot in the line of duty. I'm sure getting close enough to her is going to be like walking a gauntlet."

"I'm sure it is, but I've got an in with Porter being my godfather and all. Not to mention, she and I...we...I," Kenneth stopped, not really able to articulate just why he knew he would have no trouble getting in to see Heart. "Turns out her cousin is an old acquaintance of mine. If Porter can't get me in, then True will."

"Thank her for me," William said, hugging Merridith to him tightly. "She saved the most important thing in the world to me tonight."

Kenneth heard the shaking in William's voice before he saw the single tear slide down his face. He understood William's emotion, with all they'd both lost tonight, Merri was their one saving grace, the one thing that made the rest of the pain bearable.

Kenneth drew his former brother-in-law into his arms, the small child pressed between the two men.

"She's safe, William. Out of everything that's happened tonight, that's the only thing that matters. I have to go, I have to get back to the hospital," Kenneth said. He gave William one last hug, and then headed for Brooklyn, there was a cop that was waiting for his return.

CHAPTER 9

*K*enneth stepped off the elevator to his private parking floor in the complex. He walked toward his black SUV. He needed to be relaxed tonight, and the roomy vehicle always took the edge off when he was driving. He turned the ignition and pulled out his cell phone from his pocket. He hadn't dialed the number in his contacts for years, but dialed it anyway.

Just as always, the phone rang once and the other end clicked.

"Searlington."

A statement, not a question. He smiled when he heard True's rich alto travel across the line.

"True, I'm headed back to the hospital. Porter sent me out when Internal Affairs entered the hospital. I figured you guys were still there. How's Heart doing?"

"She's doing all right. She's still in pain in between the med dosages. I've been trying to get her to eat, but she refuses to eat any of the hospital food."

"I'm driving in, True. If you want me to stop and get her something, just tell me what."

Kenneth heard hushed voices in the background and then True was back on the phone.

"Kenneth, how are you getting back into Brooklyn?"

"Gonna take the Midtown Tunnel to the BQE. Taking Atlantic to Utica, then I'm coming down to Clarkson."

"Okay," True said. "Instead of making that right onto Clarkson, keep going down Utica for a few more blocks until you get to Snyder Ave. There's this Chinese spot there. They make the best soy-sauce chicken and pork fried rice. Can you get half a pan of chicken and half a pan of pork-fried rice? Make sure they give you a bunch of plates and cutlery as well."

"Is Heart really going to be able to eat that heavy? She was under anesthesia a few hours ago."

"Doc says as soon as she sleeps the drugs off she can have a regular diet. She sipped some apple juice and ate some clear broth a little earlier without any issues. Besides, what she doesn't eat, the rest of us will," True said.

"The rest of us?" Kenneth asked instantly feeling something tighten in his chest. He wasn't exactly sure why, but something bothered him about others surrounding her in his absence. Something was missing; something just wasn't right about that particular picture.

"Yeah, Justice and our dad just came in from D.C. In the rush to get here they haven't eaten, and neither wants to leave Heart's bedside. I was going to head out, but I kind of want to be here to liaise with the medical team."

A smile grew on Kenneth's face. He knew that True was an orthopedic surgeon in

California. He wasn't certain how much experience she had with emergency medicine, but knowing how knowledgeable she was about everything else, he was certain she was keeping close watch over the medical team caring for her cousin.

"True, you're not harassing the medical team are you?"

"I don't have to," she answered quickly. "Xavier Bradley is the chief of trauma surgery here. He's a respected colleague and a friend. I called him in personally to perform Heart's surgery as soon as I got the call about the shooting."

Kenneth shook his head. "Figures, I should have known you were pulling strings somewhere in the background."

"Aren't I always?" she asked.

"Yeah, you are," he said, and clicked the line dead.

~

*K*enneth walked to the end of the ward where he found two uniformed police officers standing in front of Heart's room. Hands filled with food and drinks, he stopped in front of the two *hulking* men.

"Kenneth Searlington to see Lieutenant MacKenzie," he said.

One officer lifted his hand up palm side halting Kenneth's forward motion. "Identification, sir?"

Kenneth went to pull his wallet out of his pocket then realized he didn't have enough hands to hold the food and get his wallet. The officer pointed to an empty cart that was next to MacKenzie's door. He placed the food and drinks down, and reached into his pocket to get his driver's license. As soon as the officer finished looking at it he returned it, then walked over to where Kenneth had placed the food and opened the containers.

Does he think I'm trying to poison her? Suddenly he realized the gravity of who Heart was, and what her job meant. She was here because someone, his mother, had attempted to kill her. In a job like hers, there was probably always going to be some sort of threat to her life. He might not be trying to poison her, but he was suddenly glad the officers in front of him weren't going to take that possibility for granted.

He walked into the room and found Heart still asleep. True, Justice, and a man who shared the same face as the other three Amare/MacKenzie family members sat with their backs to the wall, watching him as he entered the room. His eyes passed across each of them and gave a relieved nod when his gaze stopped at True.

Kenneth placed the food and bags on the bedside table and held his hand out to Justice.

"Kenneth Searlington," Justice nodded.

"I remember, you were hanging out with Faith, Genesis, and True the last time we met. I was on furlough, stopped in to see the baby sister for a minute. We all hung out for a couple of days," Justice said with a look of certainty canvassed across the features that were so similar to True's and Heart's. There was no guessing, this was a precise account of the details of their first meeting all those years ago. God, was everyone in this family some kind of trained military tactician? *Probably.* Even the little old lady that had called him on his bullshit earlier seemed just as deadly, if not more so, than the rest of her family in this room.

Kenneth nodded and moved his gaze to the oldest Amare sitting in the room. He was probably in his late fifties to early sixties. Just like Justice, he was dressed in civilian clothes, but there was no mistaking that the military was stitched into every cell of his being. Head and face clean of any hair, body rigid and alert, eyes watchful and all knowing. This man had seen and done some things.

"Hello, sir," he said, instantly feeling the need to show respect. "I'm Kenneth Searlington," he announced, extending his hand to the man.

"General Hunter Amare," he said as his strong palm gripped Kenneth's hand in a secure grasp. "Hello, son," his penetrating baritone climbed out of his throat. "I hear that you're the one we have to thank for getting my niece help when she needed it."

Kenneth shook his head. "I just happened to be in the elevator with her when she collapsed. The building was swimming with her fellow officers; someone would have found her eventually."

"But someone didn't, you did," the man said. "Thank you. This young lady is very special to us; I don't think we could have handled losing her that way."

Kenneth followed General Amare's line of vision to the sleeping woman lying still in the bed. Her hair taken out of that regulation bun, combed down so that it fell over the swell of her chest. Her skin clean, not a stitch of makeup, not even lip gloss. Here, free of all of the things that women in his experience considered a necessity, she was the most beautiful thing he'd ever seen. She was alive, she was safe, and for some reason that Kenneth was unwilling to acknowledge at this moment, that meant more to him than anything else.

"She is very special; I can't argue that, sir."

Kenneth walked over to the food and began to open pans. They all needed to eat, hopefully the food would take the edge off of all of the emotion that seemed to be filling the room.

~

*K*enneth sat in the hard plastic chair directly next to Heart's bed. True had walked her family members downstairs to their car. He somehow had the feeling that she was giving him some alone time with Heart without the critical eyes of the Amare clan bearing down on him.

He took up vigil next to her the moment the family left, stroking the same hand just as he had when she first woke up. He saw her eyes begin to flutter again and moved to stroke the side of her soft cheek.

She burrowed into the gentle touch, and lifted her eyes with a smile. When her eyes fastened on to his face a brief moment of uncertainty crossed her eyes quickly and she used her free arm to grip the hand touching her face.

"It's me, Heart," he said gently, trying to soothe the fear he saw climbing into her eyes and body. She looked him over quickly, assessing the truth, warring with her senses to relax instead of defend.

"Why do you look like you fell out of Russell Simons' closet?"

He started laughing. He knew the moment he'd dressed that he was going to have to explain himself to her. No time better than the present.

"Heart, contrary to what my background might dictate, I don't actually enjoy wearing a suit and tie every day. When I'm not working, this is how I usually dress." He watched her eyes pass over him again.

"So you normally wear Fitteds?"

"Actually, yeah. I have an entire wall decorated with them in my closet. I keep telling you, my address might be Upper East Side, but my heart has always been with

Uncle David over in Bed Stuy."

She raised a questioning brow. "You regularly spent time in Bedford Stuyvesant growing up?"

He laughed again. "Is it so difficult to believe I grew up in Bed Stuy?" he asked She nodded her head up and down in answer to his question.

"Listen, I told you that my dad and Uncle David were really close. My dad worked a great deal, and he didn't like to leave me in the company of my mother. I never really understood it at the time, but I think he just didn't want me to pick up my mother's elitist ways. Uncle David or Aunty Pam would pick me up from school on Fridays and I would spend the entire weekend with them in Brooklyn. They never asked for a bag, they kind of kept a wardrobe there for me because I was there so frequently. They bought the same things for me that they did their own son. I was never a white kid playing at being black. I was just their nephew Ken that came to visit on the weekends and everyone accepted that."

He noticed that she watched him with a cautious regard. He could almost hear the silent "yeah right," walking across her mind. He smiled at her pushing her obvious disbelief aside for the moment.

"How are you feeling?" he asked with a quiet concern.

"Not feeling much of anything. I'm pretty heavily drugged," she said.

"Is that normal for this sort of injury?" he questioned, watching her eyes close in either exhaustion or shame, at the moment, he couldn't tell which.

"I'm sure it's normal for them to be pouring heavy duty drugs into me with an injury like this. I think they're slipping it to me a little more regularly to make certain I'm out when they examine me. I nearly gave Dr. Bradley a black eye when I woke up to find him touching me."

He moved from his seat and sat down gingerly on her bed. He

tightened his hold on her hand again and lifted her chin with his finger.

"You don't like it when people touch you," he declared. There was no question in his voice when he made the statement. He knew that she didn't like to be touched. He understood that it went beyond having a preference, there was a deeply ingrained need in her not to be touched. She could not tolerate it.

Something cracked inside of him when she pulled her chin out of his reach and looked in the direction of the window, away from him. He watched her slowly shake her head no, still unable to look at him.

"I bet you've figured out my particular brand of crazy already. You just want to know why now, right?"

He watched a slow tear crawl down the side of her face, the side that she couldn't hide from him by looking at that window. He lifted a soft finger and let it trail the tear, chasing it away from her beautiful skin.

"Would I like to know what happened to you, who hurt you? Absolutely. But I don't need to know, Heart. I don't need to know anything you aren't ready to share with me. I don't need to know now, or ever. Only you can decide if it's something I should know."

She didn't move, gaze still fix on that immoveable window. He went to move his hand, to release hers and give her the space he felt she needed. When he loosened his grip to let go, she grabbed his hand, keeping him planted at her side.

His eyes rose in question to hers and saw the pleading behind her twin pools of tears.

"Please don't..." was all she said and without fail he resumed the soothing motion

his fingers had been playing against her hand all night.

"I don't want to hurt you, Heart. I thought touch..."

"Everyone else's, but yours," she huffed out on such a quick breath that it sounded like she'd only spoken one word. She took a deep breath, trying to calm herself. "I haven't been able to experience touch in fourteen years without flinching until you touched me that night in your kitchen. There was no fear when you touched me, no panic." She raised her eyes to his, they danced back and forth across his face, seeking help, seeking sanctuary. "Please, I know you think I'm some sort of freak, but I thought I would go to my grave not being able to tolerate another's touch. Please, just...until I fall asleep, just touch me."

"Aww, baby," he said. He turned lying on the bed and pulling her quaking body into his arms, surrounding her with his touch. He pulled her head into the crook of his neck letting the warmth of her tears sizzle against the anger-burning heat of his skin. He didn't know what had happened to her, or who had done it, but he did know that this was a long-festering wound that must have been eating at her soul, her mind, her body for far too long.

He kept stroking her, hoping his touch would be the balm she needed to stop the pain she'd been carrying for so long. He stroked, and soothed, and stroked some more until she was quiet, still, and sleeping the sleep of the unburdened.

They remained that way, her soundly asleep in the cradle of his arms, protected, safe, and calm. The silence of the room so welcome and loud, the soft click of the door opening sounded like a raging screech to his ears. He turned his head to find True's gaze crashing down on him with a raised brow.

"Not right now, True," he whispered. "I've just gotten her to sleep and I'm not leaving her. Say your worst, do you worst, I'm not moving from this spot." True gave him a contemplative stare and simply nodded her head.

"Try to get some sleep, Kenneth. It seems like she's in good hands, I'll go crash at my pops'. If anything changes, or if she needs something, you call me."

Kenneth nodded, she accepted his nod, and just as quietly as she'd entered, True was gone.

∽

$\mathcal{T}$he sliced light peeking through the window bounced against her eyelids, beckoning her from a comfortable slumber. She ran her hand on the side of the bed feeling nothing but cool sheet where she expected Kenneth to be.

She opened her eyes, still sensitive to the light of the new day, scanning the empty place he'd left next to her. She looked around the room, looking for a glimpse of him, even that red fitted cap he'd been wearing last night. *Nothing.*

She closed her eyes again, letting the sinking feeling that seemed to be crawling from somewhere inside her grow. He'd left. She'd hoped...thought...wanted. She shook her head in an attempt to rid herself of the ridiculous ache that seemed to settle in her gut at the thought of his name.

Kenneth hadn't promised he'd be there. She'd asked him in a rare emotional outburst to hold her until she fell asleep. It was the first time she'd felt safe in someone else's arms since she was a child. And this man, this very complicated, and unorthodox man whom she should fear, brought her the most serene sense of comfort she'd ever experienced. Why did his presence affect her so much? Why did the lack of it impact her even more?

He was a fixture in a case she was working. She knew how to separate herself from her work. She didn't take shit like this home with her, she was always able to shake this shit off when she crossed her threshold. But this, him, this was right under her skin— right on top of it if she remembered correctly.

She rubbed the fingers of her hand together, the hand she's awoken to him stroking last night. It still tingled from his touch. Or maybe that was a result of the shooting or the surgery on her arm, maybe she was imagining the fact that she could still feel his fingers ghosting over her skin. Maybe.

Somehow she wasn't so certain that the sensation she was experiencing had anything to do with medicine or surgery at all.

She was still there, just staring at the fingers, marveling at the way they felt, as if they weren't actually a part of her. So engrossed, she almost missed the slight squeak the door made when it opened. She looked up to find him walking into the room, his hands full of paper bags and a drink tray.

"Hi," he said through his wide smile. He placed the white food paper bags on her bedside table and came and sat next to her on the bed. He placed a soft hand to her cheek again, bringing forth this unexplainable need she had to nuzzle it. He leaned in, giving her a whisper of a kiss against her lips then pulling his thumb across them. He leaned in again and deepened the kiss, and without offering any resistance, she let him. She savored the feel of his skin against hers; she didn't question why she wasn't afraid. She didn't care at that moment; she just wanted to sink into the warm cloud that seemed to be surrounding her as Kenneth's lips danced against hers.

"Mmmm, morning," he said lazily. Her eyes fell to his pink lips, the edges swollen, lined with just this much red to indicate he'd been kissing.

She lifted her hand, her good arm, taking a single finger to trace around those soft lips that had just covered hers. They emanated warmth, somehow filling the chill that was growing within her.

"I went to get you something to eat. I was hoping to get back before you woke up, but the line was pretty long."

He stood up, went to the bedside table, and began pulling food from the bags. He pushed the table closer to her head and set the food before her. He handed her what felt like a wrapped sandwich. She pulled the foil and the sandwich paper away to reveal the most beautiful bagel she'd ever seen.

She looked up to find him watching her, unsure of how he knew what her favorite breakfast was.

"Cinnamon raisin bagel slightly warmed, but not toasted, with a little bit of cream cheese and a lot of strawberry jelly, cut into four sections," he said smiling, as he reached for the disposable drink container sitting in the holder. "Sugar-free vanilla iced coffee with extra cream; enough to make the coffee a shade between light beige and light tan." She could see the satisfied arrogance he often wore cloaking his shoulders.

"You must have spoken to, True or Bryan," she said as she picked up the first quarter. She took a bite, her eyes immediately closing as they always did when she bit into one of these bagels. Warm, chewy goodness filled her mouth and an almost sensual groan escaped her as she savored the texture and the flavors unique to the bagel she was eating.

"There's only one place that makes this bagel, this good, this way. You went to the diner on Linden Boulevard. How did you know?"

"The first day we met," he said. "After you threw me out of your office. I went to go complain to Porter about you, but just as I was about to walk away from the closed door of your office, I saw you pulling your breakfast out and sinking your teeth into that first bite. It was like watching a child at Christmas. Your eyes were wide, and there was a smile fixed to your face that I would have sworn you weren't capable of. In that moment, you looked like you were experiencing absolute bliss, and I just thought you should look that way every day. When I left, I asked your desk sergeant where I could get the best bagels from in the area, he said hands down, the diner at the end of Linden."

"So you figured you'd take a drive down there and get me one today?" she asked. When he nodded his head with that bright-ass picture perfect smile he always wore, she just shook her head. "Dude, you know you passed like seven fast-food places all up and down Church Ave, and Pennsylvania Ave before you even got all the way down to Linden. You know that's technically Queens right? You could have just gone down to the hospital cafeteria instead of going through all of that trouble."

"So that means you don't want it?" he asked as he extended his hand as if he was going to take the sandwich from her.

She pulled it protectively close to her. "You touch my food and you will draw back a nub, Kenneth."

He laughed and handed her the iced coffee as a peace offering. She took a long pull from it. It too, just like the sandwich, much like the man standing beside her bed was perfect as well.

~

"*I* don't fucking know, True! Now stop asking me. I'll figure it out once that damn doctor-friend of yours lets me out of here. I can't do dick from this fucking prison this hospital staff calls a bed."

Heart ended the call and tossed her phone at the foot of her bed. Her cousin could be

so exhausting sometimes. She absentmindedly began to stroke her injured arm in soothing strokes. It was something she'd taken to doing ever since she woke up to find Kenneth stroking her arm in this hospital room. The soothing circular pattern she was initiating reminded her of his comforting caresses. She needed that now.

A soft tap on the door brought her eyes up to the door. Kenneth walked through the door with severe worry lines marking his milky skin.

Damn, he heard me.

"What's wrong," he questioned.

"Nothing," she said quickly, a little too quickly if the "I call bull-shit," look resting on his face was any indication.

She rolled her eyes. Her fucking cousin True couldn't have timed her annoying call any better. That wretched busybody probably timed it that way on purpose. Knowing True, she was more than likely sitting in a dark room somewhere watching Kenneth on camera as he rang the damn elevator call bell in the lobby.

Heart looked at him again, he was still standing there, still waiting, expecting an answer from her.

"You remember a while back when you pushed your nose into some documents I was reading at your house?" she asked and watched as he nodded his yes in response.

"If I remember correctly, they were real estate papers."

"Yes." Heart nodded. "I live in a basement apartment in Cambria Heights. A few months back my landlady passed away. Her daughter lives out of state and decided to put the house up for sale."

"So you're trying to buy it?" he interrupted.

"No. It's a nice house, but it needs some significant work. I would have to make some serious renovations, with the hours I put in at work, I'd never be able to oversee them. I did decide that I wanted property of my own though."

"Have you found anything yet?"

She shook her head. "No," she said. "I was so caught up in Merri's case that I sort of forgot. I received notice almost three months ago that I would have to vacate the premises because of the sale. Essentially, I'll be homeless in three days." "Heart," Kenneth said on a long breath.

She raised her working hand up to silence the reprimand she knew he was preparing.

"I know, Kenneth, it was irresponsible of me. I just honestly forgot. Honestly that's not the worst thing I have to deal with right now. True's lackey, Dr. Bradley won't let me out of this place until I can either show proof that I've signed myself into a rehab facility or that I have someone at home willing to take care of me. He doesn't want me doing anything with my right arm."

She watched Kenneth process all that she was saying. He stood quietly, seemingly churning her words over in his mind.

"So I take it staying with your grandmother is not an option?"

She shook her head. "No, Dr. Bradley vetoed that notion. He thinks it would be too much for her to handle, and True agrees. I think my insurance will spring for a home service nurse, but there's still the little fact that I'm missing a home right now."

He nodded his head slowly. "What about your cousins and your uncle?"

"All of my cousins either live out of state or have ridiculously demanding jobs that require equally ridiculous amounts of travel. My uncle still lives here in Brooklyn, but he's a four-star general in the United States Army. His work detail requires him to spend most of his days in D.C. And my grandmother lives on the first floor, directly underneath my uncle's place. If I go there, she's going to insist on taking care of me."

He nodded again, still not really saying anything, just chewing on the things she'd told him.

"I suppose staying with Bryan or Porter is out as well?"

"I'm sure both of them would put me up, but I just don't want my boss or my subordinate to see me like this. I know they both care, I know this nonsense is in my own head, but I just don't think it would be a good fit."

He sat next to her on the bed and let his crystal blue eyes wash over her.

"I guess there's only one solution then, you're coming to stay with me," the tone of his voice solid and stiff, much like the look on his face.

"Kenneth, I didn't tell you all of that to get you to volunteer your home. I can't stay with you. I asked Dr. Bradley to suggest some long-term rehab places that can put me up while I work on my arm. I will be fine. I'm annoyed, but fine."

She watched him take hold of her good hand. He started the slow stroke that had pulled her through the haze of traumatic shock and anesthesia to find him staring down at her with happy, expectant eyes. She opened her mouth to speak again when he brought warm lips to the very tip of her knuckles. The touch was faint, it was brief, and it shortcircuited her brain and mouth.

"Heart, there's no way I'm going to let you fester in some facility alone while you heal. The solution is simple; you will come home with me."

Her brain kick-fired again, for a moment she was able to sustain a reasonable thought. She shook her head, more to free herself from the hypnotic pull of his voice and his touch than to actually say no, but the truth was, she had to say no.

"Kenneth, I wasn't hinting at—"

"I know you weren't," he interrupted. "But, nonetheless, you're still going to stay with me," his voice was confident, as if the matter had already been decided.

"I can't do that. You're a principal in a case I'm in the process of closing. For God's sake, I shot your mother; because of me she will more than likely spend the rest of her life in prison. I'm the reason your twin sister is dead. Why on Earth would you want me in your home?"

She stopped and thought on her own questions. Trying to find an answer that made sense. Then she felt a familiar sensation climbing up inside her. Inside her head there was an audible click where she felt fear taking root again.

"Why are you here?" she asked him quietly, the cold inside her crossing her lips, permeating the comfort of the room's temperature.

He must have felt it too. His hand stopped stroking hers. She used the brief interruption as an opportunity to pull her hand free of his grasp.

"Heart, I care—"

"You care, about the woman that's going to send your mother to jail? About the woman who got your sister killed? What do you want from me, Kenneth?" The last of her questions dripped with acid and accusation caused him to fall back slightly.

In that instant she saw the caring man who had been her friend and companion during her hospital stay vanish, in his place, Kenneth the businessman showed up. She'd instantly recognized this man, she'd met him that very first day when he'd come storming into her office making demands about his niece's case. She'd met him in his office where he sat at the height of his power behind his throne-like desk.

This was the person she should be dealing with; this was the man whose return she should be celebrating. Why then did she feel the beginnings of an ache inside her that the friendlier Kenneth had left— or more accurately had been pushed out of the door?

"As you know," he spoke in a level tone, void of any real emotion. "Real estate is my business. I know of a listing that is not far from Cambria Heights in Woodmere, Long Island. The owner purchased it several years ago, but his business keeps him away too often for him to actually enjoy it. It's just gone on the market for leasing with the option to buy."

"Kenneth, just remember, I'm a cop, not a banker."

"I don't think cost will be an issue. I will draw up the papers, let you look them over and give you a virtual tour of the house. If you don't like it, we can find you other accommodations thereafter. Right now, you're in a bind, and I would imagine a five bedroom home in Woodmere would sound better than a park bench."

That ache inside her was growing into a throbbing pain. She'd done this, her words had severed whatever small connection they'd been building. She could hardly move the lump in her throat long enough to draw sound past it, so she just nodded her head in acquiescence.

He stood, opened the door, and left.

Awesome, this was just one more thing on her list of screw-ups.

CHAPTER 10

Faith Bailer sat in front of the large window in her office looking out over the rolling waves of the Pacific Ocean. The hard crashing waves seemed to slap against the surf the way her memories kept bombarding her consciousness.

"Why can't you just stay away?" She let the question fill the silent room. If she could only outrun her past by demanding it stay in the past, she'd be set for life. Instead, the darkness that she fought so hard to keep at bay began to edge into her heart as it always did whenever she couldn't stop the past from leaking into her present.

She heard her office phone ringing and decided it would be better to deal with whoever was on the line, than face the blackness that was attempting to cloud her spirit.

"Dr. Bailer," she said with the practiced happiness that she'd spent nearly a decade perfecting. "How may I help you?"

"Glad I caught you before you left, Cheerleader."

Faith instantly rolled her eyes at True's annoying name for her. She was far off the mark with her assumption that the call would prove easier to handle than her current state of emotions. History had taught her that dealing with True was never easy.

"I've told you about calling me that, True," she warned.

"Yeah, but as always, I'll ask the same question I always ask when you threaten me: what are you going to do about it?"

Faith opened her mouth to speak, but thought better of it. True was a handful, more than a handful on most days. Their friendship over the years had taught her two very important lessons. The first, True was exceedingly protective of those she loved, and two, you didn't cross her if you could avoid it. Being on that woman's bad side had not fared well for most who'd dared to cross True.

"True, I'm busy. What do you want?"

She could hear the small giggle in True's voice. It made her roll her eyes again knowing True was celebrating having gotten the best of her.

"My cousin, Heart was shot on the job in New York. She's going to be released as soon as she can secure follow up care."

"Where was she shot?"

"In the shoulder, bullet nicked her axillary artery. Bradley repaired it, but she's going to need rehab, both physical therapy and occupational therapy. She was shot in her dominant arm. Heart needs the best. I need you to come out here and work with her. Get her arm back into shape so she can protect herself and others on the streets. She can't lose her gun hand, Faith."

Faith thought back to their childhood and called up the memory of True's cousin, Heart MacKenzie. She remembered a quiet girl that they'd had to force to play doubledutch with them instead of sticking her nose in one of her ever-present books. They'd all attended the same church growing up together. If Faith remembered correctly, Heart lived in the city during the week, and spent weekends on Crescent Street with them while staying at True's grandmother's house.

By the time they were teenagers, Heart had come to live permanently on Crescent

Street bringing a mountain of strange with her. The girl was always quiet, kept to herself.

But prior to her coming to live on the block, she'd play with everyone when encouraged, she'd laughed and smiled at the same stupid jokes they'd all laughed at. She was just like any other kid in

Brooklyn, happy to be outside on a sunny day, running down the street behind the ice cream man for that sacred soft-serve vanilla cone dipped in cherry or chocolate sauce, or possibly covered in rainbow or chocolate sprinkles. Something had changed when she came to stay though, something that True had never bothered to share.

"True, I don't think I've seen your cousin since the summer that Genesis and I left for college," Faith began. "Don't you think she might feel more comfortable with someone else taking over her case? We were never really all that buddy-buddy if I remember correctly. Why don't you ask Genesis?"

She felt the breath True drew in more than heard it.

"No, it's been too soon since Genesis and Drew left all that craziness behind in Brooklyn. The two of them need time away to heal and get things into perspective before they come back to the East. It has to be you."

"Can't be me, I have a ton of work to do here. I can send one of my subordinates.

My assistant director even if that will make you feel better."

"Faith, understand this. When your mother broke her fucking hip trying to foxtrot on the dance floor of a cruise ship I didn't blink when you asked me to do the surgery.

Whether you'd asked me or not, I wasn't going to let anyone cut her open and mess with her bones other than me. I expect the same of you. Heart will be ready to start therapy in the next couple of weeks. Get your shit together, let that fucking assistant director of yours earn his fucking keep, and get your ass to New York."

Before Faith could respond she heard the familiar click of the dial tone telling her the conversation was over. "Well fuck, I guess I'm going to New York."

~

*T*oday was release day. Everything concerning her release from the hospital had been organized by her cousin True, and Kenneth. True provided the medical staff that would handle her follow-up care, and Kenneth had organized the logistics of where she would rest her head at night and moving her things from her apartment to the rental house he was driving her to now.

She stole a glance at him from her peripheral vision. It had been days since she'd seen him last in her hospital room. He'd called every night to check in, but he hadn't set foot in her hospital room since she'd practically accused him of something malicious.

She still remembered that fleeting fractured look of pain across his face. It lasted only a second, and only someone with a skilled eye, taught to assess even the barest of reactions would have noticed it. It was there, and in the next moment, it was gone, and

Kenneth's business persona had emerged.

But isn't that what you wanted? She closed her eyes trying to block out the loud voice inside her head. That damned voice was annoying, but it was right. She had wanted it. She was beginning to relax too much in Kenneth's presence. In the few short days she'd been in the hospital, she'd given him more information about herself than anyone else had knowledge of. *What were you thinking giving him that kind of power?*

The fast camaraderie they were building needed to stop. She couldn't allow him to learn any more of her weaknesses. Weakness brought pain, and since she was of the belief that she'd suffered enough pain in her life, she wasn't about to hand him any ammunition to bring her more. No, this chasm that was widening between them, this was exactly what she needed to happen between then. *Then why does the thought of losing what you were beginning to build frighten you so much?*

She shook her head, trying to cut off her thoughts. She wasn't about to second guess herself now. This was what needed to happen, what needed to be done.

She turned her attention to the passenger window, focusing on the scene passing by. They exited the Belt Parkway at twenty-three B and merged into traffic on the South Conduit Avenue. She glanced again at Kenneth as he made the right turn onto Francis Lewis Boulevard.

"You drive as if you're familiar with this area," she quietly spoke breaking the palpable silence.

His eyes never leaving the road, not even for the briefest of glances in her direction, he nodded his head. "I am," his succinct declaration bristled her senses. "I've known this client for a very long time. I've had the pleasure of visiting this place several times over."

There was that business tone again. She knew it was best that Kenneth's representative was in the car with her, but every monotone syllable that crossed his lips made her ache for the caring man who had taken care of her while she lay in a hospital bed.

She turned her head back to the passenger window and watched Francis Lewis Boulevard turn in to Hook Creek Boulevard; Hook Creek became Rosedale Road when they crossed into Nassau County. He made the right turn onto Lawrence Court and took the right winding road until he reached the middle of the block.

Lawrence Court and Woodmere Drive. She looked at the intersection, a habit she'd picked up from her days walking a beat. She'd driven past these back roads often to circumvent the ever-present mall traffic on Sunrise Highway. She'd never stopped to look at anything other than the road in front of her on her way to the mall or the bulkshopping club in Five-Towns. Here on this hidden street that she never would have known about never would have cared to know about, she saw the model for normal— Middle Class, USA normal.

There was a middle-age Caucasian man watering his lawn. Bulky, muscular build

with the retirement paunch softening his middle, the salt and pepper-haired man turned around and offered a friendly smile and wave to Kenneth when he stepped out of the car.

"Good to see you, Patty," Kenneth tossed back at him, and then helped Heart out of the car and up onto the sidewalk. Kenneth led her to the brick-colored paving stones that created an S-shaped path to the white twisted staircase that ushered them to the front door. Kenneth pointed to a comfortable looking sofa sitting on the front porch and motioned for her to sit there. Once she was securely in the seat, he went back to the car and began removing Heart's suitcases.

She watched as the lawn-watering guy, Patty, moved over to the car and took one of the three bags Kenneth was attempting to juggle on his own. When Patty reached the top of the stairs, he stepped in her direction on the porch.

"Patty," he said with a gruff baritone mildly colored with an accent she couldn't quite place. She watched a kind smile light up his clean face. Wide emerald eyes sparkled at her. In them, she could see, almost feel a welcoming warmth. She returned his smile and felt a small sense of comfort in his presence. He almost reminded her of her captain.

Well…that is if Porter were a white man that was built like he used to lift cinderblocks for a living, then yeah, they resembled.

There was something about this man that spoke of leadership. Whether it was the way he stood, or the fact that he stared her straight in the eyes when he spoke to her, she could tell this man either was currently, or had been in charge at some point in his life.

Like recognized like, she could tell by the way he'd pulled the heaviest bag out of Kenneth's hand that he didn't ask, he just did. He saw a need so he fulfilled it. That's what leaders did, that's what Porter did, and that's what Porter had taught her to do with her own people. He taught her to watch out for her people. This man—Patty—was used to watching out for people—his people, whomever they might be.

He extended his hand to her in greeting, his milky complexion changing to reddishpink when his gaze fell on Heart's damaged right arm that was now completely taped to her body by an arm brace.

"I'm sorry," he quickly pulled back his hand.

"No worries," she said. "It will be a little while before I'll be shaking any hands."

She offered a smile. "I'm Heart."

"This goofball with the hippie ponytail didn't do this to you, did he?" he laughed as Kenneth put the key in the door.

A shadow from her past reached into her present and secured a firm grip around her chest. She could feel the memory trying to escape the grave she had buried it in, fighting to either free itself, or drag her in. She felt the walls of her throat, constricting, decreasing the amount of air she could comfortably pass in and out of her lungs.

No, not now.

She could hear the steadily fading voices around her.

"Is she okay, Kenneth? She's looking a little green. I don't think I've ever seen a black woman turn green," she could hear the tinge of alarm edging the tones of Patty's voice.

"Heart, are you all right?" She heard Kenneth's voice somewhere in the distance.

"Heart?"

She needed to break its hold, find something to anchor herself in the present. She placed a shaky left hand on her right arm. Its soft tremors quickly escalating into rapidly oscillating spasms. She gripped the top of her shoulder where her injury was and squeezed as hard as she could to bring the sharp ache she needed at this moment.

"Aahhhhh," she cried as the pain enclosed her. She felt herself dropping to her knees, any moment now the hard smack of the concrete slab of the porch would jump up and collide with multiple points of her body. She didn't care; it was what she needed to make this attack on her stop.

She eagerly awaited the pain, but it never came. Instead she felt strong hands grab her. They were large hands...calloused hands...the wrong hands. The panic that she was fighting so hard to control began to rise in a sharp wave ready to break over her at any second.

"Kenneth...hands...please...stop," she gasped.

"Don't touch her," Kenneth shouted as he pulled her from Patty's grasp. He pulled her tightly into his arms, stroking her back, whispering calming sounds into her ear, coaxing her to settle into his embrace.

"Kenneth, lad, did I do something wrong? I'm sorry, I was trying to..."

"Not your fault, Patty. She got hurt on the job and is dealing with a very painful injury," Kenneth said as he continued to stroke her.

"Sorry...Patty...I," she tried to turn toward the older man, Kenneth's arms still keeping her pressed against his chest.

"Lass, I know what it's like to get hurt on the job. I was a fireman for NYFD for thirty years. You just need to get inside and let Kenney-boy take care of you. Old Patty will be right next door if you need anything."

She couldn't see it for Kenneth's chest still being pressed against her cheek, but she could hear the older man smiling. She didn't know whether it was the thought of the older man's smile, or Kenneth's soothing touch that was pouring the heat back into her, getting rid of the cold that had permeated her for so long. But on that porch, in the midst of the crazy that was trying to reach from her past and into her present she'd found something she'd never felt before. Home.

~

*K*enneth stood in the kitchen pouring a cup of hot tea for Heart. It wasn't very cold inside or outside of the house, but she was still shivering, like cold was living inside of her.

He had no idea what had happened out on that porch. He kept replaying the scene in his head and he couldn't think of anything Patty had done or said to trigger such a heightened response from her. He'd never seen Heart out of control, he'd never seen her unable to help herself. Even in the hospital when she was opening up to him about her life, she had never before seemed weak, scared. But out there on that porch, she had definitely been scared.

He walked back into the living room, finding her in the same spot he'd left her on the couch. She was sitting tightly in the corner, her left hand closed in to a tight fist.

"Drink this," he said as he held out the steaming mug in front of her.

"I don't want it."

"You're sitting there shaking, like you're standing in the middle of the Arctic. Drink the tea." He pushed the cup in her direction again. This time, she took it, slowly bringing it to her lips and sipping. He could see the warmth beginning to spread through her. Her hands weren't trembling as badly, her body seemed less stiff, and her face was gaining a small bit of color. The panic was subsiding.

He took a small breath. If things had persisted, he would have had to call her cousin

True, and that was a conversation he just didn't want to have. True had been staunchly against him bringing Heart here. She had warned him that there were things Heart was likely to experience that he might not be prepared to deal with. She had warned him that victims of trauma often suffered resulting psychological and emotional issues that manifested in difficult ways at times. Even though the traumatic ordeal was over, sometimes, their minds kept replaying it, kept them living in it.

True proved to be correct. He didn't have a psychological degree, but even he could recognize that Heart was reacting to some kind of trauma. The only problem was he didn't know which one, the gunshot that had injured her arm, or the one from her past that he had not the slightest bit of information about.

He went down to bended knee and placed each of his hands softly on her thighs.

"Are you all right?" he asked.

She nodded in response, staring into the teacup, not lifting her gaze to his.

He placed a gentle finger under her chin and lifted her head, forcing her to meet his eyes. "You have nothing to be ashamed of," he said quietly.

"Yeah right." She rolled her eyes and let out a lazy chuckle. "So having a total mental freak out in front of a total stranger doesn't fall in the 'you should be ashamed' category?"

"Heart, you went through a major trauma, you have to give your head and your arm time to heal."

He watched her struggle to accept his words. The muscles in her jaw ticked an erratic rhythm.

"Kenneth," she whispered quietly. "If I can't get this under control, they're going to take my badge."

He watched her close her eyes, and saw two fat teardrops begin the sliding decent down her face.

"They can't have a frightened lieutenant with mental problems on the street," she said in a rushed voice. "I'd die if they put me on some desk duty detail. I'm going to lose everything if I can't get a handle on this."

He could see fear in her eyes and it made something inside his chest crack. He leaned forward, taking the cup out of her hand and pulled her into a hug.

"Porter would never allow that to happen. I will never allow that to happen. We're going to figure this out."

He kept her in his arms a moment more then stood up.

"Come on, let me show you around the house. Your therapist will be calling you in a few hours to get everything settled with your therapy schedule. She'll be staying with you since you wouldn't let me do it."

She took a harried breath. "Kenneth, I can't let you stay with me. It just wouldn't look right. Might also cause a problem when it comes to your mother's trial too."

Kenneth stood still in front of her. "What do you mean?"

"What do you think her attorney is going to say to all of this? He has to defend her somehow. The best way is to throw the blame on someone else. Like her son who somehow managed to steal all of her husband's money away from her. Or possibly said son used his connections with his godfather's top cop, who he's living with and therefore sleeping with to frame her. Juries are unpredictable, Kenneth, and in this day and age, they love a good conspiracy to sink their teeth into."

Kenneth shook his head as a premonition of his mother's trail walked across his mind. Heart was right; Jacqueline Searlington would have no problems using either of them as a scapegoat for her actions. He had to stop her. She'd ruined his sister, nearly ruined his niece, he couldn't let her ruin Heart as well.

"Come on, Heart," he spoke absently. His brain was already attempting to work out a solution to their problem. "Let me finish showing you where everything is, I have a few errands I need to complete before the end of business." She nodded her head, pushing up from the sofa.

"If all goes well, I will be back tonight for dinner. Dr. Bailer will be here soon."

"Bailer?"

"Yeah, one of the best OT/PT specialists I know of."

"Why does that name sound familiar to me?"

"She's renowned in her field. You've probably heard of her in the media at some point."

"Kenneth, I'm a cop, with a cop's insurance plan. Why the hell is a highly regarded specialist coming to treat me in my rented home? What did you do, Kenneth?"

He shook his head. "Heart, I'm not about to argue with you. You just sat on that chair and cried for fear of losing your badge. If your arm doesn't heal properly your prediction will come true. This is not negotiable," his tone clipped and final, leaving no room for discussion on the matter.

Heart simply nodded.

"So let's begin this tour."

~

*K*enneth drove back to Brooklyn headed for the very same hospital he'd just left. He didn't even know if he'd be able to pull off what he had in mind, but he had to try. He tapped the Bluetooth button on his steering wheel and spoke aloud. "Call A.J. Tenetti."

He tapped his finger anxiously against the wheel while he waited for the call to connect.

"Kenneth, what do you need?"

He smiled. Alexis-Jeovanni Tenetti, AKA A.J. was never one for niceties. Getting straight to the point was her way of cutting through most of the bullshit she had to deal with as a lawyer.

"This thing with my mother has to be over. I want to move on with my life, I can't do that with my mother's pending trial looming over my head. I need you to—"

"Kenneth, stop. I can't have this discussion with you." "You're my lawyer," he snapped.

"You hired me, but in this matter, I'm acting as your mother's attorney, not yours. Whatever you're planning, I can't know anything about. It could turn out to be something that could come back to bite us both in the ass later."

Kenneth took a deep breath and blew it out slowly as the buildings and houses he drove by passed around him. "All right," he said. "Get over to County's prison ward as quickly as you can. My mother's going to need her lawyer."

"Give me thirty," she said and quickly ended the call.

A.J. Tenetti may not have been able to hear his plan out, but his uncle David certainly had. His uncle David had assured him that he would move the other chess pieces in to play while Kenneth was driving. If only this would work, he might just be able to have what was fast becoming a need instead of simply a desire. His mother had stolen so much from him over the years, this he wasn't going to surrender. When he arrived, he went to the information desk that greeted him once he walked through the automated doors.

"Jacqueline Searlington please?" he asked the young woman sitting behind the desk.

She quickly punched the keys of the keyboard while looking at the computer screen. He saw a quick widening of her eyes when she looked at the screen in front of her. Kenneth would give it to her though; she quickly recovered and pasted a trained friendly smile on her face when she looked at him.

"Mrs. Searlington has a visitation restriction placed on her visitors list. I will need to see identification," she said with that same smile.

Kenneth nodded and knew he was fucked. There was no way his mother would have him on that list. He reached for his driver's license, affixing a similar smile to his face. He handed the young woman his license and waited for her to reject him. She reached for the license, checked back on the screen, and then looked up to smile at him.

"All right, Mr. Searlington. Let me just print your pass out and you can go upstairs to the patient's room."

Too afraid to show the shock on his face, Kenneth schooled his features and accepted the visitor's pass printed on the white sticker paper. He walked toward the elevator entrance and stopped briefly for the hospital officer to check his pass and grant him permission to the elevators.

When he stepped off the elevator, he was greeted by a burly corrections officer.

Apparently, Kenneth's arrival had been expected. The officer asked for his identification, and for him to remove all metal objects from his person. Once that was done, he swept an electronic wand over him in search of any contraband. When the wand remained quiet, Kenneth was directed to walk through the standing metal detector at the side of the officer's post. Once finished, the officer instructed him to remove his shoes and frisked him—smoothing his hands all over Kenneth's person in a uniform and clinical way.

Disturbed by the intimate contact, Kenneth stepped back into his shoes, and walked down the corridor. When he reached the gated door, a loud buzzing noise occurred and he heard a garbled voice through a static-like loudspeaker tell him to open the door, enter, and walk to the third door on the right.

He followed the directions and came upon another officer sitting in front of the door.

The corrections officer stood and greeted him, "Mr. Searlington." It was a statement, not a question. He was certain the officer's colleagues had warned her through whatever communications link they shared of Kenneth's arrival.

Kenneth looked down at the DOC badge high on the woman's chest to look for a name. "Hello, Officer...Dunning," he smiled briefly at the young woman. She was of average build and height with the loveliest shade of silky, mocha skin that he'd ever seen on an African-American woman.

A friendly smile curved her lips making her lifted, full cheeks round out in to a lovely heart-shaped face. She extended her hand in greeting. "Your mother's been eager to see you."

"How is she?" he asked.

"Well, she's alive. If you want to know any particulars of her health, you'll have to ask her. I'm not allowed to share that with anyone. I know she's not very happy with the accommodations at the moment or the company either," she said, still smiling as she pointed to herself.

"Don't take it personally, my mother has never responded well to authority."

"The authority thing might be a problem too, but I kinda get the feeling it's more likely the fact that I'm not her favorite color in the crayon box."

He winced as if her words had physically struck him. Wow, even here on this prison ward surrounded by corrections officers, his mother had shown her truly despicable self literally to this woman. No sense in pretending things weren't exactly as they were.

"Sorry about that, Officer Dunning. My mother hasn't been known to embrace diversity much in her lifetime. Please accept my apologies on her behalf. There are few things about my mother that I am proud of, but of all her faults, that's probably the one I'm most embarrassed by."

The officer nodded and smiled up at him again. "They called Jesus worse," she chuckled. "My skin's not so thin that I can't take a little verbal abuse from an old lady.

Especially one that's in her current predicament."

Kenneth smiled at that. This Officer Dunning had quite a bit of spunk to her, she almost reminded him of another beautiful mocha woman in law enforcement. Kenneth smiled again, and walked inside of the hospital room.

His mother sat in her hospital bed cloaked in her veneer of superiority. It didn't matter that she was essentially imprisoned in this hospital room—her freedom taken away until some judiciary figure bade her permission to leave—no Jacqueline Searlington still believed that she was better, smarter, and more entitled than anyone else.

She had a fake smile plastered to her face, the same one she'd worn for most of his life.

"So you've finally decided to come check on your mother? Really, Kenneth, a good son would have been here the minute they brought me to the hospital for surgery. I at least thought you would have had them transfer me from that hospital across the street to a more acceptable medical facility. This place is so beneath the Searlington name."

"Mother, this is a prison hospital ward. The only reason you weren't brought here to begin with is Lieutenant MacKenzie was rushed here for treatment. They didn't want the police officer in the same hospital as her assailant."

"Assailant?" She waved her hand in a nonchalant manner. "I did little more than protect myself from that tyrant."

"Mother, cut the crap," he forced through clenched teeth.

"Kenneth—"

He cut her off, "No, Mother, let's not waste our time engaging in verbal warfare. I'm here to give you an option to save your life. If you are as smart as you believe yourself to be, you'll take what I'm offering."

Just as he finished speaking, the door squealed open and the rest of his anticipated party walked through door. First, his mother's attorney—or really his attorney acting on his mother's behalf—A.J. Tenetti, a petite woman with a café au lait complexion and a youthful face that often gave her opponents a false sense of security and power. She was tiny, she was sexy as sin with curves that no woman as small in stature as she should possess, but she was also a beast in the court-room. His uncle David entered the room next, followed behind two Caucasian men that were unknown to Kenneth.

"What are all these people doing here, Kenneth?" his mother's voice drawing his attention from the door.

"Mother I'm sure you remember your attorney, A.J. as well as

Uncle David," his hand swept in the direction of both of them, then moved to the first of the unknown men in the room.

"Cecil Boothe, district attorney for Kings County and this is my executive assistant district attorney, Samuel McCoy," the man chimed in.

Jacqueline's eyes squinted in suspicion. "Why are all of you here?" she asked coolly.

Cecil stepped forward. "Mrs. Searlington, my colleague and I are here to make you an offer than you shouldn't refuse. You are currently being charged with a number of felony crimes..." he pulled a folder from his attaché case. "...not the least of which are two counts of attempted murder of a police officer. By the way, for those two charges, we're seeking the death penalty."

"Death penalty?" His mother's eyes turned to A.J. "The only person that died was my drug-addicted daughter. I had nothing to do with her death. How can they seek the death penalty when I didn't kill anyone? Not to mention there's no death penalty in New York."

A.J. glanced at Kenneth. He wasn't certain, but he thought he saw a hint of anger, maybe annoyance, in her eyes. She pulled her eyes back to his mother.

"Jacqueline," A.J. said calmly. "New York State doesn't have a death penalty. However, there are special circumstances where the United States Federal Government does allow for the death penalty to be applied to an attempted murder charge. The Federal Government has what's called the Continuing Criminal Enterprise statute or Kingpin statute. It was designed to apprehend criminals who were organizers of major drug crime syndicates. If an individual commits a murder, attempted murder, or kidnapping in order to further the organizations agenda, then the prosecution is allowed to seek the death penalty."

A.J. turned to the two prosecutors standing in the room. "So how exactly are you going to try to pin this on my client? She's a socialite for god's sake, what criminal enterprise was she running?"

"Selwyn's Drug cartel of course," Samuel said.

A.J. shook her head and rolled her eyes. She fixed her gaze on the district attorney.

"You're really going to admit that you can't handle a high-profile case like this and just hand it over to the federal prosecutor? That should do wonders for your campaign come election-time next year."

Kenneth watched a brief tick of muscle under Boothe's eye. Direct hit, A.J. always made them.

"You two know this is bullshit," she said. "You bring whatever you have to link her to Selwyn and I will shoot everything down. There's no way a jury will believe this sophisticated heiress, widow to one of New York's most esteemed citizens was in any way connected to Selwyn. She's a senior citizen, life in prison would serve the same purpose. I'm confident I could tie this bogus play up in court for a lot of years if the two of you press it."

She laid her briefcase on top of the bedside table and removed a legal pad and pen from it. She closed it with a defined click, sat down in the chair next to the bed and crossed one well-toned leg over the other. It was a move he had seen her perform many times over. It was her let's-get-down-to-business pose.

"Gentleman," she addressed the three law enforcement representatives in the room. She waved her hand dismissively through the air. "Let's cut the shit and get down to business. What is it you really want?"

The district attorney nodded to his assistant Samuel to continue. Samuel pulled a document from his case and walked it over to where A.J. was sitting.

"Ms. Tenetti, we are willing to forgo the capital punishment if your client pleads guilty to all of the charges she's been indicted for."

Kenneth watched A.J. pull a slender pair of black reading glasses from her pocket and place them carefully on her delicate nose. She read briefly through the document Samuel had given her, then raised her eyes above the brim of the glasses to look at him.

Kenneth smiled when Samuel stepped back slightly. He'd seen A.J. cut a man down to size with that glare and he wouldn't want to be on the receiving end of it.

"In exchange for what, Mr. McCoy? What does my client get if she confesses to all of these charges you're accusing her of?"

"Accusing her of?" McCoy questioned. "Ms. Tenetti, this is pretty much an open and shut case. Everyone knows what your client did, knows that she's guilty."

A.J. removed her glasses and gave McCoy her full gaze. "That's where you're wrong, Mr. McCoy, I know what my client was accused of, but no, I don't know what she did and neither do you. The law presumes her innocence until you can prove her guilt. You haven't done that yet, and I'll be there fighting you every step of the way to prevent you from doing so. Now again I ask, what do you want?"

McCoy loosened his tie slightly, a dressing down from A.J. often made one feel as if he couldn't breathe. "Life in prison without parole inside of a maximum security prison."

A.J. stood up in one fluid motion. "Everyone out. I need a moment to talk to Mr.

Searlington and my client."

The remaining three men nodded and left the room.

A.J. turned to Jacqueline who was poised to speak. "Not one single solitary word." She pulled Kenneth into a far corner in the room. "What the fuck was that about Searlington? Did you do this?" her words soft, but filled with inescapable fire.

"I need for her to pay for what she did so I can move on with my life."

"Your life, this isn't about your life, this is about your mother's life. She's either going to die in prison, or die from a needle in her arm. This is your mother. How could you want that?"

Kenneth ran a hand across the back of his aching neck. This entire ordeal was beginning to wear on him, he needed to resolve it quickly. "I was there, I saw her put a gun to my niece's head. She was afraid for her life, and the only thing I could do was stand there. I couldn't protect her. If my mother had decided to pull that trigger, there would have been nothing I could have done."

A.J. lowered her eyes briefly. When they met Kenneth's again there was a softness there he'd never seen in them before.

"I have nieces too. I love them dearly. I couldn't imagine seeing them go through something like that." She lowered her eyes again before speaking. "But Kenneth, this is your mother."

"She's the woman that bore me, but she's never been a mother to me or my dead sister. She terrorized us in that apartment, A.J., and I couldn't do anything about it. I couldn't save Merridith and I couldn't save my sister. The only person that stepped up to help, that did anything about it, got a bullet in her dominant arm for her trouble. That woman needs me, but she won't accept my help because of how it could impact my mother's trial."

He ran an angry hand through his loose tresses, gathering them at his nape—cursing himself for not carrying his usual elastic band. "The only way I can help her is if there is no trial. After all she sacrificed for me and my family, she has to be all right. I have to make certain of that."

A.J. nodded her head and pursed her gloss-covered lips. "How long have you been fucking Lieutenant MacKenzie," she paused when Kenneth raised a brow. "I'm not stupid, Kenneth. I did read the police report. Other than the lieutenant, the only other officer injured was male. She was the only 'she' hurt in that apartment that lived." She placed a gentle hand on his arm. "Are you really certain you want to do this?"

The muscles of his face tightened. "Not that it's any of your business, but I'm not sleeping with Heart MacKenzie. I'm trying to help her. This is the only way I can ensure my mother doesn't hurt any of us again and get MacKenzie the help she needs."

"You know I could fight this, you know I could say to hell with you and that bogus ass D.A. and move forward on my own. She might not go free with all of the evidence against her, but I could at least minimize how much time she went away for."

Kenneth leaned his shoulder against the wall letting it bear some of the burden his shoulders felt. He weighed the words sitting in his mouth carefully.

Alex-Jeovanni was much more than just someone he paid for services rendered. She was a long-time friend. They grew up together in the same influential circles as children. The only difference, she came from a normal family, his was turbulent at best, psychotic at worst. The people she lived at home with weren't plotting her destruction. That, and the fact that her family had more money than the Searlingtons—hell, more than God really. That fact alone forced many of the closeted bigots that they often had to deal with in their social dealings to at least pretend they had a modicum of respect for her.

But to him, she'd always been A.J., the young girl with the big brain who always had an answer for every question he'd ever asked. He'd gone to school with and played ball with her older brother John. He'd even stood as best man a few years ago when John had married the love of his life, Maxine. What he was about to say to her could rip all of that history apart.

He took a deep breath and let the words slip past his lips in a quiet whisper. "I'm sure you could," Kenneth said. "But it would have to be pro bono, because you wouldn't get a dime from me." Hard eyes fixated on him as he pushed himself to go further. "Did I forget to mention that outside of a stipend that I give to her, my mother has absolutely no money of her own? If you press this issue, I will stop signing those hefty checks I pay you."

A.J. blinked once, and then twice and just like that the hardline persona that she used in court was in place. "That was a low-blow, even for you, Kenneth. I don't like threats; you know me well enough to know I don't respond well to them. Your little play here backfires if I tell you to fuck your money and yourself, and I do this job anyway. Who do you think is more likely to win this, A.J. your friend, or A.J. the pissed off lawyer with a legal arsenal you wouldn't believe?"

He swallowed. Kenneth knew that if there was one attorney that could get his mother off of these very serious charges, it would be the woman huddled in the corner with him.

Going at her hard wasn't going to yield the results he was looking for. He needed this over, needed his mother to pay for her crimes.

Maybe if he hadn't witnessed all that she'd done, maybe if his poor sister survived. But he knew it, and he couldn't unknow it. And as long as he knew it, he also knew he wouldn't be able to live with his mother not being forced to surrender to justice for what she'd done to his family, to him, and to Heart.

"If I yank your funding now, would you legally be obligated to continue as my mother's attorney?"

She shook her head. "No, at this point there would be no violation of the law on my part. It's just, I don't know how this plays out against my own ethics. I just feel like this isn't right."

He placed a hand on her shoulder and looked into clear hazel eyes that sparkled with just a hint of green.

"If that were Darius' mother sitting in that hospital bed and you had witnessed her do the things that I saw my mother do, all for the sake of capital gain and nothing more— how far would you press to make certain she paid?"

She glanced over to Jacqueline who was hard-pressed to figure out what the two were whispering about. Then she returned her gaze to Kenneth. "I won't just sacrifice my client and abandon her. I will tell her what her options are, tell her what her odds are, and allow her to make the decision. As for not paying my fee, if that is your wish, I will refer her to some suitable legal aide attorneys to further assist her in this matter."

Kenneth remained in the corner while A.J. returned to his mother's bedside. Anxious to have this matter concluded. Anxious to be free to help Heart.

"Jacqueline," A.J. said. "You've got a real problem here. There are cops who saw you do all of the things you're accused of. Worst yet, there is footage of the things you did. The nail in the coffin of this proverbial clusterfuck is that the prosecution has every intention of calling your son as a witness and your granddaughter if necessary. Juries don't like it when kids are put on the stand. It will make you look worse if that's even possible."

"Are you saying you can't win this case?" Jacqueline asked.

"I'm telling you that it is highly unlikely that you will walk away from this without a very lengthy prison sentence. It is my legal estimation that if you don't take their deal, and they do turn this case over to the federal prosecutor, you could very likely be sentenced to death."

His mother's eyes found him leaning against the wall in the very corner A.J. had left him leaning against. They carried hatred in them. There was no pretending, his mother hated him, but more than that, she wanted his destruction.

"I bet you're so satisfied with yourself. This is your fault. If you had just given me what was rightfully mine..."

Kenneth held up a hand. "Stop Mother, we've been over this. I didn't take anything from you; my father chose to leave it to me, not you. He never intended for you to have his money. So cooking up and executing this crazy and evil scheme of yours, was all your own doing. You sealed your fate the moment you sought to bring harm to that precious little girl."

"Ken—" Jacqueline's words were brought to a stop when the doors opened, and David Porter and the two prosecutors returned inside of the room.

"Well, Ms. Tenetti, what's your client's decision?"

"In a rush, Mr. McCoy? Can't you give a woman at least a few moments to decide her fate?"

He shook his head, a small smirk pulling the edges of his mouth up. Kenneth wished the man would stop trying to show one-upman-ship and just get this deal done. Kenneth placed his gaze on A.J., knowing she lived to knock guys like this McCoy person on their asses. It was as if he saw the amber flame burst alive in her eyes, and ignite the fabulous legal mind that had made him so much money over the years.

"Yes, my client has made a decision...she'll plead guilty to all counts and take twenty-five years to life with a chance at parole at fifteen years for with each count to be served concurrently with the sentences for all the charges against her in a medium security prison."

Kenneth just shook his head and looked at his friend with a mixture of pride and frustration. Only Alexis-Jeovanni Tenetti would be able to figure out a way to both defend her client to the best of her abilities and still do as he'd ask as well—keeping his mother locked away for the remainder of her years. It was a beautiful thing to watch that woman work.

"So what's it going to be, gentlemen?" She smiled as she removed her tablet from her briefcase and tapped away at its screen. "Are we ready to put this thing to bed?"

CHAPTER 11

*H*eart remained on the sofa where Kenneth had left her. She was tired of laying around, but too groggy from her pain medication to do much else. She pushed herself up on her good shoulder and rolled until she was in an upright position. She reached for the phone on the coffee table to read the time. Kenneth had been gone for four hours and the therapist hadn't shown up yet.

A musical chiming sound pulled her attention from the clock on her phone to the door. She pushed to the end of the couch and slowly stood up. Taking a minute to gather her bearings, she walked slowly to the front door.

A twist of the knob gave way to the strange sight of Kenneth with a large rolling suitcase in one hand, a smaller case strategically secured to that. On the opposite shoulder he carried a large duffle bag and in the attached hand was a neatly folded garment bag held by its handle.

She stepped back just in time to watch Kenneth buzz past her and relieve his burdens at the bottom of the staircase that led to the bedrooms on the second level.

"Kenneth, is Dr. Bailer behind you, is that all of her stuff?"

Kenneth shook his head. "No, this is my stuff."

"Are you going on vacation or something?"

He shook his head again. "No, I'm not, I'm rooming with a friend to help her out since she was shot in the arm protecting my family."

Heart closed her eyes against the throbbing ache in her shoulder. It was time for another painkiller. She moved toward the kitchen to get her pills, but then stopped before her first step. If she swallowed a pill now she wouldn't be lucid enough to talk some sense into the man that was standing in front of her.

"You're not moving in here with me, Kenneth. We've already established that it would be a conflict of interest because of your mother's pending trial."

"Yes we did establish that, but my mother's trial is no longer a concern," he said. "Kenneth, you're mother assaulted two police officers and kidnapped a child. I'm pretty certain she's going to have a trial. The only way she doesn't get one is if she..." she raised her eyes to his. "What did you do, Kenneth?"

"She confessed, Heart; I didn't have to do anything."

She eyed him with suspicion, looking for the normal tells that people gave away when they weren't telling the truth. "I don't see Jacqueline Searlington as a woman who wishes to take responsibility for her actions." She continued to look at him through slanted eyes. "Did you give her an incentive in order to convince her to confess?"

He stood tall, looking her directly in the eye, no glancing away, no blinking, no tells.

"I didn't have to convince her of anything. The prosecutor threatened her with a kingpin charge in connection to her alliance with Selwyn. He gave her the option of the death penalty or life in prison. Her attorney was able to get the prosecution to agree to twenty-five to life with a chance at parole in fifteen years. She saw the writing on the wall. She took the plea deal, a judge was brought in, and she allocuted right there in her prison-hospital bed."

Heart heard him, but she was still suspicious of him. It just felt all too easy. She'd expected a knock-down, long fight from Jacqueline. Heart had seen her eyes when she'd held a gun to Merridith's head, there was no remorse there. She wasn't sorry; it just didn't make sense. Why on Earth would she give up? The Searlingtons had money; no doubt she had major representation on her side. "Why would she give up her day in court? Even if she were being threatened by the prosecutor, she had the clout and the muscle to drag this thing out for a very long time."

Something just wasn't adding up and she didn't like the feeling of being played, not by Kenneth, not by anyone.

"Kenneth, if you did something to make this a reality, I need to know about it. I can't have crazy shit coming back to haunt me because you did something illegal or unethical in my name without my knowledge." She took in a quick breath and continued. "Internal affairs will not care whether I knew about your scheme or not, they will say I profited from it and they will hang me. Even if they don't, the stench will follow me and taint me as a cop on the take. I can't have that."

He nodded, pulled her into the warmth of his arms, and held her as tightly as he dared with her injured shoulder.

"I promise you, I did nothing that would bring harm to you. My mother's conviction is legal and binding, and cannot be overturned. I made sure of it."

A sigh of relief left her lungs setting free the bundle of tension that she'd been holding inside. She hadn't even realized that she'd been scared. Scared of what, her professional integrity being compromised by Kenneth's actions? Or was it something she was beginning to feel would bring her more harm than the loss of her professional reputation?

She clung tighter to him, inhaling the fresh scent of his body wash and cologne. He tightened his hold on her as she burrowed deeper inside his arms, until the cold chill her fear had brought slowly ebbed away. No, she wasn't afraid of compromising herself professionally, she was afraid of losing this, losing him. The possibility that Kenneth had done something to compromise himself, compromise his ability to be here, to do this, to give her this, that was where her fear was really rooted.

When had this man become so important to her? Why? How?

Before the shooting, he'd been an annoying family member in a case she'd been working. From the moment she woke up in that hospital, his presence alone was enough to calm the anxiety that she battled every day.

That was another thing that was driving her crazy at the moment. Why was her anxiety so out of her control right now? True thought it was because of the shooting. She said experiencing one trauma could often bring the associated fears and symptoms of prior trauma to the forefront. She didn't doubt her cousin's medical knowledge, but damn, she didn't even remember much of what happened that night. She remembered the shooting, but she hadn't been afraid of that. She didn't really think her injuries were enough to bring harm to her initially. It wasn't until she felt the edges of consciousness slipping away from her that she began to panic, began to feel the fear traveling through her vessels just as quickly as the gushing stream of blood flowing from her wound.

One of the few lucid moments she had after her collapse in that nasty, piss-scented elevator was opening her eyes in the rocking ambulance, Kenneth at her side holding her hand, promising he was going to take care of her. She remembered the intensity in his cerulean gaze, felt the warmth of it wash over her. His stare made her feel as if she were wrapped in a blanket of comfort and trust.

She'd never had that before, she'd never trusted anyone. But in that bus, with the chaos of the sirens and the EMT's working on her, surrounding her, she knew she would be all right, because Kenneth had promised her he would make it so.

"Heart, your statement has already been logged. As far as all pertinent parties are concerned, this case is officially closed. I'm no longer a principal in an on-going investigation you're working on."

She tried to burrow herself inside of him even further. If it were possible, she would have been living on the inside of him right now. His proclamation had a palpable effect.

She was free to reach for the calm he alone could provide for her.

She inhaled one final breath of his aroma and slowly stepped out of his embrace.

"I guess I'd better get myself together for Dr. Bailer. I thought you were her when the bell rang," she said, her eyes concentrated on the floor beneath them.

"She's not coming today," he spoke softly. "She was only coming at this time to have an initial consultation with you. Since you're no longer staying here alone, she doesn't really need to start until your doctor says it's all right for you to begin therapy."

"So it's just going to be the two of us?" she asked quietly.

"Is that a problem? Do you want me to go? I could always hire a nurse for you if it would make you feel better."

She shook her head. "No, I can't take anything else from you. You've done way too much already. Getting the owner of this house to rent it to me, setting up my rehab, it's too much, I owe you too much, Kenneth."

He took a steady finger and lifted her chin. There again in the midst of that azure gaze was her refuge. "You owe me nothing. The only things I want from you are your recovery and your friendship. I feel like the latter is looking more and more likely, the first, we just have to work on."

He smiled at her and that inviting warmth that only seemed to emanate from him began to shroud her from the inside out again. Before she could realize or stop it, her mouth was curving into a matching smile. Before long, that smile turned into a yawn that she was quickly trying to stifle.

She saw Kenneth's smile widen and dipped her head in embarrassment.

"I'm sorry; these damn meds keep me tired."

Kenneth shook his head. "No worries," he said through smiling lips. "Let me get your meds out of the kitchen and I'll meet you in your room with something cold to wash them down. It's late anyway. It's time for the patient to get some shut-eye."

She gave a quick nod and headed up the stairs to her room. She walked over to the dresser hoping her nightclothes would be somewhere in here. Kenneth had stored away her belongings while she was still in the hospital. She hadn't gotten around to asking him just how he'd organized things.

She opened one drawer, and then another to find the t-shirt and pajama pants she was looking for. She walked over to the side of the bed and pushed down the sweatpants she was wearing. Once they were around her ankles she sat on the bed and toed them off the rest of the way. She looked down at her shirt—a wife-beater t-shirt with a built-in shelf bra. Thank God for it. She really didn't see how she was going to be able to put on a regular bra with only one working arm right now. She wiggled her good arm out of one of the straps, and then slowly pushed the remaining strap down her injured arm. When she was sure she wouldn't hurt herself, she pushed the t-shirt down her hips and took the few steps to the en suite bathroom.

She bathed and washed her hair as best she could with one hand, especially since that hand wasn't her dominant hand. She couldn't comb the tangles free from her waist-length hair. She decided to be extra generous with the leave-in conditioner instead. Hopefully she could convince True to stay in town long-enough to help her with a moderated hair routine.

After haphazardly drying herself off with one hand and arm, she padded naked over to the bed where she'd left her nightclothes. Pajama pants on, she looked at the t-shirt with the narrow head and no room for wiggling her size ten frame through. Damn, how was she going to work this? Just then her bad arm throbbed just to remind her how impossible this task was.

"Fuck it," she snapped, and sat down heavily on the side of the bed. She picked up the shirt, tried to slowly pull the injured arm through first. She bit the inside of her lip at the pain that was starting to pulse in her arm.

She figured out quickly that attempt wasn't going to work. She removed the shirt from her aching arm and decided to pull it over her head as she normally would, and just suffer the consequences.

She pulled the shirt over both wrists and attempted to lift both arms to put the shirt on. Bad idea. The pain that tore down her arm felt like a hot, jagged piece of metal slicing through the muscle and tissue beneath her skin.

The pain was too much. Darkness was threatening the edges of her sight. She hadn't heard herself calling out in pain, but she must have. She opened her eyes to see the flash that was Kenneth racing to her bedside.

He didn't say anything, the questions resting firmly in his blue eyes. He looked her over, passed a light hand over her arm to make certain she hadn't damaged herself any further.

He must have been satisfied that her injured arm was safe from her stupidity. He cradled her in his arms and pulled her to her feet. While she stood, nestled within his arms, he leaned down slightly to pull the bedcovers down. He gently sat her back down on the plush mattress and laid her against the mountain of pillows at her back. When he was certain she was stable, he pulled the cool-to-touch fabric of the covers up to her chest.

Naked. That's what her mind processed when the pain started to recede, her torso was naked, and he'd just covered her up to keep her from exposing herself further.

She felt his gentle thumb collect the tear that was hanging tentatively to her eyelash. He stood and walked from the room. She barely had time to adjust her position in the bed when she watched him walk back into her room holding something in his hand.

He sat at her bedside and unfolded the item. He gently laced her aching arm through the sleeves of a pajama shirt. From the looks of how loose it was on her arm—his pajama shirt. When he was satisfied her arm was comfortably inside of it, he pulled her torso to him gently, then proceeded to get the shirt on the rest of the way.

He worked quickly, efficiently, and gently, ever so gently. He motioned for her to rest her back against the pillows again. As she did, he went to work fastening the large buttons that pulled the edges of the shirt together and gave her the modesty she desired.

When he was done, he handed her pain pills, watched her toss them into her mouth, then handed her a cool glass of water. She swallowed the liquid and returned the glass to him.

She turned away from him, too ashamed to look into his eyes and find pity resting there. She lay half on her good shoulder, half on her back, and closed her eyes, waiting for the click of the closed door to signal his departure.

It never came.

She felt a weight press down on the opposite side of the bed. Soon, the cool on her back was replaced by welcoming warmth that begged her to submit. Without argument, without resistance, she submitted and was rewarded with a comforting arm secured around her waist. The arm tightened and pulled her closer to him. There, lying with her back to Kenneth's front, she forgot about the pain, and her embarrassment and welcomed the relief and assurance the blanket of his body offered and slept.

~

*H*eart awoke to the annoying sound of some news-radio advertisement. She went to slap the power button down when her parted eyes caught sight of a note next to a glass of water and a dose of her pain pills.

Heart, I've laid out your morning dose of pain medication. Take it. Breakfast is downstairs in the fridge, just heat it up in the microwave. I have a very busy morning and afternoon ahead, but when I get back, you and I are going to have a talk about you adhering to your physical limitations and asking for help when you need it.

Kenneth

The smart-ass comment was just about to leap off of her tongue when her hearing zoned in on the voice on the radio.

"...we watched as Kenneth Searlington, brother of the deceased, arrived nearly thirty minutes ago to pay his final respects. According to insiders, the actual services for Karolyn Searlington are not scheduled for nearly two hours. We will be here for continued coverage throughout the day. Back to you, Mike."

"Son of a bitch," she breathed heavily. "Why wouldn't he tell me today was

Karolyn's funeral?"

She found her phone and touched the picture of one of the familiar faces on her favorites list.

"Smyth," the sound of her fellow officer's voice yanked a smile from her.

"Bryan, can you give me a ride to Karolyn Searlington's funeral?"

"Sure, I was getting ready to walk out the door now. Cap says you're staying somewhere in Woodmere. Send me the address and I'll be there in twenty."

Twenty minutes later she was dressed in slacks and a camisole. She found a buttondown shirt in her closet and thought twice about attempting to put it on by herself. Not wanting a repeat of last night she decided to wait for Bryan, he would help her.

The sound of the doorbell brought her out of her room and down the stairs with her shirt in hand. The only word that could describe Bryan's expression was shock. She knew her appearance was far from what he'd usually expect of her. Her hair was always in a tight bun, not one strand out of place. Never in all the years he'd known her had she let it down. She ran her hand self-consciously over her head.

"I know I look a mess." She'd gone through nearly half a bottle of leave-in conditioner and battled with a wide-toothed comb to get her strands safely free of those blasted tangles. After that, her good arm was so tired she couldn't bother with trying to put it up somehow.

"No, actually, it looks good down. I don't think I've ever seen it down before."

She shook her head. "Don't get used to it either. As soon as I can get my shoulder halfway up I'm slapping a bun back into this stuff."

He laughed as he crossed the threshold and she closed the door behind him.

"Speaking of my bum shoulder..." she lifted her shirt in her good hand. "...mind helping your lieutenant out?" she asked.

"My lieutenant, no, my friend, anytime." He took the shirt from her hand and helped her finagle her way into it without much discomfort.

She went to grab her sling, but then thought a day trip outside would probably be better suited by the brace that strapped her arm against her body and would keep it immobilized. She wiggled it on, then closed the clips in place to keep her arm safe and secure.

"Let's be out, Sergeant," she said with a smile and lead the way out the door.

She was quiet inside of Bryan's unmarked department car. Her eyes were busy adjusting to being on the passenger side. She always drove, always, but for the last two days, and for the foreseeable future, she'd be sitting on this side of the car.

"So, you've found yourself some nice digs out here in Woodmere?"

She dragged her attention away from the window and looked at Bryan.

"I didn't find anything. I found myself temporarily homeless while I was in the hospital. Kenneth knows the owner of the house, he agreed to let me rent it while he decides if he wants to put it on the market or not."

"Damn, if Kenneth can hook you up like that on our salary, then I need to talk to that man about finding me a new place."

She laughed, Bryan was right the house was beautiful. She had no doubt that she was able to afford it because Kenneth had worked his realtor's magic.

"You and Searlington have become close it seems," he said casually, almost too casually. She recognized the tactic. They taught it in investigator 101. Get your suspect to trust you, make everything seem mundane and unimportant, then you slam the hammer down.

"You got something you want to ask, then ask it, Smyth."

She saw him glance her way briefly then return his gaze to the road.

"MacKenzie, are you seeing Kenneth Searlington?" he asked directly. No pulled punches.

"Yes...I mean...no...I mean, not in the way you're thinking," she said.

"That sounds a little convoluted," he replied.

"That just so happens to be a perfect way of describing this thing," she said, her head shaking, trying to make sense of the craziness she seemed to be in the middle of at the moment. "Some crazy things have been happening to me since the shooting. Things I never anticipated, things I never thought I would have to deal with."

"Are you all right, MacKenzie?"

She nodded. "I'm getting there. With Kenneth's help I definitely am getting there.

But this isn't something I can really discuss with anyone in the department." She hoped he understood the unspoken, *not even you*, at the end of that sentence.

"What about your fam, they would help. They've seen worse stuff than we have."

She didn't disagree with Bryan; her family had seen more trauma than most. But she didn't want them worrying about the ugliness that rolled around in her head. They'd done enough worrying about her as a child; she couldn't go down that claustrophobic road again.

"Just because my family is crazier than I am doesn't mean they're equipped to handle my issues, and it certainly doesn't mean I want them involved either. They're great, but sometimes the Amare tribe can be a little too much to handle."

He nodded; Bryan had spent a considerable amount of time with her family while dating her cousin Jussy. The family still contacted him after the breakup still to this day trying to see if there was a way to fix whatever had gone wrong between the two.

"The Amare tribe is special, that's for certain," he said distantly.

She wondered if he was reliving some of those moments that he'd spent with Jussy, her uncle, and the rest of the Amare siblings.

"I'm not even really sure why it seems that Kenneth has what I need. Right now he seems to be the only thing that pushes the craziness aside."

"Did you know him before the case, is that why you're so attached now?"

She shook her head. "No, I met him at the station when Porter gave me the case. Truth be told, I couldn't really stand him when all of this started. Hell, most of the time he still gets on my damn nerves, but there's definitely something behind the playboy billionaire façade that's reaching out to me right now." "Romantic?" he asked.

"I don't really think so, more like human kindness. The night of Merri's rescue, the two of us just experienced something in that apartment and the elevator together."

"That why you're going to the funeral?"

She was quiet for a moment. She felt for Karolyn Searlington. All the money in the world and she still couldn't save herself from an evil bitch of a mother. But Heart knew that for all of the sympathy she carried for the late Karolyn Searlington, there was only one reason she'd dragged herself out of bed this morning.

"Yeah, that's why I'm going."

Bryan nodded. "I know you've been dealing with something big since I met you in the academy. I never bothered to ask what it was 'cause you didn't really seem like it was something you wanted to talk about. If Kenneth is helping you work through stuff, helping you find your footing, then I'm all for it."

She nodded, briefly fidgeting in her seat as her one-time partner's insight washed over her.

"Whatever it is that's happening between the two of you, MacKenzie, as long as it's good, go for it. Just don't let it get in the way of your career. You know how the NYPD is. You're their golden-child one day, and being forced into early retirement or outright hung on a cross the next. Technically, there's no conflict of interest since the case is closed. Although legal, the way this case was closed could bring a shitstorm of hell on your head if the wrong person looked into it."

She turned her head in Bryan's direction. "What exactly do you mean? As far as I know Jacqueline Searlington confessed."

Bryan nodded, eyes still on the road. "She did, but some could question that if they chose to look a little harder."

"Bryan, stop with the cryptic bullshit, either tell me or drop the subject."

"Listen, MacKenzie, Porter has already put the kibosh on any of us telling you the happs surrounding the conclusion of this case. Quite frankly, I'm scared of you, but I need my pension more, so I'm not fucking with Porter just so you can be in the know. Just keep things quiet for as long as you can."

~

The room seemed to be dark except for the harsh glow of light that was hanging from his sister's casket. They were thirty-three, his sister shouldn't have a casket. He'd assumed they would have another forty years before either of them had to worry about burying the other. Apparently his math was off and they hadn't as much time as he'd believed.

His sister lay there still and quiet. Her complexion seemed off, nothing most would notice, but as her twin, he knew, this was all wrong. It wasn't that the funeral director hadn't done a good job preparing her lifeless body to stand in repose, no, considering the circumstances of Karolyn's death, the man had worked miracles. But no matter how many tricks-of-the-trade the funeral director used he couldn't bring the dead back to life, she would forever remain dead, and that would always be wrong.

They hadn't been close. That nasty fact sat in the back of his throat like bile as he looked down at her lifeless body. There would be no time to make up for old hurts and petty grievances. She was gone, and he was still here, and never would they be again together in the same place while he drew breath.

He pressed the heel of his palm in the center of his chest. It hurt, it hurt to stand here looking down on his dead twin. It hurt to think of all the lost years they had. In thirtythree years they had never found the link, the bond that twins were supposed to have.

They'd never found that invisible thread that tied them together, save for the brief few moments before she'd died in his arms.

Why had it taken so long? Why had he not seen what his mother had been doing to his sister? Why didn't he know until the very moment when it would forever be too late?

And now, now his sister, for all her flaws, and all of his regrets lay in this satin-lined box and he couldn't do a damn thing about. That pain in his chest seemed to grow. He couldn't breathe around it. He choked out, "Karolyn," before his tears escaped his eyes and fell down his face.

He kneeled at the bench in front of the casket, and leaned in, letting his forehead touch the cold, posed hands of his sister.

"I'm so sorry," he whispered. As soon as the words escaped his lips, his body began to tremble with the ache that was pressing on something vital inside him, robbing him of his breath.

He remained there, unaware of how much time had passed, unaware of how many tears he'd shed. There were only two things he knew in that moment: his sister was gone, and he should have helped her when he'd had the chance.

The pain inside grew larger, bigger, sharper. He felt like something inside him was going to snap at any moment. It would serve him right if he did die of this ache right now.

He remained there, on his knees, still hurting, still resting his head on his dead sister's hands when he felt a gentle touch run from the crown of his bowed head through the length of his hair. The touch was so light, so subtle, he thought he'd imagined it until he felt it pass over him again.

He lifted his head, and looked to the side, finding the only person who could make this moment bearable standing next to him.

"Heart," he said as relief rushed out of his lungs and through his lips. She took a soft hand and wiped his flesh free of tears.

"Sssh," she whispered. The quiet of the room demanding hushed tones. "It's going to be all right."

She wiped his cheek once more with gentle comfort. That comfort broke the fragile dam of emotions that were fighting to take him over. She used her left arm, the one free of the brace, and pulled him into her abdomen. There, kneeling at his sister's casket, he cried like he hadn't six years ago when his father died. He'd cried like he couldn't when he was a child for fear of being seen as weak. There, in this injured woman's embrace he simply cried.

❧

*H*eart held him, held on to him. She refused to let him crumble under the weight of his pain. He'd done the same for her in that elevator. He'd continued holding on to her until they'd rushed her to the operating room. She had to do the same for him.

She heard the click of the double doors at the entrance of the room and looked back. She saw William Grant there. There were questions in his eyes, but she simply shook her head and William understood her meaning, closing the door behind him.

She stroked Kenneth's hair again. The strands were so soft, so plush. Her fingers languished in the feel of them. She ran her fingers through his hair one more time, before she took her hand and raised his head with red, swollen-with-grief eyes, falling on her face.

"Kenneth, William is outside. I'm certain he has Merridith with him. If it were just William I would let you exhaust yourself here, get as much of this ache out of your system as humanly possible. But that little girl out there has been through hell and back. A hell she didn't ask for and a hell we couldn't protect her from. She doesn't know about any of the particulars; she only knows her mother is dead and her grandmother is gone. You and William are all she has, the last bit of normal in her crazy world. If she sees you like this, she won't be able to handle her own pain; she will be too focused on yours."

He closed blood-shot eyes and nodded. He took a slow, deep breath and pulled himself up to his full height of over six feet. He reached inside of his pocket, and removed the pristine looking hand-kerchief. He wiped the perfectly creased cloth across his face and removed the wet tracks of tears that had covered his fair skin just moments before.

She pulled him to her, held him for a moment longer; letting him gather up whatever stores he needed to be brave for that little girl who had lost so much. She moved in closer and pressed a chaste kiss against his lips. It was just enough to bring him back, just enough to draw him out of himself. He nodded his head once their lips parted and stepped slightly away from her. He was ready or at least ready as he could ever be to watch his only niece say goodbye to her mother.

When Heart was certain he could stand without stumbling she walked to the door and opened it, ushering in William and the tiny little wisp of a girl who was in his arms.

The little girl had her head buried in her father's neck when they entered the visitation room, but when she saw Heart, she whispered something in her daddy's ear, and he was soon lowering her to the floor.

Long midnight-black hair framed a pale face with hauntingly familiar blue eyes.

God, if she didn't know better, she would have sworn this child was Kenneth's. She was the spitting image of her uncle and now dead mother.

Just like her uncle's, those knowing eyes seemed to see through Heart, making her just this side of uncomfortable.

"Ms. Mac," the slight voice escaped tiny pink lips.

Heart couldn't help but smile at the shortened version of her name the precious child had called her.

"Hey baby girl, how you doing?"

Heart watched the tiny child look up to her with thoughtful eyes.

"Not so good. I'm sad. Daddy says that's okay though."

God something inside Heart cracked. This small little girl was carrying a weight she should never have been asked to bear, and there wasn't a thing any of them could do about it.

"It's very sad whenever you lose someone as important as a mommy," Heart said to her.

"Did your mommy go to heaven when you were my age too?"

Heart nodded. "Actually, I was lot younger than you when my mommy died. I'm afraid I don't even remember her. But you," Heart smiled as she fingered an errant dark strand behind the little girl's ears, "you have all of these fun memories of the time you and your mom spent together. And you have your uncle too. Kenneth will tell you all about your mommy so you never forget."

That brought a bright smile to the little girl's face. Heart watched her. Ice-like blue orbs locked onto chocolate ones. "And Uncle

Kenneth has you to keep him from being sad. You're going to take care of him and make him strong too."

Heart wanted to correct the child; she knew she shouldn't let the little girl latch on to ideas that might not be absolute truth in the future. Heart was just about to try to find something to say to Merridith, but then a brief glance to the side revealed Kenneth glancing her way. In that moment, every single thing she was about to tell Kenneth's niece didn't matter. She knew she would do anything to put strength and laughter back in that man's eyes.

She looked back down to little Merridith who was smiling at her, an "I told you so" smirk on her face. Heart stopped for just a minute. What was that bible verse her grandmother was always quoting to her about the things kids say? *Out of the mouths of babes and sucklings you have ordained strength.* Strength, yeah that was it…strength.

She just needed to figure out whose strength, hers or Kenneth's.

CHAPTER 12

*H*eart felt an annoying itch on her nose pulling her from her sleep. She rubbed her nose, and then tried to burrow back into the slumber she was pulled from. As soon as she'd found herself nearly there, the itch on her nose returned, followed by a dipping of the mattress.

"Kenneth, if you don't stop harassing me I'm going to take out my gun and shoot you." She felt the annoying itch on her nose again followed by warm lips against her cheek.

"Idle threats," he said. "I happen to have it on good authority that you don't have your gun right now. Porter took possession of it before the ambulance took you to the hospital."

She laughed. "As a police officer, I'm licensed to carry on and off duty both department issued and privately owned firearms. Porter has my service weapon, the one that the department issued to me."

She felt him stiffen next to her.

"You have weapons here, guns?" Was that alarm in his voice?

She opened her eyes and took in the sight of his face. Same smooth alabaster skin, same sparkling ice-blue eyes. Nothing that screamed, I'm scared, or worried. She sat up, resting against the headboard, bringing a casual smile to her lips.

"Kenneth, I'm a police officer whether I'm on duty or off duty. My weapon is an extension of me. I'm never without it. I suppose I should have warned you about my weapons."

"Heart, I didn't mean to make you feel like you owed me an explanation. I just...it didn't dawn on me that you had them in the house, especially since I'm the one that packed up your stuff and brought it here. I never even saw them."

She smiled again and reached for a lock of his midnight tresses. So amazed at how soft and silky they felt against her skin.

"You didn't transport my weapons, Kenneth. After you secured this place for me, I had Bryan go over to my old apartment and get my weapons for me. He held them for me and brought them to me when he picked me up for Karolyn's funeral."

She watched as the muscle in the corner of his eye slightly twitched. They hadn't yet talked about why she'd needed a ride from Bryan in the first place. Kenneth had been focused on taking care of Heart. Heart had been focused on letting him do whatever he needed to do to work through his sister's death.

It had been three weeks since the funeral, five weeks since she'd been shot. She hoped that both of them were edging toward a new semblance of normalcy, at least, whatever could be considered normal for this strange relationship they seemed to be building.

"I wouldn't have had you unknowingly transport them," she said, placing the smile back on her face. "God forbid you were stopped in a traffic stop. I don't even want to imagine the P.R. nightmare that would have been for the both of us." He nodded quietly.

"They are locked away and safe. I will show you where later so you can feel a little more comfortable."

He nodded again, still quiet.

Okay, enough with the quiet bullshit already.

"Kenneth, may I ask you something?" she asked, still stroking that single lock of hair. He nodded, giving her permission to ask at will.

"Why didn't you tell me about Karolyn's funeral? The only reason I found out about it was because the radio alarm was switched to radio instead of buzz. There was news coverage about it. Otherwise, I would never have known you were burying your sister that day."

He got that heavy look in his eyes whenever his sister's name was mentioned. His shoulders visibly sagged while he dragged needed air into his lungs.

"Heart, it wasn't that I didn't want you there. I did, I really did. It's just...my family had brought you such pain. My mother was going to be there. I found out from her attorney the day before that she had a legal right to attend her daughter's funeral.

Corrections only gave me a time frame that she would be arriving, I couldn't really pinpoint when."

"But, she never came."

"Yes she did," he said softly. "That's why I went so early. The funeral director agreed to have Karolyn prepared for visitation by six that morning. My mother arrived around seven. I stayed in the funeral director's office the entire time, I couldn't bring myself to be in the same room as her."

"I would have been fine being there with you, Kenneth."

"Maybe, but I didn't want to take that chance. I also considered that the media would be all over the funeral. I didn't know if you could be seen on camera or not."

She nodded, carefully weighing all the things he'd said. "I don't do much undercover work anymore. Bryan does though. We called ahead to the funeral director and had them open up the service entrance in the back. It's a garage like structure that you can drive into. We didn't get out of the car until the gates were lowered behind us and we were no longer in street view."

"I just wanted to protect..."

"I know, Kenneth," she stroked his cheek with her thumb, "I know you wanted to protect me, but here's the thing," she said with a meaningful smile pinned to her lips. "If we're going to be friends, then we've got to look out for each other, and be honest with one another. I don't ever want to know that you're hurting, and you purposely turned away from me. I don't want to be the kind of friend that only takes from you, Kenneth.

You deserve so much more than that."

At that moment she heard the chime of the doorbell ringing.

"You expecting someone?" she asked.

He nodded, a knowing smile growing on his face.

"Actually, it's you that's expecting someone. That's Dr. Bailer. She's here for your first P.T. appointment. I'll go let her in, you get dressed."

She dragged herself out of bed and headed for the walk-in closet for some sweats. She was just this side of apprehensive about beginning therapy. Her cousin True had mentioned that with her injury, the rehab would be extensive. She would have to work hard to get back to what was normal for most, let alone what was normal for her.

She couldn't worry about that now. Her arm had only been free of its prescribed brace for a week now. The muscle weakness in her right arm was instantly noticeable.

If she ever wanted back on the job, back in command, she had to be one hundred percent. Being less than could get you killed on the streets, and labeled as useless on the job. Neither of those scenarios were an option. She'd earned the title of lieutenant, and she ran her command with a tough yet fair hand. Not to mention that Bryan was losing his mind stepping in for her and acting as interim commanding officer.

When Porter had placed him in command Bryan called her up complaining. "The reason I never took the L.T. exam after you zoomed ahead and aced the damn thing was so I would never have to be a boss. Don't they know this damn sergeant's shield is just for show and the little increase in my paycheck? I'm all about being in the streets. This administrative bullshit is for the birds. You better hurry up and get your ass back to work,

MacKenzie, or you might be reading about me in the damn papers."

She laughed at the memory. Bryan was an excellent leader, he had the chops to run his own house if he wanted to, but he just didn't want to. For no other reason than that she had to get herself together. Otherwise, Bryan would kill her, or kill Captain Porter whomever he was closest to or more frustrated with at the time.

She bound down the stairs holding her stiff arm against her body, still afraid of hurting it. She made it halfway down when she saw a fit fair-skinned black woman with a pixie haircut draped all over Kenneth. There was really no other word for it. They were standing in the foyer and she was plastered all over him and for some strange reason,

Kenneth didn't seem to mind. Or at least that's what his body language was telling her.

He was embracing her warmly, smiling, obviously happy to see her.

Kenneth saw her first and stepped slightly out of the woman's embrace.

"Oh, Heart, you're here. I'd like you to meet, Dr. Bailer," he said, that goofy, happyass smile still plastered on his damn face.

Heart assessed the woman standing too damn close to Kenneth for her liking. When the woman let go of him long enough to face Heart, memory kicked in instantly.

"Faith?" Heart asked.

Heart read the young woman standing before her. There was no shock at seeing an old childhood acquaintance etched into her face. Instead there was a pleasant, professional smile—not as many teeth showing as the toothy grin she had for Kenneth— attached to her soft features.

So it's not a surprise to find me here. She'd known whom she was coming to treat. That meant only one of two things: Kenneth had asked her to be here because of their past, or her cousin had thought it would be a great way to piss her off by sending the annoyingly high-spirited Faith—a person she had never been particularly fond of by the way— to treat her. Either way, this rehab bullshit was about to suck balls. Big, hairy, ginormous, donkey balls.

~

*D*ammit, they knew each other, and from the tension in both their bodies, they weren't besties either. He'd assumed that they knew of each other, after all, Faith worked with Heart's cousin True. He hadn't banked on their being any sort of bad blood between them.

That damn, True. She'd told him in no uncertain terms that she was sending her friend to help Heart through her rehabilitation. Heart needed the best, and that meant she needed one of two people, Genesis, who was unavailable, or Faith. So by default his exgirlfriend was standing in the same living room as his...his what? Current girlfriend? Not exactly, and if this uneasy feeling that was building in the pit of his stomach was any indication, she might not ever be his girlfriend if this shit blew up in his face. *Damn it all to hell, True.*

"You two know each other through, True?" he asked. Not really certain which one he was talking to, although his eyes never left Heart's face.

"Not exactly," Heart said. Cool eyes focused on the woman standing beside him.

"Although I didn't move on the block that Faith, Genesis, and True lived on until I was fourteen, my grandmother lived in the same home since before my mother and uncle were born." Heart took another step down the stairs. "My grandmother raised me in the local church, the same church Genesis, Faith, and True attended as well." This time she took two steps. "Every Friday my father would have me taken to my grandmother's house where I'd spend the weekend playing with my cousins and the rest of the neighborhood kids. That included Genesis and her brothers, True's siblings as well as Faith." She took the final step and stood in front of Faith, shoulders back, feet planted, body taut and poised for action. "So Faith," Heart said with a chilly smile. "How the hell are you?"

❦

*H*eart didn't like this bitch, the truth was, and she never had. It's wasn't that Faith had ever done anything specifically to Heart to bring on this deep-seated contempt. No, it was just her naturally fucking chipper personality that just pissed her off to no end.

True called her the perpetual cheerleader, an accurate description if Heart had ever heard one. Heart was naturally reserved, naturally cautious. She was always watching and assessing her surroundings to make the best choice and keep things always within her control.

Not this bitch. Faith had always been the type of bitch to put everything and everyone on blast. She was loud, she was always cackling, always drawing attention to herself. Honestly, who the hell was that goddamned happy all the fucking time? No one was, no one except Faith fucking Bailer, that is.

Everything Heart had ever known about this trick had always pissed her the fuck off. Now, now she was still plastered against Kenneth like she was trying to conjoin with his ass, and that little visual was making Heart want to draw her damn weapon. Fuck, she'd do a bid just to forcibly sever the leech-like damn hold Faith had on Kenneth.

God she couldn't stand Faith, never could. She was going to slap the taste out of True's mouth the minute she saw her grimy ass. She'd set this shit up, of that Heart was certain. She didn't know why. True's mind always worked differently than everyone else's. But she was certain her cousin had purposely set her up. She'd find out why later. Sadly, right now, she had work to do, so killing this Halle Berry wannabe was going to have to wait. Heart was loathed to admit it, but she needed Faith's help—even if she couldn't stand the damn form the help came in.

"Why don't you put your things down, Faith? We can sit down in the kitchen while I get my coffee. I don't function well without it."

Kenneth's lips turned up into a smile. "That's putting it lightly. More like the rest of the world isn't safe until you've had your first cup."

A bubble of laughter began to well up inside Heart. The man was right. No one was safe until at least sixteen ounces of warm caffeinated goodness was flowing in her veins.

She walked over to the cabinet to remove three mugs. Heart reached her hand above her head expecting to feel the smooth surface of the cabinet's wood. Instead, she felt a warm familiar hand touch the small of her back. Its warmth transferred through her skin and traveled across the synapses of her nervous system, sparking electrical shocks from one nerve to the next.

It had only been a short five weeks since she'd felt the calmness that Kenneth's touch brought. But in those five weeks, in that small amount of time her body had come to ache for the soothing relief his touch brought. She was like a mewling cat, sinking back into his caress with her whole body.

"Sit down, I'll get it," he whispered in her ear. "This appointment is for you." His voice was a soft wave pushing her in the direction of the shore, to safety, to wholeness. She nodded her head, looking in the direction of the table where Faith was sitting, watching the two of them.

A flash of something crossed Faith's eyes. Some weird cross between anger and hunger, like she was longing for something. It was quick and fierce, and then gone in a moment. So quickly, Heart questioned whether she'd seen it or not.

Heart sat down across from Faith, watched her as she spent longer than necessary looking for whatever she was digging for in her attaché case. *Yeah, I wasn't imagining anything.*

Heart made a decision right there while sitting at that table. *I am Lieutenant Heart MacKenzie. Bitches fear me, not the other way around.*

~

*K*enneth sat in his executive chair looking out at the Manhattan skyline of sculptured, gothic structures climbing their way endlessly into the sky. He'd spent the last month working from home to be available for Heart whenever she needed him. He'd still be there if she hadn't literally kicked him out and demanded he stop hovering.

She said since Faith was around, there wasn't any need for him to wait on her hand and foot. She needed to focus on getting her arm well again, and he needed to get back to work.

She was right, she really was. The pile of files taking up residence on his desk was proof of that. Heart being right didn't make him feel any better about leaving her there. It certainly didn't make him feel good about leaving his ex and—his what?...his possible next?—Heart in close quarters together.

The click of his office door drew his attention. He saw two welcome faces strolling across the plush carpet.

"Drew, John." He came from behind his desk and met the two men in the middle of the room. He gave Drew and John strong hugs, loud back slaps thundering through the room.

Drew was a couple of inches shorter than his own six feet three inches. His cut body and caramel skin tone made him a popular favorite in the R&B music world that Drew was reigning supreme and ruling with a dazzling gleam in his eye. John, his dark olive tone and wavy onyx tresses gave voice to his family's Mediterranean ancestry. John was probably a hairsbreadth shorter than Drew was, but their builds were completely at odds. Where Drew was all brawn and hard muscle, John was lean with tremendous muscle definition, just not as much bulk.

"'Sup Ken-dog," Drew said. "You been M.I.A. for a minute now. Can't seem to track your ass down for nothing."

Kenneth motioned for the two men to sit in the chair in front of his desk. Once they were seated, he walked over to his in-office bar and pulled out two bottles of water.

"It's been crazy these last few weeks."

"How are you holding up since the funeral?" John asked.

"It hasn't been easy, but I've spent a good deal of my time focusing on Heart. It's helped." Kenneth knew that having her to focus on was the only reason he hadn't lost his mind yet.

"How's she doing? Genesis' dad asked me about her last night," Drew said just before taking a long gulp from his bottle of water.

Kenneth turned to Drew. "Genesis' dad?" he asked. "Give me the run down on this connection True and her partners seem to have with Heart. I thought they might be acquainted, but it's come to my attention in a very awkward way that their connection is a lot deeper than what I anticipated."

Drew shrugged his shoulders. "They grew up together on our block."

"So you grew up with Heart too then?" Kenneth queried.

Drew shook his head, "Not like you're thinking. Genesis, True, Faith and Heart all grew up together on Crescent Street in Brooklyn. Heart didn't live on the block, but she was there pretty much every weekend visiting her grandmother and her cousins. From what Genesis has told me, she came to live on the block when she was about fourteen. No one really knows why, she just showed up one day and never left. I'm about two years younger than Genesis and her crew, so by the time I came on the scene they were all off to college and beyond. Heart was the only one that went to a commuter school. So I met her on the block and in church."

Kenneth nodded, "Genesis' dad is the pastor of the church you attended?"

"Yeah. Heart's grandmother was much like my mom, very dedicated to the church. I think Heart stayed behind to help take care of her."

"What about her relationship with the other ladies?" "You mean Genesis and Faith?" Drew asked.

"Yeah."

Drew seemed to be rolling the question around in his head for a moment. "According to Genesis, Heart was just like all of them before she came to live on the block. But when she stayed, something changed. She was more reserved and cautious. She didn't mix it up like the rest of them, except for when she was with her cousins, the Amare kids. She and Genesis have always been cool, I think they both understand each other. But according to

Genesis, Faith and Heart are like oil and water. They just don't seem to mix."

Kenneth closed his eyes and leaned back in his chair. A defeated huff of breath escaping his lips, "I was afraid of that."

John leaned forward and placed his water bottle on Kenneth's desk, joining the conversation between Kenneth and Drew. "You got a problem with the ladies, Kenny?"

"I'll say. Something is building between Heart and me. Ever since she took a bullet that was meant for me, and her resulting injuries and rehab, we've been getting…close."

John's skepticism was drawn all over his olive-toned face. "Like close as in sleeping together?"

Kenneth shook his head. "No, we're not sleeping together. It's something deeper than that. I don't really know how to explain it. She needed my help with some very personal things in her life. For some reason, I think I'm the only one she's ever let get close enough to her to help. But there's this…thing—I don't really know how to describe it —building…intimacy between us. It's strong; it pulls at the both of us."

John continued. "So that's a problem?"

"No," Kenneth said. "It's not a problem at all. I'm actually very happy about it. I want to see where it leads."

"So what's your problem?" Drew offered.

"Faith is the physical therapist performing Heart's rehab. Faith is also my exgirlfriend. We dated for a few years when I was in school in California."

Both John and Drew let out long identical whistles at the same time.

"So your ex is treating your next," Drew said with no hint of a question in the sentence. "Damn, man, I do not envy you."

Kenneth didn't envy himself either. Heart and he didn't have a romantic connection, not in the traditional sense anyway. But, they did have an extremely visceral emotional connection born out of unimaginable circumstances. He wanted that connection to grow into more. Although he'd made no permanent commitments to Heart, he somehow knew Faith being here wasn't going to bode well for his current situation or his future expectations—whatever they were, he hadn't really figured them out yet—where Heart was concerned.

"Does Heart know about you and Faith?" John asked.

"I haven't told her," Kenneth said. And he never would if he'd judge the tension that he felt between the two women correctly.

Kenneth's attention was pulled from his own musings by the laughter of both his friends.

"What?" Kenneth asked them.

"You really think Heart doesn't know you two were together?" John asked.

"Hell, even if she wasn't a trained investigator, she's a woman, they have natural detective abilities," John continued through his laughter, which was beginning to piss Kenneth off for some reason.

"Bruh, even if she weren't an investigator, she's cousins with your ex-girlfriend's business partner and friend. Let me tell you, those females talk on the regular," Drew added. "Every morning those three in California have a confab over the phone. Doesn't matter where in the world they all are, they always talk at the exact same time every morning. This is all at the insistence of True, by the way. If she demands that of her friends, don't you think she would ask that of her only cousin?"

Kenneth began to feel a sinking feeling pull at the bottom of his stomach. He knew exactly what it was: his hope that this situation was going to turn out well slowly disappearing. Kenneth let out a painful moan. His life was going to shit really quickly.

"Kenneth," Drew called his attention. "Bruh, you want to at least try to get ahead of this. One thing I know, you gotta be transparent with women. Especially women like

Heart."

"What do you mean, Drew?" Kenneth asked.

"I know everyone sees Heart as tough and solid. Trust me, she really is all of those things. But one of the things she handled in the church was the children's ministry. She loved to be around kids. She was like the pied piper to all the little rugrats in the sanctuary. I think she hung out with kids, 'cause she didn't have much tolerance for adults. I've often heard her say, 'kids don't lie, they only love.' Someone that believes that has been hurt. She's skittish, don't give her a reason to run from you."

"Or a reason to beat your ass," John offered.

Kenneth shook his head and rolled his eyes. "Heart is not violent, John."

"Bullshit," John laughed out. "She's a woman with a gun, a badge, and a command. She's violent as all hell. And let me tell you, any woman who thinks another woman is trying to move in on her territory, can and will beat somebody's ass if necessary." Kenneth dropped his head on his desk and moaned again. "What the hell am I going to do?"

⤳

Kenneth walked into a quiet living room. The lights were out, the room only illuminated by streaks of light poking through the closed blinds. He sat his briefcase on the floor, dropped his keys on the hall table, and walked further inside of the house.

Maybe Heart was sleeping. Maybe she was so exhausted from her physical therapy session that she just climbed right into bed and he wouldn't have to talk to her about Faith tonight.

All hope that he wouldn't have to have this conversation with Heart tonight ended when he walked into the kitchen and found her taking plates from the cabinet and resting them on the kitchen counter.

She smiled when she caught sight of him. A smile bright and full of warmth pulled him to where she stood. He pulled her into his body and wrapped himself around her. She burrowed deeper inside of his chest and took a leisured breath when she'd nuzzled her face into that perfect spot in the crook of his neck.

She was almost mewling as he touched her. This would never get old for him. He loved the fact that she pushed into his touch so instinctively with no reservations or hesitations. She wanted to be in his arms. She trusted him, and he had to protect that trust at all costs. He lifted her chin to look in those soulful chocolate pools he'd often found himself nearly drowning in. "How was your session today with Faith?" he asked.

She took a breath and stepped back out of his embrace. "You mind getting a couple of bottles of water out of the fridge? Pizza's on the table," she said, not looking at him.

That did not bode well for this to be a light conversation. Heart didn't usually do avoidance. Not when it came to saying what she thought anyway. Avoidance of her emotions, yeah, every which way she could, but telling you what was on her mind, no issues whatsoever.

He brought the bottles to the table and sat down across from her. He watched her. She was still avoiding him, not looking at him. Instead, her eyes were focused on the task of opening the pizza box and pulling slices from the box to their plates with the pizza spatula in her left hand.

"Still not able to use your right arm?" he asked.

"I can," she said sucking the stray sauce that was on her thumb. "A little more every day since I started working with Faith. But she still wants me to refrain from using it outside of our sessions. She says after a few more sessions she's going to start giving me some exercises to work on when she's not here."

"So things are going good with Faith then?" he asked and watched as she stared at the pizza slice in front of her.

"Kenneth, Faith is great at what she does. She would have to be in order to remain partners with my cousin and Genesis. Genesis is the forgiving kind, but True, not so much. She would have gotten rid of Faith a long time ago if that was the case."

"I'm hearing a 'but' somewhere in there," he said attempting to coax more information out of her.

She shrugged her shoulders, still looking at the slice of pizza on the plate in front of her, playing with the stringy cheese pooled at its tip. "Faith really is first rate. She's even figured out a way to work through my haphephobia," Heart said.

"Through your what?" he asked her.

"Haph·e·pho·bia," she said slowly, breaking down the word into its syllables. "It's the medical term for fear of being touched."

Kenneth reached across the table and placed a gentle finger across the skin of her forearm and stroked slowly back and forth across it. She might be afraid of touch, but as long as it wasn't his touch, he knew they could work through anything.

"I'm still hearing reservation somewhere in there. What's going on, Heart? What's the problem with Faith?" he asked, reaching across the small space between then and lifting her chin and turning her gaze toward him.

"Kenneth, I'm sure you didn't know this when you hired her, but Faith and I don't really get along well," Heart admitted. "At best we're tolerant of one another, but not exactly friends."

He placed his hand atop hers keeping her line of vision on him instead of the pizza. "Did something happen between the two of you, or has she done something recently to put you off from her?"

She shook her head. "She hasn't done anything, in the past or present to bring harm to me. Our personalities just clash. Faith is very perky and annoyingly upbeat. That has never been my reality, so I just don't respond well to it. We just...we just...don't mix," she finally said.

"So why didn't you say something when I mentioned her name?" he questioned.

"I didn't connect the name. You called her Dr. Bailer; it didn't connect until I saw her wrapped all over you when I came downstairs. I know you went through a lot of trouble to hire her; I didn't want to waste your efforts or your money."

"I didn't hire her, Heart. True sent her."

Heart's raised brow questioned his revelation, but after a brief pause, he saw understanding click in to place. Her gaze fell back to the pizza, effectively closing the door on the conversation for the moment. He watched her take several small bites of the slice, pretending she was eating the pizza, and then she pushed the plate away from her and stood up from the table.

"I guess my PT session made me more tired than I realized. I'm going to head up to bed," she said quietly as she went to move away from the table.

He gently took her hand—the one connected to her injured arm—and kissed it. It was like a ritual with him, like he was paying homage to it, willing it to get better. Kenneth had never belonged to any organized religion, but when his lips touched her hand, he always prayed that someone out in the universe was hearing his supplication, and answering his sincerest prayers that she would get better.

"I know how much you love the Jacuzzi in the master bath. Why don't you go soak for a while, let this arm relax some?" he asked as he raised his eyes to hers.

"I don't want to intrude on you, you've just come home from a long day at work."

He kissed her hand again, stood, and pulled her into his arms, covering her with his warmth. "I have some work I have to do down here before I can rest. Not to mention I need to sort the garbage for tomorrow's pickup, you know how sanitation is around here." He held her again, placing a soft kiss on her cheek. "I'll be up in about an hour.

That gives you plenty of time to soak and get into bed."

She nodded her head in submission to his request and left him alone in the kitchen. He sat still listening to her move about the house on the floor above him. He listened as she moved through her room, picking up bathing and toiletry items he presumed, and then she padded quietly to his room. There was a brief pause, and then he heard the jets open and the rushing water race through the many jets in the giant tub.

He sat there, waiting as she went through her paces, waiting for the perfect time to act. Then there was silence, the chaotic rush of the water now still and silent. He counted to a hundred silently in his head, to make certain she didn't leave the bathroom, and when he heard no movement, he headed for his car in the garage. Once securely inside the car with the doors closed, he pulled his cell phone from his pocket and slid his finger across

True's name.

"If it isn't my favorite white boy?" True laughed into the phone. "What's up pale skin, what'cha need?" she asked him.

"Cut the bullshit, True, I didn't call for your games."

"Oh, somebody's feeling brave talking to me like that. What's biting you, Kenneth?"

"True, what the fuck are you playing at sending Faith here when you knew she and your cousin can't stand each other? You know what's at risk; we're talking about Heart's livelihood here. How the hell are they supposed to work together when they can barely be in the same room as one another?" he asked, trying to keep the volume out of his voice.

"Kenneth, I know you've branded yourself my cousin's champion and all, but check this hot shit out right here, don't call my phone talking bullshit like that to me, it might just get you hurt," her cool tone sailed through the phone lines, and caused the slightest shiver in his chest. He knew True, had never really seen her become violent, but understood all the same that she wasn't someone who was above using it to get what she wanted.

"True, I could give a damn about your threats right now. Why are you trying to sabotage Heart's rehab?"

He heard the woman take a long breath before she spoke. "Kenneth, my cousin can sometimes be a prickly, difficult individual to work with. Just ask Bryan, I don't know how the hell he's managed to work so well with her over the years. There are only two people I would have trusted her care to, Genesis, or Faith. Genesis is too nurturing, she takes the potshots her patients throw at her and turns them into touchy-feely words that somehow drags them out of their self-pity and right on through to rehabilitation. Faith is more the pick, poke, and annoy you until she gets you to do exactly what is best for your rehabilitation. Kenneth, you've met my cousin, exactly which one do you think she would respond best to during her therapy?"

Kenneth let his head thump against the headrest on his seat. Damn he was so stupid.

"Kenneth, understand this," she said. "My motives are always about helping the people I love, and never about fucking with your plans to sex my cousin."

"True," he said, his voice rumbling with some mix between anger and annoyance.

"Kenneth please, you thought I sent Faith out there to throw a monkey wrench in your plans to get in my cousin's panties."

"True, I'm not trying to fuck Heart over..."

"And you better not be..." she cut him off. "...if you know what's good for you. Kenneth, Heart is a grown ass woman; I could give a damn about whom she chooses to lay up with, but for damn sure, you will not hurt my cousin. Trust and believe, if you do,

I will fuck you up, no questions asked." "True...," he called her name again.

"Kenneth, no excuses," she said bluntly. "I'm really concerned about this shit between the three of you. You're the ex-man of my friend and business partner who also happens to be emotionally connected and invested in my cousin. I know for a fact that you and Faith have hooked up several times over the years since you've broken up. I don't want that shit coming back to bite my cousin in the ass."

Kenneth ran his hand over his head, and let his fingers undo the tie at the nape of his neck. He needed to run his fingers through his hair just to be able to focus. True wasn't lying, he and Faith had many hookups over the years. He thought about Heart finding out about those and what she would think of him.

"True, yes, Faith and I had dealings multiple times after we broke up. But here's the difference, neither of us were involved with anyone else during any of the times we hooked up."

"And you're with someone now?" True asked. "As far as I know, you and my cousin are barely friends, when did you become an item?"

"Heart knows how I feel about her, True."

"The fuck she does," True said. "My cousin knows nothing about feelings. If you haven't told her that you want her and only her, I guarantee you she doesn't believe you have these kinds of feelings for her. Stop punking out and tell her how you feel."

Kenneth wiped a slow hand down the length of his face as the muscles in his other hand grasped the phone tightly. "True, she's fragile. I don't want to mess this up. I can't tell here exactly how I feel and what I want when I haven't really figured it out yet for myself. What if I say the wrong thing, or drive her away?"

"Kenneth, it's obvious to anyone that looks twice at the two of you that she's important to you. If you make that one fact your priority, everything else will fall in place."

He thought about what True was saying, but before he could answer he heard the defined click of the line, she was gone. He pulled himself out of his car and went inside to finish up the errands he needed to take care of before he went upstairs. When he was done, he walked to the master bath, tapping lightly on the door and waiting for an answer. When none came, he gently pushed the door open and found the bathroom empty.

"She must have gone to her bed already," he said with the tiniest bit of disappointment. He turned the showerheads on and peeled his clothes from his tight body. He stepped under the hot spray and hoped the water would wash away the tension in his muscles. He stood under the water, washing the day away, and thinking of the beautiful woman who had just lain in his tub.

Tight athletic build, long legs meant to be wrapped around his waist or over his shoulders, with firm globes of breast and ass made perfectly for the curve of his hands. He thought about the way she responded to his touch, not in a sexual way, more like an elemental way. It was as if his touch was essential to her, she needed it, she needed him.

His hand followed the water's path down his body until he found the center of his ache. His firm hold wrapped around the turgid flesh of his cock and he gave one strong pull in search of relief. When none came, he did it again, and again, until the pressure built, until his balls were tight and throbbing, and the flesh across the head of his leaking cock was stretched and purple, so taut it was painful.

His mouth opened and a groan of pleasure climbed out of his chest through his throat and out into the air. The rumble bounced off the glass walls of the shower and the sheer power of it made him shudder.

Every night he'd stayed in this house with her, this had been his routine, this had been his saving grace. This was the only way he could lie next to her on most nights, so close to her, touching her, smelling her, and not being able to have her. Pleasuring himself in the confines of this shower, this was the only way he could rein in this almost uncontrollable lust that was buried deep inside of him for this one woman.

He imagined her warmth, the way it covered him like a plush blanket. What he wouldn't give to have her actual warmth surrounding him instead of his hand, but for the moment, his hand, and his mind were working wonders. He was almost there; he just needed one more thing, one more element to complete this beautiful sensual picture in his head. Her voice, the sound she made whenever he touched her, and she pushed into his touch with abandon and need. He called that very simple memory to his mind and just like a trigger being pulled his pleasure erupted in his hand, spurting over the rim of his finger thick and white, tapping against the glass walls of the shower. Damn, the shock of it never got old. Every night, it was the same thing, the same image, the same sound that sent him over the top in this shower. Every single time this happened, his body would quake well after his balls had run out of cum to produce. He would just shake until the spasms of the extended orgasm would finally stop, leaving him weak leaning against the wall.

He took slow cleansing breaths, dragging the air almost painfully in and out of his lungs. Giving his body the air it needed to replenish the strength he'd lost. When he could stand without the help of the glass panels surrounding him, he shut off the water and stepped out of the shower. He pulled a towel from the rack and dried himself quickly. He slung the towel low around his hips and knotted it in place.

He stepped back into his room, needing to go to her, but afraid that he wouldn't be able to control himself if he did. He wasn't completely certain if there could be more between him, he wasn't certain if there should be more between them. He walked toward the closet then noticed a flash of white silk material flash across the open doors of his patio.

She was there standing in the night, the only light present was the cascade of the moonlight against her warm brown skin. He stood there, taking in every sparkle of light, every distinct curve that the fabric of one of his borrowed pajama tops draped. And just like that, just that damn quickly his traitorous cock was fucking hard as steel again and that familiar pulsing in his rigid shaft was begging him to bury himself deeply within this woman that his body wanted so terribly.

"God you're beautiful," the whispered words crept past his lips. He was only halfaware that he'd spoken them aloud, his feet pulling him to the balcony where she stood. She turned toward his voice, hooded eyes showing how uncomfortable she was with compliments.

The light breeze lifted her hair tossing errant strands that broke free from the messy bun she had pulled to the back of her head to fall, framing her delicate face. She moved a hand to pull them back and he caught it.

"No, let them free." He let her hand go and removed the pin holding those dark tresses up and watched them spill past her shoulders in a glorious heap.

He pulled her to him and clamped his mouth over hers. If he'd been thinking clearly he would have tried to make this romantic, soft, sensual for her, for them. But the hunger, the growing hunger that he had been starving for months now, since that first kiss, the night they'd found his niece, was demanding satisfaction in this very moment, and soft, sensual, and romantic just wasn't going to cut it.

His lips locked onto hers as he pulled her tightly into his hard embrace. No matter how much he drank, he just couldn't seem to quench this soul-searing thirst he had for her. His hands roughly traveled from her face, along the curve of her shoulders, down her sides and waist, until they landed on the firm curve of her ass. He jerked her forward, his thigh between hers. He could feel the dampness gathering there at the core of her heat.

She liked this, she wasn't afraid, she wanted it.

"Holy mother of God, I'm done," he said just before he tore at the folds of the sleep shirt, needing to see, taste, and feel the mounds of flesh below it.

"Kenneth," he heard the gush of air with his name on it as it crossed her lips. He didn't let it sidetrack him, he was hungry, and she was sustenance he had to have her.

"Kenneth, please...stop."

He heard the cold words wash over him, felt the palpable chill they sent through him, stilling him, locking his muscles in a tense stasis. He brought questioning eyes to her gaze. Had he done something wrong, hadn't she wanted this too?

"Heart, you don't want to do this? You don't want me?"

There was a hard silence on that balcony. He couldn't hear anything except the drum of his loudly beating heart.

"I don't want you..." she said softly, making his heartbeat thump when it should have been thump-thumping. "...out here on the balcony in front of all of creation. Maybe we should take this inside to the bedroom."

He watched her intently, looking for any minutely discernible indication that this wasn't what she wanted. He looked, and then he looked again, needing to be certain of her desires. Then she took his hand and placed it right at the swell of her breast and pressed her flesh into his. That was it. That was all he needed. He slammed his mouth back onto hers and pulled her to him. He kneaded the curve of her ass with strong hands and pulled her up until her legs were wound tightly around his waist.

He carried her to his bed and gently planted her in the center of it. He looked at her, lips swollen from his kisses, chest heaving for air, body humming with excitement, and all of it was for him. He leaned over her, taking the moment to slow things down. He didn't want to, but he needed to. First, if he kept going at his current pace, he was going to embarrass himself by exploding the second their bodies joined. Second, there were some details they needed to address before he could make them one.

"Heart?" he questioned softly, the rumble of his baritone shaking the quiet between them.

"Hmm?" she replied with eyes half closed searching for him.

"I need to know if you've done this before."

Her eyes blinked rapidly fanning the sexual fog out of her sight. "You mean, sex?

Have I had sex before?"

He stroked her face and placed a gentle kiss on her lips. "Yes, have you had sex before?" he asked again.

"Yes," she said, her hand stroking the skin on his arm.

He swallowed, afraid to let the next word cross his lips, but knowing it was necessary. "Consensual?" he asked. He waited a beat, waited for her to process what he was really asking, the fear he'd been holding inside ever since he'd discovered her fear of being touched.

She sat up, took his hand, and laced its fingers with her own. "Kenneth, I have never been raped. I have had consensual sex before. I've had to self-medicate to do it, but I have had sex," Heart said as she dropped her head, her hair falling like a black drape, hiding the shame that was coloring her face.

"What do you mean by self-medicate? What did you self-medicate with?" he asked as he pulled her hair away from her face and pushed it behind her ear.

"Since I was fourteen I haven't been able to bear the feel of someone else's skin touching mine. As you can probably imagine, that made physical intimacy very difficult. My first year on the job I decided I had to get over it, I had to be normal, no matter what it cost me. I went to a party one of the other probies invited me to. I figured out pretty quickly after someone fed me a few drinks, that I wasn't as afraid anymore. So I drank enough that I was still technically in control of myself, but minus the fear. Anytime I've had sex I've been technically drunk.

"The first time it happened at that party, I never saw that guy again, but my second partner, we actually saw each other a few times before we both admitted that what we were doing was wrong."

Kenneth stroked her hair, attempting to calm the fire that was burning inside of him.

"That bastard took advantage of you while you were drunk?"

She shook her head and placed a calming hand on his bare chest. "No, Kenneth. It wasn't anything like you're imagining. We were sort of a bad experiment for one another. I needed to try to control my fear, and he needed to figure out his sexuality. He had some fundamental hang ups about sex and how to live his life. His family was excessively conservative and decided he would become a minister. His entire life had been planned out for him without any of his own input. Joining the force, discovering all of the things his family and his church told him were forbidden became his mission in life.

"The truth is we were exactly what the other needed while we needed it. The time I spent being with him taught me to tolerate touch, even if I didn't really like it. It helped me to hide my phobia well enough that I could do my job safely. We used each other for what we needed at the time, safe companionship, nothing more."

She closed her eyes while she spoke. "I guess after hearing how pathetic I am, you probably don't want to go through with this? I bet you're probably thinking how much easier this would be if you were here with someone normal, someone like, Faith."

He felt that criticism, the harshness of the brush she painted herself with, and he didn't like it. They'd started out on this journey with her protecting his family, protecting him, and somehow had ended up with him needing to protect her.

He wasn't exactly certain when the tables had turned. He wasn't exactly certain when it became so all-consuming and important, but protecting this woman that was lying beneath him had somehow become his purpose in life.

"Heart, open your eyes," his words were smooth and rhythmic, matching the pattern of the beat he was stroking on her hand. "There has never been another woman who has made me care about her needs more than my own. That includes Faith," he whispered. He watched the muscles in her face visibly release the tension she'd been holding.

"I've never been a selfish lover, but I'd be lying to you if I said I thought enough about my partners in the past to care about their sexual history beyond when the last time they was tested for sexually transmitted diseases. I'm asking you all of this because I want this to be right for you, because it can't be right for me if it's not right for you. That's the difference between you and everyone else. I only care that this is right for you," he said as he watched her close her eyes again. He could see the tension coming back, drawing lines on the pallet of her smooth face.

"What if this is never right for me?" she asked, her eyes still locked tightly behind her lids. "What happens if I can never be normal? I want this, Kenneth, I want you. But I don't know if I..." he kissed her, quieting the turmoil he saw building behind those worry lines.

"Sshhh," he spoke softly. "Normal is relative and it's also boring as hell. If I wanted normal, if that was what I needed, I would go out and find it. You are what I need, what I want, and if you're not normal, then normal be damned."

He kissed her again, slipping his tongue inside the warmth of her mouth, tasting the sweetness of her and allowing it to pepper his taste buds. "Right now I need you, but if you tell me you're not ready for this, then I will lie down next to you and hold you while you fall asleep, just as I have most nights since you've come home. I want you, but more than that, I want you to feel this burning need that's going on inside me too."

He kissed her more firmly, drawing out a long moan from her as he tasted and touched, never separating his skin from hers. Touch, kiss, taste: the never-ending pattern, always keeping the link between them, always anchoring her fear with his passion.

He broke the kiss and looked down at her again. "Heart, the decision is yours, whatever you need, want, just let me know."

She stilled, looked at him, through him, as if she were using his internal signals to help her in her decision process. This was who she was after all, a trained investigator, someone who was trained to notice the minute details in order to pull the puzzle pieces together.

The nod she rendered was so small, so nearly imperceptible that he was almost afraid he'd imagined it. He pulled away from her briefly, pulling open the nightstand drawer and removing the thin foil packet he knew would be there. He dropped it on the pillow next to them and reached for the top button on her pajama shirt. In one smooth motion the material opened bearing the lovely curve of her shoulders and the inviting line of her cleavage.

He stretched the material so that it cleared her right shoulder, the injured shoulder, the one that took the bullet that was meant for him and his sister. This shoulder had saved his life. It was the only thing that had stood between life and death for him. He placed a soft, delicate kiss on it, testing to see if there was any pain. When she lifted it closer to his mouth, he ran his finger along the raised skin, the skin that had been marred and broken by the projectile metal. It was circular, with uneven spikey lines stabbing out from its center. Some might call it an ugly blemish, an undesirable mark on once beautiful flesh.

For him it reminded him of a sun, warm, bright, noticeable, life-giving, life-affirming.

The fact that he could kiss, touch, and taste this scar meant that he was still here, that she was still here. It meant that they had survived it all together. That thought made him burn from the inside. He ran the tip of his tongue up the length of the scar creating a gentle wet path from top to bottom. The resulting shiver that passed through her stoked his desire, his need to worship her body.

He moved from her shoulder to the bend in her neck. He pressed a succession of kisses to the area, followed by firm, but controlled nips of his teeth. He worried the pulsepoint in her neck until her body began to struggle with want. He felt her hands traveling up his back. Being mindful of her healing arm, he secured them to her sides and whispered, "Don't move them," in her ear.

His kisses blazed a path down her chest to the bifurcating line that cleaved the two globes he couldn't wait to see, to touch, to taste. He opened the remaining buttons and watched the material fall open, leaving a trail of luscious brown skin from her neck to hips bared and opened to him.

"So fucking hot," he growled through clenched teeth, the sight of her uncovered body nearly tripping him into spasms.

He drank from her lips again while taking a firm handful of the rounded flesh of her breast. He grazed a thumb across her nipple and felt a shudder pass through her. He ripped himself from her lips, replaced his thumb with his tongue, and delighted in the near-scream that erupted from her when he closed his mouth over the pert nub and suckled.

"So responsive," he moaned as he repeated the action on her remaining nipple. "I could come just from the sounds you make alone."

He licked-kissed his way down the cleaved path between her breasts, down to her navel. He paused for a glorious moment and dipped his tongue inside, watching her body twist and shiver, listening for the erotic tones climbing from her mouth. *How could someone so unbelievably responsive to touch have been denied the simple pleasure of feeling and being felt all of this time?*

Fourteen years was too long, too long for this beautiful woman lying beneath him to go without such basic pleasures. If nothing else came from this night, it would be that she would feel him. On every inch of her skin, he would brand this electric memory on every nerve ending she possessed. He would imprint himself and their pleasure on her sense memory, and she would always be able to feel, no matter where she was, or how much time had passed.

She'd spent so many lost years on fearing touch. He would make certain that his touch became something she craved, needed, ached for in the depths of her being. His touch would follow her in her dreams and help erase the traumas that lurked behind her eyes at night. It would soothe her and delete the waking memories of her suffering. He would make certain that touch no longer riddled her with fear; instead, his touch would bring her to life. It would electrify her, make her sizzle with pleasure. And by the end of this, she would know only this: his touch was her pleasure.

*H*er skin was on fire. That was the only way she could describe the sensation. It felt like she was burning, but there was no pain, no discomfort, and most importantly...no fear. She wasn't afraid. She wanted this, wanted him. She wanted him touching her, on her, over her, in her. She just wanted. The sizzle on her skin seemed to be sending electric jolts through her body. She was lying down, but her body wouldn't stay still. It wasn't following her directions or commands; it was doing Kenneth's bidding now.

She felt him move lower, felt the wet tip of his tongue dip inside her navel, leaving a scorching sensation in its wake. She felt that cool-burn sensation travel further down her body until she felt his mouth cover her mound. In one motion he licked her from split to clit and every muscle she possessed stiffened in blessed tension.

"Ahhh...damn...ahhh...ahhh...shit." At least that's what she thought she heard through the haze of pleasure that seemed to be filling her senses from the inside out. Her brain wasn't working well enough for her to form real sentences, hell, she wouldn't be able to tell you her own name at this moment if you'd asked her.

He licked and sucked and effectively devoured the flesh of her womanhood, wet warmth covering her sliding down the crease of her ass. *God, am I really that wet, or is that just his mouth?* The truth was it didn't matter. The end result was the most amazing throb and ache that she'd ever felt. Sweet pleasure building in to the most wonderful mounting pressure she had ever experienced. *I swear I'm gonna die, I don't think I can breathe.*

He moved his tongue back up to that raw bundle of nerves just letting it draw circles on her clit. The vibrations traveled from the tip of his tongue through her clitoris and slowly spreading throughout every fiber of her being. Her thighs began to quiver with a matching rhythm, her breathing became ragged and loud, her muscles tensed in unison, and her hands threaded in the lengths of his dark hair pushing his face deeper to meet the involuntary spastic thrusts of her hips. And then he gave one last swipe of his tongue down the side of her cleft. One last lick was all it took, one last lick to the engorged flesh between her legs, while he pierced her pussy with a single finger and she was done and came undone right beneath him.

∽

*K*enneth had never seen anything this beautiful. She was splayed out before him, body tense and vibrating, muscles locked in glorious tautness. Between her cries of pleasure and the look of tortured bliss on her face, he had to fight to keep his own release at bay.

He placed gentle kisses on the nether lips of her pussy, watching her jerk at the resulting sensitivity. He stood, giving her a moment's reprieve. He dropped the towel draped around his waist and used the remaining juices of her pleasure to stroke his length. He looked down, bulging veins causing an almost painful throb. He ran his thumb across his sensitive cap of stretched skin and coaxed a pearl of fluid from himself. He took in a slow deep breath, trying to keep himself under control. He'd never been this hard, never been so ready to plant himself inside of woman as he was now.

He reached for the condom quickly dispensing with its foil wrapper and slowly rolling it down the turgid piece of flesh pulsing in his hands. He climbed on the bed and planted himself between her legs, using his thighs to widen them, carving out a space for himself. He let the tip of his hard flesh rest just inside her walls. He leaned forward and kissed her, letting her experience her own sweetness. He took her healing arm and flattened it against her chest. "I don't want you hurting yourself. Don't move it."

She nodded her understanding, complying without question.

He kissed her again and slowly inched inside her rigid walls. There was a slight resistance and then her body gave and conformed to him and within moments he was balls-deep inside the loveliest heat he had ever experienced.

"So fucking tight and hot." He fought to keep still, struggling against his body's need to release. When he felt he had some measure of control he pulled out slowly, leaving nothing but the tip of his cock in inside of her. Just as slowly, he pushed back in, attempting to give her time to adjust to him. He went to pull back again when her walls tightened around him, causing his breath to stop in his chest. His eyes winced closed as he almost succumbed to the most delicious squeeze he had ever felt.

His hips snapped involuntarily and he heard a hungry moan dance out her lips. *She liked that?* He snapped his hips again purposefully this time, and was rewarded with the same moan with an added thrashing of her head. *She does like this. Thank God, slow was going to kill me.*

He hooked one of her legs around his arm and planted his other hand on the bed, just above her shoulder. He tested the leverage by snapping his hips again in quick succession. When he was certain his place was secure, he set up a punishing pace for both him and her.

Her body was both attempting to escape but begging him for more at the same time. He kept up his brutal thrusting falling in time with the guttural sounds erupting from her mouth. He knew it was going to be like this, fiery hot. That first day he'd spoken with her, he'd felt such intensity rolling off her, the same intensity that was surrounding him now.

He could live and die in this shit right here; hot, wet, so wet it was sloppy. He could feel her juices pooling in the soft short hair grazing his testicles. She was dripping. Every time he thrust inside, more of her essence would cascade down his balls and thighs making the slide in and out so damn smooth he was about to burst.

He pulled out long enough to switch positions. He lay behind her, spooning her, cradling her to his chest, wrapping her safely in his arms. He raised her thigh over his and slide back home. Home, he'd never truly known the meaning of that word until he'd felt what it was like to rest inside of this woman's warmth.

The thought of her, of what she was allowing him to share, of what she was risking, made something inside of him tear. He felt so overwhelmed, so out of his element. He felt as if he was drowning. His lungs hurt from trying to breathe through whatever this was that was filling him up inside. His mind reminded him that he should be afraid, that he should be scared because his chest felt so full. Fear never entered the equation, instead, he reached out for her, bringing her lips to his, consuming her like a starving man with his first piece of food in ages.

"Ahh, baby," he moaned into her mouth. "You feel so fucking good." He grabbed her breast tweaking her nipple until it was almost painful, watching her squirm in his arms.

"Kenneth."

He felt her walls clamp down tighter. She was close, he was too. He didn't know how much longer he could keep up the pace. He slid his hand down her abdomen until his felt the moist juncture between her legs. She nearly bolted from the bed when his fingertip passed over the sensitive almost bulging pearl. He used one hand to keep her firmly in place, pressed against him, skin meeting skin. He used the other hand to run circles around the tender flesh with perfectly pressured fingers.

"Come for me, baby. I need you to come for me now."

He felt her tighten. God, her muscles were squeezing him so hard he felt like he might break. His balls pulled up, they were tight, painful, needed release like he needed air. He quickened his pace, the strength of his thrusts increasing, he changed his angle ever so slightly and she cried out and shattered right before him. The vice-like spasms pulled his release from him, making the thrusting motion of his hips sputter as his body peaked. He gave one last thrust and locked himself to her as blistering, pulsing jets of his cum filled the condom.

He placed his face in the juncture of her neck as his body took hungry breaths to replenish the air his lungs were craving. He placed a tired hand against her breast and felt a strong rapid pulse banging against his hand. It was beating out the matching tattoo of his heartbeat. He hugged her close one more time, making certain what they'd experienced was real. *Has to be*, he thought to himself. *Cause this...this, yeah, it just has to be.*

*H*eart wallowed in the tingly after-sensation that was zipping across every inch of her skin and her sex. There was nothing in her past that could compare to the feeling of having this man drag his cock over every sensitive nerve in her walls. *Nope, not never in the history of ever has shit ever felt this good.*

Her womb was still quivering with the tiny spasms of her recent orgasm. Shaking on the inside of its own volition, her muscles seemed to require no urging from her. She was pretty much gelatin at this point. No muscle-tone to speak of, it was an effort just to keep her eyelids at half-mast.

"Heart, are you all right?"

She heard Kenneth's voice calling to her, but again, she was gelatin, her body wasn't making any unnecessary moves at this point. He must have sensed her dilemma and pulled her into his arms so she faced him.

"Are you all right?" he asked again.

She burrowed closer into the warmth of his embrace and nodded her head. "Yes," she mumbled, not even her tongue was following her commands right now. She could feel his fingers stroking her skin, calming the electric charge that was buzzing through every one of her cells.

She let her eyes and fingers trace his skin, taking notice of things she hadn't been aware of while Kenneth was laying assault to her senses. The skin of his body was smooth, the same alabaster complexion that covered his face continued down the length of his body. For a man whose hair reached the middle of his back, his body was only lightly dusted with a fine sheen of brownish-black hair.

Her eyes followed the journey her hand was slowly taking her on. Her fingers crawlwalking down the carved swells of his abdomen and into the soft, light thatch of hair that covered his pubic area. She let her hand move lower, until her fingers were sliding down the length of his cock. It jumped at her touch, still half-erect, even after giving her so much pleasure and finding its own.

When he was erect, it had appeared menacing and angry, the lone patch of color on otherwise milky-white skin. It was red, and then a furious purple as it jutted out in front of him while he was rolling down the condom. It was wide, it had stretched her nearly to the point of pain, and long enough that he filled every inch of the cavernous walls of her pussy, making it elongate beyond its capabilities just to accommodate him. *Whoever said white men ain't packing was telling a bold faced lie.*

Her fingers curled around the width of what had to be the prettiest piece of meat there was. Granted, she hadn't seen many this close, but never had a man's genitalia made her want to touch, lick...*Did I just think lick?...shit,* she was so fucking open. Her mouth was watering and her throat muscles involuntarily squeezed. Whether she wanted to admit it to herself or not, that shit was turning her on more by the minute.

She continued to stroke and turned her eyes up to his. He looked at her briefly, closed his eyes, and his hips began to chase the rhythm she was creating. "If you're not up for receiving more of the same I'd suggest you stop. In a minute, I won't be able to stop myself from making you sit on it until I'm buried inside of you."

She sat up on her haunches, her hand still creating the careful beat his hips were rising and falling to. "Who says that I would have a problem with that?"

His eyes snapped open and he lifted a single brow in either challenge or caution, maybe both. She smiled in return and lifted herself, positioning her leg over his pelvis and gently sitting atop the stiff pipe-like dick pressing back against her folds. Her hips pitched forward out of instinct and his eyes rolled closed. He grabbed her waist and held her firmly in place.

"Shit," he muttered. "It's on."

CHAPTER 13

A piercing shrill pulled him from the haze of sleep. He stirred slightly encountering lovely warmth that moved with him, blanketing him as he climbed through layers of unconsciousness to wakefulness. Kenneth wrapped his arms around that warmth pulled it closer, snuggled deeper into it. His hands began to travel and he noticed familiar curves that brought a smile to his lips.

Heart.

The thought of her name brought back flashes of memory from the hours they'd

spent in each other's arms throughout the night. They'd made love last night for the first time, and repeated that action in several satisfying ways over and over again until exhaustion had rendered them both limp and they fell into a tangle of arms, legs, and bodies while they slept.

He went to move closer to Heart, wanting her as near as their bodies would allow, but the incessant noise that pulled him from his slumber was still screaming, demanding his attention. He reached behind him awkwardly, refusing to separate from the flesh-toflesh connection he and Heart had going at the moment. He made two or three swipes with his hand before his fingers clasped around the device.

"'Lo," was all his dry throat could produce.

"Kenneth?"

Kenneth struggled to fight through the remaining fog in his brain. The voice was familiar. He knew the voice, if he could just focus on thinking, instead feeling the curve of Heart's ass against his dick.

"Kenneth, you there? Boy you better answer me before I reach out and touch you through this damn telephone line."

Kenneth's eyes snapped open, he knew that voice, knew that gruff-ass vernacular.

"Uncle David."

"Boy, I've been trying to find you all morning. It's damn near ten in the morning on a weekday. Why the hell aren't you at work?"

"I'm home."

"The hell you are, I sent a uniform to the penthouse, no one's there."

"Shit," Kenneth hissed. He hadn't exactly told his godfather he was rooming or living with his injured number two cop. *Yeah...not really looking forward to that conversation.* "I'm in Woodmere, Uncle David."

"With MacKenzie?"

Kenneth looked down at the sleeping woman in his arms. His mind didn't readily recognize her by that name. MacKenzie was hard, foreboding, and untouchable. That wasn't the woman buried in the curve of his arm at this moment. This woman was all soft curves, welcoming, and every single thing about the texture of her skin invited him to touch, taste, lick...damn, he had to focus, Porter was on the phone.

"Uncle David, Heart doesn't really have anyone to help her out, so I've been staying here to give her a helping hand."

"Yeah...all right, tell that bullshit to someone who believes it. I know you, Kenneth, and if you're hanging around, helping my lieutenant, it's cause you're trying to figure out how to get your dick wet...if you haven't already."

Damn, sometimes the fact that his godfather knew him so well made it very difficult for him to lie. "That fact is neither here nor there. She needed help, and you didn't volunteer, so I'm here."

"Boy, don't get smart. You're not too old for me to pop you in your mouth."

Kenneth, laughed, not because he didn't believe Porter would do just what he'd threatened, but because over the entire course of Kenneth's life, the man had never changed who he was.

"Uncle D. I was up late last night, I'm tired, is there a reason you were looking for me?"

"You bet your ass," Porter growled. "Ida-Mae Amare is looking for Mac."

"Heart's grandmother?"

At the mention of her name, Heart rolled over and called his name through her sleepy daze. "Kenneth?"

Mmm, the sound of his name on her lips, especially draped in a hard-on inducing moan that was doing strange things to his anatomy at this moment.

"Was that fucking MacKenzie sounding like a bad porn actress? I can't believe..."

Kenneth pulled the phone away from his ear to spare his eardrum from Porter's rage. Heart was beginning to stir from the noise, so he slid out of the bed, quietly padded over to the dresser and pulled out a pair of sweats. The idea of talking to his godfather with his dick swinging just kind of grossed him out. Sweats loosely hanging from his hips, he tiptoed out of the room and down the stairs.

"Uncle David," Kenneth interrupted Porter's bellowing. "Uncle David, you're not helping with the screaming."

"Kenneth, I warned you to stay away from her."

"Uncle David, Heart, and I are both grown. You don't get a say in this. I'm no longer a part of her case, and she's no longer off limits. Why is her grandmother looking for her?"

"I don't know. Ida-Mae has these strange abilities to always know when something is off with Mac. She called me this morning asking to know exactly where Mac was."

"Why didn't she just call Heart?"

"She did, but MacKenzie didn't answer her phone. Apparently, wherever the two of you are in the house, Mac's cell-phone isn't with you."

Kenneth took a deep breath. "Did she say how long it would be before she left for

Woodmere?"

"Kenneth, one must always assume that when Ida-Mae Amare asks a question, she already knows the answer to it. My guess, she was probably more than half-way there when she dialed me. She was probably just seeing if I would tell her the truth."

Kenneth rolled his eyes. *How did such a beautiful morning with such amazing potential turn into this?* "All right, Uncle David, I'll let Heart know."

"Trust me, Kenneth that old woman scares even me, and I carry a gun."

Kenneth disconnected the call and turned to place a single bare-foot on the bottom stair. Before he could feel the carpeted wood beneath his foot the doorbell chimed.

"Shit," Kenneth hissed. He walked to the front door and peeked through the peephole. "Shit," he mouthed quietly afraid the elderly woman standing on the other side of the door would hear him.

"Boy, I know you're standing there, you might as well go on and open that door."

That was the second time today someone had called him, "Boy." *This shit has got to stop*. Kenneth took a deep breath, shoulders lifting, attempting to pull on his business tycoon I'm-not-afraid-of-anything façade.

He stuck his arm out, turned the locks to their open positions, and then twisted the knob with his hand. He opened the door and painted on his sincerest smile. "Mrs. Amare, how lovely to see you this morning."

The elder woman looked up at him above the tiny black frames sitting on the tip of her nose. She let her gaze travel the length of him, from top to bottom she assessed his appearance and drew her own conclusions.

She walked past him and entered the home. She looked to her left, then her right, then traveled straight down the hall to the kitchen. When Kenneth caught up to her, her old-lady purse was sitting on the counter and she was at the kitchen sink washing her hands.

"Mrs. Amare, if you need something, I can make it for you. You're a guest; you don't have to serve yourself here."

She turned toward him as she dried her hands on a nearby paper towel. "Young man, I don't need you to tell me I'm welcome here, anywhere my grandbaby is resting her head is as good as my home." She looked him over again; he could feel the chill of her gaze washing over him. "Speaking of my grandbaby, where is she this late in the morning?"

Whatever you do Kenneth, don't go all freaky pink. You start blushing and she's got you. "I think she's upstairs sleeping."

"You think? Well let's give you a question that you should certainly be able to answer. Why are you walking around in my grandbaby's home with nothing more than some pajama pants on?"

Kenneth opened his mouth to speak, but was halted, left with his mouth wide open when she lifted a skinny, aged, cocoa brown finger.

"I will remind you young man that I have spent the last nearly sixty years of my life raising children and grandchildren. So whatever you're about to tell me, make certain it's the truth. Anything else and you might find yourself on my wrong side."

Kenneth closed his mouth and looked at the elderly woman standing in the kitchen. He read people for a living; it was why his business was so successful. His bullshit meter was always finely tuned. This was not bullshit. Ida-Mae Amare was dead-ass serious.

"Mrs. Amare. I'm staying here with Heart while she recuperates."

"So you're living here...in sin with my baby?"

Kenneth raised his eyebrows. Hell, how the hell was he supposed to answer that?

"Mrs. Amare, I don't quite know about the sin part, but yes, Heart and I are living together for the moment."

"And you're sleeping with her, as in having sex with her?"

"Mrs. Amare, you are Heart's grandmother, and I have the utmost respect for you. However, Heart and I are grown, and I will not be discussing the details of our relationship with you or anyone else. If Heart wishes to discuss that with you then that's her right to do so, but I will leave that to her to make that decision."

"So you call yourself protecting her...against me, her grandmother?"

"Ma'am, I'd protect her from the devil himself if it were necessary."

She watched him for a moment with stern unshakable eyes. She pushed those scarylooking tiny glasses up her nose and a smile pulled at one corner of her mouth.

"That is what I've been waiting for all her life, a man who would stand up to anyone on her behalf," she laughed, drawing a small curl of laughter from him as well. "Including me and her crazy-ass cousin, True. You tangle with that one yet?"

Kenneth nodded; he and True had locked horns in Heart's hospital room the day she was shot and last night over the phone. "Yes ma'am, and I'm surprisingly still here."

"You got that right, 'cause that grandchild of mine ain't one to be taken lightly. If you're still breathing, she must really think you have a place in her cousin's life."

"I'm hoping I do. Heart is very special to me."

Mrs. Amare nodded and smiled again. "All right then. Since it seems my granddaughter is too tired to be up this hour of the late day, you're going to take me on a couple of errands today so you and I can get to know each other better. You all right with that, Kenneth?"

He nodded his head. "Just let me get changed and leave Heart a note."

He climbed the stairs and slowly opened the door to his bedroom. He smiled when he spotted Heart in the exact same spot he'd left her in in the middle of his bed.

He crawled into the bed and softly planted himself behind her, spooning her, pulling her warm body into his. "Baby," he whispered in her ear and luxuriated in the feel of the luscious stretch her body extended into as she responded to his voice.

"Hmm," she answered.

"We have an unexpected visitor downstairs, you're grandmother's here."

She bolted up so quickly she nearly knocked him off of the bed. "Mama's downstairs? Shit, I gotta get it together before she figures out what happened between us."

He grabbed her arm to still her, keep her from leaping from the bed. "Baby, that horse is pretty much out of the gate already."

"Noooo," she groaned. "Is she screaming, did she say anything inappropriate to you? My grandmother is like an older version of True; sometimes their mouths get a little out of hand. I'm sorry; I'll go talk to her. I'm so sorry, Kenneth."

Kenneth stroked the skin on her forearm, and then kissed the path his fingers had drawn. "Your grandmother is fine. She and I came to an understanding. In fact, I just came up here to tell you I'm taking her on a few errands; she wants to spend some time with me."

Heart began shaking her head, "Kenneth, I don't know if that is such a good idea."

Kenneth kissed her exposed neck, continuing to nibble on the tender flesh until her muscles began to relax under his touch. "Baby, trust me, let me handle this. Everything will be fine. Lie back down; get some more sleep until Faith arrives. I'll set the alarm so you will have plenty of time to get yourself together before she gets here." He continued tasting that delicate spot until he was certain she was no longer worrying and would agree to pretty much anything he asked.

"Mmm...'kay," she moaned.

He smiled; it thrilled him beyond belief that his touch made her so malleable. "I'm going to shower, and head out with your grandmother. Get some rest."

She smiled at him, then burrowed herself back under the covers. When he was certain she was asleep, he reached for the alarm clock, set it and headed for the shower.

He thought about the matronly woman sitting in the kitchen and laughed to himself.

Today was definitely going to be an interesting day.

~

$\mathcal{H}$eart heard the strange buzzing sound pulling her from the cozy sleep she was experiencing. "God, where's my gun when I need it?" The thought of her weapons and her current inability to use them made her drag herself in an upright position, pulling her legs and limbs from the warm cocoon of the lush duvet. "Well, if you ever want to use your guns again, you'd better get ready for this torture session Faith likely has in store for you."

She showered as quickly as her aching muscles would allow her to. *Note to self, no more marathon sex with Kenneth the night/morning before a therapy session with Faith.* God her aching thighs made it hard to walk.

She inched down the stairs carefully, making it to the landing just in time to hear Faith ring the bell. She rushed to the door, well, moved as fast as her aching legs and backside would allow her to. *Either Kenneth is way too talented or I need to get in better shape to deal with his ass.* She reached out for the doorknob with her weak arm and forced her muscles in her hand to grip the knob and turn. It took some major effort, not to mention a noticeable amount of discomfort, but she had done it. A week ago, that little maneuver would have set her back. As much as she couldn't stand Faith, the woman knew her business well. Heart was improving.

"Hi, Faith." Heart smiled, more at her accomplishment than the person on the other side of the door.

Faith smiled and nodded as she walked through the space Heart had made for her. Faith headed straight for the basement, it was where their sessions took place. The space was furnished into three distinct rooms. One was a home theatre. There were three rows of recliner chairs positioned on a declining angle from the back of the room to the front of the wall-sized flat screen television. The second room was a game room that housed a pool table, several high-tech electronic gaming consoles that were attached to another wall-sized TV, a cards table, and a bar. The last room, located in the far back of the structure was a completed state-of-the-art gym. There wasn't a designer gym franchise that had anything on the gym in this base-

ment. There were several resistance training machines and appara-
tuses—most she hadn't figured out how to work yet—some for upper
body, others for lower. There were cardio machines, and free weights,
as well as an indoor track that ran the diameter of the mirrored-
covered walls. Whoever the owner of this house was, he'd damn sure
spent a lot of time and money on making sure he had everything a
body could ever want to be comfortable at home. Why she was living
here instead of the owner, was a mystery she'd yet to figure out.

Once she'd agreed to rent this place, Faith had instructed Kenneth
on what equipment would be needed for her rehabilitation to take
place at home, and he had gone out and purchased top-of-the-line
everything. Apparently being rich was nice.

Faith walked into the gym/rehab room and Heart followed
tenderly behind her, being mindful of the achy muscles in her thighs
right now.

Faith straddled the workbench and motioned for Heart to do the
same. *You gotta be fucking kidding me*, her muscles screamed, but she bit
the inside of her cheek and performed a much slower version of the
movement.

"Are you all right," Faith offered.

"Hmm, just tired, it was a long night."

Faith considered her for a moment and continued on. "All right, so
how's the entire arm and hand?"

"I feel it much more, feels like it's waking up. I can grab more
things. I was actually able to turn the locks and twist the knob with
my right hand and wrist."

Faith nodded as she jotted down some things on her tablet. She did
that frequently, anytime Heart said something new about her condition, Faith noted it on her tablet.

"That's amazing progress, Heart. So what I want to do now is
change up your routine. Instead of working so much on things like
your dexterity, which seems to be getting better every day, I want to
start working on your strength."

"But what about the nerve damage you were concerned about
last time?"

"Well, the fact that you're feeling more sensation in the arm makes me optimistic that the possible nerve damage we were concerned about isn't really an issue. We'll do further testing of course before we come to a definitive conclusion, but I think over all, your arm is looking pretty good right now."

Heart couldn't help the relieved sigh that left her chest. She hadn't even realized she'd been physically holding on to it while Faith was speaking.

"Does that mean I'm gonna get my gun hand back?"

"Your hand was never really involved in the injury Heart, it was more your shoulder. The lack of feeling as a result of some of the nerve damage caused by the injury, that was our main concern in getting your hand functioning at NYPD standards."

"I'll be able to resume my duties?"

Faith took a cautious breath. "I can't promise you anything definitive, but I can say you're on the right track to making that happen."

Heart smiled. It was a positive statement—okay, a cautiously positive statement, but a positive statement nonetheless.

"All right, let's save the celebration for when you're actually back in the field. For right now, we've still got a great deal of work to do."

Heart nodded, and locked herself down focusing only on her singular objective: getting her gun hand back. She locked her teeth together and pushed through every exercise Faith tortured her with. No bitching, no moaning, she needed her gun hand back. It was the deciding factor on whether or not she would still command, or whether she would be put out to pasture before she even reached the age of thirty.

She worked through that session like a woman possessed and didn't stop until Faith put the brakes on when she motioned for Heart to lay down on the massage table. This is how each of their sessions ended, Heart lying on the table, Faith flexing and extending her recovering limb until it felt loose and noodle-like. Then Faith would attach the leads of the electric stimulation machine to her arm and she would let her muscles relax while the ache of the session eased away.

She must have drifted off to sleep because she felt the sensation of someone touching her, someone not Kenneth. Her hackles went up, her mind still a little cloudy with sleep, she reached out on instinct grabbing the offending hand in a hard vice.

"Heart, dammit, let me go!"

The voice sounded familiar, but she needed to make certain before she released her grip. She focused her eyes on the woman grabbing at her hand, face twisted in discomfort. It was Faith.

Heart's grip released finger by finger until Faith stumbled back away from her.

"What the hell was that about?" Faith asked. "How the hell did you even do that with your injury?"

"Cop instinct. I told you I had issues with touch before we started this. I told you to never touch me when I couldn't see you."

Heart breathed trying to push the fear she hadn't felt since she'd come home from the hospital. Usually during her sessions with Faith, every touch was always attempted within plain sight and Heart was able to force her panic down and work through her need to flee or defend.

"Sorry, Faith, I didn't mean to hurt you."

"God, if you can do that with an injured arm, I'd hate to see what you're capable of at full strength."

Heart sat up and jumped down from the table. She grabbed her water bottle and took a big swig.

"You had a great workout today, Heart."

She fiddled with the bottle in front of her, trying to find a reason to stay turned away from the woman across the room.

"You seemed a little tired when you came in though. Tell Kenneth he's got to keep his all-night marathon sessions to a minimum during your therapy."

Did this bitch just...? Oh hell no. "Should I know what you're referring to?" Heart asked as she slowly turned around. She and Faith were cordial enough to work with one another, but having this bitch in her business, especially where Kenneth was concerned...nah, not happening.

"It's pretty obvious that Kenneth and you are lovers."

"Is it?" Heart asked.

"I mean he's practically humping you with your clothes on every time I see the two of you together."

"Hmm, I hadn't really noticed that."

"Heart, I mean, the love bites on your neck pretty much paint a picture. That damn man was always in to leaving marks, I mean, he used to send me to school looking like

I'd been attacked by insects or vampires."

Heart put her water bottle down on the bench. The truth was, she wanted to make sure she didn't have anything in her hand that she might use as a weapon if Faith pissed her off too much.

"Hold up, I don't know how you, my cousin, and Genesis get down, but I don't discuss my personal life with anyone except the person involved in it. You are providing a service for me, we might be acquainted with one another, but we ain't friends. Don't worry about what Kenneth did or didn't do to me last night. As far as I understand it, that's no longer your concern."

Faith raised a brow while a half-smile that wasn't really a smile took control of her features. "Who Kenneth sleeps with is no longer my concern because I chose for it not to be, not because he didn't want it to be. Kenneth and I hooked up for many years after we went our separate ways."

"Faith, here's a tip. Just because something is convenient, doesn't mean it's desired."

She watched Faith visibly flinch for a second before the woman caught herself and schooled her features back into the perfect perky smile she'd been wearing since her days as a cheerleader.

"Mmm, the bitch has fangs," Faith said.

"You'd better believe it." Heart threw her towel over her shoulder and left the room.

Hopefully, Faith got the message loud and clear: back off.

∽

*K*enneth walked back into the house and slunk his back against the closed door. He'd spent most of the day running Ida-Mae Amare all over kingdom come when the only thing he'd wanted was to get back here and fall into Heart's arms. He was more than certain that Ida-Mae had sent him on a fool's journey just to keep him away from her granddaughter. But Ida-Mae was now safely home, he'd made sure of it, and now, he was home and could spend the rest of his waking hours buried in that wonderful woman's body.

Eyes still closed, he felt her presence inside before his senses had recognized her. Where did that come from? His senses had never reacted to someone like they did with Heart.

"You are an evil woman, you knew what your grandmother had in store for me and you let me walk right into her clutches anyway." Kenneth listened to the rumble of laughter coming from her.

"What did she make you do?"

"She made me drive her all over Long Island and Queens looking for these crazy items that I know she didn't really need."

"So you think she took you on a wild goose chase just to keep you away from me?"

His eyes opened wide and he took in the vision of her standing in an A-cut t-shirt that rested against her skin like a tailored glove. His eyes traveled over her full breasts down to a tapered waist. He watched the fabric of the sweatpants she wore hanging low on curvy hips that were perfectly made for holding on to. He'd dated every nationality and ethnicity of woman there was, but nothing did it for him like a woman with deep curves, giving him something to hold on to and anchor himself.

He watched her lean back against the banister and a small sliver of flesh peeked out from the gap between the bottom of her shirt and the top of her sweatpants. God, the sight of her exposed skin did things to his blood that should not be biologically possible. He walked closer to her, kneeling before her, ready to worship at her delectable alter.

He leaned forward and licked a hot swipe of his tongue from hip to hip of her exposed flesh. He felt the muscles beneath her skin tremble and that pushed him to make more contact.

He hooked determined fingers in the waistband of her sweats and slid them down to reveal smooth skin. He nibbled at her hip and let his lips and tongue blaze a trail to her navel. He wrapped his arm around her waist and dipped his tongue inside the shallow cavern. "I will never get tired of the taste of you," he whispered as he climbed back up the length of her quivering body until his hands found the firm flesh of her breasts.

He allowed his hands to knead them, the firm flesh giving under his manipulations. He felt the rigid peak of her nipple dance against his thumb. He tugged it slightly and listened to the moans falling from her mouth. He raised himself up just high enough that he could cover the stiff flesh with his mouth. He let his tongue pass over it and relished the delectable shiver her body offered.

He pulled himself off her dragging much needed air into his lungs. "Are you on birth control?" he asked, breath rushing in and out heavily before and after each word.

"No."

"Then we'd better get upstairs to where the condoms are. Otherwise, I'm fucking you right here and we're making babies tonight."

He watched as understanding poured over her and she nodded her head. She took a step back separating them, and then took off running up the stairs two at a time. He stood there for a moment smiling as he watched the twin shapely globes of her ass ripple as the underlying muscles stretched and pulled as she climbed the stairs.

"I am such a lucky man."

≈

*H*eart heard the click of the door and turned just in time to meet Kenneth's gaze as he stepped through the door.

"Damn," was all that passed through his lips. He was standing, fixed to the spot just inside of his bedroom with a hungry look plastered on his face that might have frightened her if she wasn't feeling just as starved for him.

She stood still in front of the foot of the bed skin free of any clothing.

"I'm feeling a little sticky from my PT session. I was thinking a shower might be warranted."

He leaned in to place a soft kiss on the curve of her healing shoulder. "You taste and smell fine to me, there's no way I'm waiting for you to take a shower in order to taste all of this wonderful skin."

She leaned into him, leaned into the tiny nibbles he was gracing her shoulder with, silently asking for more. "I never said anything about you waiting for me to shower. I was hoping you would join me."

She felt him still, and then he picked his head up and locked eyes with her. He placed a firm hand on the base of her neck and pulled her toward him until his lips covered hers and his tongue was pushing inside her slightly opened lips demanding access to her mouth.

She gladly granted that access and savored the taste of him. He must have been chewing gum or consuming something sweet and minty, he tasted like candy, honeyed, smooth, and addictive. She pressed into his body, pressed into the kiss, giving back the force and passion he was gifting her with. She felt a slight twinge of pain on her scalp, he'd locked his fingers in her loosened locks, holding her mouth in place just where he wanted it, just where she wanted to be.

He placed a forceful grip on her backside, pulling her close to him. She could feel the stiff yet soft flesh of his cock pressing into her belly, leaving a cool drop of pre-cum on her skin. She wrapped her arms around him, determined to keep his hot skin pressed against her nestling into the heat his skin was emanating.

He took a soft nip of her bottom lip and angled her head away from him. "Go get the shower started, I'll be right behind you." He kissed her once more and placed a light tap to her behind, sending her on her way. She walked toward the bathroom, stopping once to glance back over her shoulder and offer him one last hungry glance before she slipped into the bathroom.

She quickly turned the shower tap on and stood beneath the

powerful spray. She made quick work of washing away the evidence of her physical therapy session. Kenneth might have thought workout sweat was sexy, but she knew better.

She saw the brief shadow his muscular body cast across the glass shower door. She stepped further inside making room for him. She held out a shaky hand and he pulled her into the firm, hard sculpted muscles of his chest. He backed her up under the spray of water. She felt the drops begin to saturate her hair followed by his strong fingers massaging her tingling scalp. Like most black women, water was her kryptonite when it came to her hair, but right now she didn't give a fuck. She'd spend all day tomorrow sitting in Ms. Marisol's chair at the Dominican spot she got her hair done in. This feeling this man was giving her was worth the pain and aggravation of sitting in a salon on a Friday trying to get her 'do right.

He ravaged her mouth and secured one leg and then the other around his waist.

Before she knew it, he'd picked her up, back pressed against the wall, and he was buried within her walls. He stood still for a moment, giving her body a chance to adjust to his girth while he kept drinking from her mouth. God when had kissing become so important to her? She didn't know, but kissing him seemed more important than breathing at that moment, so she tussled and tangled with his tongue, letting it invade her with little resistance.

He began a slow roll of his hips and her head fell back against the cool tile, the pleasure of it almost too much. His length ran right over that sensitive bundle of nerves and her breath hitched in her chest as he nudged it slowly and intentionally. The pressure was just enough to send jolts of zipping electricity through her body, but wouldn't give her the release her sex was aching for. She was going to break apart in pieces and he was torturing her on purpose.

"Please…" was all she could offer, words not forming right in her head.

"Please what? Tell me what you want."

"You…" He made another slow pass inside her and the words were lost again, she was so close, if he just gave a little more force behind his thrust she would fall off the edge. Her pleasure was just within reach, but the slow push and pull he was giving her at the moment was drawing out her pleasure, preventing her from reaching that peak that was so close she could taste it.

She closed her eyes, concentrated as much as she could, and forced herself to string words together. "Fuck me, please..." That's all she could manage, all she could muster, it had to be enough otherwise she'd go crazy with this slow motion torture he was imposing on her.

"With pleasure," was all she heard before his hips snapped and she was pushed up and down the tile wall in tandem with his powerful thrusts. This was what she'd spent all day waiting for. She'd ached for this maddening sensation that was causing the most delicious pressure to build within her body. Her walls started convulsing and she could feel herself splintering.

"Shit," was all she managed before her mind short-circuited with the shocks of pleasure that were sparking throughout every nerve synapse she had.

His pace was unrelenting. He fucked her through one orgasm and right on to a second one. She grabbed on to his neck, needing purchase as her muscles locked in glorious tension for the second time in mere moments. Her cries of pleasure seemed to drive him on; he never let up, kept tapping at that elusive spot at the most perfect angle with the most precise pressure over and over again.

"Kenneth, please..."

He somehow understood and walked them over to the wide bench on the opposite wall of the shower. He sat down, their bodies still connected. He buried his face in between the cavern of her breasts and just worshipped there until he found the perfect seat within her. He pulled her hips forward. She instinctively moved with him inside of her. Her walls and muscle clutching him, moving her hips backward, forward, up, and down. He let his head rest against the shower glass allowing his eyes to close and roll back in pleasure.

He opened his eyes, focusing downward where their bodies met. He drove up, meeting her downward motion, filling every inch of her, making her insides quiver with need. He hooked his hands under her arms and over her shoulders and held her close as he changed their position slightly. She was still on top of him, but he now lay supine against the bench. He pressed up forcing her body down on him by applying firm pressure to her shoulders. She matched his intensity, her eyes watching the slow rose flush crawl slowly up from the center of his chest to his neck. He was close; she could feel the tension in his body increasing, his body becoming tighter.

She placed flat palms on his chest and used the firm pecks beneath her hands as an anchor while she slapped her sex against his, popping her ass up and out."

"Fuuuuck, baby, yes. Ride that shit," was the last comprehensible thing that crossed his lips. All other sounds were raw noises of passion that made her aching muscles continue to move and work toward one goal, his release. That's what she needed, what she wanted, for him to be as broken open by their meeting as she was. She met every one of his intense thrusts with one of her own, equal in force, adding to his pleasure while equally chasing her own.

Her skin was hot and tight, she felt like she was ready to explode. She couldn't tell if the fine sheen glistening across her skin was from the spray of the showerheads or the perspiration from her overheated body.

She glanced down at his face, muscles drawn tight, the pink flush brighter, deeper, rising to his face and ears. He was there, she could tell, he just needed...her. She bent over, wrapped his long dark locks in her hand, and tugged him forward until their lips met. She roughly covered his mouth, letting her teeth pinch that rosy bottom lip. She tugged on it, then lapped at it and sucked it between full lips while she clamped down on his thick cock one more time.

That mix of pleasure and pain was all they both needed, with it he dug his fingernails in the rounds of her ass and held her over him will he rutted up into her over and over until they both fractured into tiny pieces as the crest of both their releases peaked and fell over that deep sensual edge of pleasure.

CHAPTER 14

*K*enneth sat behind his desk tapping away at the keys of his computer. He had a crap-ton of work waiting on his desk and an amazing amount of motivation to get it done. Heart was coming to pick him up and surprise him with some after work fun only if he agreed to finish everything pending on his desk.

When she first proposed this outing he figured he would be able to decide the terms of it. After all, he was his own boss he could dictate when his workday was finished, but that crafty detective's mind of hers was a step ahead of him. She'd called his secretary and told her to personally call her when Kenneth had finished all of his pending duties for the day.

What kind of shit is this when the boss can't call the shots? He smiled as he thought of Heart. He wasn't the least bit upset that she was calling the shots. Hell, he secretly liked it when she called the shots. Like he'd woken up this morning to her full cocoa brown lips pulled tight around his dick. *Stop that Kenneth, getting a hard-on is only going to make this day longer than it already is.*

He was smiling, drifting into the memory of the blowjob he'd been fortunate enough to receive that morning when he heard a familiar voice drift into his memory.

"I sure hope that smile on your face is for me."

Kenneth blinked his gaze clear of the morning fun with Heart and placed eyes on another beautiful chocolate-skinned woman he had once known intimately. "Faith, how could the smile be for you when I had no idea you were coming?"

She held a knowing smile on her face while making herself comfortable in the chair facing his desk. "Well whose fault is that Kenneth? You've been very difficult to get a hold of since I arrived in New York. If I didn't know better I'd think that you were purposely avoiding me. But that couldn't be the problem, could it?"

Kenneth rolled his eyes and let his first and middle finger rub the slow throb that was beginning to take root at his temple. This passive-aggressive means of addressing a problem had been an issue when the two were dating all those years ago. Faith never really came out and said what she meant; she just kind of danced around the problem usually offering up a major serving of sarcasm to point him in the direction of whatever he'd done wrong that time.

"Faith, you know me, you know I hate the song and dance around the problem act that you like to play. What's the issue?"

"Kenneth, I mean, I thought we could've at least spent some time together while I was here working with Heart. Or does she monopolize and manipulate all the hours of your day?"

He raised his brow at her words, shifting in his seat attempting to check himself of his need to defend Heart all the time. "Heart does not manipulate anything. Whatever time I spend with her is because I want to give it. Why do you have a problem with that?"

Faith stood up and walked around Kenneth's side of the desk and turned his chair just enough that she was able to slide down onto his lap. "Well, I was hoping to get a little extra-friendly time in with you before I had to go back home."

"Wait, you're going home?"

"Yeah, by the end of next week," she said as she used her fingers to crawl up the length of his silk tie and landed a manicured finger on his square jaw.

"What about Heart?"

"What about her? She's finished with therapy. I'll be signing off for her to return to work as of next week. Not that I should really be telling you that, but since you've been so involved in her case already..."

Kenneth grabbed Faith's wrist and helped her out of his lap in to a standing position. "That is fantastic news; Heart is going to be so thrilled."

"Yeah, Heart is going to be ecstatic. Now, back to us..." Faith attempted to step back into Kenneth's personal space, but he stood and put distance between he and his ex.

"Faith, I'm not trying to hurt your feelings here, but what you and I had has been long gone."

She went to run her fingers through his hair and he stopped her. Heart loved his hair; she spent hours stroking it, brushing it, caring for it. It was something he adored having her play with it. It somehow felt wrong, like it was too intimate of an act to allow anyone else to partake in it. He placed a tight hold around her wrist and pulled it down from her intended target. "Faith, although I treasure the time you and I had together, I'm at a very different place in my life."

"Because of Heart?" she asked.

"I'm building something with Heart, something special, and as tempting as it is to travel down a very comfortable and familiar road, it's not what I want or need at this moment."

He watched the meaning of his words sink in and understanding take hold. "You can't honestly be turning me down for her. I mean we have always hooked up when we were in the same town at the same time."

He shook his head. "Not this time," was all he said.

She watched him circumspectly, as if she really didn't believe the words he was speaking. "She's manly," Faith laughed out loud. "And she's plain and boring as all hell.

What could you possibly see in that hag?"

Kenneth stepped close to her, speaking through clenched lips. "Watch your tone

Faith, your claws are showing."

"Kenneth, really, Heart? She's a plain Jane. You know damn well that your tastes run on the more energetic and eclectic side. Heart is a by-the-book, buttoned-up-to-herneck-conservative that wouldn't know how handle a man like you if her shiny, brass badge depended on it." She laughed to herself, lifting her eyes to see that Kenneth wasn't laughing along with her. "Kenneth, you can't really be serious can you? I mean, you can't really think you're developing feelings for that woman?"

Kenneth dragged in a deep breath before he spoke. "You don't need to know what I see in Heart, only that I do see something significant there."

Faith smiled smoothly, dragging her hands down her neatly tailored designer business suit. "But, Kenneth, we were so good together. You have to be missing that. You've always been open to that, no matter how much time passed since our breakup. No matter whom you were seeing."

"There's only one thing you need to know, Faith. And that's this; I'm not available to anyone except Heart MacKenzie." Kenneth walked around his desk taking his seat and returning to his computer keys. After tapping a few, he looked up and found Faith still standing where he'd left her.

"Was there something else you needed?" he asked. When she shook her head no Kenneth smiled and said, "Then I'll trust you'll have a good day," then returned his attention to his computer screen while he listened to her footsteps travel across his carpeted office floor. Nothing and no one came before Heart. It was time for everyone in the world to understand that.

～

*H*eart smiled as she stepped off of the elevator. Abigail had called Heart at two in the afternoon and told her Kenneth would be finished with his work in approximately an hour. Heart packed up his duffle bag and headed on her journey.

She and Kenneth had become so close over the last few weeks, closer than she'd anticipated ever getting to any other human being. Tonight she wanted to celebrate that closeness by showing him the thing that was most important in her life.

When Abigail saw her walk through the glass doors that sheltered the executive floor of Searlington Realty, she stood and smiled at Heart.

"Hello, Lieutenant, he's very anxious to see you. He's been buzzing me every five minutes to see if you'd arrived yet."

"Thanks for keeping tabs on him. I wanted to make certain he was all through with his work so he'd be free for the weekend. You can't get him away from that smartphone if everything hasn't been taken care of."

Abigail smiled brightly. "Thanks for that, if his phone is on, then so is mine. Maybe

I'll actually have a weekend of peace."

"I'll make sure of it. Can I go in now?"

Abigail nodded and Heart headed toward the double doors behind Abigail's desk.

She tapped on the door and heard a distant, "Come in," through the heavy wood doors. She slowly opened the door and found Kenneth half standing half sitting typing away at his computer keyboard.

"I can come back, give you time to finish up."

Kenneth tapped one final key like it was the last and most significant part of a choreographed performance. He clicked his mouse once, and the light from the computer monitor that was illuminating his face turned off. "As of this very moment, I am done." He walked around the desk and pulled her into the circle of his arms and claimed her mouth.

God I never get tired of that. She doubted she ever would. Being in his arms, having his lips, skin, hands, on her always made her feel calm and safe. She stepped out of his embrace and looked up into questioning eyes. "Something wrong?"

"I thought you said you were taking me out, don't you think you're a little underdressed?"

She looked down with him at her attire. She was dressed in one of those trendy sweat suits that the latest model turned fashion designer slapped her name on. It was fitted in all the right places. The crop top jacket stopped just below her bust line and the pants sat hanging low off her toned yet curvy hips. She had on a camisole that seemed to grab every curve of her breasts at the top and tapered down to hug the muscles of her abs that were showing through it. She'd worn it on purpose; this was pretty much their first foray out of the house that didn't involve police work or hospitals. She wanted to be cute, but comfortable and this was her best option considering what she had planned for them.

"No, I'm not underdressed, you're overdressed. I actually went in your closet and pulled out some clothes for you."

"Did you, now?"

"Yes, and let me just tell you, I think you've got a problem with fitted baseball caps,

I think you might need some sort of program."

He laughed. "I think you might be right. Give me the duffel; let me get dressed so we can get out of here. I'm curious to find out what you have in store for us tonight."

～

*H*eart and Kenneth exited out of the Rockaway bound A-train and headed up the stairs and out of the station. They walked down Pitkin Avenue toward the South Conduit. They crossed the street when they reached Autumn Avenue and made a left. She looked at Kenneth when they stopped in front of the large building that sat across the street from the massive mega church. She wanted to gage his reaction to this place. She was at the point where she was ready to share everything with him, even the ugliness that had marred her life for so long, but she couldn't share that if he couldn't accept this.

"What's this?" he pointed at the building they stood in front of.

"This is my place." She watched the questions ghost across his face, but whatever they were, he held them at bay and replaced them with a sincere smile.

"This is MacKenzie's Place. It's a community center that the church behind us runs."

"It's named after you?"

"Yeah, I came up with the idea and took on a major role in the fundraising for it. I also do my best to keep it safe from the neighborhood knuckleheads. This place is patrolled consistently by my officers and there are always two officers on deck working in the building twenty-four hours a day."

"How do you make that happen? Doesn't it stretch your budget?"

"Nope, it's a community affairs kind of thing. We actually have community affairs officers for just this purpose, but we haven't had a place to put them. So once a month, a select few of my guys rotate through here. They spend three weeks on the street, one here. My guys love it, and it keeps my kids safe."

He tilted his head and looked at her. "Kids?"

"Yeah, the neighborhood kids that spend a huge chunk of their time here. These are the cases that without this place would end up in my cuffs or dead in the street. This is an alternative. One I've worked hard to provide for them. They come here and they get homework assistance, physical education, use of a computer lab, and all sorts of afterschool activities to keep them busy, healthy, and safe."

He nodded his head and placed his arm around her neck, pulling her into his side.

"And you wanted to share this me?"

"Yeah, this is important to me, it's where I spend a great deal of my off time. You and I have been getting really close as of late and I want to know if you can handle this.

This place, these people, these kids, we're a package deal. You want me, you gotta want this too, or at the very least understand why it plays such a significant role in my life. Can you handle that?"

He pulled her closer, lifted her chin, and placed gentle lips across her mouth. "Baby, you have no idea how honored I am that you would share something like this with me.

Come on, I wanna go inside and see MacKenzie's Place."

Kenneth walked behind her as she led him through the doors of the community center. She stopped at the front desk to greet the two officers that were sitting down.

"Lieutenant MacKenzie?" Heart heard the disbelief in the young officer's voice.

"Officer Kimes, it's good to see you again."

The young man grabbed her hand excitedly. She saw Kenneth from the corner of her eye prepare to intervene, but she put a hand halting him. She had learned over the years to tolerate things like handshakes even though they set her teeth on edge.

"Ma'am...please...call me Manning. We were all so worried when we got word of the shooting. We're ready to get you back at your desk and in charge."

She smiled at him. "Tired of Smyth already?"

"Not at all, Ma'am, but nothing like having my boss back where she belongs." The officer looked over his shoulder at his partner. "Isn't that right, Forze?"

The other officer nodded and placed a modest smile on his face that didn't reach his eyes. She knew this man, Mancino Forze; he'd had disciplinary problems in the past with ruffing up suspects. She'd have to talk to Bryan about why he was assigned here. She couldn't prove it, but she felt Forze had a problem with the skin color of the predominant population in East New York. DL racist or not, she didn't like the feeling she had about him based on past dealings. As soon as she was back in her chair he was going back to his regular patrol.

She didn't tarry long at the front desk; she said a few more words to the two officers and motioned for Kenneth to follow her down the hall and to the large community room where she knew everyone would be gathered at this time.

She quietly stepped inside of the room and motioned for Kenneth to step inside the room with her. They stayed at the back of the room and watched. Heart allowed her gaze to move from one side of the room to the other. She saw kids huddled together at several large tables doing homework or tapping on laptops. Her attention was snatched up by the barking sound of a well-known voice that she'd missed all this time she was recuperating. "All right, you little crumb snatchers. Y'all got five more minutes before rec time.

Y'all better have that homework finished if you plan on playing in my dang house."

Heart cupped her hands around her mouth to amplify her voice. "Big Willie, why you always talking to them kids like that?"

William Seyah AKA, Big Willie turned around with murder in his eyes looking for the person stupid enough to talk shit to him in his house. He was a burly black man in his early fifties who moved with swift precision despite his age. His senses were sharp and it only took him a second to locate the source of what he no doubt would label his disrespect.

"Fuck outta here," Big Willie said as he walked to the back of the room and grabbed her hand. "How you doing, sweetheart?"

"I'm good, Big Willie, all healed up and ready to get back on the job."

Big Willie smiled at her briefly then his gaze landed on Kenneth and his smile fell from his face. "Who the fuck is this?"

"Big Willie, don't start, this is my friend, Kenneth Searlington."

"Kenneth Searlington. I don't give a fuck what his name is. You know better than to be bringing some pretty motherfucker up in my house and my wife is here. You know I don't play that shit MacKenzie. Next thing you know, Tee's ass will be leaving me for his pretty ass, and I'ma be here by my damn self. That shit ain't happening."

Heart glanced at Kenneth, watching an expression that could only be described as,

"Is he for real and, should I be worried?" run across his face.

"Big Willie, you know Tee don't want nobody, but your crazy ass. Stop tripping."

"I don't know, Heart, I mean, how pretty is his wife..."

"Is this motherfucker talking to me?" Big Willie pointed at Kenneth, but directed his question to Heart, stepping closer to

Kenneth as he did so. "You better school this pretty white boy before he gets his ass hurt."

Heart stepped in between both of them. "Willie, take your ass to the back so we can talk, I'm gonna say hi to the kids and I'll be back there in a minute."

"Is his wife back there, maybe I should go say hello?" Kenneth asked with a smirk painted across his lips. Big Willie halfway turned back around, his momentum only stopped by Heart's lifted hand.

When Big Willie was no longer in the room she turned to Kenneth. "You'd better stop poking the bear. That man is a decorated retired police officer who could break you if he wanted to. He's the person who taught me my job. He was Porter's second in command before I was." She watched as understanding dawned on Kenneth. "There are three things you don't mess with in Willie's world, these kids, his officer-brothers, and his woman."

"So you're not gonna protect me if he comes for me?"

"Hell no, I just got out of rehab. I ain't fucking with y'all crazy asses in here today."

She waved Kenneth off just in time to see a blur of color rushing at her. She heard a loud squeal and then, "Lady Cop," just as a solid thump barreled into her, pushing the air from her lungs in a harsh gasp.

Heart looked down at the quivering mass of teenager circled around her waist. "Dang

Quisha, who taught you to play the linebacker position so well?"

Heart hugged the girl to her, for so long this was the only way she could stand physical contact. There was never a perceived threat from these kids. No, not from these wonderful children who came to her to learn how to navigate their world. These kids had kept her alive and sane long enough for her to meet Kenneth. She turned back toward him and met a matching smile.

"Quisha, you gotta let me go, I need to breathe girl." Slowly the young girl peeled herself away from Heart. Heart looked down into her face and saw tears in the child's eyes.

"Quisha what's wrong?"

The teenager sniffled and then wiped her face on her jacket sleeve. "Lady Cop, we heard from Kay-Kay and 'nem that you got shot. When we asked that mean ole' Big

Willie, he wouldn't tell us nothing, said we needed to stop mindin' grown folks bidness. We thought you had died!" She sniffled again. "Nobody would tell us what had happened."

The meaning of the girl's rushed words traveled through the room and all of the contained buzzing that filled the air when Heart had entered the room had come to a halt.

The pain that this child felt, that they'd all felt by the look of all the similar expressions they all held, they'd feared for her life, and no one had told them different.

Heart raised a hand to the warm mocha cheek that was lined with a wet trail of tears.

"I'm so sorry, baby girl, sorry to all of you. I was hurt pretty badly, I'm sure that they didn't want to tell you until they knew something for certain." Heart looked around the room, putting her arm around LaQuisha and walking slowly into the center of the room. When she reached the center they all circled around her, closing in around her, and she felt not an inkling of panic. These were her kids; she felt their pain, their love, their fear.

"I didn't know no one spoke to you guys. I assumed they would let you all know that I had to go away to do rehab in order to get my arm working again." She looked out at each one of them and smiled, hoping to reassure them that she was fine, that they hadn't lost her, and that she hadn't been complicit in adding to their collective trauma.

"Listen guys, finish up your work, I'm gonna head back and talk to Big Willie for a few minutes. When I come back, we're gonna start rec time off right like we usually do up in here. Y'all ready?"

They all jumped up and down and yelled their enthusiasm to return to old routines. She laughed with them and held out a hand to Kenneth. He took it, and followed her down the hall to a closed office door.

She dropped his hand and twisted the knob, opening the door

without knocking, without asking permission to enter. Behind the desk Big Willie looked up quickly assessing the anger etched into the hard lines of her face.

"Now MacKenzie…"

"MacKenzie my ass, nobody told those kids I was alive? What the fuck Willie?

How the hell y'all gonna torment those kids like that. It was as if they had seen a ghost.

What's been going on since I've been gone?"

Big Willie ran a thick hand over his bald shiny head and looked up at her. "Shit Mac, this wasn't my idea. This shit came from brass. Something ain't right in your house and Porter shut down all intel about you and that shooting to only those that needed to know.

As much as I wanted to tell the brats, I couldn't."

"Fuck that, Willie, you ain't police no more. You don't fucking report to Porter's ass anymore."

"MacKenzie, once a cop, always a cop. I may not punch a clock in that motherfucker anymore, but trust me; Porter still has just as much pull over me as he ever had. You'll understand that shit when you become captain of that house."

She rolled her eyes. "Ain't nobody thinking 'bout becoming captain. I want to know what the hell is going on around here and at the house."

"Talk to your top cop, but I'm sure you already know what the deal is."

She nodded her head and looked up to find questioning crystal blue eyes staring back at her. "Kenneth, I think I'm about to find out something I never wanted to know."

"What?" he asked

"There's a leak in my house."

~

*H*eart walked back into the community room, glad to see the rowdy bunch of kids waiting for her. Everyone seemed to be taking their places in anticipation of their usual kick start to recreational time. She was so excited to be in the same room with her kids that she nearly forgot that Kenneth was standing next to her. *Shit, he's not gonna know what to do.*

"Hey, Kenneth, we generally kick off recreational time with dancing. We usually pick something that most of us know, something that's cross-generational that we're all familiar with."

"Oh, what dance are you doing?" he said.

She was about to answer him when LaQuisha's cousin DeAndre walked up next to her. "Don't worry 'bout it, white boy. We don't want you in here trippin' folks up cause you don't know you're left foot from your right."

Heart was trying hard to keep her features straight, trying hard to fight the inner bubble of laughter that was sitting inside her chest. "DeAndre, watch your mouth, take your butt over there, and get into position."

She turned around to find Kenneth still standing next to her. "You can watch from those seats over there. This shouldn't really take more than ten minutes or more."

"So you're not even going to tell me what the name of the dance is?"

"Kenneth, it's line dancing. That's all, nothing major."

"So you're assuming because I'm white I can't dance, and I especially can't participate in line dancing?"

She shrugged her shoulders, not really certain what the right answer was. She finally settled on, "You said it, I didn't."

Kenneth looked up and around, he must have seen similar assumptions on all the kids faces because he shook his head and took his jacket off. He looked past her shoulder and started walking toward Jaisyn. She figured Kenneth was gunning for Jaisyn because he was fiddling with the stereo in the corner of the room. She watched Kenneth whisper something to the boy and pulled out what looked like money and handed it to the smiling teenager.

Kenneth walked back over to where she was standing and looked her up and down.

"So Lieutenant, you want to put a little wager on whether I can dance or not or are you skurred?"

He's bluffing, ain't no way this white boy from uptown got skills like that on the dance floor. "All right, I'll take that bet. What's the wager?"

He smiled, leaned down, and moved his mouth next to her ear. "If I nail all of the dances that my man Jaisyn over there plays, you drop to your knees anywhere I ask and wrap those lovely lips of yours around my cock."

She snapped her head back looking to see if any of the kids were close enough to have heard his demand. They were all standing a good enough distance away that she was pretty sure they couldn't hear.

"Okay, I'll concede to that, with the exception of being in public places." She watched Kenneth take a deep breath attempting to speak, but she interrupted him. "I'm a cop; I'm not losing my badge over this bullshit." He nodded and agreed to her stipulation.

"So what do I get if you actually can't do these dances, and you embarrass yourself right here in front of me and all of these kids?"

He smiled at her and bent back down to her ear and whispered, "Anything you want."

She smiled at him and lifted her hand. "Jaisyn, do your thang boo."

Soon the room was filled with the first notes of Marcia Griffiths, "The Electric Slide." All of the kids and tutors lined up in several neat rows and everyone began dancing to the well-known line dance. Four steps to the right, four steps to the left, four steps back, dip forward, dip back, dip forward and swing kick to the right to start the first steps all over again.

She started moving to the beat and glanced over at Kenneth who was dancing to her right. She expected to see some asynchronous version of the dance, but what she found instead was Kenneth not only executing the basic steps correctly, but also adding his own little twist to the moves, something that only *experienced* electric sliders did. *What the fuck? He's actually doing the damn thing. That's all right; I know he's not going to last all of these dances that Jaisyn usually plays.* She kept smiling and dancing, waiting for the music to change up. And then almost seamlessly, the music switched into repetitive clapping and everybody moved into position for DJ Casper's "Cha Cha Slide." *He ain't gonna be able to hang with this one.*

DJ Casper told them which way to move, turn, and jump, and Kenneth missed not one answer to DJ Casper's calls. *Whatever, that's a lucky one. I know he's not gonna hang with the next one.*

Just then she heard the familiar strains of Cupid's voice initiate her favorite line dance, "The Cupid Shuffle." She moved in time to the beat and looked over to her side where Kenneth was standing. The other line dances were just steps. If you could add them in your head, you could figure out how to do them. No, the Cupid Shuffle took rhythm. You had to be able to move to really rock this dance. Kenneth was good, but she was certain he wasn't that good. *Here goes my win.*

She started moving, shaking, and walking, adding her own little spin to the dance. This was her joint and she killed it every time she did it. Then she turned her head to the side and saw Kenneth doing the exact same thing, adding in his own dash of flavor. The man was popping and locking his body to the rhythm of the music while he kept in time with steps.

This motherfucker can dance. She realized then she'd been had. Kenneth had known very well he was going to win their wager, because someone who moved like he was moving now was a dancing pro who had been at this for a long time. *Hustler.*

When the song ended, Heart went to step away from the makeshift dance floor, but

Kenneth held her hand and made her stay. "There's one more," he said through a gaping grin.

She was trying to figure out which one was next; they usually ended things with the

Cupid Shuffle. Then she heard the telltale percussive beats of V.I.C's "The Wobble" begin to blast through the speakers. She watched as he began to bounce in place to the beat of the music, still holding out a hand inviting her to dance with him. She looked at him through squinted eyes while deciding what her next move would be. *Fuck it.*

She took his hand, began to bounce with him, and they danced in tandem together in a perfect square. The kids began to form a circle around them, and all of a sudden everyone was chanting, "Go white boy, go white boy." Anyone else might have been offended, but the off-handed insult seemed to egg Kenneth on and he wobbled his ass off with her in the middle of the community center with a roomful of cheering kids celebrating his ability.

She'd brought him here to show him something new, looked like she was the one being schooled today.

~

*H*eart bounded down the stairs when the chiming doorbell signaled her guests' arrival. She'd been waiting for these two all day. She twisted the knob quickly and watched as her captain and her second walked through the door.

When they were inside she motioned for them to follow her into the kitchen. "I cooked. You guys eat yet?" Porter and Bryan just looked at each other and shook their heads. "All right, sit down and I'll fix your plates."

"What'd you make?" Bryan asked.

"Smothered pork chops mashed potatoes and some biscuits."

Captain Porter raised a brow. "You cooked that?"

She lifted her gaze from the pan on the stovetop and looked at her superior. "You seem like you don't believe me, Cap."

Captain Porter looked to Bryan as if Bryan held the key to what he was attempting to say. Bryan shook his head and lifted his shoulders as if to say, "Nope, I don't want no parts of that." Realizing he'd get no help from the young sergeant sitting at the table with him he returned his gaze to Heart.

"Mac, it's just, we've never really seen this domesticated side of you."

She smiled as she walked their plates over to them and placed them in front of them.

"I've always cooked, Cap; the only difference is there's someone else here to eat my food now. I used to bring all my excess to Smyth for lunch when we were partnered."

Bryan nodded his head. "And I appreciated every meal you've ever brought me." She laughed as the man nearly pushed his face into the plate before him.

"You seem happy, Mac, at ease. Is that my godson's doing?"

She turned over her captain's question. It wasn't that she didn't know the answer to that question. The answer was a resounding, *hell yeah*! But she wasn't really ready to expose their bond to the rest of the world. It was just perfect between the two of them, without any outside influence.

"Kenneth and I are..." She looked at her captain again, still not certain how much he should know about the developing relationship between his lieutenant and his godson.

"Captain Porter, the most honest thing I can say right now is that Kenneth has been an amazing help to me. A help I didn't really think I would ever need, and a help I was totally unprepared for needing let alone accepting. I don't think this entire ordeal would have turned out as well if Kenneth hadn't been so gracious. Instead of being put out to pasture because of a nearly career-ending injury, I'm going back to work in less than a week. I owe him a lot."

Porter nodded his head as he cut into the tender stewed meat and placed a fork full of food in his mouth. "All right, Mac, why did you ask Bryan and me to come over tonight?"

"I went to the community center last night and the kids looked at me like they'd seen a ghost. LaQuisha told me no one told them what happened to me, like at all. I chewed

Big Willie out about it and he said the order came from you. What's going on, Cap?"

Captain Porter laid his utensils down and took a sip of the cool iced tea Heart had sat next to him. "Mac, you're suspicions were right, we have a leak in the house. I couldn't risk anyone knowing anything about you, especially not when I think one of my officers may have set up your shooting to begin with."

"What do you mean, Captain? Like someone put a hit out on me?"

She leaned forward waiting for his answers and watched as captain Porter slowly nodded his head up and down.

"Yeah. Think back to that night, MacKenzie. No one knew you were supposed to be there."

"Cap, nothing out of the ordinary happened in that bust. We caught the perps off guard. I mean, we literally caught them with their pants down. No one did or said anything strange."

Porter shook his head. "To you maybe, but that's not the case according Arroyo."

Heart's thoughts traveled to the other detective who was injured during the Searlington girl's rescue. She'd heard via Bryan that he was doing well. Like her, he hadn't returned to duty yet, but was taking time out to get himself together. She'd been warned by her captain to stay away from him until the entire ordeal with Internal Affairs and their investigation of the facts of the case were done before she contacted him.

They'd spoken once or twice since the shooting, each with encouraging words for one another with respect to their individual recoveries. But there'd never been any information regarding the case shared between the two of them. Not one solitary word.

"Arroyo hasn't said anything to me about this case."

"That's because I gave him a direct order not to."

She let out a huff of air through a clenched jaw. "Cap, I'm your second, why the hell are you shutting me out?"

"Because I'm trying to keep you safe," he said. "This is about purposely setting up a cop to get killed. The only way this could have been done, was from the inside. One of our cops tried to kill you, MacKenzie. Jacqueline knew we were coming, that's the only reason she was there that night. She went there to do two things, kill you and Kenneth." Porter slammed his hand down on the table in frustration, shaking all of its contents with rumbling force. "No one knew about that bust except the cops who were assigned to that detail. That means whoever the son of a bitch is, he knew what was going down, and he let it happen anyway."

Porter pointed to her sergeant sharply. "Bryan has been investigating this quietly, but he needs a set of hands he can trust. And quite frankly, I don't trust anyone else's hands other than yours, MacKenzie's. Not even the rest of your team members. Not with a situation like this when anyone can be the leak."

She nodded her agreement. She might not like some of Porter's tactics, but what he was doing was for the best of the investigation and ultimately her precinct.

"Arroyo was on detail for the drug case with Selwyn," Porter continued. "He told us that Jacqueline got a phone call a few minutes before you and the task force pulled up on the scene. Whoever was on the phone with her, and whatever was said to her, her response was this: 'I'll take care of the lady lieutenant, you'd just better make sure I have what I need to do it. Where is the equipment I paid you for?' When Jacqueline was searched, we found another gun on her. We checked the serial numbers; it was a gun that has been in our evidence room for the last two years."

"What?" Heart stood up, she needed to move, to think. There was only a few ways that gun could have left the evidence room in the Seventy-fourth. "Are you certain the gun wasn't taken out for a court case or ballistics testing? You can't honestly think someone would purposely break the chain of evidence?"

"Mac, you know as well as I do that this is well beyond breaking the chain of evidence."

Warring emotions took over, but the one emotion that was pushing forward past the rest was fury. Someone was living dirty inside her house and that shit she just couldn't have. She sat back down at the table and turned to Bryan. "What do you have, what do you know?"

Bryan put his fork down and leaned down to where a messenger bag sat beside him on the floor. He pulled a department issued folder from the bag and handed it to her.

Heart opened it and read through some of the documents inside.

"These the cops we making for this? Based on what?" She knew each one of these officers personally; she would never have pegged any of them as someone who would sellout their own kind.

Bryan pointed to each picture in the folder. "All three of these cops had direct involvement with both the drug case and your kidnapping case, MacKenzie. We also know that the last time the missing gun can be accounted for was in evidence two days before the bust. Bryan handed her another sheet of paper with familiar names on it, more of her cops. "We came up with ten names that had access to that room in those forty-eight hours based on camera surveillance and the sign-in logs in the evidence room. These three in your hand are the only three that pop up on every cross-reference list we came up with."

Heart looked back down at the three photos in her hand and spread them across the table. "Yeah, but these two weren't anywhere on the scene when that case went to shit."

"Well, don't dismiss them yet," Bryan warned. "Why do people kill?" Bryan asked her.

Her eyes stayed fixed to the pictures on the table. No matter how many homicides there actually were, there were only eight reasons why people killed other people. "For power and position, for money, for love, anger, and revenge, for fanatical beliefs having to do with politics, religion, and racial supremacy, for self-preservation, by accident, by negligence, and finally, because they felt like it: i.e. the folks with mental issues who kill when they're off their meds." No matter what the details of a murder case, they always fell into one or more of those eight categories.

Heart raised her eyes to Bryan's gaze. "Bryan, I know these three, but I don't have a personal relationship with any of them. I'm their commanding officer, but I've never had any significant professional issues with any of these dudes. I've never given any of them a write up, so what could they be mad about?"

Bryan tilted his head back and to the side with a lifted brow and a disbelieving lopsided smirk on his face.

"Bryan, I'm not stupid. I know there are plenty of fools in the department who might not be as tolerant as others. I know the fact that I'm a black woman who's number two in the house is a problem for some. Some might not like it, but I don't think any of them feel that strongly about it that they'd try to have me killed in the field."

"I agree with you. We have some assholes in our house, some a little more verbal than others, but I don't think any of them would be trying to lose their livelihood and their freedom behind some shit like this."

She mulled over what Bryan had given her before she spoke. "As I see it guys, there are only two reasons off the why-do-people-kill list: power and position and money."

"This guy is a lieutenant." Bryan nodded and pointed at the picture in the middle of their suspect lineup. "Maybe he felt that if he got you out of the way he'd be next in line for command."

Heart looked at her captain and both of them shook their heads at the same time.

"You two really think that no one would kill to be number two in the house?" Bryan asked.

"Bryan, here's something you don't know because you've never needed to know it. It wouldn't matter whether I died, or left the department or not. Number one and number two spots in a house aren't filled from a roster. They're handpicked," Heart said. Bryan watched Heart carefully then turned his attention to their captain.

"She's right, son. Doesn't matter if she didn't set foot back in the Seventy-fourth, none of the officers would take over her command," Porter explained.

"I'm number two Bryan not because I'm a lieutenant; I'm a lieutenant because I was selected to be number two." She watched Bryan digest what she was saying. "Bryan, you remember when you and I took the sergeant's exam and passed. Well, I never had any intentions of reaching beyond that rank. But Porter told me I had to take the lieutenant's exam and ace it. I needed to take it because it was already decided I would be his number two when Big Willie retired."

"Meaning you were getting the job regardless?" Bryan asked.

"No, meaning I was the most qualified candidate the selection panel considered and the most trusted by the sitting captain and lieutenant."

"So if it's not just a matter of moving one up on the roster, who would have taken your place if you hadn't come back, MacKenzie?"

Both she and Porter zeroed their gazes on Bryan's questioning face. They stared intently until light dawned on his confusion.

"Hell no," Bryan said. "Taking over your command temporarily almost killed me,

MacKenzie. No way in hell I'm volunteering for that kind of torture permanently." "Bryan, it's just the way things go. You would have taken the job, then you would have taken the test, and I would have been happy that my command was left in the only set of hands I trust with my officers' lives other than Cap's."

"She's right, son, you're gonna do fine as number two when the time comes," Porter said.

"If the time comes, I haven't agreed to take top spot yet. I don't know if I want to be a captain yet."

Porter waved his hand dismissing her statement. "Whatever, we'll discuss that at a later time. Right now, we need to focus on this."

"Yeah, Cap's right. You're the tactical genius amongst us, Lieutenant. Why do you think one of our cops would try to off you?"

"It's not the position thing." Heart handed Bryan the photos one by one. "You can check out that angle if you want, but I don't think you'll find any of these three at the bottom of it. No, if someone is trying to kill a lieutenant in the NYPD there are only two real reasons, revenge or money. If it were revenge, it would have happened ages ago. I'm not the one out there busting heads and cuffing folks anymore, that's you Bryan, and the rest of our team. This isn't about revenge."

Bryan closed the file and tapped in on the surface of the table. "MacKenzie, we've always believed that whoever did this was getting their pockets laced for their efforts. I mean, what other reason would another cop have to betray his brothers and sisters if not for cash? All three have been having financial difficulty, all three were killing themselves for overtime, and all three very recently received large cash deposits in their accounts."

"Can the money be legitimately explained?" she asked.

"Forensic accounting is looking into that. We should hear back from them by the time you officially return on the job."

Heart shook her head. "Nah Bryan, my gut tells me to look elsewhere. I've got a price on my head it appears, a hefty one if they could partner with someone like

Jacqueline Searlington."

"Who's after you MacKenzie?" Bryan asked concern etched across his face.

Heart didn't answer Bryan immediately; instead she held her right hand out, palmside up to her captain and bent her fingers in a gimme-that motion. Captain Porter moved his dinner plate to the empty place setting next to him and replaced it with what appeared to be a metal-covered briefcase. When he clicked the case open he removed her service weapon, its ammunition magazine, and her badge. She stood, placed the badge on her hip, and then reached in and wrapped her hand around the hard body of the snubnosed forty-caliber weapon that had been her closest ally in some very difficult situations. Its weight felt familiar, and her hand and fingers caressed it as if it had been made just for her. She smiled, and then looked back up to meet her sergeant's eyes.

"To answer your question, Bryan, there's only ever been one person who's ever placed a bounty on my head."

"Who's that?" Bryan asked.

Heart pulled her phone from her back pocket, touched the screen, and slid her finger across its face a few times before placing a picture of an African American man in his early fifties with close-cropped salt and pepper hair in front of Bryan.

"Marcus Paul," she said quickly. "He's had it out for me way before I ever joined the force. Issues between his family and mine," she said tightly through a clenched jaw.

She grabbed the gun magazine and shoved it inside the handle of her weapon. She racked the slide, smiling at the familiar click-clack sound it made to signal a round being placed in the chamber. "And I say if Marcus is bold enough to use one of my own people to try to take me out, then I might just have to show up on his doorstep and show him what happens when you fuck with a cop."

CHAPTER 15

*H*eart looked at the familiar warehouse type building taking up most of the block on Glenmore Avenue between Shepherd Avenue and Essex Street. "Dr. Paul's Construction and Development," was written across it in big bold letters. The last time she had stepped inside of this building was fourteen years ago. It was a long one level flat-topped structure whose face was covered in red brick. It looked like a long red rectangle with a standard-sized door where customers entered and a larger oversized square opening in the middle of the structure where deliveries, building materials, and construction equipment entered.

Heart's fingers tingled. It was a familiar sensation she always got when her mind was preparing to protect her. It was like a big yellow neon sign that flashed behind her eyes to warn her that she would be forced to either throw hands or pull her weapon to keep herself safe.

She took a big breath calming herself. She could do this. She knew what the deal was, had known it for a very long time. There was no reason for her to fear anything on the inside of that building. She and Marcus knew each other well. She knew he couldn't be trusted, and he knew she would blow a hole in him without so much as a moment's hesitation if she felt threatened by him in any way.

She stepped out of her car and briefly grazed her hand across the holstered weapon on her hip; it was there, its mere presence giving her just a sliver of comfort. She opened the heavy metal door and listened to the long creek signal her arrival for anyone that was sitting inside.

"Anson, can you inventory those deliveries that just arrived? I put them back in the stock room. I'm gonna be stuck running these numbers for a lil' while longer."

She knew that voice, would be able to identify it whether she saw the man attached to it or not. A shiver ran through her. It had been fourteen years since she'd last seen him.

She rolled her shoulders and neck to shake off the strange buzzing running across her skin. She was in control; Marcus couldn't hurt her anymore.

She stepped in front of the office door. The same plain white walls that encased this office had been there since before she was born. Her eyes traveled down and looked at the man looking down at sheets of paper spread across his desk. It would be so easy to end him just like this, he would never even know what happened, or who had been responsible, it would be over so quick. Her tongue darted out and licked her bottom lip, savoring the thought of destroying the man who had destroyed her all those years ago. Nothing would be sweeter. Nothing would matter more. Except there was one thing that outweighed her need for revenge: Kenneth. If she let this thought form further, let it become an action, she would lose the one thing that had come to matter more than anything else in her life did.

She closed her eyes and steadied herself. Losing Kenneth just to make this pig bleed wasn't something she was willing to risk. So instead of giving into her need for retribution, she pressed it down, swallowed it until it was being burned away by the acid in the pit of her gut.

"I've been called a lot of things, but Anson was never one of them." She watched recognition take root as Marcus slowly raised his head.

"Heart," her name crossed his lips quietly.

"Don't, you don't get to call me that. Only one person does, and you're not him."

"I gave—"

"Mac or MacKenzie, that's all we're working with here today."

Dark eyes brightened and then softened before her. Understanding sunk in and he nodded slowly and extended a slow hand motioning for her to sit down in the chair in front of his desk.

"It's been a long time, MacKenzie. What brings you by tonight?"

She regarded him carefully, finally accepting the seat he offered. She sat down, adjusted her holster, and met his staid gaze with one of her own.

"Apparently someone is trying to kill me. They used one of my cops to set it in motion. Since you're the only other person that's ever tried to end my life, I thought I'd come ask if you had a hand in all of this mess."

She watched him swallow slowly. He sat back in his chair, looking directly at her. "You're the only one that thinks I tried to kill you, MacKenzie."

"I know you did, Marcus. We both know you did."

"The only thing I know is that it's painfully obvious you don't know what you're talking about."

"I know more than you think, Marcus."

"Not half as much as you believe you do."

She rolled her eyes, not really up for the innocent game the man was playing. "Look, let's agree to disagree on the past. Can you at least be man enough to admit if you had any hand in this latest attempt?"

The muscle in his jaw tightened, as if he was forcing himself to keep from saying something he shouldn't. Were her assumptions right?

"When did this so-called attempt on your life happen?"

"It wasn't so-called, I was shot Marcus. I'm just fortunate that the shooter was a terrible shot. Otherwise a shoulder wound could have been fatal. Did you set it up?"

Marcus leaned back in his chair and rested his chin on two fingers. His eyes moved over her, cataloguing her.

"No, I didn't have anything to do with that. I know you don't want to hear this, MacKenzie, but I never had anything to do with any attempt on your life. The only person that has ever wished you dead has been in the ground a long time himself."

"Luponero is dead?"

Marcus nodded slowly. "Luponero fucked up fourteen years ago. I made it so he could never fuck up again."

"Did you just admit murder to a cop?"

Marcus slowly shook his head. "No, I just said I helped a man to never make the kind of mistake he made all those years ago again."

She stood up, eyeing him slowly. "Whatever, Marcus," she crossed her arms across her chest and looked down on him, "just understand this, if you're up to your old tricks again, I will make you pay for it this time. Don't think I won't put a bullet it in you faster than I can blink."

She saw the crack in his armor, a slight flinch. She'd gotten to him.

"MacKenzie, I really hope one day you can let go of your anger long enough to find out the truth of what really happened. Everything is not always as it seems. Sometimes shit gets fucked up without much encouragement from you. When you've lived long enough, you find out that sometimes, the shit that didn't make it on the official record, is the most important and vital information that can alter perception. If you ever want to know the real deal, ask Hunter. He knows what really happened that day, so do I, but I'm sure his word will carry more weight than mine."

She turned and walked to the door of his office. She stood there for a moment and turned halfway in his direction again. "I don't have to ask Hunter shit, I was there. I know exactly what happened, I know exactly how and why it went down. The next time I see you Marcus will be one of two ways, behind bars, or the day they bury you when I piss on your grave. I really do hope it's the latter scenario."

She walked out of the office and headed toward the door. There was nothing else for her in this building. There hadn't been for fourteen years. Her hand had just touched the handle when she heard footsteps behind her. She turned around defensively with her hand reaching for the holster on her hip, ready to defend herself if she had to. She found Marcus behind her with his hands in his pocket.

"Marcus?"

"Relax, MacKenzie, I only came to say one last thing."

She watched him cautiously, then nodded her head when she was relatively certain he didn't intend her any harm. But she stayed positioned just the way she was, feet spread apart, holster unsnapped and open, ready for easy and imminent removal of her gun, hand on the butt of her weapon ready for shit to jump off. "What is it?"

"Be very careful what you wish for, you might just get it, and realize it wasn't really what you wanted after all."

A slow shiver passed down her spine again. She shook it off and left. This building was the mausoleum to a very painful past that she had buried almost a decade and a half ago. She wasn't going to resurrect it again, not for anything, not when a bright future was just at her fingertips. If Marcus wanted to come for her again, she would protect everything she loved with everything she had. She wouldn't allow that monster to take another fucking thing from her ever again.

~

*I*da-Mae stood in the middle of her kitchen staid breathless by the sharp pain gripping the center of her chest. She stood, gasping, taking shallow breaths, trying to keep from falling into the hazy black that was threatening at the borders of her vision.

She waited, that's all she could do. These attacks had been happening more and more frequently over the last few weeks. She knew that something was wrong, terribly wrong, life-ending wrong, but she didn't want to let her family know. If it was her time, then she would go home to be with the Lord. She had lived a long and fruitful life; she was ready if her time had come.

She closed her eyes, waiting for the pain to stop, because either the angel of death would come, or the attack would ease and move on.

Soon she felt a familiar tingling and then the pained that seized her released slowly, ever so slowly, until she was finally able to take in much-need air without pain.

In the distance she heard the telephone ringing. She took another breath; she had to get herself together. If it was her son, or one of her grandchildren, especially True or

Heart, they'd know instantly that something was wrong. Those girls were too perceptive of the world around them and the people in it for her to be able to fool them for long. She finally made it to the counter where the cordless phone sat in its cradle. "Hello," she said, trying to sound as normal as she could.

"She thinks I tried to kill her."

Ida-Mae recognized the controlled and angry voice coming through the line.

"Marcus, don't be so dramatic."

"I'm not being dramatic; she came here today and told me so."

"Heart came to you? Why?"

"Because apparently someone tried to kill her and she thinks I had something to do with it. Her logic is since I apparently tried to do it before I must be attempting to finish what I started all those years ago. Ida-Mae, I have sat back long enough and given you and Hunter the opportunity to fix this. The two of you didn't even bother to tell me she was in any kind of danger. I'm done. You two either make this right, or trust me, I will." Ida-Mae could feel the tension in her chest slowly creeping back in. She took more slow breaths hoping the moment would pass. "Marcus, I promise you, I will make this right. I just need a day or two to get things together first."

The line was silent for a minute. She heard him take in a ragged breath and blow it back into the phone. "Two days, Ida-Mae, that's all you're getting. Make it right in two days, or I promise you I will track her down at her precinct and tell her everything."

"Please don't do that, she'll hate me, she'll hate Hunter."

"It will finally give the two of you a taste of what I've been living with for the last fourteen years."

"Marcus—"

"Two days, Ida-Mae, two days."

The line clicked and the elderly woman felt her years and forth-coming demise wash over her. Hands shaking, she pressed digits into the phone and connected the call, waiting for the line to be answered. When she heard the familiar, "Hello," of her son's deep voice she started speaking.

"Hunter, we gotta tell her. If we don't, Marcus will."

"What happened, Mama?"

"She went to see Marcus. Thinks that boy tried to kill her. We shoulda never let things go this far or this long. The truth is the only thing that's gonna make this right."

"Mama, we did what we thought was best at the time."

"That may be true, but I'm not going to my grave with this on my heart. My soul has to be right with God when I close my eyes to this world."

She stopped talking, gathered herself and held on to the strength that one only has after living life for as long as she had. "It's time, Hunter. We have to tell Heart the truth and it has to come from us."

"All right, Mama. If that's what you want, then that's what we'll do."

~

*H*eart was luxuriating in the feeling of Kenneth's bodyweight pressing down on her. She enjoyed the leisurely kiss they were sharing while their bodies were still joined. She could feel his semi-erect dick still pulsing inside her after they'd both enjoyed bedshaking orgasms in the early morning.

"Damn, you're still half hard. Don't you ever get tired?"

"Of the sweetest pussy on Earth?" he asked as he shoved his tongue in her mouth, licking inside of her warmth, pressing himself deeper inside of her. "No... never."

She chuckled and rolled her eyes. "You really know how to compliment a woman." She turned her head and looked at the bright numbers on the digital face of the clock.

"Kenneth, we've got to get up."

"The hell you say, I plan to lay up in this good shit all day. I'm not going anywhere and neither are you." He buried his face in the side of her neck and began to lick the heated skin there.

Her insides quaked; she could feel her walls beginning to moisten again. She had to put a stop to this. "Kenneth, we both promised my grandmother we'd attend church with her today. Today is family and friends day and Ida-Mae Amare will not be made to look bad. My uncle and all of her grandkids are going to be there. Anyone who knows what's good for them never misses, neither this, nor the dinner she prepares afterward."

Kenneth rolled his hips and called her name. "Heart?" he asked sweetly. "Do you really want to interrupt what we've been doing for the last hour or so to hang out with your grandmother and cousins at church?"

She smiled, loving the feel of him growing inside of her, stretching her to accommodate him. "Let me ask you this," she said. "You've met my grandmother. Do you really want to risk pissing her off and getting on her bad side?"

She couldn't help but smile at the quick streak of fear she saw dance across his face. He shook his head quickly.

"No, let's go. I don't want your grandmother mad at me."

She laughed, "I always knew you were a smart man."

❧

Heart stood in the foyer of the Greater Mount Zion Baptist Church. It had been a long time since she'd stepped foot back into this mega-church that had once been a second home to her. Since she was born, she had spent almost every weekend with her grandmother, and her grandmother's motto was a combination of Psalms 150:6 and Joshua 24:15. She would wake Heart up early on Sunday morning no matter how late she'd stayed up watching TV on Saturday night and say: "Let everything that has breath praise Ye the

Lord because as for me and my house, we will serve the Lord." As soon as

Heart heard those words she'd known it was time to crawl out of bed—no matter how comfortable it was—and get ready for church.

So here she stood, not feeling exactly worthy of sitting in God's house—especially after the things she and Kenneth had spent most of the morning doing—waiting to walk inside a place that she had spent so much time running from since that horrible night fourteen years ago.

Oh, she'd been back within its walls over the last fourteen years, but she had never belonged to it, or anything else except the force for that matter, since the darkest night she'd ever known. She stirred slightly when warm fingers caressed her shoulders, bringing her out of her dark reverie.

"Heart, is everything okay?"

She blinked her eyes and turned to look into that soothing crystal-blue gaze that always calmed her no matter what was going on. She smiled brightly, happy he was at her side. She rested a steady hand on top of his and nodded her head. He opened the glass doors and waited for her to walk through before entering the sanctuary himself.

The first face she saw was that of the head usher, Sister Holden. The matronly woman had stood faithfully as a gatekeeper since Heart was a child. Seeing her standing there, welcoming her into this majestic place filled her with warmth she hadn't known she'd missed until that very moment.

Sister Holden's mouth curved into a wide grin as she nodded her head in welcome to both Heart and Kenneth. "Hello, baby."

She couldn't stop herself from grinning. "Hi, Sister Holden. Can you squeeze the two of us in the main sanctuary, or do we have to go upstairs?'

Sister Holden waved her hand. "Chile' you know dog-gone well I'm not going to shove Ida-Mae Amare's grandbaby upstairs in the balcony. That woman would send me to Jesus quicker than I could say amen." They both leaned in laughing conspiratorially, knowing the truth that lay within the joke. "Now who is this handsome young man standing next to you, your husband?"

Heart almost dropped the large clutch purse in her hand. Not a good idea considering she had a twenty-two caliber pistol secured away in it. *Lord I know I'm wrong for bringing a gun to church, but I'm a cop, we never leave home without 'em.* "Sister Holden, Kenneth is a good friend of mine. No, we're not married."

The older woman smiled not so shyly and placed her gaze on Kenneth. "Brother

Kenneth, I hear what she's telling me, but I see what's in front of me. The bible says, 'He that finds a wife, finds a good thing,' and you sir look like a man that recognizes a good thing when you see it."

Heart wanted to fall right through the floor. She felt Kenneth place a comforting arm around her, pulling her into his side.

"I don't know if we're there yet, but I certainly would be hard-pressed to do better than having a woman like Heart as my wife."

Heart's cheeks warmed at his words. She smiled up at him as the happy usher guided them to a pew near the front of the sanctuary. Her grandmother sat at the end near the center aisle followed by her uncle, and all four of her cousins. Kenneth stood on the outside and waited for her to sit next to her cousin True. When she was seated comfortably, he opened the single button on his suit jacket and took his place next to her.

Her heart jumped a little when she let her gaze fall down his seated figure. His beautiful midnight mane was pulled into a tight, neat, low-sitting ponytail at his nape.

She'd wanted him to wear it out—she always wanted him to wear it out—but he had gone for a more conservative and controlled look when getting ready to attend her grandmother's church.

His face was clean-shaven except for the thin goatee he had taken to having carved out since she'd mentioned briefly that she didn't hate his five o'clock shadow. He was dressed in a dark grey suit that molded the lines of his chiseled body perfectly. *God, you're in church, behave yourself.* She focused on the service. Realizing they'd entered after the requisite testimony portion she was certain she'd get to sit quietly throughout the rest of the service.

The morning notices were being given by the church secretary and the choir was about to sing in preparation of Reverend Lawrence's upcoming sermon. The first movement of sound from the choir was a song she recognized. It was J. Moss' "Restored". She watched the choir to see who would be singing lead when she heard the soft and lovely tones of Genesis Lawrence filling the massive building. She was the preacher's daughter, the prodigal daughter returned. The words of the song seemed so appropriate for Genesis' story. The composer had written about being redeemed after living in shame. God's healing love transforming their captivity into their greatest triumph and victory. All those things had happened to Genesis, who was now living a complete and happy life with Drew in California. Heart sat there asking herself the strangest question. *If this song speaks to Genesis' story, why does it feel like it has me written all over it?*

She closed her eyes to clear the watery blur distorting her vision. That's when she felt the tears drop. She felt a strong hand cover hers and a powerful arm pull her into the comfort of Kenneth's embrace. He leaned over and pressed a delicate kiss to her wet cheek and said, "It's over, whatever it is or was, it can't hurt you anymore, I won't let it.

You're free."

She smiled and nodded her head, and held on tightly to his hand. He was right, as long as she had this connection, nothing could touch her again. She wiped her face just in time to see some of her kids from the community center walking up to the front of the church.

Heart watched as Genesis stood at the pulpit and turned to the section of the church Heart and her family members were sitting in.

"Morning church," she heard Genesis sing-speak into the microphone. "We are truly blessed today. Today is family and friends day and I am so glad to be in the number to spend it with you all today. Ten years ago, I didn't think I'd ever have the opportunity to share this special occasion with you all again, but God..." Genesis waved her hand as if she was trying to shake something off. She turned around in a small circle, throwing both hands in the air as she gave a moment of praise. "But God knew my desire, and He heard my prayer, and He brought me back to the place where I first received Him.

"Our God is a God of second chances church, and he's gave us all an incredible second chance in the form of our beloved Sister Heart MacKenzie."

Heart's world stopped for a moment and she locked eyes on Genesis at the sound of her own name.

"The devil sought to kill and destroy this lovely woman who spends so much time cultivating our greatest treasure, our children."

There were several amens that filled the air, Heart wasn't quite sure where they had all come from, but she was certain one of them belonged to her grandmother at the end of the pew.

"But I'm so glad we serve a God that is in control and when Satan tried to take her life, God covered her and gave it back to her. If you didn't know before, she is proof that God is able, and all power is in his hands. Now somebody ought to stand up and give God some praise for the life of one of our own, thank Him for his mercy, thank Him for sparing her, thank Him for bringing her back home to us."

The entire congregation erupted in cries of praise and worship clapping their hands and giving life to the words Genesis had spoken. All of the church stood, her family and Kenneth included showering her with the gift of celebration for her life. Her heart was beating so loud and strong she had to put her hand over it, to feel it, embrace it, to thank God for it. She watched as Kenneth stepped out of the pew and in to the aisle, making way for LaQuisha to come and hug her. When 'Quisha had nearly crushed her with her arms, the teenager took Heart by the hands and pulled her from the pew. Heart stopped her, remembering what lay inside of her purse that was now resting on the pew. She quickly picked up her purse and handed it to her cousin True. True felt the knowing weight of the purse and held it in her hand.

Heart followed LaQuisha down the aisle and to the front center of the church where the rest of the kids from the community center were standing in matching red t-shirts, black pants, and black sneakers.

"Cop Lady," LaQuisha started. "You always give us kids the best that you got. You never make us feel dumb, never make us feel like we don't matter. When we thought we'd lost you, sometimes the only thing we could do to keep it together, keep us from crying..." she paused, taking a brief moment to sniff back her tears. "...was dance one of the dances you taught us, created with us, danced with us. So now that you're back, we wanted you to dance with us one more time."

Heart was a blubbering mess by the time LaQuisha finished her speech. She wiped the tears from her eyes again, and then looked down at her clothes. She'd chosen a pants suit out of her closet this morning instead of her customary church attire: a dress or suit with a long skirt that was fitted, but fell below her knees. The clothes she had on draped nicely against her body, but still gave her room to move so she wouldn't embarrass herself in front of God and the entire congregation in the pews.

Heart heard the familiar tunes of Joshua's Troop, "Everybody Clap Your Hands" and unbuttoned her jacket to give herself a little room and pulled the long hairpin securing her bun out. By the time her kids started moving in unison with the music, she was in step with them. Her body hadn't forgotten the steps, and there was no pain when she moved.

In those moments, moving in sync with her kids, rocking to the up-tempo beat, she lost herself in the steps, sounds, and feel of the dance. She danced the fear of losing her life away and embraced the joy of living. In a brief moment she caught a glimpse of Kenneth in the pew, he was clapping and swaying joyously from side to side like everyone else in the congregation. His smile seemed just a little brighter than everyone else's probably because he was the one who was there when she'd nearly lost her life, he was the one who'd seen with his own eyes just how close she'd come to leaving this world. That smile, it made her dance harder, made the music fill her to almost bursting.

Made her feel like she'd never felt before.

By the time the energetic horns of the band signaled the close of the song she and her kids were breathing hard with exertion from their dance, and laughing, and praising, and crying like they'd never done before. She was alive.

She was about to follow her kids from the front of the church back to her seat when Reverend Lawrence motioned for her to come stand next to him in the pulpit. She obediently followed his cue and stepped into the blue-velvet covered stage-like platform.

"If you ever had a doubt about what God can do, you ought to take a look at this young lady here." The congregation erupted in hand-claps and "hallelujahs" all throughout the sanctuary. "The last time I saw this young lady she was lying in a hospital bed, covered in tubes and probes. She slept the sleep of the gravely ill, and life was seeping out of her."

Heart looked up at Reverend Lawrence. She hadn't been aware that he'd come to the hospital to see her, no one had mentioned it.

"Yes dear, Heart. When I receive a call that one of my flock is standing at death's door, I go. Your family, including your captain, and that nice young man that's sitting next to your cousin True, touched and agreed. That young man Kenneth placed his hand on your shoulder at my request, and we all laid hands on him and prayed for your life. We stood right there in that hospital room and we waged war against the devil on your behalf, demanding that he take his hands off of you."

Heart looked at Kenneth and something snapped open inside her. She had no clue whether Kenneth was a religious man or not, but the fact that he had let the people that love her use him as a surrogate to carry out their age old tradition of laying hands on the sick in order to pray for her, well that...yeah that, it mattered.

"And so, just like I asked that day, Kenneth, I'm going to ask you to come up here and stand in her stead again." She watched Kenneth rise from his pew and follow the usher's lead up to the pulpit. He stood in between her and the reverend, waiting for instruction. "Kenneth, I want you to know something," Reverend Lawrence continued as he unscrewed a small bottle of what she knew to be blessing oil. "You may not know this, but God brought you into this woman's life for a reason, so you could take care of her. I want you to put your arms around her, protect her from all that might befall her.

You see, as long as you've got her, God's got you."

Kenneth nodded his head at the pastor's declaration; like he knew what the man said was truth without a doubt. She watched Reverend Lawrence make the sign of the cross with his oil-covered fingertips on Kenneth's forehead. When he was done, he said quietly, "Let us pray," as he laid his hand palm side against Kenneth's head.

"Dear God, we come before You once again praising You for Your mercies and Your miracles. We thank You for the life of this young woman standing before You. We thank You for the young guardian You've placed in her wake. We ask You to keep him so that he can keep her. We ask You to lead him, so that he may lead her. We ask that You provide him with strength to face the obstacles that the world will throw at her, and the ones she will erect herself. We ask that he would always know that You have placed her in his hands to care for and treasure. Lord, Your daughter shall return to an occupation that places her life in danger on a regular basis. But Lord we know that You are a God of omniscience and omnipresence, You know what dangers she will face, and only You can cover her when danger falls. Keep her protected, keep her safe, and keep her whole. Lord we ask all of these mighty and bountiful blessings in Your name, and if You would be so merciful to grant them, we would be so careful to continue to praise

Your holy name." He removed his hand from Kenneth's head and said, "...Let the church say amen."

Heart couldn't stop the tears that seemed to be falling without pause from her eyes. The water just continued to fill her eyes. She felt Kenneth tighten his arms around her shaking body. He held her to his chest and whispered to her, "I will always take care of you, always."

She'd come to church expecting the usual pomp and circumstance of the Baptist church, but what she'd received instead was something she wasn't quite prepared for, and something she'd never trade for anything in the world. She loved the man holding her in his arms. She didn't know how it had happened, couldn't explain how it had happened. But somehow, without any permission from her, her heart had gone and jumped off the deep end smack dab in the middle of love.

~

*H*eart sat in Kenneth's luxury sedan that was parked in front of her family's building. It was a two-story multi-dwelling private house on Crescent Street. Her grandmother occupied the first floor two-bedroom apartment, and Hunter resided upstairs in the four bedroom apartment. The face of the building was an ugly sky blue that Heart had begged her grandmother to change for years. Even offering her the money to finance it when she became an adult, but Ida-Mae had always said the blue suited her, and so the color remained.

Heart turned to Kenneth in the driver's seat watching him carefully, inspecting him, and looking for something that would give her insight into this man that sat next to her. "Why didn't you tell me Reverend Lawrence came to visit me in the hospital?" she asked still trying to piece together all of the missing parts from when she was incapacitated.

"I didn't really know if I should," he moved his hand across the console, reaching until she felt warm skin covering hers. "He came in while your grandmother was visiting after you'd come out of surgery. Your grandmother asked me to step outside so he could lay hands on you."

"Did you know what she meant?"

He shook his head and laughed. "Not a damn clue. I told her, no disrespect, but no one other than the doctors was going to touch you." He ran his thumb over her knuckle then brought it to his lips to place a delicate kiss where his finger had just traced. "I didn't know exactly what the issue was, but I saw how afraid you were when the medical personnel were touching you in the ambulance, and when you arrived at the hospital. The only way the EMT's were able to stabilize you was by me touching and stroking you. It was the only way you wouldn't fight them." He lifted his head and contemplated her for a moment. "I didn't know what was wrong with you, I didn't know that there was a name for your condition, I just knew that you were afraid, and I had to keep you safe. The medical team had to touch you, I wasn't letting anyone else do so."

She closed her eyes, leaned back into the passenger seat, and lost herself in the warm sensation his touch evoked. "I don't remember a lot from that time, Kenneth, but I do remember feeling safe when you touched me. It was the only time I wasn't afraid during that entire ordeal."

"I swear your grandmother and I were about to go to war until True explained what the whole thing was about. The reverend seemed to be somewhat familiar with your situation and asked if I would stand proxy for you. I didn't quite understand it at the time, but I was willing to do anything to keep them from touching you. He made the sign of the cross much like he did today and everyone in that room touched me while I touched you. They prayed and said things I didn't really understand, but I felt like somehow they were fueling me. As if they were helping me to help you. Not long after that you opened your eyes."

He softly stroked her cheek and let her burrow into his touch. His touch always made her feel connected, safe, whole. She couldn't quite explain how she'd gone for fourteen years without touch to needing his every moment of the day.

"Thank you for that. I'm not a religious fanatic, but these traditions I have been raised with have helped me cope over the years. I can't say my faith is as strong or resolute as my grandmother's is, I'm certainly not a regularly attending member, but there is something majestic about being in that place and calling on its power when in need. Thank you for that." She leaned in and kissed him lightly on his pink lips and smiled at him. "Now let's get inside before my greedy cousins eat all of the food Mama made. If I don't get at least two slices of her sweet potato pie, I might have to shoot somebody."

~

*H*eart stepped into her uncle's apartment. This place brought back so many memories. When she was little, before things turned dark, gathering with her family used to be a happy thing. True's mother, Patience, was still alive then. Sundays were the best. Patience, the aunt who had always taken a gentle hand with her and her grandmother would come home after church, send all of the kids to play in the basement or the backyard while the two cooked like an army was coming.

Heart remembered the sweet and savory smells wafting in the air signaling their bellies that a feast was waiting for them in the family dining room. She and her cousins would go running into the dining room, scrambling to find a seat around the table, mouths watering for the mountain of food the two women had labored over.

The familiar smell of sweet, warm cornbread fresh from the oven overtook her senses as she stepped inside of the house. She stood at the opened door waiting for Kenneth to step inside behind her. She took a deep breath as her mind and stomach identified the mixed aromas floating through the air.

"Mmm, that smells amazing," he said.

She nodded and smiled. "Yeah, smells like blackened catfish, black-eyed peas and wild rice," she took another sniff, "...string beans, baked macaroni and cheese, and homemade cornbread. I would also wager that there's a sweet potato pie somewhere in

Mama's kitchen."

"Baked macaroni and cheese? Gosh, I haven't had that in years. Aunt Pam only makes it for really special occasions. The last one she and Porter had, I was out of town on business."

She smoothed her finger down his knotted tie and smiled at him. "Well my friend, I'd suggest you loosen your belt a couple of notches because your stomach is about to be overloaded with Mama Amare's southern goodness."

They walked further into the apartment and were greeted by her uncle Hunter and her grandmother. She looked around for signs of the cousins, but didn't see them.

"They couldn't stay," Hunter said as he stood up from his armchair.

She lifted her neck to meet his eyes. She'd forgotten just how big of a man her uncle was. He was a couple of inches taller than Kenneth's six feet three inches with a broad solid build that made him perfectly built for the combat situations he encountered in the

Army. He shook Kenneth's hand and nodded toward her in greeting.

"True and the sibs left?" she asked.

"Yeah, True has some big-time client to operate on first thing in the morning. The rest of my kids only had liberty for the weekend, gotta be on post at zero six hundred hours."

Heart nodded her head. "That sucks, I only had a chance to see them for a few minutes after service. It's so rare that all of the Amare kids are in one place at the same time." She shrugged, missing her cousins was nothing new to her, but it wasn't something that usually weighed on her at all. They were all military, former military or law enforcement. Frequently being unavailable to family was a prerequisite for becoming involved in either of those career paths. Yet she couldn't deny the heavy block of disappointment weighing inside her chest at this moment. Why was today so different?

She looked up and found Kenneth's eyes on her. She granted him a smile in return and he enclosed her hand with strong fingers. She would absolutely never get tired of that man's touch. It did things to her that she couldn't really explain, truth be told, she'd pretty much given up on trying to understand it. The only thing she cared about was that she didn't feel broken when he was touching her, she didn't feel like the freak that she knew she was.

She saw Hunter's shadow shift slightly. The brief movement was enough to remind her senses that she and Kenneth weren't alone in the room. "So they didn't get any of Mama's food?"

"Well, you know your grandmother, Heart. No way were all of her grandbabies going to be in town and she wasn't going to feed them.

She packed them all a few travel containers. They should each be set with food for the rest of the week."

"You got that right, Hunter," Ida-Mae bustled into the living room. She smiled while wiping her hands on a kitchen towel. "Glad you two could make it." When she was finished, she slapped it against one of her shoulders and waved the two of them inside. "I just got through putting the food on the table, let's go in and get started."

They all shuffled inside of the dining room and found their seats. Hunter sat at the head of the table, her grandmother to his left. Kenneth pulled out the chair resting at

Hunter's right and waited for Heart to take her seat. When she was comfortably seated, he unbuttoned his suit jacket and took the seat next to her. A slight curve lifted the side of her mouth. He was always doing things like that for her, making her feel soft, treasured, taken care of. *I never want to not feel that way again.*

Hunter said the blessing as they all sat with bowed heads. When he was done, she glanced around the table taking in all of the full dishes sitting before them. Her eyes panned the table and saw an extra place setting. "Are we expecting someone else?" There was a strange look that passed between her grandmother and uncle.

"You know your grandmother," Hunter answered. "She's always preparing for the unexpected guest."

Heart let her gaze fall on Hunter's face and studied it. She was a trained investigator, but he was a career military man. She knew how to detect lies; he knew how to make his lies look like gospel truth. Nothing in his tone, posture, or facial expressions triggered her bull-shit meter, but there was something not quite right there.

She let it pass and began loading her plate up. Everything she'd told Kenneth she'd smelled in the air was there sitting before them, waiting for them to consume it. She watched Kenneth as he took his first bite of food. He'd taken a forkful of baked macaroni and cheese and placed it in his mouth. She could tell the minute the delectable flavor began to spread across his palate. He closed his eyes and his jaw began to move in a slow-chewing motion. He looked like he was at the height of pleasure. *God, when did a man eating food become sexy?*

"Have you ever had soul food before, Kenneth?" Heart's eyes were pulled from his blissful face by her grandmother's question.

Kenneth nodded his head in response while he finished chewing the mouthful of food. "Yes ma'am. My godparents' families hail from the Southeastern part of the country. I spent a great deal of time in their home most of my childhood." "You don't anymore?" Ida-Mae asked.

"I see them as often as I can, but with my career and my godfather being a police captain, I don't get to see my god-family as often as I would like."

Her grandmother seemed to be processing everything Kenneth had said. She took a sip of the homemade lemonade in her glass before addressing him again.

"David Porter is your godfather?" "Yes," Kenneth answered.

"So that's how you met my granddaughter?"

"Not exactly," Kenneth gave Heart a quick sideways glance. "Heart was investigating the disappearance of my niece, Merridith. That's how we met. We didn't become...close..." he said with a small smile as he looked back to Heart. "...until Heart was injured during Merridith's recovery."

"You must be very relieved that your niece is home safe," Hunter said. "How is she doing since this entire ordeal?"

"She's doing as well as can be expected. Her mother, my sister, died during the recovery. Her dad says she misses her mom a great deal, but they're working through all of it."

Hunter nodded his head and placed the fingertips of each hand together. "Kenneth, family is the most important thing in the world. You've got nothing without them. Our Heart is a very special part of this family; we've spent a lot of time worrying about her, trying to protect her from the world around her."

Heart glanced at her uncle with a furrowed brow. Was he really trying to scare Kenneth into treating her right? Was that where this conversation was going?

"Uncle Hunter, you don't need to—"

"Yes I do, Heart," Hunter interrupted her with a raised hand. "Kenneth, I know what it's like to lose a sister. I know what it's like to want to protect that sister's child, because she's no longer here to protect her child herself. I can tell just from the way you speak your niece's name how much you love her."

"Yes, sir," Kenneth nodded. "I love Merridith very much."

"And I love Heart in the same fashion," Hunter responded. "My daughter, True, tells me you spared no expense in ensuring Heart had the best of everything for her rehabilitation. I wanted to thank you for that. For protecting my family, for taking care of her when the rest of us were too far away from her to be able to give her the help she needed."

Heart sat there blinking. She'd expected Hunter to attempt to scare or bully Kenneth, but to thank him, that was totally not what she'd imagined was coming.

"Kenneth, even though we love Heart, most of the time our respective careers take us far away from her. I can tell you that life is going to present other moments where no matter how much we wish to be there to protect her as a family we won't be able to shield her. I'm asking you to stand in our place, to protect her, when her family can't.

Can you do that for me, young man?"

The air in the room felt excessively heavy for some reason. There was a cryptic tinge in the air that Heart couldn't quite understand. She looked across the table at her grandmother whose expression was much the same as Hunter's: serious, tight, and…afraid? What were they afraid of, why was fear etched in the two faces of the leaders of her family.

She felt Kenneth take her hand in his. The simple touch grounded her, even if it didn't dissolve that acidic burning that always started in the pit of her stomach when things were about to go wrong.

"Yes, sir," Kenneth tightened his grip on her hand as he spoke. "I can promise you that. There's nothing I wouldn't do for Heart to keep her safe."

"It's reassuring that someone is looking out for her."

Heart looked at her uncle and realized that he hadn't moved his lips. No way had she imagined those words, and she certainly hadn't imagined that voice. She knew that voice; it was burned in her memory. Instinct mixed in with a healthy dose of cautious fear made her stand and reach for her gun in one fluid motion. Before a second passed her gun was pointed at the intruder.

"In my family's house, Marcus? You must have a fucking death wish."

"A death wish?...No, not at all. A need to see my daughter...yes."

CHAPTER 16

"*H*eart, what's going on?" She could hear Kenneth calling her, but he wasn't her focus at the moment. Marcus was. Marcus Paul MacKenzie, he was her father, and the man who'd attempted to kill her fourteen years ago.

"Not now, Kenneth." She kept her gun arm locked and aimed at Marcus. "What do you want, Marcus? What game are you playing showing up in my uncle's home?"

Marcus put his hands in the air, showing her they were free of any weapons. "I'm not armed, MacKenzie," his voice soft, and slow as if anything about him could disarm her.

"Heart baby, please, put the gun down," her grandmother called to her.

"Mama, I'm not letting this maniac anywhere near us," she spoke to her grandmother, but her eyes remained on Marcus.

Heart stepped from the table, and walked to the entryway of the room and motioned for Marcus to turn around and face the wall. When he complied, she grabbed one of his raised arms and enclosed it with one of the heavy metal brackets of her handcuffs. Once it was secured, she repeated the action with his other wrist.

She smoothly patted him down, checking for weapons.

"Is this really necessary?" Marcus asked her.

"I could just put a bullet in your head and ask questions later. Would you prefer that?"

"Carry on," he groaned.

When she was certain that he wasn't concealing any weapons she turned him around by the shoulder to face her.

"I asked you a question, Marcus. What are you doing walking into my family's home?"

"Heart, please listen, Marcus isn't here to do you any harm," her grandmother pleaded with her.

"Mama, he's evil."

"Heart, he's here because we asked him to come," Ida-Mae answered.

"She's telling the truth, Heart," Hunter joined in the conversation. "Your grandmother and I invited him. We asked him to come."

"Why?"

Hunter stood from the table and walked over to where she held Marcus against the wall.

"Uncle Hunter, please step away from him."

"Heart, I'm a general in the United States Army, there's not a thing Marcus could do to me if I didn't let him. You've already checked him for weapons and he has none. Uncuff him, we need to talk."

She glanced at her uncle and saw sincerity in his eyes. She watched him for a moment more and then unlocked the handcuffs. She stepped back putting distance between she and Marcus. She nodded to the empty dining room chair sitting closest to them and Marcus slowly sat in it. Hunter walked back to his seat, and she leaned against the wall. She took a brief moment to look at Kenneth. *God, what he must be thinking.* She pulled her eyes from him, this wasn't the time to focus on neither him nor the questions she knew he must have at this moment. She needed to find out what was going on, why was her family involved with Marcus again.

"Someone needs to start talking to me quickly. Otherwise my first official order of business will be to bust him for trespassing and any other offense I can dig up. Why would the two of you ask the man that tried to kill me to Sunday dinner?"

The room was quiet, her father, her uncle, and her grandmother all three looking conspiratorially at one another. *What the hell could the three of them be in agreement about?*

Her grandmother fiddled with the plain gold crucifix around her neck. To anyone else it would have looked like a show of piety. To Heart it was a nervous reflex, something her grandmother did to reassure herself when she was uneasy about something. She was guilty, of what Heart wasn't certain, but she knew that nervous twitch, it was as good as a confession in her book.

"What did you do, Mama?"

Her grandmother, startled by Heart's direct question, stopped the fiddling motion her fingers were making at her neck and stared back at Heart. She took a loud breath and then closed her eyes. Her shoulders began to drop low, and then they began to shake and tremble with the weight of whatever she was holding on to, quaking under the pressure.

"Mama?" Heart's voice softened with concern as she watched the strongest woman she knew shatter in to pieces.

"I was so wrong, Heart. I was so wrong. I did what I thought was right at the time, but I was so wrong. Baby, please, sit down and let me explain."

The sight of her grandmother looking so fragile almost broke her. She reached for the chair and felt Kenneth's strong arm around her waist. She'd almost forgotten he was there, but that surge of strength that flowed through her was only because he was close enough to touch.

"Marcus didn't try to kill you, Heart. He's your father, and the only thing he has ever been guilty of is loving you and deferring to me to know what was best for you."

Heart watched her uncle's hand reach out and cover her grandmother's in a show of support. "Mama, you aren't the only one to blame, we all are." Hunter turned his gaze to Heart. "What do you remember about the night you were abducted, Heart?"

She felt Kenneth's arm stiffen around her. She hadn't told him any of this. She'd never wanted to relive it. It had completely decimated her life fourteen years ago,

Kenneth was helping her get her life back, and she hadn't wanted to sully what they were building with the darkness of that night.

She reached for Kenneth's remaining hand and faced him, not her uncle as she spoke. She couldn't do this ever again. Whatever she revealed, it would be the last time she would speak of this. She needed to tell Kenneth, so he would never have to ask her again.

"I attended I.S. 302 on Linwood Street and Liberty Avenue. The Brooklyn office for Marcus' development company was one block up and one block over to the right on Glenmore Avenue. I walked that route every day. I knew everyone one on those blocks from all the years Marcus had owned that building, all the times I'd visited him there as a child. I never thought to be worried in that atmosphere.

"Vic's candy store was in the middle of the block on Liberty and Essex. Sometimes I would make a detour after school and stop there to pick up sweets; it was a hangout for all the kids. There was this older girl I used to meet up with; her name was Sophia. She was a couple of years older, went to Maxwell high school up on Pennsylvania Ave, but she lived next door to the candy store. She would come down and tell all of us younger kids about how cool high school was.

"That day she pulled me away from the usual crowd of kids, told me she had something to show me. I don't know what it was, but the look in her eye told me something was off. This car came skidding to the curbside with doors open and Sophia jumped inside, and tried to pull me in with her. I tried to pull away from her and started screaming. Vic must have heard me, because he came running out of the store with a baseball bat. He tried to help me, but he couldn't get to me in time. They took us to some dark warehouse. I didn't know where I was, but I knew how I was going to get out of there. Uncle Hunter gave me a necklace when I was small. He told me it was magic, told me if I was ever lost, all I had to do was rub it with my fingers, and it would tell him where to find me. So I rubbed it, and I waited.

"But while I waited, the man who had organized my kidnapping came to see me. He told me his name was Anthony Luponero and that he was a friend of my father's. He told me it was my father's fault that he'd taken me, that my father was responsible for my capture. He even called my father, put the phone on speaker, and let me hear their conversation. Marcus knew who he was, and when Luponero asked him if he was ready for me to come home now, Marcus told him no. He said I couldn't see what was going on and not to bring me to him until he called. But he never called. I waited and waited for that phone to ring, and it never did.

"Luponero got bored with waiting, came back to me, and said my father had made a decision, and we would all have to live with it. He had four of his men grab all of my limbs and hold me down…"

She heard a ragged sound in the air, it was only after she saw a solitary tear coming down Kenneth's face that she realized the sound was his and not hers.

"Dear God, Heart…did they?"

"They held me down while they made me watch Luponero beat and torture Sophia. She looked like a slaughtered animal by the time that maniac was through with her, and he told me to watch carefully, because he was going to do the same thing to me. It took him days to do it, and every time he pounded on her, he'd have his men hold me down, and smile at me while he killed that girl slowly. The feel of their hands on me…it just made my skin crawl…and all I kept thinking was, this is the last touch I'm ever going to know before Luponero kills me."

She closed her eyes and reached for Kenneth's hands, holding on tightly to chase away the shadows of the dark memories that were threatening her senses. The feel of his touch quieted them, pushed them down just far enough under her surface that she could get control of herself again.

"The day after Sophia died, Luponero called Marcus again. Luponero asked Marcus if he was ready to meet up with us so he could bring me home. Marcus refused, he told

Luponero, 'I don't much care what you do. I'm not giving you a damn thing. If you want to kill her, then go ahead, because I will meet you in hell, before I give you what you want.' Luponero was just as shocked as I was. My father had just given him permission to kill me."

She turned in her seat toward Marcus. "Why did you want me dead, Marcus? What did you have that he wanted so badly that was worth my life?"

He closed his eyes, she guessed it was shame that wouldn't let him look at her.

"Your mother," he whispered.

Heart turned completely out of Kenneth's embrace and faced Marcus.

"My mother died the day I was born. How could you give her to him? What did he want, her fourteen-year-old corpse?"

Marcus nodded quickly. "Yes, that's exactly what he wanted. He wanted me to dig your mother's grave up and give him her remains."

Heart's stomach twisted at the thought of what Marcus was saying and she looked to her family for answers.

"Uncle Hunter, he's lying...right?"

Hunter slowly shook his head as he spoke carefully. "Your father, Luponero, Garrett...Reverend Lawrence, and I all grew up on this block. We were the best of friends. Luponero and Marcus had a crush on your mother. Diamond was so beautiful, every guy wanted to get close to my little sister. Although I knew Luponero and Marcus had feelings for her, I also knew they wouldn't try anything either and they'd keep the other hounds at bay that were sniffing around her."

Hunter leaned back in his chair, holding himself stiff and upright. "All four of us went into the Army. Marcus and Garrett did their time, and opted not to re-up when their contracts were up. I of course decided I wanted to be career Army, so I stayed. Luponero signed up for another four years. Well, not too long after Marcus and Garrett came home, word got back that Marcus and your mother were going to get married. Luponero was furious. In his mind, Marcus had somehow stolen what was his. Losing your mom messed with him; he wound up doing some really stupid things and got himself booted out of the Army.

"He came home, and he tried to convince your mother to leave

Marcus. When she wouldn't, he blamed Marcus and swore his revenge. He hounded your mother and Marcus for years, and for the most part, no one really paid him any attention. Until he hooked up with the local mafia, and then he had power to make his threats a reality. He kept coming for your mother, and we all kept fighting him off. When your mother died after giving birth to you, we thought it was over. We found out fourteen years later we were wrong.

"Luponero had it in his head that even in death Diamond belonged with him. So he decided that he would use you as leverage to make that happen. What you heard wasn't your father giving his permission for Luponero to kill you, what you heard was a stalling tactic. That charm I put around your neck was an electronic tracker. When you rubbed it, you activated it, and my team and me were on the way to get you. I just needed your father to make it harder for Luponero to get what he wanted, so he would keep coming back for it. That first call you heard, Luponero had led us to your mother's grave. When he asked your father if he should bring you to him, he meant to watch dig up your mother's grave. Marcus didn't want you to see that if it came down to giving Luponero what he wanted. Your father was trying to spare you trauma, not cause it."

Heart looked at the two people she'd known all her life to make this make sense. But somehow, it wasn't working. "Mama, if what you're saying is true why wouldn't you let me go back to live with Marcus? I lived with him before the abduction, I never went back afterward."

Her grandmother leaned forward, reaching for her, then halting when she saw Heart pull back away from her. "You had terrible nightmares afterward; it all got jumbled up in your head. At first we thought you were just reacting badly to the entire incident. The first time Marcus tried to pick you up, you became hysterical..."

"Because I thought the man who wanted me dead was coming for me again."

"We thought it would pass, baby," Ida-Mae said through quivering lips. "We thought maybe in a day, a week, a month you would be able to see Marcus without going into such a panic. I told him to let you stay here with me until you put this behind you."

"Mama, I never put this behind me. That abduction was the reason for everything I am, everything I became after that experience."

"I know," Ida-Mae whispered. "When it seemed to be taking you longer than we thought it should, I tried to seek outside help. I took you to the pastor and had him pray over you."

"Instead of getting me the medical help that I needed...a psychologist, a therapist, anyone that had training in helping little girls keep their sanity after a traumatic event?

You took me to your pastor and asked him to pray for me?"

Heart stood quickly, knocking the chair over behind her. It crashed to the floor with a loud thud. "You let me believe my father tried to kill me. I told you why I didn't want to go home with Marcus, and you told me you would make it so he would never hurt me again. How could you not get me help?"

"Heart, your grandmother did what she knew how. She didn't know anything about mental health professionals. She was afraid they would label you crazy and take you away from us."

She looked at her uncle, fury boiling inside of her. She'd trusted Hunter with her life, believed he would always keep her safe, knew him to be her protector, but at this moment, all she could see was someone else that was complicit in her suffering.

"You knew better, and you letter her do it anyway, Hunter." She turned to Marcus, who until that moment had remained painfully silent through Hunter's explanation.

"And you knew better too. How could you let her keep me in this emotional prison I've been living in for fourteen years? How could you just walk away from your daughter because a bossy old lady told you to do so?"

"Heart," her grandmother spoke gently. It was so unlike her usually brisk and rough tone that she almost didn't recognize that the sound had come from her. "Don't blame your uncle and your father. I did this, not them."

"Oh trust me; Mama there is more than enough blame to go

around." Heart rubbed the side of her head where her temple was throbbing in time with her racing pulse. "Why did you do this to me, Mama?"

"I wanted to do what was right for you; I wanted to take care of you like I promised your mama I would before she died."

"And this is how you think my mother wanted me taken care of? Separated from my father for fourteen years all based on a lie of omission that you allowed to continue for more than a decade. Consequences be damned, as long as you got to take care of me, everything was just fine?"

"Heart, I needed to take care of you."

"You needed...what about what I needed...what my father needed? None of that mattered did it? As long as you got what you needed, nothing else mattered. You say you did this for me, but I think you did this for one reason alone, your daughter died, so you thought you'd just keep me as the reincarnation of her." "Heart?" Hunter's question dripped in sorrow.

"Hunter, we all know it's the truth. I'm the spitting image of my mother, having me live with her filled a void that death had opened. Well here's a newsflash, when your daughter dies, you don't get to steal someone else's. I am not Diamond." She said her mother's name so loud against the silence in the room that she felt the walls tremble with its echo.

"Heart..."

"Baby..."

"Heart..."

All three of them were calling her at the same time. All three of their voices were clawing at her insides. She'd lost the ability to touch and be touched fourteen years ago and now it seemed her ability to process sound was leaving her as well. Everything sounded like noise. She was losing herself again. Her senses were drawing her back into that torture chamber. She could feel the pressure of the hands of those four thugs holding her down. She could feel the panic rising again.

"Nooooo," she screamed, trying to cancel out the chaotic sounds in her head. She needed to find an anchor. She looked to Kenneth and saw him rising from his seat, slowly reaching out to her. She wanted so desperately to hold on to his hand, to let it pull her above this emotional sea that seemed destined to drown her. She was just about to seek out his calming touch when she caught sight of his eyes. Inside of them, there was fear mixed with something else, something she'd never wanted to see in those beautiful cobalt eyes; there was pity.

She shook her head, and stood up, grabbed her bag and turned on her heel. She headed straight for the door, down the stairs, through the front door, and out on the street. Her chest hurt, she was breathing too hard, trying to force air in and out of her lungs. She made it up a block or two, she couldn't even be sure, she just needed to put as much distance between that house, those people, and her aching heart.

She found herself at the Euclid Avenue train station. She hurried down the stairs, flashed her badge at the attendant, and waited for the screaming buzz indicating the gate was unlocked. She ran down the Manhattan side just in time to meet the arriving train.

She didn't really care where it was going; she just needed to get away from this place, from these people.

~

*K*enneth let his gaze walk around the dining room. The walls were covered in a maroon color. The table and the rest of the furniture were made of a dark colored wood that complimented the walls. There were pictures of various family members that lined the walls. He could make out Heart and her Amare cousins in several pictures at several different ages. They were all happy, all smiling. This room exuded warmth, like the memories of happier times that lived within its seams. She had been happy here. She had known love here. This had been a place of refuge for her.

Yes, it had been a safe haven for her, but today, today it held the source of her pain. He looked at the three other people in the room. All shocked quiet, not certain what to say, or who should say it first.

This was Heart's family, the people she was supposed to be able to trust, yet they were the ones responsible for her betrayal.

He knew what that felt like. He understood the hot fire that sliced through your chest when you realized your own blood betrayed your trust. His mother had been the one dragging the hot iron sword down the middle of his torso when his bout with betrayal had arrived. Now, an estranged father, a conspiring uncle, and a grandmother with wellmeaning intentions sat in front of him facing the aftermath of their collusion.

Kenneth stood, placed both hands on his waist. He looked at the three coconspirators and shook his head. The words just wouldn't come. He didn't have time for this, he had to get to Heart. Kenneth turned toward the doorway when he heard, Hunter utter, "We love her" from behind him.

Three words, simple in their joining, were strong enough to pull Kenneth's gaze back to them. "General Amare," Kenneth answered. "With all of the crap that has gone on in my family as of late, I've no room to judge you. What I can tell you is that your silence has caused so much damage to that young woman. She's hurt every single day of her life since the abduction, and you all perpetuated that hurt, kept her drowning in it by letting her believe that her father had a hand in her trauma. I know you all love her, but I think it would be best if you all gave Heart a little space for the moment. Give her some time to work through this."

Hunter nodded his head, accepting Kenneth's words with little resistance. Ida-Mae was staring at nothing; she seemed locked inside herself unaware of the world around her. Marcus seemed contained. Kenneth could see the anger he was fighting in the tightly pulled muscles of his jaw and neck. The man was not happy, and he was fighting to keep his shit together.

"Marcus, I need you to give Heart some time," Kenneth said. "I've given her fourteen years and look how that's turned out." "If you push her, you could lose her," Kenneth offered.

"I've already lost her; don't think you can get much lower when your daughter believes you've tried to kill her."

Kenneth scraped his nails across his scalp as he tried to gauge the words he needed to speak. He understood Marcus' need to make things right, but he wouldn't let him traumatize her further, that wasn't an option. "Marcus, if you go charging after her, she will fight you. In the end, you will lose her, possibly forever. She needs time."

"Young man, no disrespect, but what gives you the right—"

"Marcus," Kenneth called the elder man's name with the same authority he commanded in his day-to-day business dealings. His father may have left him an empire, but that empire stood strong and thrived because Kenneth knew how to lead and stand his ground. He called forth the same calmed power that disarmed his competitors and kept him in control of his business to emerge. "This is not up for discussion. My only interest is keeping her safe. If you want to get to Heart and she's not ready to receive you, you'll have to go through me to do it."

"Are you threatening me?" Marcus stood placing his palms flat against the table as he rose from his seat.

"Mr. MacKenzie, I'm not threatening you. I'm stating fact. I won't let you hurt Heart any more than she's already been hurt. You don't want to tangle with me, especially not on this issue."

"What the hell gives you the right to keep me from my daughter?"

"That's simple; I'm the only person in her life right now that she trusts that doesn't have an agenda."

Kenneth took a deep breath and tried to remember that the people in the room with him did love Heart, they hadn't hurt her intentionally, and there had been no malice when they'd agreed to this illformed plan. Kenneth relaxed his shoulders and rolled them briefly attempting to decompress the fiery anger that was building inside of him.

"Marcus, trust me, she's gonna need a little time."

Kenneth reached inside of his jacket pocket and removed his cell phone. "Give me your number Marcus, when she's ready, I'll call you." Kenneth programmed the number into his phone, and sent Marcus a text containing his number.

"What if she's never ready to talk to me?" Marcus asked.

Kenneth watched him, saw the fear he harbored over the broken relationship with his daughter.

"All I can promise is that I will talk to Heart. If she's not ready, I'll call and let you know that too."

Marcus regarded Kenneth carefully then he nodded his head, and held out his hand.

I'll hold you to that."

Kenneth grabbed hold of his hand and returned the firm handshake. He turned and offered the same gesture to Hunter, and stopped abruptly in front of Ida-Mae. She still sat there, staring intently at nothing, still playing with the delicate crucifix around her neck.

He went to extend his hand to her, but stopped, she wasn't there, wasn't focused on him at all. He looked between the two men hoping they would read his silent message to tend to this woman. As much as he felt for Ida-Mae, as much as he could feel for her considering her part in all of Heart's pain, she wasn't his focus. Heart was his priority; he needed to get to her.

~

*H*eart entered the darkness of the house and let a silent breath of relief escape her lips. Either Kenneth wasn't there yet or he was asleep. She embraced the silence that surrounded her. There had been way too much noise today.

She quietly climbed the stairs and stopped at the top of the landing. If she continued straight she'd end up in Kenneth's bedroom—the one she'd been sharing with him since they began sleeping together. If she turned right, she'd find herself in her room, the room where they'd grown to care for each other, grown to become friends.

She headed to the right, to the safety of solitude. She felt too raw to be in Kenneth's presence. He'd seen her weak before, but this, this… thing she felt was beyond weakness. She felt broken, as if the pieces of her soul and mind didn't fit together any more.

She pulled off the pantsuit she'd worn to church, let the pieces of it fall to the floor, and headed for the shower. She needed to wash this disaster of a day away right now. She stepped inside of the blistering water and let her head hang beneath the spray. She didn't care about her hair; she just needed to be clean, to wash the stench of distrust and betrayal from her senses.

Her eyes watched the circling rivulets of water going around and around the drain before falling into the oblivion of the pipes. If only it were that easy, if only she could make it all disappear down the drain just like the water.

They'd lied to her, all three of them. Her uncle and father had perpetuated the lie, but she knew full well who had generated it to begin with. Ida-Mae Amare, her grandmother.

Ida-Mae was the only mother Heart had known, and she'd betrayed her, lied to her, and crippled her. How was she supposed to ever trust anyone ever again if she couldn't trust the woman who had raised her?

Raised you or trapped you? She squeezed her eyelids tightly and began fiercely washing herself, scrubbing her skin with the exfoliating puff of material in her hand to the point that it was painful. Her skin would probably be irritated later, but right now she needed some-thing...anything to distract her from the ache in her heart, even if it was physical pain. The sting of the bristles made her feel alive, made her feel something other than the tragic numbness that had been pouring into her soul since she'd left her family's home running to be free of them.

Aren't you supposed to run to family in the times of crisis?

She assumed that was true for most people, and up until earlier today, it had certainly been true of herself. Now though, now she didn't really know where to turn. She didn't know if she really had a place to be safe, to find shelter.

Heart finished her shower and dressed quickly in loose sweats and an A-line tee. She padded her bare feet against the soft carpeting and climbed into the bed, falling with a solid thump. Her body was tired, her limbs left heavy by the weighty emotions that plagued her since the afternoon. She turned over on her back, tired, but her mind still dancing, too active to find rest. Then she noticed the change in the air and her skin crackled. The familiar scent of spice and man that was unique to Kenneth Searlington wafted into the room. The truth was even without his scent she would have noticed him.

Her senses were always aware of him.

"What are you doing in here?"

"How'd you know I was standing here, I didn't make a sound when I came in?"

"You didn't have to, I'm a cop, I use all of my senses, not just my sight. I smelled you. I felt you."

"Then we share something in common because I felt you the moment you walked in this house. I waited for you to come to me, you didn't."

She felt him move closer to the bed, felt the dip on the side of the mattress when he lay down next to her.

"No, I didn't," she whispered.

"Why not?"

"It's late; I didn't want to disturb you."

"Sleeping without you disturbs me. Especially when I know you've had an unbelievably difficult day."

His body pressed against hers and without thought she burrowed into the hard muscle of his chest. It was reflexive. When had this become second nature to her, they'd only been in this house for a few months, had only been intimate for possibly half that.

Yet, she instinctively knew her place was in his arms.

"We should talk about what happened today."

She shook her head. "No, we really shouldn't."

"Heart...bottling this up is not going to help anyone. You need to talk about it, so you can figure out what you're going to do when you see your family next."

She pulled out of Kenneth's arms and headed for the bathroom. She popped open the medicine cabinet and pulled out a bottle of ibuprofen. Just thinking about what the elder members of her family had done to her made her head throb. They were supposed to lead her; instead they'd lied to her and deceived her.

She swallowed the pills and headed back into the bedroom where

Kenneth was waiting for her in the middle of the bed, body braced on his elbow. He was shirtless, but still wore a pair or boxer briefs. Even in her current state her womb clinched in excitement at the unobstructed view of strong muscle covered by smooth skin.

What the hell is wrong with me? I've had my world blown up today, yet I still want to hump the dude lying in my bed.

He patted the bed and motioned for her to climb in next to him, and of course she did, because all he had to do was even hint that he wanted her near him, and she would be there. Her body didn't know fear or rational thought around him, it just knew want and need.

She sat in the bed, knee bent, looking down at the man who'd entered her world, and changed everything she'd thought she'd known about herself. The tranquil blue gaze met hers and that raging ire that had chased her out of her family's home and through the streets of Brooklyn seemed distant and muffled, like sound passing through water. She could feel it, knew it was still there, but it wasn't as sharp or as clear as it had been only moments before.

She felt his free arm snake up her chest and wrap around the curve of her neck. She felt the tugging pressure he applied and went willingly to meet the soft pink lips waiting for her.

He kissed her hard, keeping his hand firmly in place on her neck. He didn't need to though, once their lips met, she couldn't have moved if she'd wanted to. Everything she needed was right there pouring life back into her through their kiss.

Kenneth finally released her, and her lungs drew in a ragged breath. She hadn't realized she was air-hungry, she just knew that keeping his lips pressed against hers was far more important that providing life-sustaining oxygen to her blood and cells.

He kept his hand cupped around her neck, allowing his thumb to slowly stroke her cheek. "You get a pass tonight, Heart. I know you're too overwrought to deal with all of this drama tonight." His voice followed the pattern and tempo of the touch he was skirting across the skin of her jaw and lips. Soft and slow, soft and slow, this was the way his words slipped out of his mouth. Each word was spoken in a gangly stretch to meet the next.

"I don't want to think about this ever again."

He nodded, but kept stroking her skin. "I know you don't, but you can't avoid your family forever, and you shouldn't. You need answers, answers that you won't be able to process right now because you're so angry. But, Heart, you still have to face this…you still have to face your family."

She nodded her head. *Why the fuck am I nodding my head? How does he do this fucking mind-control trick over me? I've really got to get my shit together. The dick cannot be this good.* Kenneth leaned in again and pulled her body down until it rested on top of his. She could feel the granite-flesh between his legs pressed against her abdomen and the walls of her pussy instinctively did that open-close-open motion that it always did when it anticipated that she'd get a taste of him. *Who the fuck am I kidding? Yes the hell that shit is in fact just that damn good.*

She straddled his hips and ground the lips of her sex down on top of him. Just the pressure she felt from that move alone was almost enough to push her over the edge of orgasm. A low moan escaped her lips; she had to still herself to prevent the threatening climax. She wanted him inside of her when she peaked; it always felt so much better that way. She needed him that way tonight.

Just as she reached down to free the monster hiding behind the snug fabric of his boxer briefs she heard the landline ring. It shocked them still for a moment, and then she saw his arm reaching toward the night table for the cordless phone.

"Kenneth, do not answer that phone."

He picked it up and glanced at the caller-id. "It's your uncle."

"Don't answer it, Kenneth."

"I'm not ignoring your uncle, Heart." He connected the call and answered her uncle quickly. "General?" A few seconds passed and Kenneth nodded his head as if her uncle could somehow see him through the telephone line. "We're on our way."

He hung up the phone and moved her off of his lap and onto the bed. "Get dressed, we're leaving," he said as he dashed toward the doorway.

"I'm not going anywhere. I could give a damn about whatever

326

demands Hunter is making. That shit might work on his kids and his military underlings, but not me. What kind of bullshit did he tell you to get you up and out of my bed?"

Kenneth stopped, standing eerily still. The flushed rosy pink that was just beginning to tint his skin was replaced by a grey sallow color that made him look almost ill. "He said your grandmother had a heart attack and they're rushing her to the hospital."

CHAPTER 17

*H*eart sat in the waiting area of the cardiac care unit and let her guilt form into a solid boulder sitting in the bottom of her stomach. Every time she thought about the way she'd spoken to her grandmother, the cold words she'd uttered...

Dear God, don't let her die. Please, not like this. I promise if You keep her here with me, I will do whatever I have to in order to make up for the last words I said to her.

Please, just don't take her from me. Not now, I'm not ready, I still need her.

She'd been praying those same words over and over in her head since Kenneth had delivered the news. She needed her grandmother to live; if she died...she couldn't die.

There was just no other option. None that Heart was willing to acknowledge anyway.

"Where the hell is this doctor? We need to know something. I'm going back there and find out what the hell is going on." She made it as far as the door before she felt familiar fingers wrap around her arm and press into her flesh.

"Harassing the doctor and the medical team is not going to help your grandmother right now. You need to sit down and wait this out.

Ida-Mae is in the best hands. It seems your cousin True has so many medical connections that only the best of the best is touching your grandmother. Let them do their work. Let them…"

There he went again with that damn mind-control trick he always used to keep her from doing what she wanted to do. She'd thought it had only worked during sex, apparently even when they weren't humping she just couldn't say no to him when he spoke to her like that.

She nodded her head, realizing he was right. Flashing her badge could get her a lot of things. Unfortunately, her grandmother's restored health wasn't one of them.

Just as she was about to return to her seat, the door swished open and a woman in frog-green scrubs stepped inside of the room. "Lieutenant MacKenzie," the doctor said. Hunter was Ida-Mae's son, but they'd all decided years ago that Heart would be her healthcare proxy. Although busy, her work usually didn't take her all over the world like her general uncle's often did.

"Yes," Heart turned toward the doctor and was immediately flanked by Kenneth and her uncle. She could see Marcus standing on the outskirts, with them, but not with them, much like he had always been over the years.

"I know you've been waiting to hear something so I'll get right to the point. Your grandmother suffered a heart attack. She has blockages in two of her cardiac arteries that are decreasing blood flow to the cardiac muscle."

Heart's chest hurt, none of what this woman was saying seemed good.

"What does that mean, and how will you fix it?" she muttered.

"The two arteries in question have become stiff and have plaque buildup in them that have narrowed the available space that blood can flow back to her heart through. Under normal circumstances we would perform a cabg procedure which is short for coronary artery bypass graft. But we have some concerns about performing such a procedure on your grandmother."

"Like?"

"Her age," the doctor answered. "Your grandmother is elderly and because of that, plus her health history, we don't think she would survive the surgery. If she did, she would more than likely succumb to post-op complications."

Heart felt a wall against her back, then realized she hadn't been standing next to a wall. The warm familiar touch was Kenneth's. He'd just sort of appeared to keep her standing under this onslaught.

"What…what are you going to do for her then?" she stammered. "What alternatives do you have if the bypass isn't an option?"

"There's what we call angioplasty, but we can't do that because one of the arteries that's being blocked is the left main artery. It's too risky to hazard further damage to it. I'm afraid our only real options are medicinal therapies such as beta-blockers, calcium blockers, and nitrates. And even those won't cure or fix the problem."

The pain in Heart's chest increased a little more. She placed a hand where the pain was, trying to make it stop.

"Are you saying my grandmother is going to die from this?"

"Yes. She could last an hour, she could last a year. There's no way to tell how long she can survive under these conditions, but ultimately, her heart will fail completely. I'm sorry, there's nothing more I can do."

Kenneth's hand appeared and Heart latched on to it. She was sinking, and she needed an anchor. The doctor's words were turning over slowly in her head. Her grandmother was going to die.

She felt the doctor place a delicate hand on her shoulder, bringing her attention back in focus.

"The nurses have settled your grandmother in. You can go see her for a few minutes.

Please, don't excite her. No more than two of you at a time at the bedside."

Heart turned to her uncle. Hunter stood stoic, the rigid lines of his face and body tight and immovable, except for the slight twitch of his jaw.

"You go ahead and see her first, Uncle Hunter."

Hunter shook his head. "No, Heart. You're the only person she's been asking for since she collapsed at the house."

She nodded, the broken pieces of her soul fragmenting a little more. She walked toward the door and realized that Kenneth wasn't moving behind her. "Please?" was all she could muster, but it was enough for him to understand her request. He took her hand and led her down the hall and into her grandmother's hospital room.

She shivered when he pulled her into the room. She wasn't certain if there really was a chill in the air, or if the frighteningly still image of her grandmother just made everything inside her shiver.

There were plugs and tubes, and probes, their wires tangling as they covered every visible area of her petite and fragile looking frame.

Fragile?

She's not supposed to be fragile.

That was never a word she'd associated with her grandmother. Strong, yes, determined, yes, controlling, absolutely, but never fragile, never weak.

I did this.

The thought reverberated loudly through her head. She closed her eyes to try to quiet the noise. She blinked it away long enough to focus on the chair next to the bedside. She went to it, sat carefully, and extended a slow hand to cover the stilled fingers resting atop the bed sheet.

"Mama?" she waited for a response. Her heart so uncertain if the woman she had loved still resided in the quasi-lifeless husk. "Mama?" she called again. This time there was a shift in her eyes. A small and simple sign of life that Heart was almost overwhelmed to see.

"Heart? That you?" The elderly woman's voice was quiet and small, but its presence somehow filled the entire room.

"Yes, ma'am."

"I didn't think...thought you..."

Heart smoothed calming circles on the small patch of skin that was free of tubes, catheters, and cords. She looked down at where her hand was joined with her grandmother's and realized that this was the first time she had voluntarily sought to touch her grandmother in more years than she could count. Somehow, at this moment, her fear of never feeling the elderly matron's warm skin beneath hers again far outweighed her fear of skin-to-skin contact.

"Sssh, I'm never too anything to come to you when you need me."

"But...I lied..."

Heart nodded her head. Ida-Mae had always demanded straight answers, trying to sugarcoat things now would not help their collective emotional debacle.

"Yeah you did, and you hurt me...more than I can say. But no matter how much I'm hurting right now, I will always love you, I will always need you." "I'm not long left for this world," Ida-Mae whispered.

Heart shook her head, fighting the reality the doctor had already painted for her. Fighting what her grandmother seemed to have accepted already.

"Mama, we are not going to entertain that. We are going to get every specialist we can in here. We will find someone to fix this, to fix you...we..." Her words were caught in her chest. She could see that her grandmother had accepted her fate, even if Heart couldn't.

"Baby, doesn't matter who you bring in here, or what they do to me, God is already calling me home. My time is near. I've lived a good life; I carried and raised two beautiful babies who gave me five more beautiful babies. I had a husband who loved and took care of me and I've experienced joys in this life that no other human being can claim. I've lived a full life. It's time that I left living to you young people."

Her grandmother curved her lips in to a tired smile, her soft, sleepy eyes drooping, slowly succumbing to the heavy burden of keeping her eyes open.

"There are only two things I regret in this life. Not fixing this situation a long time ago between you and your daddy is one of them. I shoulda found a way to help you understand. I was wrong."

"Mama, that's not important right now. The important thing is that you get better."

"The important thing is that you fix things with your daddy. Don't punish him for what I started." When Heart nodded her head in acquiescence, Ida-Mae continued. "I also regret that I'm leaving you here alone, with no one to watch out for you. Your cousins, your uncle, they've all known love; they all know how to lean on each other. You don't. You keep it all bottled up inside you and just shut down. Carrying so much on the inside will tear you up."

"Mama, I'm fine…"

"No you're not, you're lonely, and overworked, and…I just wish I could have kept my promise to your mother that I would make sure you were loved, with a family of your own before I left this world."

Heart saw wet tracks of tears begin to break free of her grandmother's closed eyes.

"Mama?"

"I'm so sorry I failed you, Diamond, so sorry I failed your baby girl." Heart heard the beeping from the cardiac monitor speed up.

"Mama, you've got to calm down. Excitement is not good for you right now." "I shoulda…done better…by you, baby," Ida-Mae choked out.

Heart watched a shadow move to the other side of Ida-Mae's bed. Kenneth leaned down and placed a gentle kiss on a brown wrinkled cheek.

"You don't have anything to worry about, Mrs. Amare. You didn't fail either of them. I'm here, and I'm going to take care of her, just like you've always wanted someone to do."

"You…mean?"

Kenneth nodded his head and flashed a full mouth of white teeth through the brightest smile she'd ever seen him produce.

"Yes, I proposed this morning before we came to church."

Heart's eyes caught Kenneth's across the small frame of her supine-lying grandmother.

What the hell did he just say?

"We were going to tell you at dinner after church, but things got a little out of hand."

Heart opened her mouth to interrupt, to stop this man from lying the way he was, but he locked eyes with her, and signaled her to look up at the cardiac monitor. The beeping sounds that had become maddeningly fast were now slowing down. Her grandmother looked less distressed, and there was a tiny hint of pink tinting her cheeks.

"It was a very spontaneous proposal. I don't think either of us expected it, but I just looked at your granddaughter and knew that there was no one else I wanted by my side.

When she woke up, I asked her, and she smiled and said yes. I didn't even have a ring; I just wanted to let her know what was in my heart. We decided we were going to tell the family and have a formal engagement party later."

Heart was speechless. She knew damn well none of what Kenneth said had actually taken place. She had woken up to him smiling at her which had led to another steamy session of lovemaking, but everything else was fabricated. She knew this entire tale he was weaving was fictitious. *Why does it feel so real then?*

Ida-Mae turned to Heart, smiling, but seeking corroboration. The truth was on the tip of her tongue waiting to jump off. The beeping of the monitor called her attention again.

She looked at it for a second longer and then back to her grandmother's face: oxygen cannula in her nose, hair pulled back in a half hazard bun, lips dry and cracked, and never looking more beautiful in all the days Heart had known her.

Heart smiled, and reached across her grandmother with her free hand and laced her fingers with Kenneth's.

"Surprise, Mama, I'm getting married."

~

Kenneth watched Heart as she spoke briefly with her uncle and her father about IdaMae's condition. He was anxious to get her alone so they could talk privately while equally afraid of what she was going to do to him once they were in fact alone.

Heart walked up to him and motioned toward the elevators. She pressed the call button, waited for the doors to open and stepped on without making a single sound. They walked out of the hospital and toward the parking lot. When they neared his SUV, he clicked his key fob and they each climbed easily into their respective seats.

Once the doors closed, there was a beat of silence before she turned in her seat.

"What the fuck were you thinking?"

He'd known she was going to explode. He'd hoped she would just laugh it off and quietly go along with it. He'd hoped she'd see the overture for what it was, a way for him to comfort her by comforting the person she loved most.

"Baby..."

"Baby my ass, Kenneth! You have no clue what you've just done, what you've made me a part of."

"Heart, all I did was give a dying woman a little emotional comfort on her death bed."

She raised her hand to rub her neck. He reached over and replaced her hand with his and began massaging the tense and strained muscles. He needed to touch her while having this conversation, she always responded better when he had his hands on her. It was an observation he'd come to understand as their relationship had developed, and he wasn't above using that knowledge to get himself out of hot water either.

"Heart, what was so bad about me seeing a way to make your grandmother feel better and executing it?"

She took a breath; he could feel some of the tension bleeding out of her neck. He continued to rub her there, giving her something soothing and pleasurable to focus on, instead of the anger that was just beneath her surface.

"Kenneth, you don't understand. To my grandmother, marriage is something sacred.

It's like Holy Communion and the Bible as far as she's concerned. It's sacrilege to speak of any of those things unless it's from a place of sincerity. My grandmother is also a master manipulator. Although she is deathly ill, don't think she won't use that to her advantage to twist folks into doing exactly what she wants them to do. It has been her dream to marry me off to a man she believes would take care of me the way my granddaddy took care of her."

"What's so wrong if she believes that you have that?"

"You don't get it. You didn't just give her comfort, Kenneth you fed her expectation. She's going to expect us to get married, Kenneth. What's going to happen when that doesn't come to fruition?"

He had to admit, he hadn't thought that far ahead when he allowed those words to slip from his mouth. His only concern had been to make Ida-Mae happy. He knew that if she died before she and Heart had a chance to fix things, Heart would never be able to bury the guilt that she'd been carrying since they learned of Ida-Mae's condition. Now, in the light of day, maybe he had been too hasty.

He sat back and watched the woman next to him, really watched her. She was strong and fearless, risking her life and limb to protect the public. But Ida-Mae was right, she didn't fight for herself the way she did others, she just buried everything, refusing to acknowledge it. She was lonely; he recognized it because he saw it in himself. Yes, he'd had plenty of bed companions before Heart became something more than just his roommate, but he'd never had the kind of connection they had, where someone else's happiness meant more than his own.

"Heart, I'm willing to take this thing as far as necessary, even if that means us actually getting married. Don't you know by now that there isn't anything I wouldn't do to help you?"

She turned her head, the rest of the earlier anger she carried seeping out of the lines of her face.

"I know that you've been an amazing friend to me in these last few months, but I can't ask this of you. I can't allow you to legally tie yourself to me and all of my garbage."

"This is not about what you will allow, but what I am determined to do. Like it or

not, you've got yourself a new fiancé."

She pinched the bridge of her nose and turned to him.

"If we tell this lie, Kenneth, no one can know it isn't real. Not even my cousins. Especially not True. If no one else believes it, neither will my grandmother. I can't bring her anymore harm. Not after this.

Whatever tomorrow holds, I need for her to leave this world with no regrets where I'm concerned."

He nodded his head and pulled her into his arms. It was settled, he'd won the argument, they were engaged now, or at least that's the lie they were going to tell the world. He'd gotten his way, turned her way of thinking around to his. There was only one question that remained rattling around in his head. *What the fuck am I going to do now?*

CHAPTER 18

*K*enneth stood outside of the closed door waiting for someone to answer. He shoved his hands in his pockets fiddling with his set of keys, hoping the clinking sound of metal would somehow distract him from the jittery sparks of nervousness traveling through his system.

He needed to get a grip. Nervousness wasn't his thing. He never questioned his decisions, always entered into every choice and action with a decisive confidence rolling off of him in currents. Yet he stood here feeling like his body and mind were in shock.

He heard the pattern of heavy footsteps coming to the door followed by the tinkling of the locks turning.

"Kenneth?" his old friend John Tenetti stood there with a happy but puzzled look on his face.

"Hey, John, you got a minute?"

John titled his head to the side, giving Kenneth a contemplative stare, and then he stepped aside and waved Kenneth in.

"For you? Anytime. You seem like you've got something serious on your mind.

Follow me to my office, Max and the girls won't bother us in there."

Kenneth nodded and the two men headed for John's office in the back of the house. John motioned for Kenneth to sit on the large black sofa against the far wall. Kenneth sat and loosened the knot of his tie and unbuttoned his shirt collar trying to relieve the claustrophobic sensation he was experiencing at the moment.

John walked to the bar in the corner and held up a clear decanter filled with an amber liquid. "You look like you could use a little liquid courage." Kenneth held up his hand, but John waved him off.

"Don't worry, if you get sloshed I'll make sure you get home."

Relieved of his responsibility to drive after this, Kenneth nodded his head and fell back against the sofa cushions with his eyes closed. He didn't open them again until he felt the cool glass being pressed against his hand. He took the drink from John, and downed all of it in one gulp.

"Damn, that bad, huh?"

Kenneth looked at his friend and nodded. He sat the glass on a nearby table and leaned forward bracing his elbows on his knees.

"What's going on, Kenneth? I don't think I've ever seen you looking like this."

"John, what I'm about to say to you can never leave this room. You can't even tell your sister, 'cause if A.J. knew what was going on in my head right now, she would kill me." John nodded and motioned for Kenneth to continue. "Long story short, I'm engaged."

"What...when?"

Kenneth held up a hand to halt his friend's questions. He needed to get this all out, wasn't certain if he could say it more than once.

"Heart and I have gotten very close since the shooting, intimately close. And I don't just mean physically, emotionally too. Her family laid some big emotional time bomb on her recently that kind of blew up her life. It ended with her having an ugly argument with her grandmother. A few hours afterward, her grandmother had a heart attack."

"Damn," John whispered.

"I know it's not looking good for Ida-Mae. Doctors have basically put the kibosh on any hopes of recovery. They're basically sending her home to die because they can't do anything for her. Heart was...is a mess. We rushed to the hospital when we got the news. The grandmother was lying in that bed, frail and weak. We could see it was a struggle just to breathe let alone speak and yet all she could do was lament about failing Heart, leaving her in the world alone without anyone to take care of her.

"Man, she was going that night. I stood there in that hospital room and I knew that woman was about to die. I also knew that if she died before she and Heart had a chance to fix things, Heart would never forgive herself."

John took in a long breath. "So you jumped in to save the day and told the grandmother you and Heart are getting married and you're panicking because you don't want to be caught in this trap?"

Kenneth shook his head. "I did tell the grandmother we were getting married, but

I'm not afraid because I don't want to marry Heart, I'm shook because I think that maybe

I do want to marry her. I don't think I want this engagement to be fake."

John looked surprised. "Kenneth, you're really feeling this woman this way? I've never heard you talking about marriage with anyone, not even Faith."

Kenneth nodded his head. "I've never thought about marrying anyone else. But

Heart...she...she just does something for me, something I can't even seem to name. I just know that I want to be with her all the time. I want to protect her all the time, give her everything, all the time. It's like an obsession, John; I can't seem to stop myself. What the hell is wrong with me?"

Kenneth looked up meeting his friend's eyes and saw a gleam of mirth looking back at him.

"Kenneth my friend, there's only one thing that's wrong with you, and the truth is, you're not going to be able to do much about it."

"What is it?"

John smiled wide and placed a strong hand on Kenneth's sinking shoulder. "You my friend are in love. Welcome to the club."

⁓

*H*eart checked around the house for the hundredth time attempting to make sure everything was perfect. In just a short while, Kenneth would walk through the door with her grandmother.

If it were up to her, she would have been the one picking up her ailing grandmother, but reinstatement paperwork had to be completed if she was to return without any administrative issues blocking her way. Ask her to stand in front of a bullet, she'd do it all day smiling, ask her to spend all day filling out a few forms, and she'd cower like an infant.

Heart heard a big clanging noise coming from the backyard. She peaked through the blinds of the kitchen window and saw a crew of workman milling about. Kenneth had mentioned that the next-door neighbor, Patty, was having some work done in his own backyard and asked if his workman could set up a second workstation in their yard to help expedite the work. He'd promised the workers would set everything up in a large covered tent and that they would do their best not to disturb her. They'd been relatively quiet this morning and again this afternoon when she returned home.

She released the blinds and walked back into the living room. Everything had to be perfect. After two weeks in the hospital the doctors had finally deemed Ida-Mae stable enough to come home. She wasn't cured, she wasn't healed, she was essentially a ticking time bomb waiting to go off. Ida-Mae had said if she were going to die, she wanted to be at home and not in the hospital, so Heart and Kenneth had made the necessary arrangements to bring the woman home to live out her days in comfort.

This whole ordeal with her grandmother's health was so surreal. Ida-Mae was still sick, but her mental faculties were still as quick and sharp as ever. The only reminder of her ailment came by way of spontaneous bouts of difficulty of breathing and an accompanying grey-ish-blue tinge that colored her lips and fingertips when the oxygen levels in her blood were too low.

The doctor had informed them how difficult things might get with Ida-Mae at home, but Heart didn't care. She would have done just about anything to grant Ida-Mae's wish, but she didn't have to. Kenneth had stepped in and handled all of the arrangements. She'd given him her credit card and told him to charge whatever expenses her grandmother needed to the card, but he said it wouldn't look right if he didn't pay for it. Him being disgustingly rich and her being his *fiancée* somehow meant that he had to take care of her even when she was perfectly capable of taking care of herself.

She had to admit though, even though this was a completely fake engagement, she'd never felt so at ease. Kenneth did that for her, made everything happen so she could just...be.

She seldom had to worry about anything if Kenneth was near. There was not a thing she needed to concern herself with as along as Kenneth was around, except for the fact that this made-up engagement was somehow going to be the destruction of her.

It felt great to let someone take care of her, but this...this lie was going to blow up in their faces. She knew it and she could feel it. It had to disintegrate into nothing, it was a lie, and when everyone found out, Kenneth was going to go his merry way and she would be left looking like a fool.

The day her grandmother had a heart attack, also happened to be the day she made a crippling realization, she loved this man that had moved into her life, and taken over. She loved him, and although he was fond of her, although he'd done some extraordinarily nice things for her since she'd come home to recuperate from a bullet wound to the shoulder, Heart knew two things: Kenneth Searlington wasn't in love with her, and when he left, it was going to destroy her.

How could it not? How could she experience what it felt like to be safe and secure in her life for the first time in nearly two decades, and go back to being who she was before she knew what this was like? She couldn't, so she expected things were going to become very painful for her in the near future.

Thank God for work. Porter had given her a few extra days off to get her grandmother settled into her rented house. Her workaholic tendencies left her with way more vacation time than human resources was comfortable with and so even though she'd just returned to work, Porter was happy to grant her more leave. That thought posed another issue that she knew she had to address. She was renting this home, but hadn't yet attempted to buy it. Now that her grandmother was going to be living with her fulltime, she'd need to make more permanent living arrangements than a month-to-month rental. What if the owner decided to sell this house tomorrow? She'd been through that already, she wasn't about to let that happen again now that her grandmother was in her care.

She was just about to run upstairs and change her clothes when her phone rang. She looked down and saw Kenneth's name flashing across the screen. The usual smile that his presence elicited grew without much effort from her.

"Hey Kenneth, are you on your way?"

"Soon, I'm waiting for the doctor to fill out a few more forms and then Ida-Mae's

discharge will be complete." He paused for a second, "I need you to do me a favor."

"What's that?"

"Go upstairs to the bedroom; I left something there for you to put on. You and I are going to have a very special dinner tonight and I want you to wear something pretty that I picked out for you. It should be hanging in the closet."

She started to laugh a little, her skin beginning to tingle with familiar warmth that only surfaced from his touch, or his words, or thoughts of his touch and words.

"You do know my grandmother is going to be here, don't you? We can't exactly play dress up while she's downstairs recuperating."

"I like where your mind is headed, but I actually wasn't talking about playing *that* kind of game. I will have to take a rain check, because I so plan to take you up on that a little later. We're not going out; we're having dinner at home. Just go upstairs, put my gifts on, and I will see you as soon as I can. I promise you'll understand when I get there."

The line clicked and the call was disconnected. She stopped for a second and contemplated what Kenneth could possibly be up to, but when she came up with nothing she decided her energy could be better used by getting dressed as he had asked.

She ran upstairs; she showered quickly and then walked over to the walk-in closet.

She found a black garment bag hanging on one of the closet's double doors. She pulled opened the flaps of the bag and found the most beautiful chiffon cocktail dress.

She removed the dress from the bag, still resting on its hanger and stood in front of the wall-length mirror. The one-shoulder dress was a brilliant royal blue with occasional flecks of silver beading accenting the goddess-style garment. It was beautiful, elegant, and…short. She laughed when she held the dress in front of her. It would probably fall somewhere just below her mid-thigh. She wasn't a short girl, at five-nine in her bare feet, if she wore heels, she would stand as tall as Kenneth's six feet three inches.

Her smile brightened when she thought of how fixated Kenneth was with her legs. He was always telling her how much he loved when she wrapped them around him.

You probably asked the damn dressmaker to only provide just enough material to keep me from getting arrested.

Her phone chirped and she saw a text from her cousin True. *I'm coming up the stairs now don't shoot me.*

"Then you should learn to ring a doorbell and stop sneaking into people's houses," Heart screamed over her shoulder.

"Whatever chick, you're a cop; your doors shouldn't be so easy to get past." Heart shook her head, if True only knew the veracity of her own words.

You ain't ever lied about that cousin.

Heart turned around just in time to see her cousin walking

through the bedroom door. She watched True raising her arm in preparation for the fist bump they usually gave each other in salutation. It was as far as Heart had been able to go in the physical affection department. For years it was the only way she'd ever felt her cousin's touch. Unless they were sparring, she hadn't known what it felt like to be in her cousin's embrace.

Before her abduction she remembered that True always gave these whole-body hugs. Hugs that were so tight they stopped her breath. Hugs that let you know you were loved without question. How had she gone her entire teenage and adult life without experiencing one of those? Her life might have been so different if she had.

True stopped in front of her, dropping her raised fist and regarded Heart with careful eyes.

"Hey, everything okay?" True asked, still watching Heart with slow assessing eyes. Heart nodded, and blinked back the wetness suddenly threatening to spill.

"Yeah, I'm fine. I was just remembering the last time you hugged me when we were kids. I was just thinking how much I missed being able to experience those hugs of yours."

"You know my hugs are always available for you."

"Yeah…I'm just…one day," was all Heart could get out. As jumbled as her words were, her cousin seemed to understand and she smiled at her.

"So, I get a call from that sexy white boy you smashin' and he tells me I need to get my butt over on this side of the country to help my cousin get ready for this special night he's got planned for her."

Heart rolled her eyes. "Can you get anymore inappropriate? I can't believe people actually pay you to cut them open with half the shit that comes out of your mouth."

True gave a carefree shrug. "One thing has nothing to do with the other. I'm awesome at what I do." True wiggled her eyebrows and turned her attention to the dress on the bed. "That's hot; I'm taking it you didn't pick that out?" Heart shook her head.

"Let's see what other types of goodies Kenneth left you." True opened the garment bag up completely and found two more items: a thin circular shaped velvet blue box and a beige shoebox.

"Get the fuck outta here!" "What?" Heart asked.

"You don't know what these are?"

Heart shook her head as she watched her cousin gingerly pick up the beige shoebox with white writing on its lid. True opened the box and removed two red shoe bags and laid them on the bed. Then she gently pulled a stunning set of closed-toed six-inch platform heels—one in each hand, careful not to let them touch each other as she removed them—that seemed to be adorned with some kind of crystals or jewels on them.

True turned them upside down so that the vibrantly red soles glared at her.

"You really don't know what these are?" True asked again.

Heart lifted her shoulders in question and shook her head. "Should I?"

"You've got to be kidding me. Don't you know anything about fashion?" When Heart shook her head no, True rolled her eyes in apparent frustration. "These are a pair of CL Redbottoms, these shoes cost like six and change on sale."

"You mean to tell me Kenneth spent six hundred dollars on some shoes with pretty crystals on them?"

True shook her head and started laughing. "Nah, boo, Kenneth spent like six grand on some celebrity designer shoes. This particular pair right here, CL only makes for specialty clients. You can't find them in any retailer, they're exclusive."

Heart sat slowly on the bed with her mouth hanging open. She carefully took one of the shoes out of True's hand and turned it slowly from right to left assessing all of the angles and contours.

"These damn shoes really cost six thousand dollars?"

True pulled out her smartphone, opened up an internet browser, and called a photo of the exact pair of shoes they were looking at. The picture was pretty, but it didn't do the real product any justice. True directed her line of sight while she scrolled down to the bottom of the picture and read, "MSRP $6,000."

"What the fuck was he thinking? I can't wear these damn shoes."

"Girl, if you won't wear them, I will. I've been trying to get an appointment with this man for two years to get this exact pair of shoes. I don't have that kind of clout. I even tried to use Drew's R&B celeb status to get in the designer's door. Apparently awardwinning singers don't have that kind of clout either. You have to be like royalty to sit down with this dude."

"Why would he spend so much money on shoes? All I'm going to do is walk on them."

"Yes, and let me tell you, you will be stepping pretty with these mofos on tonight."

Heart stared at the expensive shoes, wondering why Kenneth would spend what for some was the sum total of their monthly income.

"Because he cares about you," True answered.

Heart looked up. Had she asked that question again out loud?

"No, you didn't say it out loud, but it was written all over your face. The man cares, Heart. There's nothing wrong with him showing you how much he cares about you. But damn, if he spends this kind of money on shoes, I can't wait to see what your engagement ring looks like."

True motioned for Heart to stick out her hand in a "show-me" motion.

"I'm not wearing an engagement ring."

"Why not?"

"Um…in case you forgot, your grandmother did have a heart attack not too long ago.

Kenneth hasn't had the chance to get one for me."

Heart's insides trembled just a little. She looked down and started fiddling with her clothes on the bed. If True had the slightest inkling of what she and Kenneth were up to she'd smack fire out of her. No need getting the crazy cousin mad at you if you didn't have to.

"Stop worrying about my engagement ring. If his taste in shoes is any indication, I'm certain whatever Kenneth chooses will be phenomenal. Now, didn't you say Kenneth asked you to help me get ready? We'd better be quick; he should be here any minute."

She walked over to the vanity with her cousin still watching her. She sat down and turned to face True again, this time with a painted smile. "Coming?"

~

*H*eart looked at herself in the mirror and had a hard time recognizing the woman that smiled back at her. True had worked wonders. Heart could do basic makeup, a little gloss, a little mascara. The artistic masterpiece True had been able to create was something out of a fashion magazine. Her lower lids were painted with an electric blue that shocked the senses. The blue bled up into the contour of her eyelid where a darker transition color—a mix between a navy blue with some ginger-brown undertones. On her upper brow, there was a soft, yet glittery translucent tan color that made her eyes look sultry. True topped it off with a pale rose color on her cheeks and just a hint of a whisper pink gloss to her lips.

The makeup accented the entire look, including the high sitting ponytail that rested atop the crown of her head. True found a way to bind the ponytail with a metallic-like string that wove in and out of the bend of the curl of her gathered tresses. She looked like a goddess and she felt...she felt. There wasn't a word that could accurately explain what she was feeling right now.

She turned to the side and her crystal-laden red-bottomed shoes sparkled in the mirror.

I can't even lie, this six grand looks good as hell on my feet.

She was smiling so hard at her reflection she almost missed the arrival of that familiar, electric sensation that filled her from the inside out. Kenneth was near; it was the only time her body reacted that way. She lifted chocolate-brown eyes in the mirror to meet the cool azure gaze watching her from behind.

"You look amazing," he said as he walked across the room, touching her shoulder and neck carefully.

She turned in his embrace and let her eyes take a cautious pass over his appearance. His ebony locks were bound in a polished ponytail that rested at the nape of his neck, the remainder of his mane falling down the center of his back. He wore a royal blue collared dress shirt with white slacks and matching shoes. His necktie was a swirling pattern of white and royal blue. If it were anyone else wearing those colors it would have been comical, prom-worthy, but on him, on the magnificently sculptured lines of his body those clothes looked regal, majestic. The term tailor-made didn't seem quite right. The material of his clothes caressed every sinew of muscle in his broad shoulders down his lean chest to his neatly tapered waist and powerful thighs. Fuck, she was jealous. It just didn't seem fair that some material other than her skin was able to touch him so closely, so intimately.

"I'd say that it's a good thing you dressed both of us tonight, now I at least look like I belong with you." She dropped her lids, needing to shield herself from his intense stare for a moment.

She felt his light touch at the tip of her chin and he slowly bent his head to place a soft peck on her lips.

"You always belong with me," he whispered, the low rumble of his voice making her tremble.

He took her by the hand and walked her over to the bed where he sat down, and then pulled her into his lap. He held the small circular shaped velvet case in his hand and slowly opened it for her.

"I went to the jeweler's with the express purpose of buying you a diamond tennis bracelet today. But when I saw it, I knew it wasn't you."

He pulled her wrist to his mouth and placed a warm gentle kiss on her pulse point.

"So I asked her to show me what other pieces she had for the wrist. I told her whatever it was needed to reflect all the things you were, all the things I treasure about you."

He took another breath and placed another gentle kiss at her pulse.

"I told her I wanted something bold, yet delicate, sassy, yet sophisticated, and above all else, it had to be as breathtaking as you are."

Again, at the end of his sentence, he took a breath and kissed her wrist. The simple interaction was making her burn. Blistering prickles of anticipation and excitement electrified her skin. She wanted to melt into the heat he was stoking in her. She watched him look down at her wrist again followed by a jolt from cool metal meeting scorching skin. She looked at her wrist, it seemed almost foreign for her to be adorned with his offering of a delicate bangle made of a white metal—maybe white gold, maybe silver. At the top of the bangle rested an infinity symbol made of diamonds.

"Kenneth, this is too much," her voice shaky with the emotion he was igniting inside of her.

"This is not enough. I told you, you will always belong with me. This platinum infinity bracelet just proves it." He kissed her wrist again, and motioned for her to stand up. "Now, let's go get this evening started."

"What is all of this about, Kenneth? We can't go anywhere. You just brought my grandmother home from the hospital."

He placed a single finger in front of her lips silencing her.

"Just trust me." He smiled. "As long as you trust that I will always have your best interest in mind, nothing can break us."

She nodded her acquiescence. This whole thing was a matter of trust; it had started out that way from the very beginning. From his very first touch, her body, her soul had known that he wouldn't bring harm to her, that his touch brought soothing and calm.

She followed him down the stairs. He led her to the back of the house, and finally opened the kitchen door that led into the backyard. The last step off of the deck began a long white aisle runner that covered the stone path that led to where the workman's tent was sitting.

The tent looked very different under the mask of night. She could see the soft glow of lights humming under its cover. She turned her head sideways to look at Kenneth.

"I'm not going to find workman in there...am I?"

They'd reached the tent, he shrugged his shoulders and lifted his hand, ushering her inside the tent.

"I guess you're just going to have to step inside and see.

Kenneth lifted one edge of the thick veil material covering the entryway. When she stepped inside there were softly glowing lights illuminating the darkened space. She couldn't place any specific lighting fixtures; the glow just seemed to emanate from the billows of chiffon material that covered the roof and walls of the tent. There were no banquet tables, the room looked more like a modern styled lounge with crisp sleek lines of royal blue piping chasing the perimeter of the tent. The furniture consisted of elegant lounge chairs covered in white, ranging in varying geometrical shapes and sizes: square, rectangular, and circular. They all sat low to the ground and were topped with mountains of white and royal blue decorative pillows.

When she stepped inside, her heel clicked on a solid surface. She looked down to find a shiny royal blue floor. *What the hell has he done?* She walked further inside the tent, finding what appeared to be a white cushioned backdrop for what seemed to be a fashioned dais. On the side, movement caught her eye and she realized they weren't alone. The entire left side of the tent was made into a serving station where several members of the waiting staff stood at attention in white attire with royal blue neckties and aprons. On the opposite wall was the bar with three bartenders in the same white and blue uniform as the rest of the servers. Behind her, she saw the DJ dressed in the same colors as everyone else and everything else in the tent, including them.

"This is beautiful, Kenneth. I'm still a little lost with respect to the occasion though?"

"It will become clear soon. Until then, dance with me."

She looked around the hall, yes the DJ was standing behind his equipment, but the tent was silent.

"Kenneth, there's no music playing."

"You sure about that?"

She looked around again, still a little puzzled by his behavior. But when she returned her gaze to his, his eyes bade her to trust him. Without thought, she stepped into his embrace, pressed herself against his chest, and melted in the feel of his arms wrapping around her. She walked her hands up his strong arms until they rested on the expanse of his shoulders. They stood cheek to cheek as he led them in to a slow sway from side to side.

She closed her eyes as they moved in sync. She didn't need to see where she was going, not as long as Kenneth was holding her. She heard the smooth tones of a man's singing voice fill the air. She recognized the words to the song; it was Javier's "In Your Hands." But there was something different about the song, that voice, it was familiar to her. She opened her eyes and watched as Drew stepped into the tent dressed completely in white with the exception of his microphone, his belt, and his shoes, both the same vibrant blue that was accenting the rest of the tent.

As Drew sang, other people she recognized began to enter the tent from all directions. Her four cousins and her uncle were there, all dressed in the requisite white with royal blue accents. She saw Bryan step inside and her captain, and even their neighbor Patty. Each time they moved around on the dance floor, she recognized more of the people stepping into the tent. Her eyes passed the room again and saw John T., the pop singer walking in with a young black woman whose face Heart couldn't place at the moment. As the song was beginning to wind down, her eyes made one final pass and her heart lurched. Merridith, the tiny girl who had brought this lovely man into her life stepped inside accompanied by her father. As the last note of the song passed, Heart watched Marcus push her grandmother's wheelchair into the tent.

She watched a proud sparkle dance in the broken woman's eyes and it made Heart's eyes water. She didn't know why, but everything about that moment told her that her grandmother was happy to be in this room sharing this moment with them.

She pulled her gaze back to Kenneth's, the designer shoes she was standing in kept them eye to eye.

"Kenneth?"

He kissed her cheek and motioned to someone standing on the side of them. She saw someone pass him a blue microphone. She assumed it was Drew; there couldn't be that many blue microphones in one tent. She stepped back a bit, giving Kenneth room to place the mic in front of his mouth.

"Heart, we didn't meet under the most traditional of circumstances. If I remember correctly, I didn't really behave as well as I could have and well, everyone knows you don't really suffer foolishness." The other attendees began to laugh as she shrugged her shoulders. Kenneth was speaking the truth there was no denying it.

"I learned really quickly that you didn't take crap, but I also learned that you were the type of person that would put her life on the line for a total stranger. I know it to be true, because you did that for me, more importantly, you did it for a little girl that you'd never met before."

Heart took a moment and spared a glance at Merridith. She was so pretty and delicate in her beautiful white dress. She was turning back and forth in a half circular motion the way little girls who are happy and cared for do.

"Heart, last week Merridith called me and said she wanted to do something really special for you, because you are a very nice lady, and nice ladies deserved nice things. Since I completely agreed with her, we thought about it really hard, and came up with something extremely special."

Kenneth looked at Merridith again and motioned with a flick of his wrist for her to meet them in the middle of the dance floor. Once she was there, he picked her up with one arm and gave her the microphone.

"I wanted to give you something really nice," the small voice said. "But the nicest thing I have 'sides Daddy is me and Uncle Kenneth. But Uncle Kenneth says you can't give one people to another people, so we had to come up with something else." The little girl gave the mic back to Kenneth, then dug her tiny fingers into the chest pocket of his shirt. "So since I can't give you Uncle Kenneth, cuz he's a people and you're a people, Uncle Kenneth let me pick this out for you."

The little girl smiled and shoved a small closed fist in Heart's face. Kenneth uncurled the child's small hand and revealed a sparkling ring resting in the child's palm.

Heart peaked through half-closed eyes. The ring so bright it almost hurt to look at it directly. She looked back up at the child and her uncle, twin pairs of crystal blue eyes staring back at her in stereo making her heart clench. *No, he's not doing this now...please.*

"Uncle Kenneth says the one way that's okay for people to belong to each other is if they get married. He says getting married means two peoples come from different families and build one big family. So you wanna marry us so we can be one big family? That way, I can give you me and Daddy and Uncle Kenneth and we can all be a big family and it will be okay for us to belong to each other."

Heart dropped her hands to her chest, then pulled them back up to her mouth. She just couldn't find the right place to put them. They were shaking with so much energy. She finally wrapped them around herself. She was a veteran police officer, a detective, a lieutenant. She instinctively knew how to deal with the unexpected, never had to question what her next move was in a bind. Yet here, surrounded by their very small circle of friends and family, here in front of this man and this precious child, she had no clue what to do.

Kenneth plucked the ring out of Merridith's palm and bent down to let the little girl skip back to her father's side. When he stood, he took one of her hands in his and brought it to her lips for the briefest of kisses. He moved to his knee in one smooth motion and looked up at her.

"I never thought life would find me here, in this moment, in this position. It never occurred to me that I could want someone so much...need them so much."

God her chest hurt so much, watching this man kneel before her. It was fake, her head knew this. *Then why does it feel so real?* Why were her tears flowing, why did she want so much for this to be exactly what it looked like to everyone watching them? Why couldn't he really love her, and really want her for his wife?

She shut her eyes against the image of him there on bended knee.

It was too much for her heart to bear. It was too much for her mind to control and compartmentalize into her it's-not-real-so-it-doesn't-matter category. It mattered, it mattered more than anything else had ever mattered, she wanted this, and it was all just a charade to make a dying woman feel better about leaving her pathetic granddaughter alone in life.

She felt him stroking her left hand, coaxing her out from behind her closed lids. She looked at him and ached for the veracity of the sentiment he was portraying, she wanted so badly for this to be her truth, their truth.

"Heart, I never thought I would want this, but I'm so happy life decided to surprise me with you. Now all I need is for you to help me…help me give us both what we never thought we'd have. Help me by giving me the opportunity to spend the rest of my life taking care of you."

"Kenneth," she whispered. She was so torn between losing herself in the fantasy kneeling before her, and begging him to stop the painful lies.

"Believe in me, Heart. Believe me when I tell you that all of this…" he waived his hand around the room, "…is not for show, it's not for anyone else's benefit other than yours. I want this, more than I have ever wanted anything, or anyone. Please…believe in this…in us. Please…let me spend the rest of my life taking care of you. Heart, will you marry me?"

CHAPTER 19

S he was engaged to Kenneth Searlington.
How the hell had this happened?

Heart sat at her desk getting absolutely nothing done. The only thing she had accomplished was sitting there, staring at the monster-sized engagement ring Kenneth had placed on her finger a few nights before. God was the thing huge, but so beautiful she could hardly look away from it. Its center was a sparkling light blue stone whose head sat on a high mounting secured by five prongs. She had mistakenly referred to it as a blue topaz. The center stone was surrounded by a double halo of pave set clear stones. The shank was composed of a white metal and held several clear round accent stones in a channel-like fashion.

The day after their engagement a well-dressed man with a brief-case knocked on their door. According to Kenneth the man had come to pick up the appraiser's report and finalize the insurance documents for her ring. Once all of the documents were signed, Kenneth was pulled away by a business call and she was left alone with the insurance agent. She'd almost chocked when the man congratulated her on their engagement and told her Kenneth must really love her to spend so much money on a single purchase.

She saw the man to the door and went upstairs to find Kenneth in their bedroom. She closed the door and waited for him to finish his phone call.

"Kenneth, how much did you spend on this ring?"

He gave her a devilish smirk. "It's not really tactful for a woman to ask for the bottom line on her engagement ring, Heart." Heart shook her head.

"Kenneth, I'm not playing. That man just told me that you must really love me to have spent so much money on this ring." She held up her hand and looked down at the flashing stones. "How much money could a ring made of blue topaz and zircons cost?"

"Zircons?" he said with laughter. "You think those stones are zircons?"

"Aren't they?"

He slowly shook his head and took her left hand into his.

"Heart, that center stone is not a blue topaz, it a very rare six-carat heart-shaped blue diamond. The stones that are surrounding the blue diamond in the double halo, as well as the stones in the channel setting are all diamonds and they total about four carats in weight. Altogether, you're walking around with about ten carats of diamonds set in platinum on your finger."

Her breath nearly stopped, Kenneth had to guide her to the bed to sit down before she fell.

"How much, Kenneth?"

"Heart, you really shouldn't worry about the cost."

"How much, Kenneth?"

"It's nothing that should really concern you."

'Kenneth!"

He stilled when she called his name and he looked her in the eye.

"The seller wanted six; I was able to talk him down to four-point-five."

"Hundred-thousand?"

He shook his head. "Million."

She looked at the ring, looked back at him and then the ring again. Her head was throbbing with so many questions. "Kenneth, why on

Earth would you spend four and a half million dollars on an engagement ring for a woman you aren't really engaged to?

Did you forget we're just doing this for my grandmother's benefit?"

His voice was quiet, but full of strength and sincerity. "What if I want it to be real?" he asked her. "What if I bought you a real ring, because I wanted it to be a real offering for your hand in marriage?"

"Kenneth—"

He threw up a hand to silence her. "Heart, I know this engagement started out as a way to appease your grandmother, but the truth is, everything I said to you when I was on my knee, I meant. I want us. I want us now, tomorrow, for as long as you'll have me. This thing between us has grown in to something I never imagined it would. It's vital to me, I need it, and I need you."

"Kenneth—"

He held up his hand again, quieting her objections. "I know you feel this thing too, Heart. I know that this relationship means as much to you as it does me."

'It does, but I don't want you to get trapped into a marriage with me because you're trying to do something nice for a dying woman or because you feel obligated to me because of the shooting."

He pulled her into his arms and held her until the stiffness in her body waned away.

"I might have told your grandmother we were getting married to appease her, but I proposed to you because I wanted you to marry me. I meant it when I told you that entire production wasn't for show, it was for you. As for feeling obligated toward you, my wanting to be with you has nothing to do with the shooting. I wanted you from the first time we met, getting to know you just made that need even stronger. Heart, spending these last few months with you...that just made it crystal clear to me that I don't want any other woman in my life except you."

He set himself away from her and kneeled down on the floor in front of her. He took her left hand in his and kissed the top of her engagement ring softly. He looked up to find smooth yet unsure chocolate eyes watching him, questioning him.

"Heart, I obviously wasn't clear enough when I dropped to one knee in front of our family and friends, so let me be clear now. You and I are not temporary in my eyes. We are permanent, and you are a permanent fixture in my world. I want to share everything life has to offer with you right there next me. So, for the second time, and hopefully for the last, I'm going to ask you if you'll agree to be my wife. Marry me, Heart? For real.

Be my wife, and let me be your husband in the truest, sincerest, meaning of those terms."

And here she sat, in her office, really engaged to a man she secretly loved. She was getting married. She sat there, trying to call up the usual anxiety she had about her personal life, and she just…couldn't. She felt good, she felt strong, she felt happy.

Kenneth had done that for her. Kenneth had made this their truth.

"You still can't stop looking at it, can you?" Heart blinked at the sound of the familiar voice.

"Cap, I promise I'm going to get my head outta my ass, I just…I can't believe it's real."

"The ring, or you and Kenneth?" he asked her as he sat in front of her desk.

"Both. I didn't expect any of this. It hasn't even been half a year yet and we're together and getting married." She looked at her boss, a little uncertain if she should follow her current train of thought. "Cap, you okay with all of this?"

"Mac, I did everything I could to get my godson to stay away from you. With the exception of your cousin's friend Faith he hasn't had very many relationships. He's usually been a one and done kind of man. He saw the kind of marriage that his parents had and he wanted no parts of that. But from the day he met you, he's always wanted more, even when I threatened him with bodily harm. He didn't care though, he went for what he wanted and dared anyone to get in his way. I can't get mad at a man for that,

MacKenzie. As long as you two are happy, and treating each other right, I couldn't be more thrilled for both of you."

He leaned forward a bit which was always his tell for when something was not necessarily right. She leaned forward, mimicking his motion.

"What's wrong, Cap?"

"Not wrong, I'm just concerned. You know I'm pushing for you to take the captain's exam so you can take over my command when I retire soon."

She nodded her head. He'd been hounding her almost since the day she got her results for the lieutenant's exam. Up until now she had consistently said no. One of the reasons was she lived for being in the streets. There was never anything for her to come home to, so she focused all of her energy into being as hands on as she possibly could.

The higher up in rank she went, the less she would be allowed to do that. That fact had never sat well with her, but now, the weight of her marriage finger beckoned her to give Porter's request a little more consideration.

"I gotta tell you, Mac, this is probably not the best choice you could have made before you became captain. It could be a PR nightmare."

"I know I'm marrying the son of a woman convicted of trying to kill me. Brass is going to flip. How should I handle it?"

"Quietly, very quietly. I don't know what kind of wedding plans you and Kenneth have in mind, but quiet would be better. I also suggest you take that exam as soon as possible. There's one coming up in a couple weeks. Make sure you're signed up for it, make sure you demolish it. As soon as we get your test scores back, I'm turning in my retirement papers."

"Cap..." Porter had guided her career from her very first day in the academy

If his plan worked—as they usually did—she would be the youngest captain in NYPD history. That was a lot to take on. "I'm not ready. I thought we were talking a couple of years or maybe even five. Not now...I'm not ready to do your job."

He nodded casually. "Yeah you are, you've been ready for a while now. These cops in this house, they respect you, they would follow you anywhere you asked. That doesn't mean that they won't fight you every step of the way, but they will take the path you carve out for them."

He was right, her cops were loyal, even the ones that couldn't stand her. All of them would follow her lead, all except one apparently.

"Cap, speaking of my cops, I'm having a hard time finding out about our current undisclosed problem."

"That's gonna be the thing that will smooth over your marriage to a former principal in your case. You find that son of bitch who is doing dirty shit in your house and you crucify him. Brass won't be able to kiss your ass fast enough. Make it happen,

MacKenzie."

She leaned back in her chair and crossed her arms against her chest. "I'm working on it, Cap. I spent most of yesterday and today looking through the surveillance footage from the evidence locker. I can account for everyone that went in and out of there, except for one person."

"Who is it?"

She shook her, shoulders raised up in answer. "I don't know. I can't make him. The bastard has his lid on and he's pulling the brim over his face. The only thing I can tell you is that he's white and young, but he managed to take advantage of the camera angles. Kept his face turned and covered the entire time. The only thing I could get a clear view of was a partial of the tattoo on his wrist. We're running it now to see if we can make any connections."

Porter stood and nodded. "That's my girl, track this bastard down. Got any idea what the tattoo is yet?"

She shook her head. "The image gets distorted when we try to blow it up. Lab techs are working on it now to clean it up. It's looking like it could be some sort of dog, but so far, there's nothing in the database that matches it."

"You'll get him." He nodded. "That bastard has no idea that all you need is a tiny whiff of his scent to track his ass down. He just gave you your first sniff."

She smiled at her captain, always in her corner, always believing in her ability to get shit done. "He surely did, Cap, surely did."

~

*H*eart rubbed the tips of her thumb, forefinger, and middle finger together. It was a nervous habit she had, and right now she was nervous as hell sitting in the passenger seat of Kenneth's big ass SUV.

"Kenneth, do we really have to do this?" "Yes," he answered.

"But you know I'm not one for parties."

"I don't know why, I've seen you dance, I know you know how to shake your groove thang."

She rolled her eyes and gave him a sideways glance. "Kenneth, your outer white boy is showing."

He reached over the center console and surrounded her hand with his. "Why are you so worried about having a little get-together at Drew and Genesis' place?"

"Who's going to be there?"

He blew out a breath and shook his head. His hair was pulled into a ponytail and then woven into on long thick braid, so the only thing that moved with the motion was the long braid draped over his shoulder. She hated that his hair was bound, had begged him to set it free several times, but he'd told her he didn't really like wearing it out on occasions like this when he knew he'd be moving a lot.

"Genesis and Drew of course, and your cousin, True. I think True said the rest of her siblings are coming too. Genesis' brothers will be there, and John, Maxine, and AlexisJeovonni too. Bryan just texted me before we left the house that he and Ramirez are heading over too.

She kept knowing eyes on him, watching him as he watched the road. "And who else, Kenneth?"

He kept his eyes fixed on the road, never glancing once in the direction of her voice.

Nobody is that focused of a driver. "Who else, Kenneth?"

"I'm not sure; I would guess that Genesis and Drew probably invited some of their other friends over as well."

"So Genesis and Drew, two people I share at best second or third degrees or separation, just decided to throw us a party celebrating our engagement?" She crossed her arms over her chest and fixed her line of sight in his direction. "I call bullshit, how the hell did this party really come about?"

She watched Kenneth twist the end of his braid around his finger. It was something he did when he called himself "protecting" her for her own good.

"I was on the phone with Drew last week," Kenneth began. "He suggested that we should get together to celebrate our engagement."

She rolled her eyes again. "Kenneth, Drew and Genesis were both at our engagement party. Why would they need to throw us a second one?"

"That party was respectable, for the 'rents and the superiors. This one, this one is for us and our peers."

She raised her brow questioning the veracity of his statement. "Kenneth, Drew and I have never been all that close."

"Maybe not, but he does have a great deal of respect for you. Not to mention, he and your cousin are really good friends from what I understand. Maybe that influenced his decision as well. Or maybe he just needed an excuse to get some common acquaintances in the same room. Hell, I don't know. The only thing I do know is he has a sweet ass mansion with all the trimmings and I'm about to go enjoy myself. I've got the baddest chick in the game on my arm, and my boy is picking up the booze tab. Life just doesn't get any better than this."

She started laughing. Couldn't help herself really. By day, the man that was seated next to her was a button-down businessman who navigated through high society like he was born to it, probably because he *was* actually born to it. But at home, or anywhere out of the office for that matter, he turned into the ambassador for urban culture. Hell she was still mad that he'd won that dancing bet at the community center. She'd never seen a white boy with so much rhythm, okay, maybe with the exception of Channing Tatum, or those dudes that played the villains in You've Got Served, she'd probably have to add K- Fed and Vanilla Ice to that list of white boys who can move on the dance floor too.

"Baddest chick in the game, huh?" she laughed again. "Sounds to me like someone has been listening to too much Jay Z."

He shrugged his shoulders. "I don't know what you're talking about, there's no such things as too much Jay-Z. That still doesn't mean it isn't true though."

"You think you're so slick trying to distract me with compliments. You still haven't answered my question. Who else is coming to this party? Wait a minute, since you've been breaking your neck not to say her name let me guess, Faith?"

He shook his head. "I really don't understand why the two of you don't get along,

Heart."

She rolled her eyes. Just the thought of that woman pissed her off. "Kenneth, Faith and I didn't care for each other as children because our personalities have never mixed.

But there's only one reason we don't like each other now, and that's you."

Kenneth slowed the car and pulled into a parking space on the street. He put the car in park and turned to her. "What do I have to do with this unspoken war between you and Faith?"

"Kenneth, that woman still wants you."

"No she doesn't, Heart. Faith and I broke up ages ago."

Men are so fucking blind. "I don't care when you broke up. She still wants you and she's pissed that I'm standing in her way."

"Heart, listen..."

She raised her hand to silence him. "Kenneth, look. That woman had a claim on you once, and she wants to reclaim you. Now up until you placed this ring on my finger, I never assumed that just because we'd had some amazing sex that I had any rights to you." She jiggled her ring finger with the hefty diamond engagement ring on it. "But since you placed this bad-boy on my finger and asked for a real engagement, know that I don't share. As long as I wear it, I'm yours, and you're mine. Now if Faith is more your speed then I'll gladly step back. The only thing I ask is if this ever isn't something you want, that you let me know. I just don't want to stand in the way of something that you want."

He turned toward her, facing her. She watched the muscles of his face draw tight and the line of his mouth pull straight. He looked...*angry. But why?*

"Heart, I'm a grown man, and a grown man always knows what he wants. The only *thing* I want, the only *one* I want, is *you*. Now if that's too much for you to handle, then let *me* know. Otherwise, don't presume to tell me what I want."

He turned back to the road, put the SUV in drive and continued up the next few blocks until they were turning into the gates of Drew's home. She felt like a scolded child, only she wasn't quite certain what she'd done wrong. Kenneth stepped out of the vehicle and walked to the other side of the car where the valet held her door open. Kenneth held out his hand waiting for hers. When she was out of the car, he pulled her to him, locked a hand in her hair, and tugged with just enough force to keep her head where he wanted it. He slammed his mouth against hers moving with determined strokes of his tongue, demanding entry. He continued to press until she relented and just let him own her mouth the way he wanted.

And boy did he own it. He licked, nipped, sucked, and then outright bit her lips. He was so rough, so hungry, so in control. Her body was beginning to tingle. She liked this.

When did aggressive caveman antics become my kink?

It didn't really matter when it happened, only that it actually had. At this moment she could feel the buds of her nipples tightening under the fabric of her bra and she was certain she was going to have to head straight for the bathroom in search of some wet naps to clean up the growing puddle that was forming in her panties.

Her brain was beginning to get foggy; it was either from the sizzle of pleasure racing through her veins, or the lack of oxygen from this powerful kiss. Didn't really matter, she had no intention of stepping away from the electric current that was passing through his lips right on through every cell, nerve, vessel, tissue, bone, and organ she possessed.

When he finally ripped his mouth away from hers he looked down into her hooded eyes and said, "The only one I want."

She licked her swollen, tender lips and did the only thing her brain would give her leave to do at that moment: nod in agreement. When they entered the house, they were instantly enveloped by loud music and dimmed-dark lighting. Heart looked around the room taking note of its occupants and layout. This was her usual tendency—being a cop and doing cop-like things didn't end just because she was off duty or surrounded by friends.

She expected a multitude of hangers-on that should be present at an industry party. What she got was a small intimate number of people that she knew personally. All persons that Kenneth had mentioned were present and accounted for. Everyone that is, except Kenneth's ex.

Maybe that bitch decided to keep her ass on the left coast?

The sofas were all lined against the wall, and the center of the room had a dance floor on top of it. Genesis, Drew, True, Ramirez, and Bryan were on the floor dancing to some familiar circa 1990s R&B classic, while the rest of her cousins sat down on one of the sofas with longnecks in their hands, nodding their heads simultaneously to the beat.

She and Kenneth made their way through the room talking to everyone, accepting their offered congrats. This was something new for her. Experiencing this kind of satisfaction outside of her job was a completely original and unfamiliar occurrence. These people that were gathered here, they were genuinely pleased that she and Kenneth had found happiness together.

Together.

They were really together, an authentic couple, engaged and making plans to marry. The thought still managed to make her feel a little dizzy in the head. She instinctively reached out for Kenneth's hand and felt no doubt that he would clasp onto hers. He always caught her.

She turned around to meet his smile with a matching one. She leaned in to whisper something to Kenneth when she saw Drew approaching them.

"How are the guests of honor? You guys enjoying the party?" Drew asked smiling back and forth between the two of them.

"It's a great party, Drew. Thanks for doing this. I just wish you hadn't gone through all of this trouble for Kenneth and me."

She watched the corners of Drew's mouth rise in to a wide grin. He slapped Kenneth's back and gave a hearty tug to his shoulder.

"Are you kidding me? You just made my man here the happiest I've ever seen him. It's my pleasure to do this for you guys."

The beat of the music changed and the intro to Chub Rock's "Treat 'Em Right" began blasting through the speakers. Heart felt her body beginning to sway back and forth involuntarily to the music. This song was a favorite that she and True used to dance to all the time when they were kids. She scanned the room, meeting True's eyes across the dance floor. True smiled and winked at her like she did when they were girls and a spontaneous smile beamed on Heart's face.

"Hey guys, keep each other company. My cousin owes me a dance." She briefly saw Kenneth nod his head and she was headed to the dance floor. As soon as her heels touched that hard floor her body moved on its own. The beat made her feel alive and moving in a call and answer motion with her cousin had felt fun, and silly, and alive, and...normal.

All of this, hanging out with friends, experiencing happiness, sharing a connection with Kenneth, it all felt normal. It was something she'd never thought she'd feel in her life, something she didn't really think was a possibility in the reality of her world. But here, on this floor, dancing with her cousin, stealing glances at the man she loved standing in the corner of the room, she felt normal. And there was nothing more exciting than that.

~

"*T*hat girl got your nose wide open," Drew laughed loudly in Kenneth's ear in order to be heard over the music.

Kenneth grinned; he could feel that stupid pink blush crawling up his neck and face.

Truth was he didn't even care. He couldn't deny how amazing it felt to be with Heart, really be with her, without fear that she was going to run from him. He'd always carried that fear when it came to her. She was always on the defense. Always waiting to protect herself from something, including him. All of that had changed since she accepted his proposal. Well, since she'd accepted the second proposal anyway.

She was his, in every way, and nothing was going to change that. In a couple of weeks they would be married. They'd decided that neither of them wanted to wait to plan a huge wedding. Heart being as private as she was, even if they didn't have Ida-Mae's declining prognosis hanging over them, he was certain his fiancée's tolerance for picking out china patterns would only serve to frustrate the woman if they planned something long, big, and drawn out. Nope, short and sweet was the way to go, and he couldn't wait.

"Yeah, no denying how I feel about her," his face was still pulled into that permasmile that seemed to take over whenever he thought of Heart.

"Everything okay with the planning?" Drew asked. "You've got what?...Two weeks?"

Kenneth nodded. "Yeah, all the plans are taken care of. Just need to get you guys measured for your tuxes and we're good. Glad it's about done too, the wedding planner was driving Heart crazy."

"About what?" Drew asked.

"Heart likes the color blue. It's significant to her because of the cop thing. She wanted True's dress and all of the arrangements to be designed with some sort of royal or navy blue theme. The wedding planner told her that was drab and no one did blue anymore for their wedding. Instead she was going to design the perfect lilac wedding for the two of us."

"I assume that didn't go well?" Drew laughed.

"Well, only if you consider Heart telling the woman that she bleeds blue and if the wedding scheme wasn't dipped in Heart's blood, it would be dipped in the wedding planner's blood—literally, a good thing."

Drew held his stomach as his shoulders shook with laughter. "Damn, your woman is no joke. You sure you're all right with marrying a woman that can back up a threat like that?"

Kenneth bit his bottom lip and laughed. "I think that's what draws me to her. Danger is seductive."

Kenneth's eyes scanned the dance floor until they found Heart. She was still on the floor dancing with her cousin. The music had changed; he recognized the tones of

Jaheim's "Ain't Leavin' Without You."

Kenneth's eyes were fixed on Heart's movements. Her body kept in perfect time with the sultry bass line filling the room. The movement of those strong hips, thighs, and legs that pulled at the memory of what it felt like to have them wrapped around him called to something inside of him.

He heard Drew calling his name. It sounded distant, like Drew was far away from him.

Did Drew go somewhere? I could have sworn he was right here? Where did he go?

Why can't I remember?

His eyes fell on to the roundness of her ass and suddenly, without any signals from him he felt himself moving toward the dance floor.

"Kenneth, you didn't hear a thing I said, did you?"

Drew's intrusion pulled him away from the vision of his woman on the floor moving as if she was made for sin.

"Sorry man," Kenneth countered absently. "I gotta go."

He didn't even look back to see Drew's reaction. He could hear his laughter traveling behind him as Kenneth walked closer to the dance floor. He couldn't care less if the entire room was laughing at him in that moment. He needed to touch Heart or explode from watching her move this way and that.

She turned and saw him walking toward her and she put her hands out in a welcome motion. Kenneth took them as he fell in step in front of her. He twirled her around until her back met his front and they were pressed together creating blessed friction on just the right parts of his body.

He leaned down and whispered in her ear, "I swear, if we do this much longer I'm going to lose my shit, right here in front of all of our friends, and it's going to be all your fault."

She leaned back against him, pressing her body even closer to his. "Well, we can't have that. What would you suggest we do about your little situation that's developing?" He pressed a kiss to her neck, and let his teeth lightly graze the skin. "I suggest we find one of Drew's many vacant rooms and deliver the agreed upon terms of our bet at Mac's Place."

She smiled and turned to him. "We've got an audience right now, my cousins are watching us. If we disappear right now, they'll know what we're sneaking off to do and knowing the Amare kids, they'll find some way to ruin it for us. Give me a few more dances, and then we'll go find that room so I can give you everything I promised and more."

She raised her eyebrow, seeking confirmation of his agreement to her terms. He gave a single nod and returned to her neck to kiss her again. This woman was going to be the death of him—a very slow, sexy, orgasmic death that he would be delighted to suffer at her hands.

~

True sat at the very end of the couch and took the single remaining free seat next to her three seated siblings. She turned her head to the right to look at them. She smiled; they were all sitting in their order of birth. Law was at the other end, Free next to him, and Justice in between Free and True. The four Amare siblings had always been close, seeking out each other wherever they ended up in the world. Their father, Hunter had taught them early that family was all you could depend on in life. They took that lesson and held it close to their hearts. It was hard to enter into their circle, but if you were granted entrance, then you were as good as family.

Four similar sets of eyes with just enough minute variation to differentiate one set from the other three were all focused on the spectacle of their cousin Heart and the man she was practically humping on the dance floor.

"So, do we know this dude well enough to let this shit go down?"

True didn't have to look three bodies over to know that voice came from her oldest brother, Law.

"Yeah, Kenneth's cool, I've known him for a long time."

"He better be. On your word, True, that motherfucker better be the best there is in the world the way he's painted all over Cousin," Free chimed in.

"I don't think I've ever seen Cousin like this," Justice added. "She's so loose and..."

"Happy?" True offered. "Is that the word you're looking for, Jussy?" Justice nodded while still watching the engaged couple on the dance floor.

"Justice, you of all people know what can happen, how a person can change when they find the right kind of love," True said.

She watched Justice's eye travel across the room and cast a longing glace on Bryan Smyth. Those two always found each other in a room. It didn't matter how many or little folks were gathered together. If Justice and Bryan were both there, they would somehow always find each other amongst others. It also didn't matter that they'd been broken up for over a year. The heart wanted what it wanted, and those two hearts belonged together. Anyone watching could see it.

True watched as Justice beat down the thick emotion that passed between the two of them and refocused on the safer topic of Kenneth and Heart.

"Yeah, I know what happens when you find the *one*. Those two definitely look like they are heavily connected. Just look at the two of them together. It's as if their movements are in sync. Like they chore-ographed and practiced that shit before the left home."

True gave Justice a sideways glance and rolled her eyes.

"True, you know I'm telling the truth, they look like they're in one of those dance flicks like, "Step Up.""

True shook her head, she knew this shit was about to turn in to a giggle fest between her older, yet less mature sibs.

"I know, right?" Free responded. "That motherfucker moves like the white boy in the movie, Tatum Channing."

True rolled her eyes again. "Free, I believe that man's name is Channing Tatum."

"Whatever," Free answered with a tilt of his head. "Right now Channing is over there plastered all over Cousin. My question is should we do anything about that? Cousin has been through a lot. Is Channing over there going to help her or hinder her?"

True turned her eyes and looked at her siblings. The one thing that was constant for all of them was the love they held for their cousin, Heart. Law, Free, and Justice were pains in the ass, but they loved the hell out of Heart.

"Kenneth is a good man, Free. He used to date Faith. The relation-ship kind of ran its course and they both moved on. He's been really good to Heart. He's been really good for her. That looseness Jussy was talking about, that's all due to him. She's still dealing with a lot from the past, but at least she's able to grab a small piece of happiness for herself."

The other three Amare siblings nodded their heads, but Law was the only one to speak.

"He's good, as long as she's good," he said. "The minute that shit changes, is the minute Channing has a problem."

True shook her head again. "That man's name is Kenneth."

Law, Free, and Justice all uttered one word simultaneously, "Whatever."

*H*eart placed a soft kiss on Kenneth's cheek and asked, "Are you ready?"

"If I were any more ready I'd embarrass myself in front of all these people."

Heart smiled with the most amazing mix of innocence and seduction blended together. He needed to get her into a room where they could be alone and he could watch her wrap those beautifully full lips around his cock.

Heart said nothing, simply nodded and began walking to one of the doorways that exited out of the room. He followed her and they found themselves inside of one of the many guest rooms on the second floor of the house.

As soon as the door clicked Kenneth felt himself pushed back against the door. Heart draped herself over his front and laid assault to his lips. She mashed herself against him, taking from his mouth. There was no request for permission, there was no hesitation, it was hers, all of it, and she knew it, and that sexy little piece of knowledge had him ready to spill in his pants.

She moved to his neck, biting the sensitive skin there. When she nicked just the right spot he grabbed two handfuls of her ass and pulled her closer to him, providing the friction he needed against his aching cock. She continued to kiss and bite his neck while her deft hands worked quickly to unfasten his belt and pants. Before he knew it, a soft warm fist was surrounding his meat and his dick instantly twitched in its hold.

"Mmm, fuck!" he said.

She looked up into his eyes with smiling mischief dancing all over her face.

"No, no. The terms of the bet were for a blowjob, wherever, whenever you wanted as long as it wasn't in public. No fucking, just a blow job, that's all you're getting."

Before he could respond she was on her knees pulling his pants down just below his ass and balls and used her hands to widen his stance. She gave one long pull to his hard flesh and proceeded to rub the cap of his sensitive head across and around the lips of her opened mouth spreading a clear stream of his pre-cum.

"Shit!" The sight of his cock pressed against her lips—lips that were now glistening with his juices—that shit was threatening to send him over the edge. Thankfully she chose that moment to take mercy on him and she let his painfully stretched skin glide inside the welcoming warmth of her mouth.

She pulled off allowing her tongue to cup the underside of his dick like a gentle hand caressing him. She added her hand to the base of his dick twisting it up and down matching the rhythm to her scorching mouth.

Her stretched lips spread over the width of his girth were the sexiest thing he'd ever seen. He would never get tired of watching this image unfold before his eyes. He loved watching her do this. It was always a tossup for him. He could never determine what the more rewarding activity was, watching the sensuous picture of utter debauchery she became when she took him into her mouth, or experiencing the absolute torturous skill of her lips, mouth, and throat.

He dragged his thumbs around the path of her lips and gently hooked his thumbs into the corners.

"Come on baby, open up for me." She did as he asked without a second's hesitation and he pressed all the way inside her mouth until her lips were touching the base of his cock and he could feel his agonizingly taut head tickling the back of her throat.

He wove his fingers through her loosely falling curls, taking a secure grip.

"Are you ready for me?"

"Yes," the one syllable hissing from her lips as he tightened his fingers in her hair. This had become their ritual, she had learned what he needed from her, and she gave it willingly. She wasn't concerned about what she looked like when she was pleasuring him, she cared that he was satisfied, and knowing that heightened the pleasure he experienced with her to sensual summits he'd never reached before.

He took himself in hand and rubbed his purple head against her lips. He watched her eyes close and her mouth open wide, her long tongue hanging in open invitation. Damn if the wanton image before him wasn't enough for him to bust a nut.

Her hands grasped onto his hips and urged him forward. He sank forward adding a matching pressure to the two hands now entwined in her hair. He pulled her forward and snapped his hips in a matching motion. He wasn't gentle; he never was, not when it came to loving her. She'd never wanted him to, she always demanded everything he had, and he took the sincerest pleasure in being able to give her that.

The fiery friction her mouth was creating was making his balls ache. They were pulled tight close to his skin; it wouldn't be much longer before he exploded.

"Fuck, baby. I'm so close."

She grabbed his ass, and pulled him forward into her mouth, she knew what he needed. He slammed into the heated cavern of her mouth, balls slapping against her chin sending an almost painful zing of sexual electricity through his scrotum, up his testicles, to his shaft. He just needed one more thing and he could reach the height of his pleasure. He felt her tongue curve the long vein on the underside of his shaft. She swirled her tongue around his girth, how she ever managed to do that with a mouthful of long, hard dick, he would never know. When his tip was finally sitting inside the very top of her throat he felt the walls of her throat contract. That shit right there… that was what he'd needed. There was no holding back after that.

"Shit, I'm coming."

He went to pull out of her mouth but she held him in place and swallowed around him again. Shit, he wouldn't have been able to move after that if he'd wanted to. He fell back against the door as the first jet of his orgasm exploded out of him. With each contraction of his testicles she swallowed the thick cream erupting from him. It was copious, too much for her beautiful mouth to hold, and coming too quickly for her to continue to swallow. It began to spill out of the sides of her mouth and drip down her chin. Her mouth was a sexy, fucked-out mess and he had never seen anything more beautiful in his life.

He took his spent cock out of her mouth and rubbed it into the milky residue on her face. He was marking her, she was his, and if he wanted to paint her lips with his cum, then he would, because before the night was out, he was certain he wasn't coming up for air until he wore a face full of her juices slathered all over him.

He helped her off of her knees and kissed her, tasting his own flavor mixed in with hers. Nothing tasted better. He led her to the bench at the foot of the bed and motioned for her to take a seat. He went into the bathroom, washed his hands and face, looking in the mirror trying to affix some semblance of respectability on his features.

He took a clean washcloth from one of the shelves in the bathroom, wet it will warm water and returned to Heart in the bedroom. He gently wiped the traces of his pleasure from her lips and face. The only thing left to witness to their hurried coupling was her red, slightly swollen lips.

"I'm afraid your makeup is gone."

She moved his lingering hand away from her face.

"No you're not. You enjoyed every moment of messing it up."

He laughed. "Yeah, I did. Can't even lie about that."

"Well you've had your fun. Go on back to the party first so my nosy ass cousins won't suspect what we've been doing. I need to go fix my face before I walk out into our audience."

Kenneth leaned down again and joined their lips in a heated kiss. "You can if you must, just know I plan on messing it up every chance I get."

∾

It had taken Heart an additional fifteen minutes inside of that bathroom to reapply her makeup. She pulled the wide toothed comb through the haphazard disarray of wavy strands on her head and finally, twenty minutes later, she looked as she did when she'd walked into this room. The folks downstairs could assume what they'd been doing, but none of them needed to look at her and know for certain. Now if she could only get this stupid grin that screamed satisfaction off her face, she might actually pull off the subtle look she was going for off.

She left the room and headed toward the stairs. She needn't have worried about her smile giving her away, as soon as reached the top of the stairs the smile dripped from her face one angry muscle at a time.

"Faith...Heart and I are together—" Kenneth was backed into the wall with his hands up, palms in the air. Faith was pressed against him, far beyond that imaginary line that marked acceptable contact.

Faith leaned in closer—if that was even possible— and locked her lips onto

Kenneth's.

This bitch obviously wants to die.

Kenneth pulled his lips from Faith's the angles of his face pulling in to angry lines.

"Faith...what the hell?" He pushed past her.

"What the hell indeed?" Heart said from the top of the stairs. She felt both sets of eyes fall on her as she walked slowly down the stairs.

"Heart..." Kenneth said eyes wide with apprehension.

Faith on the other hand stood there looking at heart with a shit-eating grin.

"Shut up, Kenneth," Heart stepped off the last stair. She put her hand on Kenneth's chest and pushed until he stepped behind her, effectively placing herself between Kenneth and Faith.

"Heart, I'm sorry you had to walk in on that," Faith said while her lips were still curved into a satisfying smile.

"Bullshit, you're not sorry. If I had to take a guess, I'd say you planned it like that."

Heart saw Faith's eyebrow rise in response and knew instantly that she'd hit the mark. Faith had planned this little seduction. "So you did plan this. What? Were you listening to us upstairs too? Is that how you get your kicks these days, Faith? Does listening to your ex screw his current do it for you?"

"From what I did hear, I don't think there was much to brag about. I can remember him making far better...louder sounds when he was with me."

Faith turned her back and walked back into the room where the party was taking place. Still smiling at Heart as if she'd won some sort of prize.

"Nah, bitch, this ain't hardly over."

Heart followed behind her and heard Kenneth's footsteps quickly followed suit.

Heart grabbed Faith's arm, turning Faith around to face her.

"Let me explain something to you. Whatever you and Kenneth had is over. It is done. Don't let me catch you in his face again, touching him again. I promise if you do you won't like my reaction."

Faith looked around them, realizing they now had an audience to their little melodrama and that seemed to make her voice get louder.

"Are you threatening me, Lieutenant?"

"I don't have to threaten you, Faith, I'm explaining fact. Keep your fucking mitts of my man or deal with the very ugly consequences."

Heart saw Genesis walk up to them and place a hand on Faith's shoulder.

"Faith, maybe it's time for you to leave. I'll come with you," Genesis said. Faith was apparently enjoying the performance she was in the middle of because she pulled her shoulder away from Genesis and returned her focus to Heart.

"I'm not going anywhere, Genesis. This bitch thinks that she can just come in and take what was mine. She thinks I'm supposed to be scared of her because her family and her cop friends are here."

"You shouldn't be afraid of me for any of those reasons, Faith; you should fear me because I will break you," Heart spit out.

"You talk big shit because you got a gun and a badge on your hip, Lieutenant. I bet you wouldn't be so flip at the lip if that wasn't the case."

The room suddenly went silent. The music stopped and suddenly they were surrounded by the other guests at the party. Heart felt Kenneth take hold of her hand and attempt to pull her away. Heart snatched her hand back in a fast and angry motion, never taking her eyes off the problem in front of her. Self-defense one-oh-one, if you can't see the danger, you can't protect yourself from it.

"Smyth," Heart called for her sergeant and he was at her side instantly. Without looking, she removed her badge from her hip and handed it to him. Then she withdrew her weapon from her holster, made sure the safety mechanism was engaged, removed the ammo clip and ejected the lone round from the chamber. She handed the disassembled gun to Smyth and dropped her hands to her waist.

"No badge or gun to worry about, princess. So if you're feeling frogfish, bitch, then leap."

Heart stood there waiting for Faith to make her move. Heart understood one thing in life, if people came for you; you stopped that shit in its tracks. Otherwise, they would keep coming for you. If this bitch took a swing at her, Heart was going to put her down hard, and fast. This bitch was going to learn that Heart, and more importantly, what belonged to Heart, was not to be fucked with, now, tomorrow, or ever.

Faith drew back her arm in an angry motion, and that was as far as Heart was going to allow it to get. She grabbed Faith's arm with one hand and used her other to wrap around the front of Faith's throat. In a move that seemed reminiscent of one of those wrestling entertainment shows, Heart lifted Faith in the air by her throat and planted her through a table that was behind her.

Glass and wood splintered everywhere around Faith as she lay dazed from the impact of the collision with the table and floor. Heart extended her hand out to Bryan and he placed her badge and her gun back in her hand. She secured them while keeping her eyes on Faith still lying on the ground.

"Understand me, bitch. I catch you near him again, being put through a fucking table will seem like a picnic compared to what I will do to you. Don't fuck with what's mine."

Heart lifted her eyes and sought out Drew. "Drew, come to the house tomorrow, I'll write you a check for the cost of the damages. Thank you for attempting to do something nice for us, I'm sorry that this is the way I repaid your kindness."

Drew shook his head in a don't-worry-about-it motion. Heart

turned around and walked to the door. When she didn't hear foot-steps immediately behind her she called,

"Kenneth!" in a sharp tone and heard the quick, hard fall of his feet as he followed her out of the door.

One thought filled her mind as they entered the car and drove off.

Shit has just gotten real.

CHAPTER 20

*K*enneth watched Heart climb the stairs two at a time. She went into what had now become their bedroom and headed straight for the walk-in closet. He heard the keypad beeps from the gun safe as she dialed in the combination code.

He felt a slight sense of relief. Heart was silent-angry. That was never a good thing. At least if she was this mad and her weapons were locked away, he stood a chance of surviving to see the next day.

She re-entered the bedroom and walked directly past him. He heard her quick footsteps run down the stairs. He followed, saw her head for the basement door, and disappear into the lower level of the house.

He walked downstairs to find her standing in the middle of the gym with her arms crossed against the expanse of her heaving chest.

"Baby, I..." She put up her hand and stopped his words. She turned toward the stereo, turned it on, and fiddled with the dials until he heard Maxwell's "Bad Habit" pouring from the speakers.

It was late and she had the sound turned up on *damn*. Fortunately for their neighbors, the basement was soundproofed. When the house was built, the original owner had wanted a place in the house where he could make as much noise as he wanted without disturbing the neighbors. By the looks of it, Heart planned to benefit from that fact. He wasn't quite sure if he was going to benefit from it or not yet.

"What's with the music being so loud?" he yelled over the driving base.

"I want to make sure that the neighbors don't hear you scream," she said, face straight, muscles tightening in her arms as she squeezed her hands into tight fists.

"Shit," was all he could say. He knew he was in trouble now.

She rushed him…that was the only way to explain how she was standing across from him one moment, and sitting on top of him the next. In a matter of seconds he was on the floor; face up, with her sitting on top of him.

"Heart, this is not funny. Get up so we can talk."

She didn't move, didn't even make a sound. She just looked at him, through him with sharp brown eyes cutting into his soul. His hands had somehow ended up near his head when he fell. He went to pull them down and felt resistance. He tried to move them again and heard a metal clinking sound above his head. He moved his head around until he could see the shiny glint of handcuffs. She'd cuffed him to the weight machine they'd landed in front of when she'd taken him to the floor. This was the very same weight machine that was bolted to the floor and immovable.

"Heart, this isn't funny. What are you doing? Why did you cuff me?" Her face was still tight with anger, her body stiff and poised for attack.

"Kenneth, do you know that I hate watching you get dressed. I hate it because I hate that anything else in this world gets to touch your beautiful alabaster skin as closely as I do. I want to be the only thing draped over you so intimately. Not the fine garments you wear, and certainly not that bitch, Faith."

He watched her pull something from her back pocket. At first it looked like a heavy handle, but with a flick of her wrist, it became a knife.

"Heart?"

She ran the dull side of the knife across his lips and said, "Ssssh."

He swallowed carefully as he watched her remove the knife from his lips and slice the sharp side down the length of his shirt, causing the two sides to peel away from his body like water.

She continued the slide of the blade through his pants until he was lying beneath her naked and at her mercy.

"I'm an only child, Kenneth. I never really learned how to share. I'll be damned if I'm going to share you. So hear me now. If you want that bitch, be with that bitch, then leave me the fuck alone. But if here is where you want to be, keep that bitch, and any other out of your face. I. Don't. Play. That. Shit."

He nodded his head quickly. He knew he hadn't perpetrated that kiss with Faith, but him lying naked beneath her while she had a sharp blade dancing between her fingers didn't seem the most appropriate time to point out whose fault this entire fallout was.

She brought down the hand holding the knife with a hard and fast stabbing motion. He flinched, anticipating pain, but realized soon that there was no pain. She hadn't stabbed him. He turned his head slightly to the side and saw the shiny blade next to him, sticking out of the floor.

Heart grabbed him by his chin and allowed one word to slip through her tightly ground jaw, "Mine!"

She slammed her mouth down on his and kissed him hard, sharp teeth biting into his flesh. His skin rent and he tasted the bitter metallic tang of blood. He should have been pissed, he really should have felt afraid, after all, this woman had rendered him helpless and brandished a weapon in front of him. He was shaking, his heart was pounding, and his breath was coming out in rapid tufts of air from his heaving chest. But surprisingly, there was no fear, only…interest.

His dick jumped beneath her. He was handcuffed with a knife sticking out of the floor next to his head and he was so turned on his dick could cut granite.

What the fuck is wrong with me?

He didn't have time to come up with an answer to his own question. He watched as Heart stood to remove her pants and her panties. She resumed her spot perched atop his crotch and swiveled her hips in a looping motion until she found her comfortable spot. His cock pulsed and he could feel a small pearl of pre-cum bubbling up on his tip.

He was either going to die tonight, or have the best fucking orgasm of his life. Either way, he didn't care, as long as she kept grinding against him like this, she could pretty much do anything she wanted, and he would be good with that.

Heart placed strong fingers around his cock, leaned forward and within a breath he was inside the sweltering heat of her pussy. In one quick motion he was fully seated inside her, her fire surrounding him, sucking all the air from his lungs by way of his dick.

I wonder if people really do die from good sex? If they do, I'm certain my ass is gone tonight.

She rose up again, and slammed back down onto him. She kept repeating the motion with a speed and power that were causing his muscles to spasm and his toes to curl. He wanted so badly to use his hands, to touch her, to grab her, to use her hips as leverage so he could fuck up into her the way he wanted, the way his body craved. But this was her show, she was running it, and she wasn't giving him an ounce of control. All he could do, the only thing she would allow him to do was moan. *Fuck, who was he kidding?* He wasn't moaning, he was screaming like a bitch, the sounds falling from his open mouth with every twitch of her round ass.

His muscles burned, his balls wanted release so bad, they ached with tension and need. She slammed down on top of him, palming his thickly braid hair and wrapping it into her fist. She pulled hard, sharp pain seizing his scalp. She planted her mouth back on top of his, stealing his breath as she shoved her tongue into his mouth again. God the taste of this woman, even in anger there was nothing sweeter than the flavor of her.

She ripped her mouth from his lips and sought out his nipples, sharp teeth grazing the pointed nubs. When she left both aching and red, she moved her mouth to his shoulder clamping down on the pulse she found there. He screamed out from the mix of intense pleasure peppered with just a touch of pain. He could feel her walls contracting; she was just as close to eruption as he was.

She bit his neck again, and placed her lips next to his ear as she pounded on top of him. "Mine…you hear me…mine! Don't ever let another bitch touch what's mine. You understand?"

She bit down into his shoulder, extracting his answer from him on a long moan.

"Yes…baby…yes."

She bounced up and down on him, walls closing in tighter and tighter around his girth, drawing his orgasm out of him as she raced toward her own.

"Remember…that…shit!" she said when her body locked into one long contraction of muscle as she rode her orgasm and him.

Her release triggered his. The muscles of his body rippled and jerked uncontrollably beneath her. He poured out his release into the seeping wet heat of her cavern. Nothing in life had ever felt this good. He saw blinding white heat behind closed lids as his muscles kept clenching and releasing, spurting one long stream of cum after another. He couldn't breathe, he couldn't think, all he could do was feel this amazing, overwhelming tidal wave that he was certain was going to end his life tonight.

And when his senses couldn't withstand the onslaught of sensation, he saw the black edges of unconsciousness quickly pulling at his mind. He fought, tried to stave it away, but light bled into the dark and then just as quickly as his orgasm had flooded his senses, the dark had taken him over until there was simply nothing left.

∾

*H*eart secured her weapon in her holster and took one last glance in the mirror. The haunted eyes that looked back at her were almost unrecognizable to her.

What the hell did you do?

Her stomach began to twist in uncomfortable knots as visions of last night trampled across her brain.

She'd been so angry.

She was angry that Faith had dared to touch Kenneth, she was angry that Kenneth hadn't put up a more firm resistance, and she was angry that she'd allowed herself to lose her cool the way she had.

She didn't regret putting Faith through that table, hell that was the only positive thing she could remember from the entire night. Hell, if she could, she'd put that shit on instant replay just for giggles at a later time, but the way she'd manhandled Kenneth afterward, the way she'd taken her frustration out on him—it made her sick.

Kenneth had been a willing participant last night. Once he'd realized that she wasn't crazy and she wasn't about to kill him, he'd gotten off on her aggression. He'd liked every minute of it. He'd said yes more times than she could count. The way his body responded to her, the way he begged her...she came so hard hearing those beautiful cries of pleasure crawl out of his mouth and into her soul. The power was heady, and she'd enjoyed every minute of it. But if she enjoyed it so much, why did she feel so afraid of it, afraid of him.

~

*K*enneth heard the distant sound of a ringing phone tugging him from wherever the fuck his dark mind had dumped him. He closed his eyes tighter hoping to pull his scattered thoughts together. He patted the surface around him with open palms until one of them landed on his cell.

He tried to open his lids but the bright lighting in the gym felt like a hot knife against his eyes. He cracked one eye open—slightly—and saw Drew's name flashing across the front of the screen. He slid his finger across the screen and put the phone to his ear.

"'Lo."

"Kenneth? You all right man?"

"Yeah, mm'fine. Long night."

"John and I are on your doorstep. Can you let us in? We just wanted to check on you."

"Okay, gimme a sec."

Kenneth place the phone down used his hands to help him push himself up into a sitting position. When he was finally able to open his eyes, he realized he was sitting on a floor, not in his bed where he should have been if he felt this fucked up.

He blinked through the fogginess of his mind when memories from the night before emerged.

"Shit!" he said to the open room and stood up quickly.

Faith had kissed him last night and Heart had put her through a table for it, and fucked him straight into a blackout.

He felt his naked flesh swinging and realized he needed something to put on. He slowly ambled over to the gym closet, body stiff and ridged, muscles tight, and ruffled through the items until he found a pair of basketball shorts. He stumbled as he put them on, needing to lean against the wall to remain upright as he dressed.

He knocked against the walls on his way to the door, needing something fixed to keep himself standing. He opened the door for his friends and heard a collective,

"Daaammmnnn," coming from the two men in perfect harmony and pitch.

He hid his eyes from the glaring sunlight rushing in the door walking back into the house.

"Fuck both of y'all songbirds, I need coffee."

He made his way back to the kitchen and found a full carafe of coffee waiting for him. "Mmm, Heart," he whispered. He managed to pour himself a full cup of the rich black substance without spilling any—a feat he was absolutely proud of considering his current state.

"What the fuck happened to you, dawg?" Drew said as he and John ogled the bruises that were covering his upper body.

"Damn, Ken, did she beat your ass? You look like tenderized meat," John added.

Kenneth planted his hands on the counter and looked at his friends. "No, she didn't beat my ass. There's really only one way to explain what Heart did to me last night...she fucked me within an inch of my life and I loved every moment of it."

~

*H*eart sat at her desk working. Work cleared her head, forced her to think, it made her calm. She needed those things after the night she'd had. She shuddered at the thought of how out of control she was last night.

She looked up in response to the light tapping on her door and saw Bryan standing in front of it. She motioned with her hand for him to enter.

"Rough night?" he asked.

"Bryan, I'm not up for talking about last night. I'd rather just forget it."

"You may not be able to. I understand why you did what you did, but you gotta know she was baiting you. She wanted to make you look bad in front of Kenneth. I don't think she accomplished that, not by the look on his face last night, but what she did do was get you to put yourself in a situation where she could fuck with your job."

Heart rolled her eyes at Bryan. She knew what he was saying was true, but honestly, at that moment, even now, she could give a fuck.

"Bryan, that bitch had it coming. What would you have done if someone put their lips on Jussy like that when the two of you were dating?"

"Oh, I would've beaten somebody's ass, that's for certain. I'm just saying she could come at you with a lot of shit depending on how vindictive she wants to be. Don't let her get the better of you again, and if she does, make sure there are no witnesses. I don't want

I.A. hounding my ass about this shit."

"I know, it's just she pissed me off so much. I had a Big Willie moment. Now I see why he's always flipping out over dudes trying to get at Tee's ass." She waved her hand at him as she laughed. Bryan was always her voice of reason. Heart was tactically sound, but she was a hothead at times. Bryan was always her calming force. She would need him to keep her from killing people if she went for top cop position in the house. Fortunately for her, he always had her back.

"Bryan, do me a favor. When you go back out, can you tell Kimes and Forze to come in here?"

"Something up?"

She shook her head. "Not really. The two of them were at Mac's place when I brought Kenneth through while I was on leave. Kimes seems okay, but I've heard and continue to hear too much shit about Forze harassing young black urban men. I can't prove anything, but I don't really think he's the best person to have around my kids."

Bryan nodded and exited out of the door. Soon after she heard a double tap on her door and Forze and Kimes were walking in.

"L.T.," Kimes said as he greeted her with a smile. "Sergeant Smyth said you wanted to see us."

"Yeah, as of today I'm switching your rotation, the two of you won't be on site at

Mac's house."

"Is there are a reason for that?" Forze added.

She turned her eyes to him, assessing his body language. He was standing in her office, in front of her desk with his hands on his hips like he was demanding an explanation.

Oh, I guess he didn't get the memo, I run this.

"Yeah, the reason is because I said so."

"So you get to jerk our schedules around without notice just 'cause your badge is gold?"

Heart stood up slowly and looked at Kimes. "Officer Kimes, would you give your partner and I a minute?"

Kimes looked from one to the other with wide eyes, as if he wanted to say something, but thought better of it after fully assessing the situation. He simply nodded and left the room, closing the door with a quiet click.

Heart returned her eyes to Forze. After the night she'd had dealing with Faith, and the way she'd handled her anger with Kenneth last night, today really wasn't the day for folks to get on her bad side. Not if they knew what was good for them.

"Officer Forze, I don't know what they taught you in the academy, but let me explain how shit goes down in the real world." She walked around the expanse of her desk and stood eye-to-eye in front of him. "I am in charge of every aspect of command in this motherfucker. I tell everyone where to go, when to be there, and what to do when they arrive. The only person I answer to, the only people who get to question my decisions and attempt to come at me with any bark are the captain of this house, and brass. And if I'm not mistaken, you don't fall in either of those categories. So let's get this shit straight. I don't have to consult you; I don't have to give you warning. I do what the fuck I want and you…you've got one viable option…you handle it."

She walked back to the opposite side of her desk and sat down in her chair, quiet and calm like, as if nothing had just happened. She picked up the files on her desk and uttered an indifferent, "Dismissed," at him and went back to her work.

∾

*H*eart and Kenneth sat in Reverend Lawrence's office waiting for the seasoned clergyman to enter. Heart sat stiffly in her seat, gripping the arms of the chair tightly.

"If you hold on any tighter to those arm rests you're going to break them," Kenneth leaned in and whispered.

She turned to him and gave an apologetic smile. Why the hell was she so nervous?

She'd known Reverend Lawrence since birth. She'd grown up in his church. The man had always been kind and supportive, yet sitting here waiting on him for a mandatory pre-marriage counseling session was shredding her fragile nerves.

If it had been up to her, she would have hired a judge to come out and perform their marriage, but her grandmother had gotten wind of that plan and told her it would be sacrilege. Ida-Mae actually wanted the wedding to happen in the church, but Heart had drawn the line at that. She did very much believe in God, but organized religion was something she really questioned. She saw the good work the church did in the community, and she loved the alliance she had with Greater Mount Zion Baptist Church with respect to the shared work they did with the kids of Mac's Place, but she didn't think that was enough for her and Kenneth to stand at the altar and exchange their I-dos.

Kenneth had suggested a reasonable compromise, have Reverend Lawrence perform the ceremony in their backyard. Kenneth would have another tent constructed, much like the one their engagement party had taken place in and their grandmother would be satisfied that her long-time minister would be blessing Heart and Kenneth's union.

It had seemed like such a perfect idea until Reverend Lawrence demanded they attend at least one session of pre-marriage counseling before the ceremony. She'd stared down armed criminals, she'd fought in hand-to-hand combat with some of the deadliest people on the streets, she'd spent almost every day of the last nine years of her life on an urban battlefield and had never really thought twice about any of it. But this, sitting to talk to this mere man, a humble man of God was making her nervous system twitch.

"Why are you so nervous?" Kenneth reached for her hand stilling the repetitive tapping motion it was making against the armrest.

"I'm not nervous," she answered quickly.

Kenneth looked down at their joined hands and then met her eyes again. "I'd tell you what I call on that particular statement, but seeing as we're in a house of worship I will refrain from telling you you're full of it. What's going on? You've known Reverend Lawrence all of your life."

"Kenneth, we're not your typical couple. This engagement didn't come about via traditional circumstance." She rolled her neck trying to relieve some of the tension that was building there. "What if he decides that we shouldn't be married and refuses to marry us?"

Kenneth took a gentle hand and pressed it against her aching neck. He rubbed comforting circles at the base until the knot of tension that was taking up residence there dissolved.

"Baby, there isn't a man on this Earth that can stop me from marrying you as planned, next week. I would love for Reverend Lawrence to marry us. Especially knowing how much it would mean to your grandmother and to your family. But understand this, even if he says no, there will be an officiate standing ready to perform this sacred rite. You will be my wife, Heart. No one will interfere in that."

She smiled and nodded her head. Kenneth's promises were facts written in stone as far as she was concerned. They were going to be married, that was the only thing that mattered.

Reverend Lawrence entered the office from a door on the side of his desk. He shook Kenneth's hand, and then hesitated as he reached for hers.

"I'm sorry," he said quietly.

She shook her head and waved a passing hand. "No worries. I'm actually working on that." Her eyes passed quickly over Kenneth's face. "Ever since my family explained the details of my abduction to me, Kenneth has been encouraging me to seek help for this phobia. He found a therapist for me that specializes in treating people with Post Traumatic Stress Disorder."

The reverend sat up a little straighter. "PTSD? I thought—"

"That only people who were active participants in a war came home with PTSD? Yeah, I thought that too. Turns out anyone who has experienced a traumatic event can suffer from the same condition."

The reverend nodded. "Do you feel like therapy is helping?"

"It's still very early in the process. It's only been a few weeks of intensive therapy. I see her five times a week. She's been working on coping techniques with me. Things I can use to help me withstand normal everyday touches without going on the defensive."

The reverend nodded his head and looked at Kenneth. "I'm glad to hear you're working so hard to keep her healthy. That's what being married is all about...helping one another with the trials and tribulations of life."

Heart felt Kenneth's gaze pour over her and she smiled, the corners of her mouth tugging her lips wider as she found a matching smile on Kenneth's face.

"Now, if we're all ready to begin, let's bow our heads in prayer to start this session off right."

～

*K*enneth felt Heart's gaze on him. They'd just left Reverend Lawrence's office and were grabbing a bite to eat at the diner on Linden Blvd.

"What, do I have something on my face?" he asked with a cheek full of the cheeseburger he was currently chewing on.

"No...I...Kenneth."

Kenneth wiped his mouth with a napkin and took Heart's hand. "What's wrong?"

She stumbled over her words for a moment, sitting there with her mouth open, producing no sound. She finally closed her eyes, took a breath, and forced air through her mouth.

"I'm sorry for the way I behaved the night of Drew's party."

"You mean for putting Faith through a table?"

"No, she deserved that, and I enjoyed it. I'm talking about the other thing."

Kenneth lifted a brow and thought back over that night. It had been a pretty unforgettable night, he was certain he wouldn't ever forget it.

"Are you talking about what happened in the basement?" he asked, confusion marring his face. He watched Heart nod her head up and down.

"Kenneth, I should have never come at you like that. I should never have restrained you. I would completely understand if you wanted to call this entire fiasco off."

"Heart, you're apologizing for the most erotic experience of my life? I don't get it. I could have sworn I was a willing participant in all of it. Then again, you kind of fucked my brain to mush so my words might not have been all that intelligible."

She looked around them to see if anyone had overheard him. When she saw no one looking, she hid her eyes behind her hand.

"Kenneth..."

He put up a hand silencing her. "Heart, I enjoyed it. Hell, I wouldn't be opposed to doing it again. Except next time, you think you could just let me take my clothes off instead of cutting them off me? I really did like that outfit."

~

*K*enneth stepped in front of the mirror and assessed the image looking back at him. Raven hair slicked back into a neat, low-hanging ponytail, a thin goatee framing pink lips and a square chin. He continued his perusal over the navy blue two-button tuxedo jacket with its satin navy blue lapel and nodded his head in approval. Heart would love him in this. The navy silk tie knotted at his neck was the perfect accent to the stark while pointed collar of his formal shirt. Slim fitted navy pants that fell perfectly over the top of his pointed patent leather shoes and he was an impressive vision to behold, tall, lean, confident, and happy as fuck.

A month ago, he hadn't envisioned this day. He hadn't even known he'd wanted it. He just wanted Heart, all the time, every way he could have her.

Isn't that the reason people get married?

Perhaps he had wanted this day, and just hadn't realized it? It didn't matter now. Their wedding day was here, and he was so excited that Heart was finally going to be his. Kenneth and Heart decided on a small intimate affair for their nuptials. That included the two-person wedding party consisting of her cousin True as maid of honor and his childhood friend, John as best man.

The ceremony was about to start, John had left Kenneth alone for a few moments to gather his thoughts and emotions before joining his life to Heart. John had told him to ask himself three questions before he left that room and headed down to the alter inside of that tent and to be certain of their answers before he said *I do.*

Am I ready to do this? Is she the one I should be doing this with? Do I love her enough to do this?

His mouth curved into a bright smile as one answer passed his lips with blessed ease.

"Yes."

Kenneth saw the door open through the mirror and watched as a smiling True entered the room and closed the door.

"What's up, Cousin?" Kenneth threw over his shoulder with a small chuckle of laughter passing his upturned lips. He stepped away from the mirror long enough to see the navy blue blur of True's cocktail dress coming at him.

True pushed Kenneth into the wall, his back slamming against the flat surface with a hard smack. Shocked by her sudden aggression, he froze, and that was just enough time for her to position her forearm across his throat. He went to move off the wall and he felt her hand snake down the front of his tuxedo pants and grip his cock and balls in a firm hold. The hold didn't hurt, at least not yet, but it certainly made him aware that she could change his gender with the right—or wrong depending on whose perspective you were looking from— amount of pressure.

"I see Faith wasn't lying when she said you dispelled the myth that white men ain't packing. According to her the dance floor wasn't the only place you had rhythm."

Kenneth watched her carefully unsure of why she was damn near assaulting him moments before he was about to marry her cousin.

"True, what the he'll are you doing?"

"Kenneth, as far as I know you treated Faith right when she was with you. I also know that before and after Faith you ran through women quicker than you changed underwear. Let me be very clear, from this day on, *this*..." she emphasized the word with a firm squeeze to his groin, "...belongs to my cousin. If I hear nary a tale that you are giving this to anyone else, I will slice it off, put it into a pretty package, and ship it to

Heart. You got me?"

He nodded quickly giving a breathless, "Yes."

"Good, then I only have one other thing to say...Welcome to the family."

∽

*H*eart walked outside onto the deck and saw her father standing at the bottom of the stairs. He held out a hand to assist her. She looked down at the sparkly, electric blue, sixinch CL Redbottoms that covered her feet and decided the helping hand might not be such a bad idea.

She smiled to herself as she slowly took the steps while holding on to Marcus' hand.

Kenneth had seen how much she loved the silver shoes he'd purchased for their engagement and decided she needed the blue version to fulfill the *something blue* item on the familiar bride's wedding day list.

When she reached the bottom step, Marcus let her hand go and took a slow look at her.

"You remind me so much of your mother on our wedding day. You're so beautiful."

Heart looked down at herself and smoothed a careful hand down the length of her short dress. Her grandmother hated her dress. Heart thought the woman was going into cardiac arrest again the way she behaved when Heart had walked out of the dressing room in this short little number.

Ida-Mae had envisioned Heart in something big and frilly and big for this wedding. Heart had tried to appease the ailing woman, but those tent-style dresses just made her itch. She felt like she couldn't breathe with all of that material covering every inch of her body.

In response to Heart's reaction, the boutique consultant had suggested something a little more modern for Heart's next selection. It was short, cocktail dress length in fact. It was made of the traditional wedding dress bridal satin with those same artfully decorated patterns that you would see on any bridal gown. It was everything a traditional, strapless, square neckline, A-line cut wedding dress was, except, its hem stopped at just above her knee. Heart nearly leapt when she saw herself in the mirror. It was perfect, and she didn't feel like she was being strangled by all of the material.

Her grandmother was livid, but Heart told her she had two

choices, either Heart wore the gown she loved, or she'd show up to the wedding in her police-issued dress blue uniform.

Ida-Mae must have known Heart was serious and just scrunched up her face in a painful looking scowl.

Now she was standing in the dress, ready to walk to her future and the first person to see her in it was praising her appearance. It was a much needed confidence booster.

"Thanks, Marcus," that was all she could get out. Afraid that more words would mess up the flawless makeup job True had done.

"No," he said through a shaky smile. "Thank you for allowing me to be a part of this."

Heart nodded her head. Her therapist had helped her take some very important steps to making sense of her past, to help rebuild a relationship with her family, including Marcus. They were small steps, but they were meaningful. She'd asked him to give her away and he'd readily accepted. He'd even sat in on a session with her therapist to figure out the best ways not to aggravate her phobia. The three of them together had sat in her therapist's office and worked out ways that he could touch her that wouldn't drive her insane and she'd felt a grain of closeness sprouting, something she knew had the possibility of growing into something bigger and stronger if nurtured in just the right way.

They heard the music change, signaling her entrance into the tent. Marcus pulled the short blusher veil that stopped just at the apple of her cheeks over her face. He gently fingered the curtain of loosely formed curls draped over one shoulder and extended his elbow to her.

She looked down, and touched light fingertips to his offered arm. It wasn't much, but it was more than she'd been able to give in her past. She was getting better, her life was moving in the right direction, and it was all because of the man that was waiting for her at the end of the aisle.

"I'm ready if you are, Heart." Marcus smiled.

She closed her eyes and took a deep, calming breath.

"Let's go, Marcus, my future is waiting for me on the inside of that tent."

~

 *K*enneth had been a wall of composed happiness. He'd walked down that aisle, and stood in front of their makeshift group of family and friends and Reverend Lawrence and smiled with ease. He had no doubts, this was what he wanted and needed. He'd not had a moment of nervous energy during the entire preparation of this wedding until the heavy curtains at the back of the tent opened and he saw the loveliest vision of feminine perfection he'd ever witnessed.

He felt his breath catch in his throat with the tightening of his heart. His eyes started burning, and then he felt the warm sensation of wet tears sliding down his face. The last time he'd cried had been at his twin sister's funeral. Today his tears were his body's way of processing how much joy was bursting from the seams of his full heart.

That overwhelming fullness left a sweet ache in his chest. He literally ached for her, ached to be near her, ached to have her, ached to make her his in every way. It was agonizing to watch her take that slow saunter down the aisle on her father's arm.

He felt John lean closer to him.

"There's your future walking toward you," his long-time friend said to him.

Kenneth nodded, John was correct. There she was, his future, unstoppable, certain, and looking more lovely than he could bear.

His Heart.

Once she stood before him, the ceremony passed pretty quickly. They answered in all of the appropriate places with all the appropriate answers and then it was time for them to share their vows with one another.

"Kenneth, I know that I'm the lucky one in this relationship. I know that I'm the one that's getting all of the benefit. Most people would probably think, 'Who wouldn't jump at the chance to marry a billionaire?' But see, your money doesn't even enter into the equation for me. The truth is…I'd marry you even if you were destitute. What you give me…is something no amount of money can buy."

She extended a shaky hand and let it rest on his lapel, just above his heart. Warm brown eyes looked at him wide with happiness and unshed tears.

"You see, the way I feel when my face is pressed against your chest, and the sound of your heartbeat is thumping against my cheek, and your arms are wrapped around me, that's why I'm marrying you. That feeling is safety, it's assurance, it's trust. It's something I've never had before, something I've never experienced with another human being. It's something I've never wanted to share with anyone, yet it's something that happens so easily with you. When it comes down to the heart of the matter, there's no real logical reason why I should feel this way. The truth is I'm well past the point of trying to figure out why I do. All I know is this, I love you, Kenneth. That may have not been part of the plan, but it's certainly my reality today. It's the only reality I want. It's the only reason I agreed to this crazy idea of yours for us to marry, and it's the only reason I'm standing here with you now."

She turned to True and held out her upturned hand in anticipation of the platinum ring with large channel set diamonds on its face. She held it between her thumb, middle, and forefingers, and held it at the bottom of his marriage finger.

"So that's what I'm promising you today, my love. I want you to rest in my love, the way I have yours. With this ring, I pledge you the safe haven of my love today, tomorrow, and always." She glided the ring upward and over his knuckle until it rested at the very base of his finger.

He took the hand she used to put the band on him and kissed it gently, needing to touch her in even the slightest of ways. He was so full right now, her gift, so precious, so priceless. Her love, she was giving it to him. Freely, without compulsion, without him even asking for it, she'd opened her heart and allowed him inside of it.

He turned briefly to John and took the female match to his ring. He placed it at the bottom of her marriage finger and lifted smiling eyes to her.

"You were not expected," he said softly. "but once you were here, I didn't want to let you go. I wanted to keep you with me, no matter the cost, no matter who I had to walk through to make it happen."

He rubbed a soft circular pattern on the top of her hand, soothing her, as he always seemed to do.

"Heart, we started out on this path together for various reasons. But please know, the only reason I'm standing here, is the only reason that matters. I love you. I love your strength. I love how well you do your job and how seriously you take the responsibilities of your command. I love the way you care for the people and the community you serve. I love the compassion you have for those who are victimized, and I love the selfless way you put the needs of others above your own. But mostly, I love the way someone who has seen so much misery and pain still manages to give light to those who are struggling in the darkness. I love the meaning you bring to my life, but most of all, I love the man I am when I'm in your presence. The man you've made me. I promise you that as long as I live, you will have my love and devotion, today, tomorrow, and always."

He pressed the ring forward slipping it easily over her knuckle and stopping when he reached the base of her finger. He took her hand and pressed his lips to the cool metal resting against her skin, consecrating it with his love.

He placed a soft hand against her cheek and watched her press into its warmth. The smile on her lips filling her eyes with brightness, hope, and expectation of happiness. He knew then that nothing could ever damage this sacred joy their hearts had found.

CHAPTER 21

*T*he rough chopping sound of the helicopter mimicked the raging trepidation in her head.

Ida-Mae was dying.

The truth, her grandmother had been dying since the day she'd had a heart attack nearly a month ago. They'd known then that this day was eminent, but to know that undeniably that day was here, the last moments of her life dripping quickly away like sand in a timer… that was almost too much for Heart to bear.

She'd wanted to stay home after the wedding. But Ida-Mae had insisted that Heart and Kenneth go on a honeymoon, she hadn't wanted to keep the young couple from enjoying their new marriage. Heart had fought with the old woman, but just as most times the two women disagreed, Ida-Mae decisively won the argument.

Kenneth encouraged her to listen to her grandmother. He'd even agreed to a staycation of sorts. He'd secured accommodations at a premier hotel in Manhattan and managed to get them tickets to some of the exclusive Broadway shows and events that she couldn't have gained access to even with her badge and a warrant.

They'd been having a lovely time. They'd laughed, eaten, made love, and explored Manhattan like tourists. It was everything she could have ever wanted in a honeymoon. Then forty-five minutes ago her uncle had called her with devastating news. Ida-Mae had collapsed and been rushed to the hospital. The doctors weren't holding out much hope and she needed to get back to Brooklyn quickly.

She was an emergency responder, yet she was always amazed that it was Kenneth and not her who always planned ahead to keep her sane during moments of personal crisis. He'd arranged to have a helicopter on standby for the week they were staying in the city. If worst came to worst, the helicopter would meet them on the hotel's roof and scurry them away to the hospital's helipad in a matter of moments.

His plan had come together perfectly. As soon as Hunter's call came through, Kenneth had dialed the pilot to set things in motion. He'd packed up their belongings while she'd showered and dressed and then took his turn getting ready as the porters came to remove their luggage.

In less than twenty minutes after she'd hung up with Hunter she was sitting in a helicopter being whisked back to Brooklyn. She stepped inside of the large building and was enveloped by cold. She didn't know if it was her imagination, but she felt the chill pour down into her, filling her up. Her body contracted in a hard shudder. It almost paralyzed her, her muscles fighting against her brain's commands. Kenneth wrapped an arm around her, blanketing her in his warmth. Reassuring her that she wouldn't face whatever waited for her beyond those white metal doors alone.

Heart walked into the room, filled by familiar faces. Her four cousins, Reverend Lawrence, her uncle Hunter, Marcus, and even Genesis all stood in various parts of the small CCU room. Heart knew that a hospital usually had restrictions on the number of visitors a patient could have at one time. The fact that there was a small crowd gathered in this room...Heart knew it wasn't good.

"Mama?" the small word slipped out of her mouth.

"I knew you would make it."

The small figure in the middle of that hospital bed drew Heart's eyes to her face. Ida-

Mae's skin had a greyish blue tinge to it that confused Heart. How could a black woman with a dark complexion look grey?

Because she's dying.

"I love you, mama," Heart said as her grandmother's tired eyes met hers.

"And I love you too, baby. I love all my babies. You were the one that I worried most about Heart, but now, now I don't have to worry. Kenneth's gonna take real good care of you. I can rest now."

Heart felt Kenneth press against her back and place a strong hand on her shoulder.

She needed his strength. She was losing the only mother she'd known.

"I'll take care of her, Ida-Mae...always."

She smiled up at Kenneth and closed those tired eyes of hers. "I know you will,

Kenneth, I know you will."

Ida-Mae took a painful noisy breath. She reached for Heart's hand and held on with all the strength her small, frail frame could muster.

"Love you, Heart...don't want to leave you...so tired."

Heart felt her soul crack and splinter in to tiny fragments. She wanted to scream with rage, keep her grandmother here with her, hold on to her beloved *mama* with every single ounce of strength she possessed. But looking down into that lovely aged face, all she could do was release her from her pain.

"It's all right, Mama. You can go. I'm gonna be just fine. We're all gonna be just fine. You rest. You've spent so long taking care of all of us; it's your time to rest. It's okay, be with Diamond, be with Granddaddy."

Ida-Mae looked around the room, wet eyes smiling at them all. She looked at Heart one last time before fixing her eyes just beyond Heart's shoulder. She took one long ragged breath and when she released it, the monitor that had been beeping in time with her weakened heartbeat emitted a final long monotone sound.

Just like that, in the shifting of a brief moment, her grandmother was gone.

~

*H*eart sat in the first pew of Mount Zion Baptist with her uncle, Marcus, her cousins and Kenneth and felt nothing. She was aware that the church was full, she was aware that the front of the church was filled with huge floral arrangements and she was aware of the white pearlized metal casket sitting in front of her. She was even aware that her beloved grandmother's body was in that pretty metal box—if one could really ever call a casket pretty. But still, inside, there was nothing.

In a matter of moments her grandmother had slipped through her fingers and there was nothing left of her but an empty shell. Eight decades of living, and the only thing left was the stiff husk lying face up in that cushion-lined metal box.

How could that be the only thing remaining, shouldn't the world stop and take notice that someone so vital was gone?

She sat there, still and unfeeling, her insides empty, cold, hollow, much like the remains of her grandmother's lifeless body. *Is this what it feels like to be dead?*

She sat quietly through the service, clapped and smiled in all the appropriate places. She accepted well-meaning condolences from the throng of attendants, mourners, and church folk. She did all the things one was supposed to do at a funeral, except feel.

She watched the funeral directors come forward to open the casket for the final viewing. She watched the tall man dressed in all black lift the lid and stick a key near the top of the head to elevate her grandmother's body in to view.

From where she was sitting, Heart could see the gloved hands of her grandmother resting over the white bible lying face down in her lap. If Heart hadn't known the truth she would have assumed her grandmother had just fallen asleep reading her bible. How many times over the years had she witnessed that very same occurrence?

Whenever she'd spy her grandmother nodding off with the bible in her lap she'd softly nudge her and encourage her to lie down.

"Mama, you're tired, why don't you go in your room and rest yourself?"

Ida-Mae would shift out of her dosing state, glasses hanging on the very tip of her nose just this close to falling off. The very sight always made Heart smile.

"No, baby. I'm sitting here fellowshipping with the Lord."

Heart would chuckle. If Ida-Mae was fellowshipping with anyone, it was the Sandman, not the Lord.

"Mama, I'm sure the Lord wouldn't mind if you took a little break. Go get some sleep and when you get up, you can go back to fellowshipping."

Her grandmother would nod her head and remove those thin-framed rims that had been perilously hanging from her nose and lean back into the sofa.

"I 'spose you're right, baby. I'm just gonna shut my eyes for a few minutes and get right back to my bible study."

Within moments, Heart would hear soft snoring coming from her grandmother's lips. Kenneth nudged her from her memory with a gentle hand on her arm.

"It's time," he whispered.

All of her family members had walked to the casket to say their individual goodbyes and now it was her turn. She stood in front of her grandmother's lifeless body. Dressed in one of her favorite white missionary uniforms, she looked as close to angelic as any human being could manage.

She stood there, just there, her mind unable to process what she was supposed to be doing at this point. This was all wrong. The funeral director was motioning for her to say her final goodbyes, but she couldn't make herself. This was so counterintuitive; she couldn't be saying goodbye to the woman who had mothered her all her life. No, this was so very wrong.

She watched the funeral director reach for the key to the casket.

He was going to lower her grandmother into that box and seal her in there for all eternity.

She reached a hand out. "No, no, no, no," the repeated word came out as a painful, strangled cry.

She leaned down and pressed her forehead to the cold cheek of her grandmother. This was all wrong. The cold flesh beneath hers was stiff, hard, and unyielding. Heart took in a deep breath and her senses were overwhelmed with a strange odor. Even the smell of this body was off. Her grandmother had always smelled like fresh baked goods and cinnamon. The aroma had been embedded in her pores from the constant baking the woman always engaged in. This empty shell smelled wrong. There was a mixture of something floral and some sort of chemical cleaner wafting off the body.

"Mama, no...no," she wailed. Something clicked inside of her, this wasn't wrong, it was reality, her grandmother was gone, and she was left here to live without her.

The numbness she'd been carrying throughout the entire process of preparing for this funeral began to slowly creep away. In its place, a sharp pain began to hack at the edges of her soul slowly bleeding in, slowly filling her up until everything hurt.

Her skin, her teeth, the follicles of her hair, her eye lashes, her blood, every single part of her ached with an agonizing throb that pulsed quickly against her senses, too quickly for her to process the world around her. The pain was going to swallow her up she couldn't fight it off. She felt herself sinking into it, cold spasms cramping her insides. There was nothing she could do; this pain was going to kill her. She was going to die right here in front of her grandmother's casket and there was nothing she could do about it.

If she were honest, she wasn't exactly certain she wanted to do anything about.

Maybe if she gave in to the pain, maybe it would swallow her whole and she would be free of this. It hurt too much, she couldn't do this, didn't want to feel this agony for another moment.

She felt strong hands surround her waist and felt Kenneth's lips against her temple.

"You will survive this; I promise you're going to get better."

His voice, strong and soft, tethering her to reality—a reality she wanted to walk away from. A tug began inside of her. One side of her mind began pulling her to the darkness that would bring the sacred peace she needed. The nothingness that would silence the sharp ache was so tempting, luring her into the onyx abyss that would bring her serenity. The other side was the lull of Kenneth's sweet voice. It was full of love and promise and safety.

She'd held on to that safety to pull herself out of an emotional prison that had held her captive for fourteen years. She'd grappled that safety, using it as a shield to wage war on an injury that sought to steal her livelihood from her. Kenneth's safety had always done as he'd promised, had always kept her through some of the most difficult times of her life.

She turned over her shoulder to peek through slit lids as the funeral director closed Ida-Mae Amare's casket. Her grandmother was gone, nothing could bring her back.

Realizing that, she turned her head into the comfort of her husband's strong chest and reached for the safety only he could offer. There was nothing left in that shell for Heart. The only gift she had left for the woman who had sacrificed so much to raise Heart was to live life. Now if only her broken heart would cooperate with that plan.

~

*K*enneth watched his wife sleeping. It was an activity he'd enjoyed since before he'd ever known they would end up like this, naked, bodies pressed together, nothing between them but the trust and love they held for each other.

God he loved this woman.

He loved every inch of the person lying in his arms, reassuring weight pressed slightly on top of his body. He loved every measure of the soul that danced behind those deep mahogany eyes.

It had nearly killed him to watch this beautiful woman ache for the grandmother that she'd loved and lost. But he'd survived it, they both had.

Losing Ida-Mae had been a terrible blow to them, especially to their new marriage.

But he'd promised Ida-Mae that he would be there for Heart, and he'd meant it.

It wasn't easy. Heart had fought him every step of the way. She was a frustrating, scared, combative piece of work throughout most of it, but deep down he'd known that it was all just because her heart was broken. So he'd fought with her and for her to drag her through to the other side of the aching wound that seemed as if it was going to swallow her whole at varying points. She was still grieving, there was no way the passing of three months could erase the ache you felt when a part of you was lowered into the ground. He knew that. It hadn't yet been a year since his sister had passed and some days…well some days were better than others were.

He'd held her hand, even when she hadn't wanted him to, he held on determined to be her anchor to the world they were living in. They were just finding normalcy again.

Getting to a point where she could at least speak Ida-Mae's name without allowing her grief to swallow her whole.

"Stop watching me and go to sleep. You have to get up early tomorrow so you can get to the office early for the Ellery purchase."

He smiled down at her and snuggled closer to the warmth of her body. "What are you, my secretary? I thought Abby was the only one who knew my schedule better than me."

"Well, Abby keeps me filled in so I always know where my husband is."

"She's on my payroll, but spying for you? How did that happen?" She turned in his arms until her lips were a breath away from his.

"Well, happy wife, happy life. I keep you so happy that you want to come running home early every night, she gets to come home early every night. It's really a mutually beneficial situation for everyone involved. I didn't even have to twist her arm, or bully her with my badge to get the info."

Kenneth smiled. He ran gentle fingers through her hair and pulled her lips to him. "You make me very happy indeed." He continued stroking her hair and gave her a contemplative stare. "I was worried about you for a long moment there."

She nodded and placed her head on his chest, long fingers drawing swirling patterns across his vanilla skin.

"I know, I scared me for a time too. You told me not to hide how I felt during this entire ordeal, so I'm gonna be truthful. It still hurts. I don't know that I'm ever going to get to a day when it won't hurt. I just feel as if the hole isn't throbbing and seeping the way it was when she first died."

He understood. It was progress, she might not reach the next level of the healing process for months or even years to come, but she was moving in the right direction. Her head and her heart were slowly making sense of the loss that had nearly consumed her.

"I'm functional right now, Kenneth. And that's largely because of you. Just bear with me. As long as I have you, I know I'm going to be fine. Just don't give up on me yet."

He rolled her onto her back and looked down into her beautiful face. She was such a sight, lying there with her hair fanned out against the pillow, her eyes watching him with vivid expectation.

He dipped his head down to drink from her lips. His tongue pressed into her warmth, savoring the sweet taste that was uniquely hers.

"There is nothing on this Earth that could make me ever give up on you. You're it for me. Whatever life throws at you, I'm always going to be right there, fighting side by side with you. What happens to you…happens to me."

He kissed her again and nipped at her bottom lip before he set her lips free. "So, while you and Abby were discussing my schedule, did the two of you leave enough time for me to make love to my sexy-as-sin wife?"

"Of course, that was the first thing we finalized when we sat down to plot in your calendar."

He ran his hand down the length of her body and shivered at the spark of electricity that passed between them.

"Good, because I call hot-sex break with the boss' wife right now."

~

*H*eart sat starring at the image on her computer screen. The lab technicians had cleaned this image up months ago and she still had no clue what it meant—if it meant anything at all—to her case.

Why the fuck was this image of a black wolf's head with dark blue eyes so intriguing to her? She didn't know what it was about this image, but it just seemed familiar somehow, like something she'd forgotten. Frustrated and tired of looking at the computer screen, she closed the image and reminded herself to talk with Bryan about this later when she caught up to him.

She felt her phone vibrating in her back pocket. There was a text from Abby, waiting for her. The executive administrative assistant had become her ally in keeping her husband from working too hard. She laughed when she thought about it, being a workaholic herself it was comical that's she'd actually try to keep Kenneth out of the office as often as possible.

He's finished with his meetings; he should be done in another forty-five minutes or so.

Heart smiled and looked at the time on her phone. It was almost nine, there would be no traffic headed into Manhattan this time of night.

Don't let him leave. OMW.

Abby sent her back a smiley face emoticon. Heart grabbed her keys and headed for the parking lot. Hell, if she couldn't solve a case, she might as well spend some time with the pretty-ass man she was married to.

~

*K*enneth heard the familiar sound of designer shoes padding across the carpet of his office. The sound snatched his eyes away from the paperwork he was attempting to complete so he could go home to his wife.

Faith stood in front of his desk, tailored suit hugging the slim curves of her perfect body. A body that used to elicit so much pleasure from him, but now, sitting here watching her saunter in front of him that same body left him cold.

"How did you get in here?" he asked.

"You're secretary wasn't at her desk when I stepped off the elevator."

Kenneth rolled his eyes. "What do you want, Faith?"

"Is that any way to treat someone you once loved?"

Kenneth watched a satisfied smile climb her lips as she lowered herself into the chair opposite his desk.

"Faith, you tried to set me up the last time I saw you. I'm not about to give you another chance. Get out."

She smiled at him again. "Are you saying the Amazon you married wasn't happy with you the last time we saw each other? Maybe she was so upset because she saw what kind of chemistry we had together and it made her jealous?"

Kenneth's jaw ached from the constant clenching of his teeth. He usually gave Faith a great deal of leeway. Even during their relationship he'd overlooked some of her overthe-top personality traits and just shrugged them off as Faith being Faith. He'd never really seen her willingness to do whatever she wanted no matter what as a bad thing. She was always cheery, always bright, and always happy. Now standing here in front of her, he wondered how much of that never-ending happiness was at the expense of others.

He'd always taken a soft hand with her, always given in to her requests without much resistance. It didn't hurt that most of her requests had fallen in line with what he'd wanted. But this…no, nothing was going to harm his marriage. And if Faith thought she could destroy what he and Heart had built, what they were still building…she'd soon find herself on the wrong side of his anger.

"Be very careful how you speak about my wife, Faith." Her name left his lips on a low growl. The deep rumble of his voice penetrated her, making her visibly shiver and take a cautious step back from him.

She looked down at her feet, trying her best to keep her eyes off of his face. "You're really going to throw everything we had away because of her?"

Kenneth gripped the side of his desk to keep from putting his hands on Faith in anger. He'd never been a man to use violence against a woman, his father and uncle had raised him better than that. But Faith was doing her very best to try every last nerve he possessed. He closed his eyes to center himself, to reign in the anger that was beginning to pulse like drums through his vessels.

"So exactly what part in this little melodrama that you've created have we reached, Faith? Are we at the point where I tell you how much I love you and can't live without you? Or have we gotten to the part where I admit that I'm trapped in a marriage of obligation secretly pining away for you? Or are we at the part where I beg you to take me back and tell you I'm leaving Heart for you?"

Faith's eyes locked on his, the sultry, conniving expression gone and replaced with a growing ire. She didn't like his tone. She'd never liked not getting her way, and she hated it even worse when anyone dared correct her. Well that was just too damn bad for her because he was just getting started putting her in her place.

"First off, understand that none of the aforementioned will ever take place in this lifetime or the next. I love my wife; she is it for me, period. I didn't marry her for any other reason than I love her more than any other person in this world. I love her in a way I never could have loved you, Faith."

"Kenneth, you loved me," she shouted while slicing a dismissive hand through the air.

"Yes, I did love you…once. But we both know I was never in love with you. You were too self-centered to ever allow that to happen. There were plenty of times where I tried to get closer to you, but you didn't want that. You wanted to keep things light, fun, nothing heavy. Dating was okay, being my girlfriend was okay, but you never wanted anything beyond that. When things got serious, when my father became ill, you dipped really quickly. You didn't even blink when I told you I had to go home, didn't offer to come back to New York with me to support me, nothing. If I remember correctly, you fucked me good the night before for old time's sake, but you couldn't even rearrange your schedule to drop me off to the airport in the morning."

Faith dropped her eyes making an effort to look contrite. She moved from foot to foot attempting to shift the weight of Kenneth's scrutiny.

"You want to know when I knew Heart was the one for me? The day of my sister's funeral I left Heart sleeping in her bed, sedated by painkillers nursing a surgically repaired shoulder after a bullet tore through her. I didn't tell her about the funeral because she'd just been released from the hospital the night before. She was in no condition to be anywhere but in her bed. But she heard about the funeral over the radio and realized I'd gone by myself without telling her. She called a friend and had that person come all the way to Woodmere to get her and drive her to the funeral. When we talked about her attendance she said to me, 'I don't want to be the kind of friend that only takes from you, Kenneth. You deserve so much more than that.' She was the first person in my life other than my father and uncle that wanted to take care of me."

Faith kept her head turned from him; he could see her well-polished façade cracking. The truth was cracking her porcelain veneer in to tiny pieces, each line branching off in to a separate direction, bisecting and trisecting from one fracture to another.

"You liked dating me, you for damn sure liked the perks of dating me like good sex, and my money, but other than that, you didn't give a damn about me. So if you think I'm gonna leave that amazing woman to go back to your superficial ass, think again."

Kenneth saw sadness creep up into her eyes. She'd heard him this time, she'd finally heard what he'd been trying to tell her for months—

more than heard him if the pain dancing across her features was any indication. She felt it this time.

"Kenneth, I'm so tired of people taking things from me. When do I get to have what

I want?"

A rare bit of vulnerability shone in her eyes. He knew what was behind that look, had always known that he was nothing more than a means to soothe that ache. But no matter how much he cared for her, he could never be that for her again.

"Heart didn't take anything from you," Kenneth said softly, letting his locked muscles finally relax. "You and I were over before Heart ever walked into the picture. We were over before we even started and we both know why, Faith. I'm not him...I will never be him. All I ever have been to you was a comfortable spot to rest while you ran from what you really wanted and needed. I didn't mind being that before, but I can't do it now. Not when it means endangering what my wife and I have."

He watched Faith press her lids closed against the truth. As if her inability to see it, to see him, would make their truth any less real.

"If you're honest with yourself, Faith, you know where your heart has always belonged, and it was never with me. Please, stop this; don't twist the friendship that we've always had in to something ugly just because you're afraid to grab hold of what your heart really wants. Go back to California; go back to your life."

He looked at her, head still turned away from him, arms folded tightly across her chest. He could see pain washing all over her, but he knew there was nothing he could do to stop it. This was a war she had to fight herself. Faith had been running too long, and life had a way of making you crash when you refused to stop on your own.

"Please, Faith," he begged. "Stop all of this noise before the wrong person overhears this madness, before someone is irrevocably hurt."

"Too late."

Kenneth and Faith turned to the door to see Heart standing casually against its frame.

"Shit," he muttered. This was all he needed. The last time Faith violated his personal space Heart had taken extreme exception. He looked around quickly, just making sure there was no glass furniture that Heart could throw Faith through again. "Heart, this isn't what it looks like."

Heart raised her hand to silence him. She stepped in between him and Faith and stood in front of his ex with her arms crossed, feet spread wide. It was a fight stance, or a preparation for one. Either way, this didn't really bode well for the night ending in a quiet and peaceful resolution.

"*K*enneth, I think it's exactly what I'm thinking," Heart watched a corner of Faith's mouth hitch in satisfaction.

God it would feel so good to slap that smirk off that bitch's face.

Heart's hands tingled with the need to strike. She pressed her fingers into tight fists, her nails biting into the flesh of her palms.

"It looks to me like some desperate chick just can't seem to recognize when she's been dismissed."

Faith rolled her eyes and stepped closer to Heart. "Say what you want, Heart. We both know that the only reason you lost control and put your hands on me was because you were insecure. You were worried about Kenneth's feelings for me."

Kenneth opened his mouth to speak, but was silenced again by Heart's upturned hand. She used the same hand to push Kenneth farther behind her giving her clearer sights on Faith.

"You're right, I was insecure," Heart laughed. "But then about two weeks later Kenneth stood in front of God and man and told me he loved me and married me. And if you'd asked me if I still had doubts about our relationship, I still would have said yes. But these last three months, what Kenneth has given me, what he's been through with me that only happens when you love someone. My husband loves me, only me, and I know it.

Especially after watching him dismiss you like he just did."

Heart smiled and stepped a tad bit closer to Faith who responded in kind by taking a step back as well.

"Now, this pushing up on my man...that shit is going to stop. I put you through a table before, no telling what other piece of furniture I might put you through next."

Faith took a careful look around the room then returned her eyes to Heart, glaring at the truth she saw resting in them. Faith turned and exited the door without another word to either of them. When she was gone, Heart turned to a waiting Kenneth.

"Baby I—"

She pressed her lips to his and took advantage of his open mouth to pierce it with her tongue. She felt Kenneth wrap his arms around her and the tension of a few moments ago just bled out of her. Nothing else in the moments prior to this one mattered. Her man was here for her, as he always was and she was right where she was supposed to be, pressed against his heated flesh with no room between the two of them.

She pressed in even closer to Kenneth; she always wanted to be closer to Kenneth. She was just about to bury her fingers in those soft midnight tresses hanging down his back when she heard the irritating beep of her phone. She pulled herself away from the velvet of Kenneth's lips and pulled her phone from her pocket.

"This is a text from Big Willie. He needs me to stop by the center before I head home."

"Ugghh, tell that evil old man to go home to his wife so I can go home with mine."

She gave Kenneth a quick peck on his lips and laughed. "You'd better stop talking about that old man. I keep telling you Willie is not to be fucked with. If he's calling me, he needs to see me. It's late, take a car service home; I'll meet you there as soon as I can."

Kenneth pulled her into his embrace and ground his hips against her, his hard cock pressing through his tailor-made slacks and into the groove of her crotch.

It's just not right that this man always feels so fucking good.

416

"You'd better, I'm in need of assistance that I can only get from you," Kenneth moaned against her parted lips.

She placed sure fingers on the bulge behind his zipper and gave a firm squeeze. "I promise I'll take care of you as soon as I get home. Now let me go, or I'll never get home."

He kissed her once again and gave her ass a final strong squeeze before letting the sting of a quick slap settle across the solid globes.

Yeah, Big Willie better have something important to tell me for walking out on this shit right here.

~

*B*ryan sat at his desk going over the case files MacKenzie had left for him. She was home snuggled up with her husband, and he was here tired and lonely. How had that shit happened? A year ago, their roles were reversed. He had Jussy to go home to, to love. Now, because of his own stupidity, he had nothing but these damn cases that were lining his desk. He picked up the digitally enhanced picture that Mac had left for him. It was the only thing they could identify about the cop who'd tried to have Mac killed. He held the picture of the tattoo in his hand and continued to study it line by line. He heard a light tap on his door and gave the visitor permission to enter.

"Sergeant Smyth," the uniformed officers acknowledged Bryan. "Have you seen the L.T.?"

Bryan shook his head. "I think she left a while ago, Forze. What do you want with her? Last I heard you guys weren't exactly on friendly terms."

"Sir, we need to find MacKenzie, we've got a big problem, I need to talk to her about. Her moving me from the community center detail was a big mistake."

Bryan let his hand drop to the desk. "Forze, you're really skating on thin ice here," Bryan said as he let the hand with the picture fall to his desk. Forze's eyes fell on the image as he scrutinized the intricate design.

"I know that marking," Forze said.

Bryan sat up. "From where?"

"That's what I've been trying to tell you, Sergeant Smyth. I know who bears that mark. I told you, we've got a really big problem and we need to find the lieutenant now."

Forze pulled a folded leather wallet from his pocket and handed it to Bryan. When

Bryan flipped it open he saw Forze's face, but not the name Mancino Forze.

"Who the fuck is Timothy Grazzo?" Bryan asked.

"He's me, the real me. I'm I.A.," slipped out of his mouth quietly as he looked across the desk at Bryan.

"Why the fuck is Internal Affairs in my house without my knowledge or the knowledge of my superiors?"

"Because we figured it out, we knew Mac was set up to get shot by a cop. I was sent in to find out who that dirty bastard was, and I have, and we need to get MacKenzie now before that rat bastard tries to kill her again."

~

*H*eart walked into Mac's Place and was greeted by the young officer, Manning Kimes. The young man stood up to greet her with a big smile and an extended hand. The only person she'd ever seen so damn chipper was Faith, and even her happy-all-the smile seemed low-watt compared to Kimes.

Ahh, the enthusiasm of youth and being new to the job.

When she didn't extend her hand in return the young rookie rolled his sleeves to the middle of his forearm.

"Kimes, what are you doing here? I seem to remember taking you and your partner

off of this detail."

"Yes ma'am. One of the guys covering had an emergency so he asked if I would help him out by covering the rest of the shift. My shift ended about an hour ago, so I didn't mind picking up the O.T. here. I was about to lock up and walk out now."

"Where's your partner?"

"Home I think, he said he was pretty beat after our shift."

Heart nodded her head. "You seen Big Willie?"

"I think he might be in the back, said something about needing a beer after the day he'd had with the kids."

Kimes grabbed a knapsack from behind the desk and headed to the door. "I'll see you tomorrow, Lieutenant."

Heart nodded again and watched the young man leave and lock the double doors behind him. He bounced down the stairs and disappeared out of sight a few moments later. Heart opened the door to the common room of the center. The lights were low and the room was empty and quiet, not necessarily a strange occurrence for this time of night. But something was off.

An uncomfortable tingling sensation traveled from the base of her neck down her spine, to the tips of her fingers. Her fingers moved of their own accord with anticipation of action. Her hand went to her sidearm, unhooking the strap that secured her pistol to her holster. She took a slow step in a circular motion to look around her.

Something ain't right.

She drew her weapon and kept quiet, softly stepping toward Big Willie's office. The door was slightly ajar and she couldn't see Big Willie from the door. She lightly pushed the door until she met resistance behind it. She swept the room, her senses still demanding that she remain alert.

She let her eyes dance off the walls from top to bottom looking for anything strange and out of order. Nothing jumped out at her; the office was intact, kept neat, and orderly by Big Willie's neat freak ways. The bookcases were neatly lined, the files were stacked neatly on his desk, the chair was pushed in. This was how Big Willie's office looked every day. She was preparing to ease out of the uninhabited room when her eyes landed on a single dark muddy-red spot of something wet on the floor just on the edge of the desk.

Blood.

She stepped farther into the room and there just behind the desk she saw Big Willie splayed out on the floor with a dripping crimson line trailing from his head on to his face.

She dipped down to one knee, quickly pressing two fingers at the base of Big

Willie's throat.

You'd better be alive you old bastard. No way I'm telling Tee you died.

She released a long breath as she felt a strong thumping beat under her fingers. He was alive, and his heartbeat was steady. She pulled her radio from her belt, turned the volume low, and pressed the talk button.

"Dispatch this is Lieutenant Heart MacKenzie of the NYPD. Do you copy?" she said in a whisper.

"Copy that, Lieutenant," a female voice crackled through the airwaves.

"I've got a possible assault. Vic is former NYPD lieutenant William Seyah. Vic is unconscious with what appears to be a head wound. Requesting medical assistance at

Mac's Place Community Center on Autumn and the Conduit."

"Copy that, Lieutenant. A bus is on the way."

Heart went to acknowledge the dispatchers statement when the lights went out. It wasn't just the lights in the office. She could see the dim emergency generator lights were now lining the hallway with an eerie, soft glow.

"Dispatch, perp may still be on the premises. Ten-thirteen to this location."

She heard muted footsteps coming toward the door. She stood and raised her weapon, ready to defend herself and Big Willie if it came to it.

"Lieutenant?" she heard Kimes' voice. "You still here? I forgot something and saw all the lights out. Lieutenant? Are you still here?"

When he reached the door he had his weapon drawn too. They watched each other for a moment and then both dropped their gun arms.

"Big Willie's been assaulted. The power just went out; I think the perp might still be here."

Kimes nodded his head and raised a hand to his hair, ruffling the strands a little. The action pulled his sleeve down exposing a dark marking on his arm.

"I know Big Willie can be a bit of an asshole, but why the hell would someone wanna bash in his skull and leave him for dead in here?"

Heart shrugged her shoulders. "I don't really know, all I do know is we've gotta get him some help and secure this building. You take point; I've got your six. Let's go out front and see if we can find this asshole," she said quickly and motioned for him to walk first into the hall.

Kimes nodded, wrapped his hand around the handle of his pistol, and began walking in front of her. When they were free of the small corridor and standing in the middle of the community room, Heart raised her weapon and firmly placed it against Kimes' skull.

"Lieutenant?" he asked so innocently that she almost believed his act.

"Kimes, drop your weapon, lock your hands behind your head, and kick the piece away from you."

"Lieutenant, what are you doing?"

"I'm about to arrest the man that attacked my friend in there, and the person that set me up to get shot."

"Lieutenant...I...I don't know what you're talking about." He slowly placed the weapon on the floor then locked his hands behind his head and kicked the gun away from them. "Let's just relax here, put down your gun and we can talk about this."

"That sweet-as-pie act that you have going on is really good. Up until two seconds ago, I never suspected you. I would have thought your boy Forze would have tried something like this, but never you. There were only two things that just gave you away. I never mentioned Big Willie had a head wound, and you couldn't see it from the doorway.

So if you knew, it's because you put it there."

She saw his muscle pull with tension as his posture became stiffer.

"You said there were two things that gave me away," his voice low and dangerous, "what was the other?"

"The tattoo above your wrist," she said. "It's a black wolf with blue eyes; the cop who stole the gun from our evidence room which was used in my shooting had the same tattoo. You should probably really learn to keep that thing covered up if you're going to commit felony crimes."

Kimes spun around, pushing into her, knocking her weapon from her hand. He rushed her and took her to the floor with a hard thump, driving the breath from her. He reared back and landed a hard punch at the side of her mouth. She felt the skin inside her lip tear and the bitter-metallic taste of her blood fill her mouth.

Oh, this motherfucker wants to grapple...let's.

When he drew back his arm for another punch, she thrust her fist upward and caught him in his throat. He staggered back, giving her time to scramble to her feet. He caught his breath and came for her again. She blocked his jabs and struck quick repetitive blows to his face and eyes. Kimes was a solidly built man. They were equal in height, but he outweighed her by at least sixty pounds of defined muscle. If she went for body shots, they'd probably have little effect. She needed to keep him dazed and off of his feet, and that's exactly what she did.

Hands and feet, hands and feet, she wasn't just a street brawler, she had skill, she had technique. She'd been trained in hand-to-hand combat by the best. Hunter had made certain she was prepared to walk the streets of New York as a cop. Yeah, the job provided training on how to handle your own in a fistfight, but that shit was nothing like the military-grade shit that Hunter and her cousins used to train her. If this motherfucker wanted a fight, he was about to get one.

She kept at his face, relentlessly targeting his eyes and mouth. He stumbled a little, the face shots beginning to daze him a bit. She saw an opening and applied a punch at the perfect angle to the bridge of his nose and felt the splintering bone fracture beneath her fist. When he grabbed for his nose, she used her feet to sweep his legs from under him. When he was down she jumped on top of him and continuing to land blows to his face and injured nose. When he could finally get his hands up, he pushed her off and climbed to all fours. Before Kimes could raise himself up, she landed a hard kick to his side.

"You think you can into my house and make it dirty!" she yelled as she kicked him again.

"You think you can come for me and win!" she landed another blow to his side, keeping him on the floor, unable to use his hands, unable to defend himself or strike at her.

"I don't know what the fuck this was all about, but I know that this will be the last time you think of coming for me."

Kimes collapsed on the floor. Arms and legs spread out his face bloodied and pummeled. She jumped on top of him and forced his limp arms around his back binding each one with the metal of her handcuffs.

"You took him from me," the mangled words were almost unrecognizable coming from Kimes' bloodied mouth.

"I've never taken a damn thing from you. What the hell are you talking about?" She stood and climbed over the prone man and retrieved both their weapons.

"My father, you took him from me."

Heart looked at the beaten man who'd managed to use the wall to help himself into a sitting position.

"Who is your father?"

He turned wide eyes to her, a mix of his tears and blood painting a horrid mosaic across the lines of his face. She'd seen beaten men before, but this man, this man was broken, and not by the blows she had landed either. There was something else that had destroyed him, something else that had left that hopeless look on his face.

"Anthony Luponero."

The two words shook her and drew her back to that day fourteen years ago when Anthony Luponero had snatched her off of the street and had his goons hold her down while he made her watch him kill a childhood acquaintance. She saw the first blow that Luponero had landed on that poor girl's face. He reached out to keep her head in place while he rained angry blows to her face. There, on his forearm, there was a tattoo, a black wolf with blue eyes.

A pained moan coming from Kimes' mouth pulled her back into the present. How had she not recognized it? The tattoo she'd been staring at for months, it had seemed familiar, like she'd known it, recognized it. Why didn't the image immediately take her back to that night? She should have known that mark. It had haunted her for so long. She had dreamt of that awful night over and over again and she had always seen that ferocious wolf baring its angry teeth from its place on Luponero's arm.

She searched herself for the answer to the questions running through her mind with rapid-fire speed. Through the noise she found one simple thought that seemed to emerge, quieting the chaos that was filling her.

You moved on. You are healing.

She looked at Kimes again, recognized the wild pain behind his eyes. She had lived in a similar state of hell all of these years, she knew that look quite intimately.

"I didn't kill Luponero, Kimes. He died shortly after I was rescued."

"He didn't die, your family had him gunned down like a dog in the street."

She didn't know how true that was. It was very possible her uncle had done it or set it up to be done. She didn't have the details to how Luponero died, the truth was, she wasn't all that concerned, only relieved when she found out her captor had been eliminated.

"Did it ever occur to you, Kimes, that if your father hadn't kidnapped me, my family wouldn't have had to have him killed, if that's even true? Your father was a member of the mafia, any number of the people he associated with could have had him killed."

He bared his teeth at her, the truth adding to his rage, as if the rational thought she'd offered wasn't an option.

Madness doesn't understand rationale.

"I didn't kill him, Kimes, and you didn't need to come for me. But madness usually never sees what's right in front of it. You have a choice. You can choose to move forward, or you can choose to let

your demons overrun you and destroy you. You chose the latter. Me…
I'm gonna choose the first. Your father has stolen enough of my life,
from this moment on, he gets no more."

"Police, don't move!" Bryan Smyth's voice bellowed through
the door.

"It's just me, Smyth, the perp is down and cuffed." She watched her
fellow officers spill into the room. It was over, all of it. She was done
with letting a single occurrence define her life. No, she would no
longer allow the past to conquer her; she was the one that would be
conquering that bitch. After all, she was Lieutenant Heart MacKenzie;
she ran shit, not the other way around.

EPILOGUE

*H*eart woke up to the feel of her husband's lips traveling down her body, leaving a blistering trail of kisses from her collarbone down to her navel. The nub of sensitive flesh resting behind the closure of her nether lips throbbed with anticipation. He wasn't even there yet, hadn't even stroked her yet, and her body was already in flames.

This was what happened every morning, what she hoped would continue to happen every morning for the rest of their days together. He would wind her up slowly and watch her ache until she couldn't contain the sensual flames licking at her core, threatening to incinerate her.

He dipped his head to her mound, parted her lips wide, and lapped at that sensitive pearl that was pulsating with her building passion. He licked his tongue in one long motion down the expanse of her exposed center. Her muscles tightened in response and he moaned as he watched the cavern of her walls close and then open in a hungry swallow.

He rubbed a gentle finger softly around her opening. He slowly slid it in until it was fully seated inside her. God she was so hungry for him, for any part of him. Her body clamped down on that finger begging for the pleasure she knew it would render her. After a few careful pumps, he allowed a second finger to slide in next to the first causing a blessed burn as her flesh yielded to him. Her hips snapped up in a quivering motion as his moving fingers glided over the delicate bundle of nerves inside her.

"Shit, Kenneth, I'm there...I need..."

She couldn't voice it, the pleasure was so overwhelming, so consuming, her electrified body shut her mind out, leaving only her ability to feel and respond with the most guttural noises being ripped from her throat.

Kenneth latched on to her clit and sucked it roughly into his mouth. He licked, laved, and sucked until her body was just a shivering mass of skin and limp bones. He crooked his fingers upward and stroked at the perfect angle and her orgasm ripped through her with screaming force tipping her over the edge of sanity. Her muscles locked and her body stiffened into rigid contractions as the wave of sweet release pushed through her body from her core outward.

When the passionate spasms began to ebb slowly away he kissed his way back up her body until his lips were on hers. She opened to him, allowed his tongue entry. It was smooth and strong and flavored with the taste of her. She could feel wetness pooling at the very door of her gate. She felt the hardness of his cock waiting there, nudging her to open to him.

She let her legs fall wide and open, giving him access. He nestled himself between her legs and pushed the prominent head inside her.

God that thing is like a python.

He eased slowly inside of her, inch by inch until he was balls-deep inside of her. She flexed her muscles and watched his face contort with lines of welcomed torture. She did it again and a huff of breath escaped his clenched lips.

"If you keep that up, I'm going to come."

"Would that be such a bad thing?"

"A bad thing...no...a little embarrassing...yes. Stop cheating, let me do what I do.

You know we'll both thank me in the end."

He was right, she couldn't really argue with his lovemaking skills. She never left their bed unsatisfied. Usually she was the one begging him to stop, telling him she couldn't take anymore. But Kenneth never gave in to her, he always pushed her past her threshold and she had received more pleasure than she'd ever had in her lifetime because of it.

She surrendered, gave in, let him have his way, and he rewarded her with an agonizingly slow thrust, pulling himself almost all the way out, leaving only the tip of his cock inside. He lifted her legs and pushed them back, bending her almost completely in half. He snapped his hips, over and over, each thrust stronger than the last, the pace so furious she could hardly breathe through the intense pleasure coiling its way through her body. The muscles of her core were pulling together, tighter and tighter and she couldn't stop them. She was beyond caring about trying to stave off the orgasm that was threatening to take over.

She felt Kenneth press his torso to hers. He placed a hard kiss on her lips and began his furious pace all over again. She reached around him, her hands gliding on the smooth skin of his back, fingers caressing the mounds of hard, stiffened muscles sewn together like expert latticework.

He changed the angle of his hips and pressed perfectly into her pleasure pot and a second and more powerful orgasm swallowed her whole. She felt like someone pulled her underwater too quickly for her mind and senses to recognize what had happened. Everything was a swirl of colors and sounds, all muted through the foggy haze of her climax.

Somewhere, just beyond the edge of her mind she felt Kenneth's pace falter and then he collapsed onto her with a loud groan. If she hadn't been aware of what was going on, she would have thought he was in pain, but here, nestled inside of her, he was giving into the most perfect pleasure either of them had ever known.

He collapsed on top of her, a welcomed weight she had come to enjoy. He kissed her again, firm pink lips moving over hers with knowing ease. "I was so afraid," he said, body still grasping for air in hard puffs.

"I know it's not easy for you when I'm on the job."

"Heart that maniac almost took the most precious thing I have and I wasn't even aware of it until you walked through the door last night."

He ran gentle fingers over the bruises on her face. They were probably purple by now. The certainly felt like they should be purple with lots of dull achiness to boot.

"You're not always going to know when I'm in danger, Kenneth. Just know, when

I'm out there, I'm being as smart and as safe as I can be so I can come home to you."

He kissed her again and stared down at her like he was cataloguing every inch of her face.

"You seemed different last night after you visited Big Willie at the hospital."

"I was. I talked to Big Willie for a while, made sure he was all right, and then I came home. The entire time I was on my way home I just kept thinking, what if I hadn't pieced it all together in time? What if Kimes had gotten the drop on me? Kimes was a mess last night. He was consumed by his demons. I looked in his eyes and I saw the same demons that have been chasing me for the last fourteen years dancing in his eyes. I knew if I didn't do something, I would wind up just like him, obsessing over a ghost who could only hurt me if I let him. I just decided I wasn't going to let him. It turns out; I've got too much to live for."

"Yeah?"

She nodded her head and feathered her fingers through his midnight strands of hair.

"Yeah, I have a family that loves me, I've got a job I'm really good at and love, and most of all, I've got this wonderful husband that loves me, all of me, even the ugly sides of me. I didn't see him coming, didn't even want to let him in, but now, when you get down to the heart of the matter, he's the only thing that matters in my world."

She watched that brilliant pink blush climb from his neck to face as he smiled. "I love you too, Captain Searlington."

She rolled her eyes. Captain Porter had delivered the news yesterday when she'd come home after all the chaos had settled. She'd passed her exam, aced it really, and the committee would be officially offering her the position in the next few weeks. The entire process would probably take about six months, but soon, she would be top cop in her house.

"I still have to get through the committee and I haven't changed my name legally to

Searlington yet."

"Well maybe you should, maybe now that you're transitioning into another position, maybe this is the right time, unless you just don't want to."

"We married so quickly, I don't think we ever discussed whether I would or not. MacKenzie has never held any real emotional meaning for me. I mean, things are getting better between Marcus and me since my grandmother died, but honestly, I could give it up without much thought."

He nodded then kissed her again. "Then why haven't you taken my name?"

The hoods of her lids dropped for a moment. When she reopened them she was caught in the wave of that crystal blue gaze. She'd fought that wave for so long, and when she couldn't fight it any longer, she'd struggled to navigate it, often thrashing against its power, holding on to anything that would keep her afloat.

"I was afraid to."

His brow furrowed as he leaned in. "Why would you be afraid to take your husband's name?"

"I was afraid to take your name because I wasn't certain I had your heart. We don't exactly have what most would call a traditional history. I was always afraid that you would wake up one day and realize you didn't want this anymore. That you would realize that you didn't want me."

He parted his lips to speak, but she silenced him by leaning up and passing her bruised lips over his.

"I *was* afraid of that Kenneth, but not anymore. I know I'm not in this thing alone, I know that you love me." She reached up and tucked a loose tendril of hair behind his ear and smiled. "But most importantly, I know that I deserve your love."

"You do," he said softly, his voice a low rumble in the quiet of the room.

"I realized while I was fighting Kimes that I wasn't just fighting for my life. I was fighting to get back to this, to us. It didn't matter how hard, or how long I had to fight, I wasn't going to let him take me away from this."

Kenneth rolled on to his back and pulled her tightly into his arms. The embrace was warm and strong, making her feel like she was tucked safely away in a tightly swaddled blanket.

She wallowed in his touch for just another moment, and then she pushed him onto his back and sat on top of his lap.

"Mmm, Captain, ready for round two?" he asked with fiery devilment dancing behind those cool blue eyes.

She secured his hands above his head and smiled. "I would love to. But Captain Searlington has to go take a shower and put on her gun and her badge to and keep the city of Brooklyn safe."

"So…you're not going to cuff me to the headboard and fuck me within an inch of my life?"

She shook her head. "This morning…no, but tomorrow is another day."

"And tonight is even better."

"Yeah, tonight sounds like it might be better."

He pulled his wrists from her grasp and pulled her back into his embrace. "You give in way too easily, Captain."

She smiled, and burrowed into the safety of his touch. "Only to you, Searlington. Only to you."

he End

ABOUT THE AUTHOR

LaQuette is an erotic, multicultural romance author of M/F and M/M love stories. Her writing style brings intellect to the drama. She often crafts emotionally epic, fantastical tales that are deeply pigmented by reality's paintbrush. Her novels are filled with a unique mixture of savvy, sarcastic, brazen, and unapologetically sexy characters who are confident in their right to appear on the page.

This bestselling Erotic Romance Author is the 2016 Author of the Year Golden Apple Award Winner, 2016 Write Touch Award Winner for Best Contemporary Mid-length Novel, 2016 Swirl Awards 1st Place Winner in Romantic Suspense, and 2016 Aspen Gold Award Finalist in Erotic Romance. LaQuette—a native of Brooklyn, New York—spends her time catering to her three distinct personalities: Wife, Mother, and Educator.

Writing—her escape from everyday madness—has always been a friend and source of comfort. At the age of sixteen she read her first romance novel and realized the genre was missing something: people that looked and lived like her. As a result, her characters and settings are always designed to provide positive representations of people of color and various marginalized communities.

She loves hearing from readers and discussing the crazy characters that are running around in her head causing so much trouble. Contact her on:

Website: LaQuette.com
Email: LaQuette@LaQuette.com
Amazon: www.amazon.com/author/laquette
Facebook: www.facebook.com/LaQuetteTheAuthor
Twitter: twitter.com/LaQuetteWrites
Instagram: instagram.com/la_quette

OTHER TITLES

Wicked Wager: Texas vs. Brooklyn 1
Bedding The Enemy
Lies You Tell
Heart of the Matter: Queens of Kings: Book 1
Divided Heart: Queens of Kings: Book 2
Protected Heart: Queens of Kings Book 3
Power Privilege & Pleasure: Queens of Kings: Book 4
His True Strength: Queens of Kings: Book 5
My Beginning: Trinity Series: Book 1
Love's Changes

NEWSLETTER SIGNUP

Hello,

If you're interested in staying current with all the happenings with my writing, previews, and giveaways, sign up for my monthly newsletter at www.LaQuette.com.

Keep it sexy,
    LaQuette 💋

COMING SOON...

LOADED LONGSHOT

Texas vs. Brooklyn 2

Kandi Adkins, the executive manager of Sweet Sadie's Cosmetics, has her roots planted firmly in Brownsville, Brooklyn. Kandi knows what it's like to have nothing. Education and her friend's late mother, Sadie King, pulled her out of the mire of poverty and enabled her to grab hold to personal and professional security.

Life has taught Aaron Nakai to play his cards close to the vest. Reaching for more than you need only invites trouble into your life.

That's what happened to his father, a man who died young attempting to make his mark on the world. He finds comfort and security living in his adoptive brother, Slade's, shadow. Aaron refuses to allow lofty dreams to rob him of the gains he made in life. Being Slade's lawyer and right-hand man suits him just fine.

When Slade needs Aaron to step out of the background and take care of an unexpected problem in New York, Aaron's quiet existence back in Texas is blown to bits by a quick-witted, sassy-mouthed fireball named Kandi. Their attraction is just as palpable as their distaste for one another, making the decision to wager their hearts and their careers a high-stakes game with potentially disastrous outcomes.

Will they fold? Or will they reach for a loaded longshot to win it all?

COMING SOON.

SEDUCTIVE STAKES

Texas vs. Brooklyn 3

Azure Carlisle is simply tired. She's tired of always struggling to do the right thing only to have life slap her down time and time again. She climbed her way out of the projects of Brooklyn by getting an education. Her Ph.D. in Chemistry was her ticket out of the 'hood, but the lingering student loans from both her undergraduate and graduate degrees crush any dreams of personal advancement.

When the financial juggling game she plays every month begins to topple, Azure stumbles upon a way out. With an offer to clear her debts in hand, Azure is nearly burden free. The only thing she must do to escape financial ruin is simple: betray the trust of the woman who offered her a job, and friendship.